THE

# ABC

OF

# AWT

*Also by Antony Worrall Thompson*

The Small and Beautiful Cookbook

Supernosh (with Malcolm Gluck)

Modern Bistrot Cookery

Sainsbury's Quick and Easy Fish

30-Minute Menus

Ready Steady Cook 1 (with Brian Turner)

Sainsbury's Quick and Easy Winter Warmers

Simply Antony

# THE

## ABC

# OF

## AWT

Antony Worrall Thompson

Photographs
by Steve Lee

**HEADLINE**

'JANE GRIGSON'S CURRIED PARSNIP SOUP' AND 'ONE-EYED BOUILLABAISSE WITH PEAS' ARE TAKEN FROM JANE
GRIGSON'S VEGETABLE BOOK (PENGUIN) 'ELIZABETH DAVID'S EVERLASTING SYLLABUB' WAS FIRST PUBLISHED IN
THE BOOKLET SYLLABUBS AND FRUIT FOOLS (1969) AND REPRINTED IN AN OMELETTE AND A GLASS OF WINE (1984)

FIRST PUBLISHED IN 1998 BY HEADLINE BOOK PUBLISHING

10 9 8 7 6 5 4 3 2 1

CATALOGUING IN PUBLICATION DATA IS AVAILABLE FROM THE BRITISH LIBRARY
ISBN 0 7472 2116 2

ENDPAPERS: *ROASTED PEPERONATA* (SEE PAGE 257)

EDITED BY SUSAN FLEMING
HOME ECONOMY BY JO CRAIG
FOOD STYLING BY MARIAN PRICE
PHOTOGRAPHY BY STEVE LEE
TYPESET BY LETTERPART LIMITED, REIGATE, SURREY
DESIGN BY DESIGN/SECTION

PRINTED AND BOUND IN GREAT BRITAIN BY BUTLER & TANNER LTD, FROME AND LONDON

HEADLINE BOOK PUBLISHING
A DIVISION OF HODDER HEADLINE PLC
338 EUSTON ROAD
LONDON NW1 3BH

# CONTENTS

**To my wife, Jacinta**

They say that behind every successful man is a great wife, and behind every wife is a successful mistress. I have discovered the best of both worlds, wife and mistress in one glorious package.

# ACKNOWLEDGEMENTS

To SUSAN FLEMING, my editor, for her amazing coolness faced with an author who promises and eventually comes up with the goods. To LORRAINE JERRAM at Headline, for her persistence; I am now having withdrawal symptoms without my daily phonecall fix. To HEADLINE'S TEAM OF DESIGNERS for producing a book with great style, no mean feat when the author has ideas of his own. To HEATHER HOLDEN-BROWN, also at Headline, the big bad boss who was heard to exclaim 'I don't believe it' when I finished the book. To STEVE LEE, our photographer, who, knowing my style, kept his cool when others around him were losing theirs; they are great photographs. To my agents, FIONA LINDSAY and LINDA SHANKS, who sensibly listened to my wife and not me, refusing bookings when it was obvious I was under pressure towards the end of the book. To AMIE PRIOR and her front-of-house team, ADELE, STEVE, IAN, CONXI, AMANDA, MARIA and MARK, and to DAVID MASSEY and his team of chefs, BIG JOHN, MARK, MATT, BEN and CLAUDIA at Woz, for patiently tolerating my various absences from the restaurant during my marathon writing sessions (secretly I think they were quite relieved). To INGRID McCARROLL, LUISA ALVES, our nanny LIZZIE WILSON, and JO HYNES, my PA, who collectively became the *ABC* typing-pool harem under the watchful eye of her indoors; a huge thanks to them for often working late into the night to meet various deadlines. To my new courier service, KATY FINGRET, NICOLA NARDELLI, DAVE CANNON and SUE RICHARDS, who ferried bundles of papers from Henley to Headline when deadlines seemed to appear from nowhere. To my children, BLAKE, SAM, TOBY-JACK and BILLIE-LARA, who always manage to put things in perspective, either with a letter or an unconditional smile. And finally to JACINTA, who is still my wife despite not seeing me, apart from feeding time, for the best part of twelve weekends on the trot. When I needed tea she was there, when I was feeling down she lifted my spirits, and whether I needed advice or not I got it regardless! All in all, a tower of strength.

PS. Oops, I'd better not forget the 'little old lady' from Malahide, my mother-in-law MAEVE SHIEL, who was constantly on the phone from Ireland reassuring her daughter that I would eventually become a husband again.

# ASSUMPTIONS

When using this book, please assume the following unless otherwise stated.

- Potatoes, carrots, onions, shallots, garlic, celeriac, turnips, swede are all peeled.

- Peppers and chillies are cored and seeded.

- All vegetables and salads have been washed and dried.

- Beans, mangetouts and sugar-snap peas have been trimmed and strings removed.

- I have generally stated 'season to taste', as this aspect of cookery is so subjective. Everyone's taste buds are different, so in this area of cookery, experimentation is the name of the game. Where I have stated quantities, including spices other than salt and pepper, feel free to increase or reduce the amounts.

- **Ⓥ** at the top of a recipe means it is suitable for vegetarians. Unless otherwise stated, please assume all puddings to be vegetarian.

Throughout the text and recipes, if a term or method is printed in **bold type** this refers you to a sort of glossary, Chef Talk, at the back of the book, where everything arcane will be revealed!

# INTRODUCTION

I never really see the point of an introduction. On a recent poll of twenty avid cookbook reader friends, the majority said they never read an introduction. The ones that did were very foodie, the sort you might find on the judging panel of the André Simon or Glenfiddich awards.

While some foodies may enjoy this book, it has not been written especially with them in mind. It was written for real people who enjoy the occasional spell over a hot stove, glass of wine in hand, chilling out as they produce flavourful food for friends. Thumbing through the finished book I can honestly say there are only a handful of posey chef recipes where more than a modicum of skill is required.

The book is a collection of ingredient-led dishes that have become favourites of mine over the years. When I wrote my first book, *The Small and Beautiful Cookbook*, at the height of *nouvelle cuisine* in 1984, I probably wrote it as an ego-trip and for other chefs to say, 'Gosh, what a clever chappie he is', but unfortunately it was not written with the public in mind. It was a pretty book but totally impractical, with the reader having to refer to about five different recipes before any dish could be completed. And the food content . . . well, all I can say is, 'designer food', dishes that I thought the reader should eat rather than dishes the reader actually wanted to eat. And what was worse, looking back, there were only a handful of dishes that I would actually want to eat myself!

*The ABC of AWT* is different – these are all dishes I love to eat. I have not covered every ingredient, nor indeed every letter of the alphabet. I have written about ingredients *I* love, so don't go looking for tripe or sago, for instance, as they won't be there. It is a book I have enjoyed writing, and a book that has taught me a lot. Researching ingredients has thrown up a wealth of information I confess I had no clue about. As well as the main recipes each ingredient has a potted history and a series of 'bites' or small paragraphs that are 'skeletons' of dishes in their own right, suggestions that might inspire you. Thus it is a useful reference book that I hope will remain in your kitchen for a long time, growing old with greasy-thumb-stained pages, just how a cookbook should be. This is definitely not a book that will remain on the coffee table.

# ANCHOVY

In a list of ingredients essential to my cookery skills, anchovies would feature near the top. An all-time favourite, I find them indispensable. Most people know them only in canned or bottled form, swimming in a sea of inferior oil, and it's only recently that chefs have been able to find them fresh or salted. Strange when you think how many millions of the little fellows have been caught and canned or turned into an essence or the gentleman's relish, *Patum Peperium*.

Anchovies belong to the herring family, and shoal in the warm waters of the Mediterranean, and around Spain. (There are various species around the world.) Fresh anchovies do not transport well as they are fragile and tend to disintegrate quickly, so it will only be the rare occasion, perhaps on holiday abroad, that you are likely to find them. Salted anchovies are growing in popularity among chefs, thanks to Rose Gray and Ruthie Rogers at London's River Café, who have always sought out and demanded the best of everything. In my opinion salted anchovies are much superior to the oiled varieties. To use, simply soak for a couple of hours in water or milk, and then lift off the fillets, discarding head and bones. Use for any recipe that demands anchovies in oil.

As to those in oil, by and large you get what you pay for. There are some delicious ones from Spain which I can eat straight from the tin, but be selective and get to know the variety that best pleases your palate.

Anchovy side-kicks include anchovy essence and anchovy paste, both of them useful products.

## Anchovy Butter

*Anchovies marry well with grilled steak. Make a roll of this anchovy butter and store in your freezer.*

● *Cream 225g (8 oz) unsalted butter with 2 tablespoons chopped capers, 2 tablespoons lemon juice and 1 crushed clove of garlic. Press 8 anchovy fillets through a fine sieve and fold into the butter.*

● *Roll up in clingfilm, then refrigerate or freeze.*

● *Serve a slice on top of a grilled steak.*

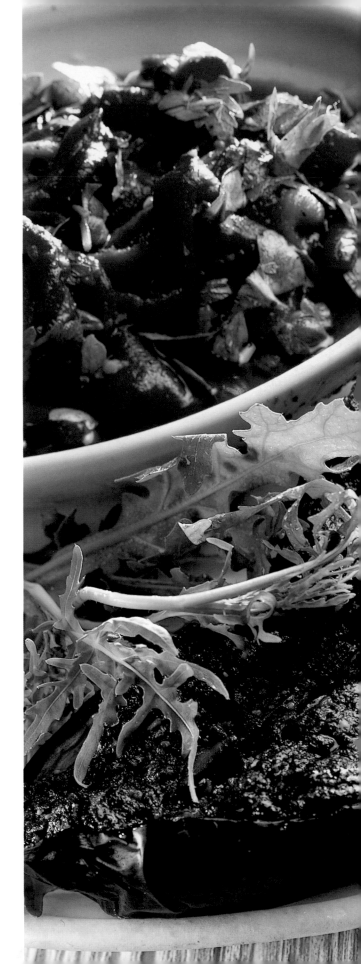

# Anchovy and Roasted Pepper *Compote*

Perfect on *crostini* or *bruschetta* with a few rocket leaves and shards of Parmesan, or served as a side dish with grilled fish or lamb.

**Preparation and cooking: 1 hour**
**Serves: up to 6**

150ml (¼ pint) extra virgin olive oil

6 red peppers, roasted or grilled (see page 254), peeled, seeded and cut into 5mm (¼ in) dice

1 teaspoon soft thyme leaves

15 anchovy fillets, chopped

4 cloves garlic, crushed

12 basil leaves, ripped

2 tablespoons roughly chopped flat-leaf parsley

2 tablespoons small capers, drained and rinsed

½ teaspoon ground black pepper

1 teaspoon balsamic vinegar

**1** Heat the olive oil in a medium saucepan over a low heat. Add the pepper dice with the thyme and cook for 12 minutes. Add any of the delicious juices that escaped when peeling and seeding the peppers.

**2** Add the anchovies and cook until they have 'melted' into the *compote*, about 10 minutes. Remove from the heat and fold in the garlic and basil. Allow to cool to room temperature.

**3** When cool, fold in the remaining ingredients. Because of the anchovies this *compote* will not require any further salt. Refrigerate until required. Serve at room temperature.

• • • • • • • • • • •

*Fold a little of the anchovy butter opposite into a white sauce or Béchamel Sauce (see page 60) with some parsley for the perfect sauce to partner lamb or mutton.*

• • • • • • • • • • •

Anchovy and Roasted Pepper *Compote* with Grilled Nutty Aubergine (see page 23) – two tempting *antipasti*.

# Anchovy Dipping Sauce

I could have called this *anchoïade*, but it's not *quite* the classic French recipe. A versatile sauce for those of you who worship anchovies. As good for raw vegetables, especially cauliflower, as it is for boiled or grilled fish, or just spread on a slice of toast, or dolloped on to a hunk of steak.

**Preparation: 15 minutes**
**Serves: up to 6**

2 egg yolks

1 teaspoon Dijon mustard

12 basil leaves

8 anchovy fillets

3 teaspoons capers, drained and rinsed

1 clove garlic, roughly chopped

4 tablespoons finely chopped parsley

juice of 1 lemon

½ teaspoon ground black pepper

300ml (½ pint) extra virgin olive oil

**1** Place the first nine ingredients in the bowl of a food processor and blend until semi-smooth.
**2** With the machine running, add the olive oil little by little as you would if you were making mayonnaise.
**3** For a more substantial sauce add a couple of tablespoons of soft white breadcrumbs before you add the oil. Check seasoning and serve at room temperature. Refrigerate if not required immediately (keeps for 2 weeks).

• • • • • • • • • •
*2 tablespoons of*
*anchovy essence folded into*
*600ml (1 pint) melted butter*
*is a great accompaniment to*
*asparagus or boiled*
*artichokes.*
• • • • • • • • • •

# Caesar Salad Dressing

I was going to make a Caesar salad, but then I asked myself 'Which section would it go in?', Salad Leaves or Cheese, so I decided on the dressing. Here it is, then, in the Anchovy section, a little controversially, as there are those who insist that anchovies are wrong for a Caesar salad. I think they're *vital*. Traditionally the dressing would be made with a one-minute coddled or boiled egg yolk but perhaps life is too short to be that pernickety.

**Preparation: 10 minutes**
**Serves: up to 6**

2 egg yolks

1 tablespoon red wine vinegar

1 tablespoon freshly squeezed lemon juice

5 tinned anchovy fillets, mashed to a paste

1 teaspoon anchovy essence

3 cloves garlic, mashed to a paste

1 tablespoon Dijon mustard

1 teaspoon English mustard powder

½ tablespoon ground black pepper

2 teaspoons Worcestershire sauce

300ml (½ pint) good olive oil

**1** In a food processor blend together all the ingredients except the oil. I like my dressing quite peppery, so reduce the quantity of pepper if this is not to your liking.
**2** With the machine running add the oil in a slow trickle as you would for mayonnaise. Serve at room temperature. Refrigerate until required.

**N.B.** To make a Caesar salad, tear into bite-sized pieces washed and thoroughly dried leaves of 2 crispy cos lettuces. Add enough dressing to coat the leaves, fold in 85g (3 oz) freshly grated Parmesan and 85g (3 oz) Parmesan *croûtons* (see page 53). Toss to combine. Don't faff around with marinated anchovies or shards of Parmesan; a Caesar salad made well does not need unnecessary adornment.

## Anchovy Powder

*This is an ancient recipe that I've found useful for sauce thickening, folding into stews or casseroles or adding to the flour when making a batch of fresh pasta. You can also dust your fillets of fish with it before frying.*

● *Pound some anchovies, some grated lemon rind and a little cayenne, pass through a fine sieve then fold in enough flour to make a dough.*

● *Shape into a roll, then cut into 1cm (½ in) discs.*

● *Bake in a very low oven until the biscuits are brittle. Allow to cool.*

● *Break up with a knife, then process in a blender or a coffee grinder to a fine powder.*

* * * *

*Instead of using salt in your gravy, add a dash of anchovy essence.*

* * * *

* * * * * * * *

*When roasting a leg of lamb, spike the flesh with some slivers of anchovy as well as garlic and rosemary.*

* * * * * * * *

## Quick Spaghetti

● *Fry 6 cloves of smashed garlic and 6 tablespoons of extra virgin olive oil with 2 finely sliced chillies and 6 chopped anchovy fillets for 5 minutes over a low heat. Discard garlic and chillies.*

● *Add a splash of white wine, the cooked spaghetti with a little of the cooking water still clinging, and a handful of chopped flat-leaf parsley.*

● *Season with plenty of black pepper.*

## Anchovy Mashed Potatoes

*An excellent accompaniment to plainly cooked fish.*

● *Fry 1 chopped onion in 85g (3 oz) unsalted butter and fold in 8 chopped anchovies.*

● *Cook for a couple of minutes then add 150ml (¼ pint) double cream.*

● *Fold in 900g (2 lb) of dry mashed potatoes and a handful of finely chopped spring onions or chives.*

## A Sauce for Fish

*A quick hot sauce to go with a chunk of cod, halibut or turbot.*

● *Cook 1 tablespoon crushed garlic, 4 chopped anchovy fillets, 150ml (¼ pint) dry white wine and 1 tablespoon lemon juice together in a saucepan over a high heat.*

● *Reduce by half, then fold in 150ml (¼ pint) double cream and a handful of shredded sorrel and cook for a further 5 minutes.*

● *Liquidise or serve as is.*

* * * * * * * * * * *

*If you do find fresh anchovies, wash and dry them well. Cut off the heads and remove the innards. Remove backbone by gently pushing along the spine from the skin side, then pull out the bone as you would for sardines. Dip them in milk, then in cayenne-seasoned flour. Deep-fry in hot dripping until golden. Serve naked with a wedge of lemon.*

* * * * * * * * * * *

THE ABC OF AWT

# ARTICHOKE, GLOBE

The globe artichoke (actually no relation of the Jerusalem artichoke) is a type of thistle native to the Mediterranean. It can be grown in sunny positions further north, and the plants can reach a height of some 2m (7 ft). The vegetable, at the top of long sturdy stalks, consists of the unopened flower bud of the plant. The scale-like leaves are too tough to eat except at the very base, and these must be pulled away to get at the delicious heart. This heart is the base of the infant thistle flower, and its fibrous 'stamens' – known as the choke – must also be removed.

Globe artichokes still grow best around the Mediterranean, and are loved by the Italians and the French – why not the British? The trouble is that they are often sold in Britain a little past their prime, too large and too woody. In their countries of origin, small – even tiny – artichokes are available in season (summer and autumn), often so immature that the choke has not yet formed. These are tender and delicious, and can be eaten whole. Occasionally they are seen here, when they are known as mini violet or *poivrade* artichokes.

The preparation of artichokes is off-putting to many, but once you know what to do, you'll repeat the experience on a regular basis.

## For Plain Boiled Large Artichokes

1   If the leaves are not tightly closed, soak in a bowl of salted water to expel any insects. (Some cooks pull off tougher outside leaves. Generally that is not necessary.)

2   If the artichokes are young and fresh, the stalks can be eaten, otherwise they are cut off at the bottom of the leaves.

3   Prepare a bowl of cold water diluted with lemon juice or white vinegar into which you place each prepared artichoke until ready to cook. (The leaves discolour easily when cut, and the **acidulated water** will prevent this.)

4   Prepare a large pot of boiling salted water into which you pour 2 tablespoons of vinegar for every litre (1¾ pints) of water. Some chefs add a *blanc* to preserve the colour which is made by whisking 2 tablespoons of plain flour into every litre (1¾ pints) of water. Discoloration of the artichokes makes no difference to the flavour, however.

5   Cook the artichokes for between 15 and 30 minutes, depending on size. To test whether they are cooked, pull off an outside leaf and if the bottom, thick part of the leaf is tender when nibbled or sucked, it is ready. (If eating the artichokes cold, allow them to cool down in the cooking liquor.)

6   Make hollandaise (see page 113) or melted butter to eat with hot artichokes or vinaigrette (see page 240) to eat with cold.

7   Give each of your guests an extra side plate on which to place the discarded leaves.

8   To eat, pull away the leaves starting at the bottom and suck or nibble the thicker fleshier part at the base of each leaf after dipping into your chosen dressing. The remainder of the leaf can be discarded.

9   When you have eaten the final leaf you will be left with the heart and the choke, a tuft of whitish fibres. Remove these fibres by scooping them off the flesh with a teaspoon or just pulling them off with your fingers.

10   You are then left with the heart, in a way the whole point of the exercise, which is delicious.

Artichokes cooked and served in this way are excellent for dieters as they take so long to eat that you rarely feel like having anything else! Don't be tempted to buy canned artichokes or hearts as they are fairly tasteless. However, wood-roasted artichokes in olive oil are very pleasant and excellent in a char-grilled vegetable salad.

And never try to drink a good wine with artichokes. A chemical constituent, cynarine, makes everything taste sweet.

*Mash cooked artichoke bases or blend in a food processor, pass through a fine sieve and mix with a little garlic paste (see page 194), lemon juice and extra virgin olive oil for a mixture to top pasta or spread on crostini (see page 53).*

# Baby Artichokes
## *en Barigoule*

A classic dish from Provence that I have enjoyed on many occasions in the South of France but rarely in England. In many restaurants down there you are given a massive dish of them as a starter, and made well they are extremely moreish.

**Preparation and cooking: 45 minutes**

**Serves: 4**

| |
|---|
| 16 baby artichokes |
| 2 lemons |
| 150ml (¼ pint) good olive oil |
| 2 carrots, cut in thin slices |
| 2 onions, thinly sliced |
| 1 bay leaf |
| 1 teaspoon soft thyme leaves |
| 8 cloves garlic, 5 finely chopped |
| 300ml (½ pint) dry white wine |
| 12 basil leaves, finely chopped |
| 3 tablespoons chopped flat-leaf parsley |
| salt and ground black pepper |

**1** Cut the stems of the artichokes leaving about 4cm (1½ in) remaining. Cut 1cm (½ in) from the top of the leaves, peel the artichoke bases and stems, and remove two or three rows of leaves from the base. Gently spread the remaining leaves and with a teaspoon or small melon baller remove the choke. Rub all cut surfaces with wedges from 1 lemon then place the trimmed artichokes in a bowl of **acidulated water** (use the juice of the second lemon).

**2** In a large heavy saucepan or casserole dish heat the olive oil over a medium flame, then add the carrot, onion, bay leaf and thyme. Stir to combine. Add the 3 whole garlic cloves. Cook slowly until the vegetables have softened and are just turning golden.

**3** Add the artichokes in one layer, leaf side down, then pour in the wine. Top up with water until the artichokes are just covered. Cover with a lid, bring to the boil, reduce the heat and simmer for 15–20 minutes or until the artichokes are tender.

**4** Remove the artichokes and set aside to keep warm. Increase the heat and boil until the liquid has reduced by half.

**5** Remove from the heat and fold in the chopped garlic, basil and parsley. Season with salt and ground black pepper. Pour the vegetables and juices over the artichokes. Serve hot or at room temperature.

## Preserved Artichokes

● *Place cooked baby artichokes briefly on a barbecue to brown all over, then allow to cool.*

● *Place in a large Kilner jar, layering them with garlic slivers, chopped rind from pickled lemons (see page 171) and some sprigs of thyme, then cover with extra virgin olive oil.*

● *Leave for one month before using, as a starter, part of an* antipasto, *or to garnish grilled fish.*

## Artichoke *Salsa*

*Good with grilled fish.*

● *Chop 4 cooked artichoke hearts in small dice and combine with diced tomato, chopped flat-leaf parsley, some chopped garlic, a chopped fresh chilli, ½ a diced red onion, a little lime juice, some chopped coriander and olive oil.*

*Cold cooked artichokes mixed with cooked jumbo prawns, cooked haricot green beans, raw peeled broad beans and raw podded new peas and tossed with a mixture of half soured cream, half mayonnaise, chopped chives and chervil, some diced tomato, a dash of Tabasco and a squeeze of lemon make a great starter.*

*A superb dish for vegetarians is to make a pie with layers of baby artichokes, potatoes, Swiss chard and a savoury egg and cream filling.*

. . . . . . . .

*Toss cooked baby
artichokes with honey,
lemon juice and olive oil
for a great salad.*

. . . . . . . .

## Deep-fried Artichokes

*A classic dish from Rome.*
- *Take some very young baby artichokes, then remove the tough outer leaves and 1cm (½ in) off the top.*
- *Carefully remove any choke with a melon baller then pull each leaf down slightly so that the artichoke resembles a flower.*
- *Heat a decent amount of oil over a low flame, then fry the artichokes slowly without colouring, turning from time to time.*
- *When cooked, push leaves down even more to spread them out.*
- *Increase temperature under the oil and deep-fry until crisp.*
- *Drain well and serve hot.*

. . . . . . . . . . . . . . . . . . . . . . . .

*If you have a glut of artichokes in the
garden you might like to dry them. Trim
them, remove the chokes, boil them in salted
water for 15 minutes, then drain. Place in a
low oven – 140°C/275°F/Gas 1 – for 1 hour
then cool them. Repeat the oven procedure
several times until completely dried out.
Perfect for folding into Mediterranean
stews or grinding to a powder and
folding into fresh pasta dough.*

. . . . . . . . . . . . . . . . . .

# Stewed Artichokes with Spices and Apricots

I'm a bit of a fan of North African cooking and I was given this dish (and its recipe) by a friend who spent a great deal of time in that part of the world. It's packed full of flavour and textures, and with a mass of spices with a sugary aftertaste.

**Preparation and cooking: 45 minutes**
**Serves: 4–6**

4 large globe artichokes
1 lemon, cut into pieces, plus juice of 1 lemon
2 cloves garlic, finely sliced
10 black peppercorns, crushed
12 coriander seeds, toasted
¼ teaspoon ground turmeric
⅛ teaspoon cayenne pepper
¼ teaspoon cumin seeds, toasted
2 onions, cut in eights
2 bay leaves
50ml (2 fl oz) extra virgin olive oil
pinch of saffron stamens, soaked in cold water
2 carrots, sliced
300–600ml (½–1 pint) vegetable stock
8 dried apricots, sliced
55g (2 oz) raisins
25g (1 oz) sliced almonds
1 x 400g (14 oz) tin chickpeas, drained and rinsed
225g (8 oz) baby spinach
2 tablespoons roughly chopped coriander
4 tablespoons roughly chopped flat-leaf parsley
salt and ground black pepper

**1** Trim the artichokes by peeling the stem until all woody matter has disappeared. Pull off all tough outer leaves until you reach the pale green ones. Cut about 2.5cm (1 in) off the top of the artichoke. Cut the artichoke vertically into four and cut or pull out the choke. Rub all cut surfaces with squeezed lemon pieces and place the artichoke quarters in a bowl of water to which you have added the lemon juice.

**2** In a mortar and pestle or coffee grinder crush together the garlic, peppercorns, coriander seeds, turmeric, cayenne and cumin seeds.

**3** In a saucepan cook the onions and bay leaves in the olive

oil over a medium heat until soft but without colour, about 8 minutes. Add the spice mix and cook for a further 3 minutes.

**4** Add the artichokes and the saffron with its soaking liquor and toss to combine. Add the carrots, 300ml (½ pint) of the vegetable stock, the apricots, raisins and almonds, and simmer, covered, for about 20 minutes, stirring from time to time. You may need to add more stock.

**5** When the artichokes are tender, add the chickpeas, spinach, coriander and parsley, and stir to combine. Cook until the spinach has wilted, a couple of minutes only. Season to taste. Serve hot or at room temperature with steamed couscous or rice.

*Trim artichokes, thinly slice, then cook on a griddle pan or barbecue to achieve a wonderful smoky flavour.*

# Raw Artichoke and Parmesan Salad

There are times when all you want to eat is something light; there are also times when you fancy something healthy, but often healthy has connotations of boring. This little salad is far from boring, but being made with a raw vegetable, you feel a warm sense of satisfaction after eating it. Only make this dish just before you wish to eat as it discolours quickly.

**Preparation and cooking: 15 minutes**
**Serves: 4**

3 lemons

8 *poivrade*, violet or baby artichokes

50ml (2 fl oz) extra virgin olive oil

2 egg yolks

85g (3 oz) Parmesan, freshly grated

salt and ground black pepper

couple of handfuls of rocket leaves

**1** Prepare a bowl of **acidulated water**, using the juice of 1 of the lemons. Reduce the stems of the artichokes to about 4cm (1½ in) in length, then peel them with a potato peeler. Cut about 1cm (½ in) from the top of the artichokes and discard. Rub the cut artichoke from time to time with a second lemon, cut in half. Remove any tough outside leaves. Spread the remaining leaves and use a small spoon or melon baller to remove the choke. Place the artichokes in the acidulated water until ready to use.

**2** Make a dressing by combining the olive oil, the grated zest and juice of the third lemon, the egg yolks and Parmesan. Season to taste.

**3** Drain, then finely shred or slice each artichoke. As you complete each one, place the artichoke in the dressing. Stir to coat with dressing.

**4** Arrange the rocket leaves on the bottom of a salad dish or on four plates. Top with the raw artichoke in the dressing, and serve immediately.

*Cut large artichokes down to the base, cut bases into quarters and stew with peas, sage, pancetta bacon, baby new potatoes, baby onions and olive oil until the vegetables are tender. Finish with lemon juice and flat-leaf parsley. A starter or a vegetable accompaniment.*

*Mix cooked chopped artichoke bases with loads of parsley and Parmesan. Pour in beaten eggs and cook a frittata (see page 115) or tortilla.*

*Slice some trimmed baby artichokes and new potatoes, toss with some chopped garlic and soft thyme leaves and place under a leg of lamb when preparing your Sunday roast.*

# ARTICHOKE, JERUSALEM

These small tubers are not related to the globe artichoke, but they may have acquired the name artichoke because the flavours are said to be similar. I don't think my palate is shot, but I can't discern it frankly. Neither are they from Jerusalem, but from North America, and that sobriquet is probably a corruption of *girasole*, Italian for sunflower, the botanical family to which the vegetable belongs.

We should see more Jerusalem artichokes in our greengrocers and supermarkets because they are a special root vegetable. Treat them much in the same way as you would a potato although their texture does become a lot softer. Interestingly enough, unlike the potato, they contain no starch, but the carbohydrate inulin, which is composed of fructose units, so these vegetables could be useful for diabetics. One small downside to the Jerusalem artichoke is that, like beans, they create wind.

They look akin to knobbly potatoes or bulbous ginger, grow well in northern countries, and are at their best in the winter. When buying, look for the least knobbly, otherwise you are in for serious waste. They should also be very firm, with no give when pressed. Try to buy just before you need them, but if stored in a dark dry place they will keep for up to a week.

To prepare, peel as you would a potato, removing any stringy roots, then drop them immediately into **acidulated water** so they don't discolour. Or, if they are very knobbly, wash and scrub and drop them into boiling salted water for 10 minutes, then run them under cold water until you can peel away the skins. Now you can proceed with your recipe.

## Jerusalem Chicken

*Jerusalem artichokes have a natural partner in chicken.*
- *Fry some chicken thighs until golden, and place in a deep casserole.*
- *Fry garlic with onions, oregano and capers, add peeled and thinly sliced Jerusalem artichokes, some white wine and stock and cook for 30 minutes.*

# Jerusalem Artichoke Soup with Crispy Bacon

These tubers make one of the finest soups around, perfect comfort food on a cold winter's day.

**Preparation and cooking: 40 minutes**
**Serves: 4**

6 rashers streaky smoked bacon, cut into **lardons**
450g (1 lb) Jerusalem artichokes, peeled, diced and submerged in **acidulated water**
225g (8 oz) floury potatoes, diced
1 onion, diced
2 cloves garlic, diced
1 stick celery, diced
115g (4 oz) unsalted butter
1 teaspoon soft thyme leaves
1 litre (1¾ pints) chicken or vegetable stock
300ml (½ pint) double cream (optional)
pinch of freshly grated nutmeg
2 handfuls baby spinach, washed
salt and ground black pepper

**1** In a heavy-based saucepan over a medium heat cook the bacon until it releases some of its fat and becomes golden and crisp, about 8 minutes. Remove bacon and set aside.
**2** Drain the artichokes and put them into the bacon fat, then add the potato, onion, garlic, celery and half the butter. Stir to combine, add the thyme, and cook for 10 minutes, stirring regularly until the potatoes start to soften.
**3** Add the stock and leave to simmer until the vegetables are soft, about 10 minutes. Blend everything in a liquidiser until smooth, then pass through a fine sieve if you want a squeaky smooth soup. Return the soup to the saucepan.
**4** Add the cream, nutmeg and spinach and reheat, stirring, until the spinach has wilted, a couple of minutes only. Fold in the remaining butter, cut in small cubes, if desired. Season to taste with a little salt and a decent amount of black pepper.
**5** Serve in hot bowls and scatter with the crispy bacon pieces.

*Instead of using potato for a salt cod brandade, fold in mashed Jerusalem artichokes.*

# ASPARAGUS

Asparagus is one of those vegetables that almost everyone enjoys, so much so that unfortunately it is available all year round . . . I say 'unfortunately' because I am a vigorous defender of the seasons. There is nothing nicer than eating the freshest of fresh asparagus in the latter half of May and throughout June, for British asparagus is infinitely better than imported varieties. Part of the reason may be psychological, but undoubtedly asparagus doesn't travel well, and the flavour diminishes as the hours of travel increase.

Asparagus, a member of the lily family, is native to southern Europe, North Africa and parts of Asia. It is a shoot vegetable, growing from underground rootstock. Originally eaten for its curative values, it has now become a valued member of the luxury vegetable category. This wasn't always so, for in the nineteenth century it was often used as a substitute for peas. Various old books that I possess state, 'Take one hundred heads of asparagus and cut off about 2 inches of head ends, cut them into pieces about the size of peas . . . sufficient for five persons.'

So what do you look for when buying asparagus? Firstly the colour: white or green? They are the same variety, only the white is blanched by 'earthing up' or cutting while still under the ground. I must admit that I prefer the green for a sweeter, stronger, asparagus flavour, although the French prefer the white. Whichever, only buy the freshest available. Never buy asparagus with wrinkled or dried-out ends; the spears should be crisp (without too much flexibility), green (or white/purple), with the tips dry and tight. Size is of some importance as asparagus that is too large will tend to be woody. Very small spears, called sprue, are deliciously sweet and can be picked up for a song (Cockney traders call sprue 'grass', from 'sparrow grass', a corruption of asparagus). Try to buy asparagus, whether fatter or thin, with each spear much the same thickness as this will help the cooking process.

To prepare asparagus, cut away or snap off the woody end if applicable. Green asparagus may need a further 2–5cm (1–2 in) thinly peeled to make every bit edible; white asparagus generally needs peeling from tip to tail as the outer skin is far tougher.

As for cooking there is a variety of views expounded about the correct way. Some books tell you to tie them into bundles, but from my experience you tend to overcook the outer layer, the string cutting into it, and the centre spears are under-cooked. Some books (for those with deep pockets) advise the purchase of a special boiler where the asparagus stands upright in a narrow basket with 5–8cm (2–3 in) of the stalk base submerged in water. This works well, but how many of us need or want an extra pan in the kitchen? No, the simple and perfectly effective way is to throw asparagus spears into boiling salted water in a suitable pan (a friend uses an enamel coffee pot to keep the tips out of the water), and cook over a high heat for 5–12 minutes, depending on its thickness. Drain and serve immediately.

The classic combos include hollandaise sauce (see page 113), melted butter or *sauce Maltaise* (hollandaise sauce combined with reduced blood orange juice). For cold asparagus, don't plunge the spears into iced water as this tends to reduce the flavour even if it does retain the bright colour. Allow to cool naturally and serve with herbed cream, *Mayonnaise* or vinaigrette (see pages 239 or 240).

And the downsides to asparagus? There are only two to my knowledge: the sulphur content makes your urine smell very strong, and, because of that same sulphur, asparagus is very hard to partner with wine, making it taste metallic (a herby spicy wine such as an Alsace Gewürztraminer is probably the best choice). The upside is that asparagus is rich in vitamins A, $B_1$, $B_2$ and C and, a bonus for the diet conscious, an average portion without any dressing will yield only about 35 calories.

*Instead of serving toast 'soldiers' with soft-boiled eggs,*
*serve warm or cold asparagus spears for dipping.*

# Asparagus 'Peas' Cooked in their Own Juices Ⓥ

Quite the best recipe I've tried to get the full flavour of asparagus. Despite what I say in the introduction about smaller asparagus being sweeter, for this dish I use a larger variety, as they juice better.

**Preparation and cooking: 30 minutes**
**Serves: 4 as a starter, 6 as a side dish**

1kg (2¼ lb) medium-large asparagus
55g (2 oz) unsalted butter
¼ teaspoon salt
1 teaspoon caster sugar
¼ teaspoon ground black pepper

**1** Cut 7.5cm (3 in) off the base of each asparagus stalk and set aside. Cut the remainder of the asparagus, including the tips, into 5mm (¼ in) pieces, the 'peas'.
**2** Extract the juice from the asparagus base pieces by placing them in a centrifugal juicer. Discard the pulp.
**3** Place the asparagus 'peas', the juice, butter, salt, sugar and pepper in a saucepan so that the liquid just covers the asparagus. Add extra water if necessary.
**4** Cook uncovered over a high heat, stirring from time to time, for about 8–10 minutes. The asparagus is cooked when the liquid has all but evaporated, leaving behind the concentrated buttery juices. Season to taste.

## Asparagus Soup

*Some asparagus hasn't much flavour, so you can add some extras.*
● *Melt butter and cook shallots, garlic and soft thyme leaves until soft.*
● *Add some diced potato and vegetable stock and cook until the potatoes are soft. Add trimmed asparagus, some fresh peas, a handful of spinach, and cook for 7 minutes.*
● *Liquidise and pass through a sieve, then season to taste.*
● *Serve topped with a dollop of whipped cream and a few **blanched** asparagus tips.*

# An Asparagus Stir-fry Ⓥ

There are times when you want to treat yourself and you don't fancy any meat or fish. Asparagus lends itself nicely to oriental flavours and the crunchy texture is perfect for a stir-fry.

**Preparation and cooking: 30 minutes**
**Serves: 4**

1kg (2¼ lb) small-medium asparagus, trimmed and peeled if necessary
salt and ground black pepper
1 tablespoon sesame oil
1 tablespoon vegetable or groundnut oil
½ fresh red chilli, finely sliced
1 clove garlic, finely chopped
4 spring onions, sliced diagonally
1 tablespoon lemon juice
1 tablespoon soy sauce
1 tablespoon chopped coriander
55g (2 oz) cashew nuts, chopped
½ tablespoon sesame seeds, toasted

**1** Cut the asparagus into 2.5cm (1 in) pieces. Cook for 1–2 minutes in boiling salted water.
**2** At the same time heat the two oils over a medium heat in a wok or frying pan. Add the chilli, garlic and spring onion and cook over a high heat for 1 minute.
**3** Drain the asparagus and add to the oil base with the water clinging to the spears. Stir to combine, and cook for 2 minutes before adding the remaining ingredients. Warm through and serve immediately or allow to cool to room temperature and serve as a salad.

*For brunch serve crunchy hot asparagus with poached eggs, a dribble of reduced hot double cream and a scattering of breadcrumbs fried crisp in clarified butter (see page 60).*

## Asparagus Sauce

*Good with fish or chicken.*

- *Chop up the stalks, retaining tips, and cook for 10 minutes.*
- *Blanch the asparagus tips for 5 minutes.*
- *Make a butter sauce by folding butter into reduced vegetable stock with a teaspoon of caster sugar and the juice of a lemon.*
- *Fry the cooked asparagus in butter with a handful of spinach leaves for 3 minutes and liquidise with the butter sauce, then pass through a fine sieve. Season.*
- *Fold in the blanched asparagus tips.*

*__Blanch__ asparagus then pan-fry it and serve with nutty brown butter, chopped hard-boiled egg and some deep-fried capers.*

*For a totally different taste and texture, roast asparagus in a hot oven for 20 minutes with a decent amount of butter, shredded pancetta and grated Parmesan.*

*Wrap cold cooked small asparagus in slices of Parma ham spread thinly with Tapenade (see page 243) for delicious finger food.*

# A Warm Salad of Asparagus, Field Mushrooms and Fresh Peas Ⓥ

Warm salads were all the rage during the *nouvelle* 1980s with, more often than not, weird and not so wonderful combinations. This one was made to last, fresh and vibrant with clean flavours. Perfect for a light lunch, for supper or as a starter.

**Preparation and cooking: 30 minutes**
**Serves: 4**

20 medium asparagus spears, trimmed and peeled if necessary

175g (6 oz) shelled young peas

4 tablespoons extra virgin olive oil

1 clove garlic, mashed to a paste with a little salt

8 small field mushrooms, stalks removed, peeled if necessary

salt and ground black pepper

1 *ciabatta* loaf, cut into two horizontally then in two from top to bottom

1 shallot, finely chopped

3 tablespoons Dry Martini

55g (2 oz) unsalted butter, cubed

1 tablespoon chopped flat-leaf parsley

1 tablespoon snipped chives

1 teaspoon chopped tarragon

1 tablespoon freshly squeezed lemon juice

25g (1 oz) each of rocket and watercress leaves

**1** Cook the asparagus in boiling salted water for 1 minute, remove and set aside.

**2** Add the peas to the asparagus cooking water and cook for 2–5 minutes, drain and set aside.

**3** Prepare your barbie, grill or griddle pan.

**4** Combine the olive oil and garlic and brush over the asparagus and both sides of the mushrooms. Season the asparagus and mushrooms with salt and black pepper.

**5** Grill or barbecue the mushrooms for 4 minutes on each side, and the asparagus for 2 minutes on each side. Keep both warm. Brush the *ciabatta* slices on both sides with the garlic oil and grill until both sides are toasted.

**6** In a saucepan heat the remaining oil infusion, add the shallot and over a medium heat allow to cook without colour. Add the Dry Martini, increase the heat and cook for a further minute. Remove the pan from the heat and whisk in the butter a little at a time. Fold in the peas, parsley, chives, tarragon and lemon juice. Season to taste. Return to a gentle heat to warm through.

**7** Combine the rocket and watercress and divide between four plates. Top the leaves with a slice of the grilled bread. Divide the asparagus and mushrooms between the bread slices, arranging them attractively on top of each slice. Spoon the peas and buttery juices over the salad leaves.

## Deep-fried Asparagus

● *Season some flour and put on a plate.*

● *Beat an egg with 150ml (¼ pint) milk, a dash of Tabasco, some grated nutmeg, a teaspoon of chicken stock powder, salt and pepper.*

● *Combine 25g (1 oz) grated Parmesan with 55g (2 oz) fresh breadcrumbs.*

● *Dip the asparagus into the flour, then the egg, then the breadcrumb mix.*

● *Deep-fry in hot oil for 4 minutes until golden.*

*Try char-grilled asparagus with mollet eggs (6-minute boiled, see page 112) and Parmesan shavings with a dribble of extra virgin olive oil, a splash of balsamic vinegar and a few grinds of black pepper.*

*Hot asparagus with crispy bacon fried in butter, a handful of chopped flat-leaf parsley and a squeeze of lemon juice is a marriage made in heaven.*

*Serve cold asparagus with Mayonnaise (see page 239) into which you have folded some whipped cream and a little grated orange rind.*

# AUBERGINE

The aubergine, the fruit of a tall shrub native to Asia, is known in various countries by a host of names. The British know it as aubergine, but this name was originally used by the French . . . or was it? The Spanish called it *berenjena*, the Arabs, *al-badinjan* . . . Then there were the imaginative Americans who named it the 'eggplant', probably because the first one they saw was small, white and looked like an egg. The Australians also adopted the name eggplant.

It is an ancient vegetable. The Chinese first encountered it in the third century AD, but it was not greatly appreciated, as it had a reputation for high toxicity. Possibly this could be connected to the fact that it has a host of troublesome relatives of the Solanaceae family, including deadly nightshade (or belladonna) and tobacco. Some of its more friendly relatives include the tomato, potato and red pepper. There are also tiny varieties available, including the 'pea' aubergine; some are green or white or streaked pink, and are seen mainly in Indian shops.

The aubergine finally made its way to the Mediterranean, where it developed into the vegetable we all know and some of us adore, the long, rounded, lustrous purple variety. It obviously still had a dubious reputation, because it was known as *mala insana*, or 'mad apple'. To this day, the Italians call it *melanzana* and the Greeks *melitzana*. It grows best in sunny countries.

Most of the aubergines seen in Britain come from Holland. But try, where possible, to buy Spanish or Italian aubergines during the summer and you will appreciate what a bit of natural sun can do. You will learn to enjoy a vegetable that is probably more versatile than anything else we can buy on our shelves.

Look for aubergines that are shiny-skinned, taut and deeply purple. When in the greengrocer or supermarket, sneak a little squeeze, they should be firm and feel heavy for their size. Never buy a wrinkly one or one that is bruised or has a dull skin. Buy when you want to use or, failing that, keep them in the salad drawer of the refrigerator for a few days.

How do you prepare them? For a start, this is one of the few vegetables that you don't boil, as they taste disgusting. Jane Grigson felt that aubergines were best peeled unless you were going to stuff them. In this I beg to differ, as the skins nowadays are rarely leathery. Always remove the green calyx at the top with caution as it can give you a nasty prick. Do you salt the vegetable after slicing, cubing or wedging? The general rule is yes. Having said that, most aubergines we can buy these days do not have the bitter juices which the salt is meant to remove. However, it would appear from research that salting for half an hour, draining and drying will reduce the amount of oil or fat that the aubergine absorbs when cooking by up to one-third. This also obviously reduces excessive moisture, therefore cooking time as well.

I urge you to get to know the aubergine, as it will give you years of cookery pleasure. Dieters can rejoice as well, as a portion size yields only 25 calories; unfortunately the cooking medium, oil, will quadruple that. The aubergine also has healthy qualities: while relatively low in vitamins, it is extremely rich in minerals and essential amino acids.

. . . . . . . . . . . . . . . . . . . . . . . . . . . . . . . . . . . . . . . . . . . . . . . . . . . . . . .

## *Caponata*

*Probably one of the most famous Italian aubergine dishes and widely found in many other cookbooks. As with all classics there are hundreds of variations, but the rough gist of the dish is to deep-fry cubes of aubergine and combine them with blanched cut celery, a tomato sauce made by cooking down peeled tomatoes, garlic, onion and a decent slurp of good olive oil, with some white or red wine vinegar, black or green olives, a decent amount of baby capers, some chopped anchovies, chopped flat-leaf parsley and some ripped basil leaves.*

. . . . . . . . . . . . . . . . . . . . . . . . . . . . . . . . . . . . . . . . . . . . . . . . .

*To make a more spiced version of* caponata, *omit the celery, olives, capers and anchovies, and add some ground cumin, ground allspice and cayenne pepper to the sauce, and some toasted pine kernels, some currants, and chopped coriander and mint.*

# Aubergine, Red Pepper and Herb *Salsa*

*Salsa*, while being an 'in' restaurant word, really just means sauce. The word is generally used for a raw diced tomato relish, usually containing onions, lime juice and coriander with a hint of chilli. Thailand has inspired this delicious recipe, which makes a refreshing salad tossed with a few jumbo prawns and some salad leaves, or it makes an equally great partnership with plain grilled fish.

**Preparation and cooking: 1¼ hours**
**Serves: 4 as a salad, 8 as a garnish**

1 large aubergine
90ml (3 fl oz) vegetable oil
90ml (3 fl oz) soy sauce
90ml (3 fl oz) rice vinegar
2 red peppers, roasted (see page 254), peeled, seeded and diced
2 tablespoons *nam pla* (fish sauce)
2 tablespoons soft dark brown sugar
1 teaspoon chilli sauce
6 spring onions, finely sliced
1 tablespoon grated fresh ginger
2 tablespoons chopped coriander
1 tablespoon chopped mint
2 tablespoons chopped flat-leaf parsley
3 cloves garlic, finely chopped
1 teaspoon finely grated lemon rind

**1** Cut the aubergine lengthways into 5mm (¼ in) slices and combine with the vegetable oil, soy sauce and vinegar. Allow the aubergine to marinate for 1 hour, turning and basting regularly, then drain, if any juices remain.

**2** Cook the aubergine slices ideally over a barbecue, but failing that in a griddle pan or frying pan over a high heat for 4–5 minutes on each side. The aubergine slices should be very dark and thoroughly cooked. Allow to cool.

**3** Cut the aubergine slices to match the red pepper dice. Combine the pepper and aubergine dice with any remaining marinade and the remaining ingredients. Check seasoning. Refrigerate until just before you wish to use. Serve at room temperature.

# Grilled Nutty Aubergine  Ⓥ

I've eaten a variety of spicy aubergine dishes in both Chinese and Japanese restaurants, usually accompanied by either a peanut or sesame sauce. The one that always grabs my fancy is the Japanese dish which is grilled with a *miso* and sesame paste. It tends to use ingredients that are quite difficult to get, so I've created a similar dish that is more accessible. (See the photograph on pages 8-9.)

**Preparation and cooking: 50 minutes**
**Serves: 4 as a starter, 2 as a main course**

2 medium aubergines
1 tablespoon olive oil
salt and ground black pepper
1 tablespoon chopped garlic
3 tablespoons chopped coriander
175g (6 oz) crunchy peanut butter
2 tablespoons sesame oil
90ml (3 fl oz) soy sauce
85g (3 oz) soft dark brown sugar
2 teaspoons rice vinegar
1 tablespoon chilli oil

**1** Preheat the oven to 220°C/425°F/Gas 7.

**2** Cut the aubergines in half lengthways. With a sharp knife score the surface of the cut flesh with criss-cross hatch marks. Brush the cut surfaces of the aubergines with olive oil and season with a little salt and some ground black pepper. Cook in the oven for 20–30 minutes or until the aubergines are very soft.

**3** Remove from the oven and allow to cool. Meanwhile, in a food processor blend the remaining ingredients to a smooth paste. The mixture should be as thick as double cream so if necessary thin down with a little warm water. The recipe can be prepared ahead to this point.

**4** Spread the cut surface of the aubergine halves liberally with the nut paste and cook under a hot grill with the cut surface towards the heat. Cook until the aubergines have warmed through and the top is bubbling with a few charred patches. Serve with a rocket salad.

# Aromatic Aubergine Purée

Aubergine is the perfect vehicle for carrying other flavours as it is pretty bland in its own right. Here is a wonderful purée that is good as a dip or as an accompaniment to grilled chicken or fish.

**Preparation and cooking: 1 hour**
**Serves: 4–6**

| |
|---|
| 2 large aubergines |
| 3 tablespoons peanut or groundnut oil |
| 2 tablespoons finely chopped garlic |
| 1 tablespoon grated fresh ginger |
| 8 spring onions, finely chopped |
| ¾ teaspoon dried chilli flakes |
| 5 tablespoons light soy sauce |
| 4 tablespoons soft dark brown sugar |
| 1 tablespoon rice vinegar |
| 2 tablespoons *mirin* or dry sherry |
| 1 teaspoon sesame oil |
| 1 tablespoon chopped coriander |
| 4 tablespoons Greek yogurt (optional) |

**1** Preheat your oven to 220°C/425°F/Gas 7, then prick the aubergines all over with a fork. Bake the aubergines on a roasting tray for 30–40 minutes or until completely collapsed, turning once or twice during cooking. That is one way, but my preference – and I know this won't be appropriate for everyone – is to char-grill the aubergines all over on a hot barbecue until you achieve the same effect: collapsed aubergines. This latter method gives a much smokier flavour.

**2** If you have oven-roasted, split the aubergines lengthways and scoop out the flesh, discarding the skin. Mash the flesh with a fork. If you have char-grilled, run the aubergines under a tap and scrape off the charred skin, place the flesh in a food processor and blend until smooth.

**3** In a wok or frying pan heat the peanut oil, then add the garlic, ginger, spring onion and chilli flakes and stir-fry for 30 seconds. Add the soy sauce, sugar, rice vinegar and *mirin*, and stir to combine. Cook for 1 minute.

**4** Fold in the aubergine purée and cook over a low heat, stirring continually, for 15 minutes or until most of the moisture has evaporated. Remove from the heat, taste and add extra of any ingredient that you think it needs . . . it shouldn't.

**5** When it has cooled a little, fold in the sesame oil and chopped coriander. When completely cold, fold in the yogurt if you want a milder flavour.

• • • • • • • • • • • •

*Aubergines are essential for one of my favourite dishes, Moussaka (see page 218).*

• • • • • • • • • • • •

• • • • • • • • • • • •

*Aubergines are perfect for stuffing. Roast whole as described on the right, cut lengthways, scoop out flesh and chop. Combine the flesh with a cooked stew of onions, garlic, tomato, olive oil, cumin and flat-leaf parsley. Put mixture back in the skins and bake with a sprinkling of grated Parmesan.*

• • • • • • • • • • • •

• • • • • • • • • • • •

*If you are having a barbecue, thrust whole small aubergines into the hot charcoal and allow them to become charred and blistered, turning them from time to time. Cut open, and eat hot with a spoon after dousing with some extra virgin olive oil, lemon juice, chopped anchovy, salt and pepper.*

• • • • • • • • • • • •

# 'Ratatouille' Fritters

Vegetarians often get a raw deal unless they are prepared to cook for themselves. They will find this recipe attractive, but it shouldn't put off carnivores because it can also serve as a delicious starter.

**Preparation and cooking: 1 hour**
**Serves: 4**

| |
|---|
| 1 medium aubergine |
| 1 small onion, finely chopped |
| 1 clove garlic, finely chopped |
| ½ teaspoon soft thyme leaves |
| 1 tablespoon good olive oil |
| 1 tablespoon tomato purée |
| ½ green pepper, cut into 5mm (¼ in) dice |
| 1 courgette, cut into 5mm (¼ in) dice |
| 1 tomato, seeded and diced |
| 2 tablespoons chopped flat-leaf parsley |
| 1 tablespoon chopped basil |
| 1 teaspoon salt |
| ½ teaspoon ground black pepper |
| 1 egg, beaten |
| 2 tablespoons freshly grated Parmesan |
| ½ teaspoon baking powder |
| 4 tablespoons fresh breadcrumbs |
| oil for frying |

**1** Preheat the oven to 220°C/425°F/Gas 7, and prick the aubergine several times with a fork. Roast on a baking tray in the oven for 30–40 minutes or until the aubergine is very soft and on the point of collapsing. Remove and set aside to cool slightly.

**2** Meanwhile, in a large frying pan over a medium heat cook the onion, garlic and thyme in hot olive oil until the onion is softening but without colour. Add the tomato purée, pepper and courgette, increase the heat, and cook for 5 minutes. Allow to cool slightly.

**3** Cut the aubergine in half and scoop out the flesh. Discard the skin. Mash the aubergine pulp to a purée with a fork or use a food processor. Combine the purée with the fried vegetables and the remaining ingredients except for the frying oil. Check the seasoning.

**4** Heat 5cm (2 in) of frying oil in a deep frying pan or saucepan. Take tablespoonfuls of the aubergine mixture and drop into the hot oil; do not overcrowd. Cook until brown on all sides, about 4–5 minutes. Keep warm in the oven on kitchen paper while frying the remaining fritters. Serve with a salad or your favourite tomato sauce.

## Aubergine and Potato Curry

- *Fry some onions and grated ginger in clarified butter, add turmeric,* garam masala, *salt and cayenne pepper.*
- *Cook for a few minutes then add some skinned tomatoes, halved small new potatoes, and cubed aubergine.*
- *Cook over a medium heat, stirring often until the vegetables are cooked.*
- *Season, fold in lemon juice and some yogurt if required.*

*An aubergine bake is a lovely winter warmer. Make by combining layers of cooked aubergine, cooked rice, a thick cooked tomato sauce, slices of mozzarella, finished off with tomato sauce and grated Parmesan. Bake in a hot oven until bubbling and golden.*

*An elegant starter can be made by layering cut and grilled slices of aubergine with thinly sliced roasted red peppers, slices of buffalo mozzarella and a dressing of olive oil, balsamic vinegar, anchovies, oregano and seasoning. Pre-layer your 'sandwiches' then bake in a hot oven for 10 minutes or until the mozzarella is starting to ooze. Drizzle with the dressing.*

# AVOCADO

Avocados are the fruit of a tropical tree native to central America and Mexico, and botanically are classified as vegetable fruit but nowadays, more often than not, they are used for savoury purposes. They have since migrated to Hawaii, Australia, Africa, Israel and to other parts of the United States, including Florida, which has a flourishing avocado industry. There are over 700 varieties of avocado, but for my taste, not that I've tried all 700, the Haas avocado is best, followed by the Fuerte then possibly the Sharwill. Don't be put off by the lumpy textured skin of the Haas as the flesh has good flavour and a wonderfully buttery texture. Tiny cocktail avocados are occasionally seen, which are seedless.

To choose an avocado ready for eating, cradle one in your hand and gently push the surface which should be slightly yielding. The stem end should be quite soft. If you don't need to eat it immediately buy one that is harder and keep it in an airy place. If you need to ripen an avocado quickly, pop it in a brown paper bag and seal the top. The avocados give off ethylene gas which aids ripening. Once ripe, the avocado can be held for a couple of days in the salad drawer of the refrigerator.

To prepare all avocados cut the pear lengthways into halves, going around the stone. Twist the two halves to separate. The large stone is easily removed by cutting into it with the blade of a knife and twisting. If not using immediately rub the cut surfaces with lemon juice as avocados discolour quickly. The skin comes away very easily if you strip it from the narrow end: a ripe avocado will not require the services of a knife for peeling. If you don't want perfect peeled halves, then take the avocado half in the cup of your hand and ease the flesh away by slipping a tablespoon between skin and flesh. The flesh can now be sliced, chopped, cut in wedges or mashed. If you are preparing an avocado always remember to do so at the last minute because of discoloration. You can slow down the process by adding a citrus juice, covering the surface with clingfilm and, the Mexicans say, by returning the stone to the mixture.

I'm told that avocados are fattening. They do contain some 15–25 per cent oil, but half an avocado costs you about 135 calories, so it is not exactly deadly; unfortunately it's what you eat with the 'avo' that is the problem. Think on the bright side, though; the avocado contains at least eight essential vitamins and five important minerals.

# Avocado and Charred Corn *Salsa* Ⓥ

A delicious topping for nibbles or *tortilla* chips, this recipe is based on *guacamole*, a dish originating in Mexico. So many people have had bad experiences in restaurants with *guacamole* that, although tempted, I decided you would prefer this recipe.

**Preparation: 20 minutes**
**Serves: 4–6**

2 Haas avocados, peeled, seeded and mashed
1 corn cob, **blanched**, char-grilled and nibs removed
1 fresh red chilli, finely diced
¼ teaspoon ground coriander
¼ teaspoon ground cumin
½ small red onion, finely diced
2 plum tomatoes, seeded and diced
½ bunch coriander, leaves only, finely chopped
juice of 1 lemon
2 tablespoons good olive oil
salt and ground black pepper

**1** Combine all the ingredients. Do not place in a food processor. *It should be chunky.* Season to taste.

• • • • •
*Diced avocado mixed with segments of pink grapefruit and vinaigrette is refreshing.*
• • • • •

• • • • • • • • •
*Combine a couple of bunches of washed rocket that you have ripped up with 1 diced avocado and drizzle with extra virgin olive oil, a drop of lemon, a splash of balsamic vinegar and seasoning. Serve immediately.*
• • • • • • • • •

• • • • • • • • • • • •
*A delicious sandwich is made by creaming butter with chopped coriander, spreading this butter on thinly sliced wholegrain brown bread, and topping with sliced tomato, crumbled crispy bacon, avocado slices, some extra virgin olive oil, a squeeze of lemon juice, black pepper and snipped chives.*
• • • • • • • • • • • •

# Avocado and Goat's Cheese Soup

You get lots of avocado soups which are all much of a muchness, based on avocado, stock and cream. This one needs a little more effort, but it creates a dish that is very special.

**Preparation and cooking: 40 minutes**
**Serves: 4**

140g (5 oz) parsley sprigs
55g (2 oz) baby spinach, washed
salt and ground black pepper
3 tablespoons extra virgin olive oil
225g (8 oz) very soft young goat's cheese
300ml (½ pint) double cream
2 ripe medium-sized Haas avocados, stoned, peeled and diced
600ml (1 pint) vegetable stock
1 teaspoon lemon juice
½ teaspoon Tabasco sauce
½ teaspoon ground coriander
½ teaspoon ground cumin
1 tablespoon chopped coriander

**1** Remove any thick stalks from the parsley and spinach. Boil a pan of heavily salted water and cook the spinach for 2 minutes, then add the parsley and cook for a further 2 minutes. Drain and plunge into cold water. Drain and squeeze out most of the water. Blend in a food processor with 2 tablespoons of the oil. Pass the purée through a fine plastic sieve, forcing through as much as you can. Refrigerate until ready for use.

**2** For a garnish purée, place half the goat's cheese in a bowl with 3 tablespoons of the double cream and 2 teaspoons of the remaining oil. Mash to combine. Season with salt and pepper. Refrigerate until half an hour before use.

**3** Place the avocado flesh, stock, lemon juice, Tabasco, ground coriander and ground cumin in the bowl of a food processor. Blend until smooth. Add the remaining goat's cheese, cream, oil, the parsley and spinach purée and the chopped coriander, and pulse until smooth. *Do not overprocess or the soup will split.* Pour the soup into a tureen, thin if necessary with more stock, and refrigerate.

**4** Serve the soup in chilled bowls with a dollop of the goat's cheese purée and a little extra diced avocado if you require.

## Chicory with Avocado
*An elegant salad.*
● *Slice a quarter of an avocado, fan-shaped if you wish.*
● *Arrange with a pile of chicory spears and a pile of ripped radicchio, and dress with a mustardy dressing. The sweet creaminess of the avocado contrasts pleasantly with the bitterness of the leaves.*

## Avocado Vinaigrette
*You can fuss around with avocados, but this is still one of my favourites. Don't just pour your favourite dressing into the hollow left by the stone, though.*
● *Scoop out the flesh in small amounts with a dessert-spoon and place in a bowl.*
● *Mix with dressing, a little diced shallot, some snipped chives, chopped flat-leaf parsley and plenty of black pepper.*
● *Put the flesh back into the empty skins or serve on a plate with some picked watercress leaves.*

## Hot Bacon Dressing
*Great with a peeled, sliced half avocado.*
● *Fry chopped bacon until crisp then add diced shallots and a diced skinned tomato.*
● *Cook for 5 minutes, then add a tablespoon of grain honey mustard, some extra virgin olive oil, lemon juice and seasoning.*
● *Pour hot over the avocado.*

## Avocado Mayonnaise
*Makes a wonderful accompaniment for shellfish or smoked fish.*
● *Mix together 2 mashed avocados, the juice of ½ lemon, 1 teaspoon horseradish, a dash of Tabasco, 2 chopped spring onions, 1 tablespoon snipped chives, 150ml (¼ pint) Mayonnaise (see page 239), 150ml (¼ pint) soured cream and seasoning.*

*Make a small amount of my version of gazpacho (see page 295) and serve as a sauce around half a sliced avocado with a scattering of fresh white crabmeat or crumbled crispy bacon.*

*What, no hot avocado dishes? I hate hot avocado!*

# BACON AND HAM

Bacon and ham are cured cuts of pork, and curing was practised originally in order to preserve the meat of the autumn-killed pig throughout the winter. Nowadays it's done because both types of meat are delicious!

Basically the curing process involves an initial salting – which partially dehydrates the meat, drawing out its liquids, as well as preserving it from bacterial attack – followed by drying and/or smoking, which further dehydrates the meat, and also, fortuitously, adds colour and flavour. The salting could be through immersion in dry salt or in a brine (both with additional flavourings) or, as often nowadays, by injections of brine. The latter ensures the meat is salted throughout, but the subsequent drying process often does not eliminate all the liquid, making for a slightly soggier and heavier product.

Hams, correctly speaking, come only from the back legs of the animal (although some shoulders are now cured as ham). Bacon is any cured part of the pig *other* than the back legs. If the back legs are still attached to the whole sides of bacon pork during curing, they are detached later and sold as gammon.

## BACON

Bacon is probably one ingredient that most meat-eaters could not do without, and one many vegetarians yearn for. The smell of it cooking in the mornings is one of the most attractive cooking smells one can experience. In fact if I was to appear on *Desert Island Discs*, I would probably classify bacon as my little luxury. As bacon is widely available, this might seem a little strange to you, but with some bacon and perhaps a few seed potatoes, life wouldn't be so bad on a desert island.

But there's bacon and there's *real* bacon. Too much of the bacon produced today is designed to be cheap. Modern production methods and regulations enable producers to increase the weight of the meat by pumping it full of water, phosphates and other additives which can contribute over 50 per cent to the weight. The result is a wet and flabby product that oozes a nasty white liquid when frying. Bacon ain't what it used to be.

What you need to look for is bacon that is labelled dry-cure. Traditionally it is cured by rubbing with dry salt, a procedure which can last for up to two weeks, then it is either air-dried, cold-smoked, or hot-smoked. (Air-cured or cold-smoked makes for a raw product, whereas hot-smoked is fully cooked.) My local butcher, Machins, produces a superlative product by old traditional methods. (If of interest to you, he does a great mail-order business: 7 Market Place, Henley-on-Thames, Oxfordshire RG9 2AA. *Tel*: 01491 574377.) Other traditional makers can be found in Henrietta Green's *Food Lovers' Guide to Britain*.

When choosing bacon, look for a product that has very white fat and pinky-red meat. I prefer to go to a butcher where it is sliced for you as I like my bacon cut quite thick; most packaged varieties are cut much too thin. If you want to use bacon for flavouring stews then it is sensible to buy bacon in the piece and cut into **lardons**. I prefer to use smoked streaky as the fat content is vital for flavour.

Storing bacon is simple, just wrap in a double layer of foil and refrigerate. Rashers will keep for about a week, with streaky lasting longer than back. Bacon bought in one piece will last for about a month. Don't worry if white crystals appear on the meat, these are just salt crystals which can be wiped off with a damp cloth.

For your morning bacon rashers, fry or grill. I prefer to fry decent bacon by just brushing my frying pan with a coating of oil as bacon often sticks, and cooking for 2–3 minutes each side until the fat starts to become crisp. Use the fat that comes out of the bacon for frying bread or sliced

## Bacon and Mustard Dressing

*Combine 3 rashers of crumbled crispy bacon with 1 tablespoon grain honey mustard, 1 tablespoon snipped chives, 1 tablespoon sherry vinegar, 4 tablespoons extra virgin olive oil and seasoning.*

*A winning sandwich for children is to wrap half a banana in bacon and grill for about 10 minutes until the bacon is crisp and the banana is softening. Slap in a long soft roll and wait for the oohs and aahs!*

tomatoes. Those who want the healthier approach should grill the bacon, but beware, the spitting fat can make a smoky mess of your grill.

Bacon is often used for **larding** poultry or game, and strips of fat pork or bacon are used for larding lean pieces of meat such as topside of beef or venison.

When talking bacon, we must not ignore all the other various cuts, including boiling joints. There are eighteen different cuts of bacon, ranging from the small hock at the front of the pig to the gammon hock at the back. Many of these bacon joints need soaking before cooking, to draw out some of their saltiness. And several bacons from abroad can be very useful indeed if you can get hold of them: *pancetta*, a flavourful bacon from Italy, and *speck*, a fatty and tasty German bacon.

## HAM

Hams come in different styles the world over. Basically, pork is salted, then is hung to dry before being smoked or not. Some are sold raw for cooking; some cooked in steam-injected ovens; some remain, and are eaten, raw. Most of the cheaper ham we buy in Britain is cooked, whereas Parma ham, for instance, is a raw ham which has only been salted, and then air-dried for several months or, in some cases, years.

As with bacon, get to know which ham is your favourite, as there are many varieties which look the same, but it's the taste that counts ultimately. To me there is no comparison between cooked and raw hams, with raw winning hands down.

When buying raw Italian ham it is important to remember that if you ask for *prosciutto*, this can be confusing to a knowledgeable shop assistant as the word simply means ham. To be offered a selection of raw you must add the word *crudo*, or ask for ham by name – *prosciutto di Parma, di San Daniele* etc. Or buy the other raw hams, including Bayonne from France (this is lightly smoked), *jamón serrano* from Spain, or the German Westphalian (very smoky in flavour).

• • • • • • • • • • • • • • • • • • • • • • • • • • • • • • • •

*One of my favourite breakfasts is to halve tomatoes, sprinkle with a little salt and pepper, thyme leaves and dot with butter, place in a combination grill/oven and cook until the tomatoes are very soft. I then top them with rashers of streaky bacon and cook until the bacon is crisp and the bacon fat has flavoured the tomatoes.*

• • • • • • • • • • • • • • • • • • • • • • • • • • • • • • • •

## Dublin Coddle

Coddling means slow cooking, and this slow-cooked dish is wonderful winter comfort food. I married my Dublin-born wife, Jacinta, hoping she would cook this dish (it wasn't the only reason), but unfortunately she had never experienced the delights. The dish dates from the seventeenth century, a typical dish of bacon, sausages and potatoes. I have since added cabbage, sorry Dublin.

**Preparation and cooking: 2½ hours**
**Serves: 8**

| |
|---|
| 1 x 1kg (2¼ lb) unsmoked bacon joint, soaked in cold water overnight |
| 450g (1 lb) pork and leek sausages |
| 1kg (2¼ lb) potatoes, diced |
| 450g (1 lb) onions, sliced |
| 1 teaspoon soft thyme leaves |
| ½ teaspoon ground white pepper |
| ½ teaspoon English mustard powder |
| 4 tablespoons chopped flat-leaf parsley |
| ½ Savoy cabbage, chopped |
| 2 bay leaves |
| chicken stock |
| 55g (2 oz) unsalted butter, cut in small cubes |

**1** Preheat the oven to 170°C/325°F/Gas 3.

**2** Cut the bacon joint into 5cm (2 in) pieces. Cut the sausages into quarters.

**3** Combine the potato, onion, thyme, pepper, mustard, parsley, cabbage and bay leaves in a bowl.

**4** Make several layers using the bacon, sausage and the potato mix in a deep casserole and pour over enough stock to come level with a final layer of potatoes. Dot the surface of the coddle with the butter cubes.

**5** Place the casserole over a medium heat, bring to a simmer, cover and place in the preheated oven for about 2 hours or until the bacon is tender.

**6** If required, increase the oven temperature and remove the lid to brown the top layer for the last 30 minutes. This drastic step would not be considered traditional in Dublin. Serve with wedges of soda bread.

## Boiled Bacon

● *Boil a soaked bacon joint for 15 minutes per 450g (1 lb) with a couple of bay leaves, 2 whole onions pierced with a couple of cloves, 1 carrot per person, a quarter heart of celery per person, a couple of turnips, and some large chunks of peeled floury potatoes.*

● *When cooked, remove meat and vegetables and keep warm.*

● *In the cooking liquor, fast boil some wedges of Savoy cabbage.*

● *Carve the bacon and serve with the vegetables and some of the broth for delicious one-pot dining.*

*Pancetta is basically streaky bacon, but because of its flavourful curing, it is quite superior – drier, purer, much tastier. A carbonara made with pancetta is to die for.*

*Add crispy bacon pieces to a potato salad with soured cream and dill.*

*Add crispy bacon to some raw peas, broad beans, gratings of fresh Parmesan, extra virgin olive oil and lemon juice.*

*Add crispy bacon bits to a baby spinach and sliced button mushroom salad tossed with a grain mustard dressing.*

# Bacon Sandwich

It may seem odd, having a bacon sandwich recipe, but when it is part of my culinary life, why not? There can't be many meat eaters who don't enjoy a bacon sarnie. Apart from using the best bacon, an indispensable factor has to be factory-made sliced bread, rather than any of the purist products. And, as a southerner, I'm a ketchup rather than a brown sauce man, but the choice is yours.

**Preparation and cooking: 15 minutes**
**Serves: 1**

4 rashers smoked streaky bacon, rindless

25g (1 oz) pork dripping or butter

2 slices sliced white bread

ground black pepper

butter (optional)

ketchup or brown sauce

**1** Fry the bacon over a medium heat in the dripping until the bacon fat starts to turn golden, turning the bacon once. Remove and keep warm.

**2** Take the two slices of bread and liberally pepper one side of both. Place the peppered sides down into the fat in the bacon pan and cook until the bread is golden.

**3** If required, butter the uncooked side of the bread. Place the bacon on to the uncooked side. Season with ketchup or brown sauce, then top with the other slice of bread, uncooked side down.

**4** Eat immediately – particularly good after a heavy night's drinking.

## Crispy Bacon Bits

*Perfect for scattering over soups or folding into a salad. If time is of the essence you can now buy ready-crisped bacon in supermarkets.*

● *Place streaky bacon on an oiled baking tray in a slow oven and cook until deeply golden.*

● *Pour away any fat from time to time.*

● *Place the bacon on a cooling rack and when cold you can chop or crumble it.*

## Bacon and Bread Fricadelle

*A 'new' sandwich I found in an eighteenth-century cookbook. Put streaky bacon between slices of bread, season and dip in a batter of egg, milk and flour, and deep-fry over a medium heat for 7–8 minutes . . . I serve it with Branston pickle!*

There is not much that
hasn't been wrapped in bacon
without a modicum of success –
oysters, scallops, prunes, chicken
livers, cooked new potatoes and
asparagus, to name but a few.

# Baked Ham with Kentucky Glaze

I have tested various glazes for Christmas hams, and this one is a clear winner. Remember to baste regularly during the baking process. This quantity of glaze will do for a ham of about 3.5–4.5kg (8–10 lb); cut the quantity of glaze for a smaller piece.

**Preparation and cooking: depending on size**
**Serves: depends on size of the ham**

| | Ham glaze and garnish |
|---|---|
| boiling ham or bacon | 225g (8 oz) soft brown sugar |
| 300ml (½ pint) cider vinegar | 55g (2 oz) polenta or cornmeal |
| 600ml (1 pint) dark beer | 1 tablespoon English mustard powder |
| 2 oranges, studded with 2 cloves | 1 tablespoon ground black pepper |
| 2 bay leaves | 3 tablespoons bourbon whiskey |
| 2 apples, cut in half | 425ml (¾ pint) apple juice or cider |
| 2 onions | 225g (8 oz) dried stoned apricots |
| 2 carrots | 150ml (¼ pint) Madeira or Marsala |
| 2 sticks celery | |
| 2 sprigs thyme | |
| 1 cinnamon stick | |
| a few cloves | |

**1** Weigh the ham and place in a large saucepan. Pour in enough water to cover. Add all the ingredients except the cloves to the pan and bring to the boil. Simmer gently for 15 minutes per 450g (1 lb).

**2** Allow the ham to cool in the cooking liquid. Cut off all the rind, score the fat in a diamond pattern and insert a clove in the cross point of each diamond.

**3** For the glaze, in a bowl mix together the brown sugar, polenta, mustard and pepper. Moisten the mixture with the bourbon. Spread the mixture over the ham.

**4** Place the ham in a baking tray and pour in the apple juice or cider. Bake in the oven preheated to 190°C/375°F/Gas 5 for about 15 minutes per 450g (1 lb), basting frequently.

**5** Meanwhile, combine the apricots and Madeira or Marsala in a small pan, bring to the boil, cover and leave to infuse.

**6** About 30 minutes before the end of cooking, add the apricots to the baking tray with their juices. Continue to bake and baste the ham.

**7** Serve the ham sliced, with the apricots and pan juices.

## Hambled Eggs

● *Chop some cooked ham into small pieces and for every 55g (2 oz), fold in 2 eggs.*

● *Melt 55g (2 oz) butter in a saucepan, add the ham–egg mixture and season with cayenne and salt.*

● *Stir until hot and partially set as you would scrambled egg then spoon on to buttered toast.*

## Pea and Ham Soup

*Use boiled bacon stock (if not too salty) as the basis for pea and ham soup.*

● *Boil together split peas, onions, carrot, a ham hock, and a sprig of thyme.*

● *When the split peas are cooked, remove ham hock and shred meat.*

● *Liquidise the remainder of the soup and return the shredded ham to it.*

● *Serve with crispy bacon and/or snippets of bread cooked in bacon fat.*

## Ham Spread

*Makes a great sandwich spread.*

● *Mince ham in a food processor and combine with grain mustard and a splash of Worcestershire sauce.*

● *Add half the weight of the ham in butter and blend to combine, and then add a dusting of powdered mace and nutmeg.*

*Serve raw ham thinly sliced with melon, figs, pears or rocket for a healthy low-calorie starter or light lunch.*

*Slice cooked ham on the bone and serve with butter-fried eggs and thick or thin chips for a delicious lunch.*

# BEANS, DRIED

Dried beans, together with chickpeas and lentils, are often referred to as pulses. A selection of bean varieties is a necessity in a well-stocked store cupboard, as they are all nutritious and inexpensive, providing essential carbohydrate, protein and roughage. Except for baked, the British seem to be a bit reticent about eating beans, which are more associated with the peasant cooking of the Mediterranean, the Middle East, Latin America and the West Indies. Most dried beans come from varieties of fresh bean that are eaten with both seed and pod. All the kidney beans, for example, come from *Phaseolus vulgaris*, also known as the French bean. (See Beans, Fresh.) All, apart from the broad bean, are originally native to the Americas, and were only introduced to Europe in post-Columbian times.

Varieties of beans include:

ADZUKI or ADUKI, a tiny browny-red bean with a light-coloured seam;

BLACK-EYED, creamy with a black eye (actually a pea), popular in the southern states of America;

BORLOTTI, a large kidney bean, wonderful fresh and dried. When fresh, the pod is streaked with claret-coloured markings; the beans inside are similarly marked, but lose their vivid colour when cooked;

BROAD, a large flat bean known as fava or shell bean in the States. Colours can vary from pale green through beige to brown. It needs lengthy cooking to break down the tough skin, and is often used in purées;

BUTTER beans (the American Lima beans) are similar to broad beans, although smoother in taste and with a much creamier texture;

CANNELLINI, a white kidney bean much used in Italian cookery, with a mild butter taste;

FLAGEOLET, a small green haricot, is expensive, but great in soups and stews and goes well with lamb;

HARICOT, a creamy kidney bean, smaller than the cannellini, is very often used for making baked beans;

PINTO, a kidney bean, beige flecked with brown, similar to the RED KIDNEY and BLACK BEAN;

SOISSON, a small French variety of haricot;

SOYA, used in many forms of vegetarian cookery, the easiest bean to digest and the most nutritious (the only vegetable source of complete protein), a small oval bean with a beige colouring. (Soya beans are fermented, when they can be known as brown, yellow or black, and used in sauces.)

If possible, buy beans from a specialist shop such as those run by Middle Eastern immigrants, where you can be sure the turnover is good. Buy loose where possible, as it is impossible to tell how old beans were when they were bagged. Store in an airtight container away from direct sunlight.

The preparation of beans involves for the most part soaking overnight in cold water to rehydrate them. As the beans release indigestible sugars, raffinose and stachyose, never use the soaking water for cooking, as this is wind-inducing. (According to my Gran, the soaking liquor reduced down, cooled and bottled, makes an excellent cleansing solution.) Rinse the beans, discarding any that have floated to the top. Cover the beans by a couple of inches with fresh unsalted water (salt toughens the skin), and simmer for 45 minutes, then drain and discard the water. Repeat the exercise and cook until tender, up to a further 1¼ hours.

Flavourings such as herbs or root vegetables can be added at the second stage of cooking. You can cook the beans all in one hit, but I think the two-stage cooking makes the beans less windy, as well as rendering them safer, for beans contain what are known as antinutrient substances. These are destroyed if proper soaking and cooking procedures are followed. Broad or faba/fava beans are responsible for a form of anaemia known as favism; this occurs mainly around the Mediterranean (and in China), and is the result of a genetic enzyme deficiency.

# Cassoulet

The classic bean dish from Toulouse has differing versions from Carcassonne, Castelnaudary and Castelnau, and arguments rage worldwide as to how it should be made. Who cares, as long as it tastes great. Basically it is a delicious amalgamation of dried haricot beans, sausage, pork, occasionally mutton, and *confit* of goose or duck, flavoured with herbs and garlic.

**Preparation and cooking: up to 2 days**
**Serves: 8**

## Beans

1.3kg (3 lb) soisson or white haricot beans, soaked for 2 hours

900g (2 lb) belly or salt pork, in the piece

1 pig's trotter (optional)

2 onions, studded with 1 clove each

2 carrots

1 stick celery

4 sprigs fresh thyme

12 peppercorns tied in muslin

3 bay leaves

4 sprigs parsley

225g (8 oz) pork rinds, tied together

8 cloves garlic

2.3 litres (4 pints) chicken stock or water

450g (1 lb) boiling garlic or Toulouse sausage

## Meats

4 lamb shanks or ½ shoulder of lamb or mutton

900g (2 lb) pork blade bone

4 tablespoons duck fat (see page 111)

salt and ground black pepper

4 onions, chopped

2 sticks celery, thinly sliced

8 cloves garlic, smashed

1 x 400g (14 oz) tin chopped tomatoes

3 tablespoons tomato purée

3 sprigs thyme

2 bay leaves

600ml (1 pint) dry white wine

900ml (1½ pints) chicken stock or water

## To finish

6 legs of *Duck Confit* and some of their fat (see page 111)

1 tablespoon soft thyme leaves

about 175g (6 oz) fresh breadcrumbs

extra stock or bean cooking liquor

## The day before

**1** Drain the beans then cover with fresh water and bring to the boil. Simmer for 5 minutes, remove from the heat and allow to stand for 30 minutes. Drain and discard the water.

**2** Return the beans to a large saucepan with the other bean ingredients, except for the sausage. Place the pan on a medium heat and bring to the boil. Reduce the heat, cover the pan and simmer for 1¼ hours. Add the sausage for the last 30 minutes. The beans must be cooked through but retain their shape. Drain the beans, retaining the liquor. Discard all the other ingredients except for the sausage, the pork rinds, the pork belly and the trotter. Cool and then refrigerate everything.

**3** Meanwhile, preheat the oven to 120°C/250°F/Gas ½. In a large casserole, brown the lamb shanks and pork blade bone all over in the duck fat. Remove the meats, season and set aside. Add the onion, celery and garlic to the fat in the pan, and cook until soft but not brown. Add the tomato, tomato purée, thyme, bay leaves, white wine and stock. Return the meats to the pan. Bring the liquor to the boil, cover and place in the oven to braise for approximately 2½ hours.

**4** Remove the meats and set aside. Strain the cooking juices, pressing down on the vegetables to extract the fullest flavour. Return the liquor to the heat and **reduce** until you have about 1.2 litres (2 pints). Allow the liquor and the meats to cool, then refrigerate.

### The next day

**5**   Remove all the meats from the fridge. Cut the meat off the blade bone into 5cm (2 in) pieces; discard the bone. Cut the meat from the lamb shanks to the same size; discard the bones. Remove the skin from the garlic sausage and cut into 2.5cm (1 in) rounds. Cut the pork rinds into small dice. Remove and discard the skin and bones from the duck legs.

**6**   Combine the bean cooking liquor with the meat cooking liquor. Warm the beans through with the belly of pork and the pig's trotter and a little of the liquor. Remove the belly and the trotter; cut the belly into cubes and place in the food processor with the meat and skin from the pig's trotter. (When removing the bones from the pig's trotter be very careful as there appear to be hundreds of little bones as well as the toe nails!) Blend the meats until you have a smooth paste and fold this paste back into the beans. Check the seasoning.

**7**   Take a large earthenware dish, 6.75 litres (6 quarts or 12 pints) capacity and 15cm (6 in) deep. Place a layer of beans in the bottom, followed by a ladleful of the cooking liquor, a couple of spoonfuls of diced pork rinds and a few pieces of each of the meats, including the duck *confit*. Cover with beans and cooking liquor and continue to alternate until the casserole is full. (Make sure there is plenty of liquid in the casserole.)

### Finishing the *cassoulet* (at least 2 hours before sit-down)

**8**   Preheat the oven to 180°C/350°F/Gas 4. Sprinkle some thyme leaves and breadcrumbs on top of the *cassoulet*, dot with melted duck fat and place the dish in the oven. As soon as a crust forms, break it and push it into the beans. Add a little more cooking liquor and extra breadcrumbs. Repeat every 25 minutes.

**9**   After the first addition of breadcrumbs, reduce the oven temperature to 150°C/300°F/Gas 2 and cook for a further 1½ hours. The juices at the finish should be reduced and thickened by the starches from the beans.

**10**   Present the bubbling dish as is to your guests and allow them to tuck in. A large bowl of salad is all that is needed.

## Tuna and Bean Salad

*An all-time popular Italian salad.*
● *Simply combine 1 drained 400g (14 oz) tin of cannellini beans, ½ red onion, finely sliced, 1 tablespoon roughly chopped flat-leaf parsley, 1 x 200g (7 oz) tin of flaked tuna in olive oil, 4 tablespoons extra virgin olive oil, ½ tablespoon freshly squeezed lemon juice, salt and ground black pepper.*

## Italian Bean Soup

● *Make a quickie bean soup by frying 1 teaspoon chopped garlic in 7 tablespoons good olive oil in a heavy saucepan, adding 2 x 400g (14 oz) tins of drained cannellini beans, cooking for 10 minutes, then puréeing a third of the beans with 300ml (½ pint) chicken stock.*
● *Fold the purée back into the bean mixture and then add 3 tablespoons roughly chopped flat-leaf parsley and season to taste. Serve with grilled bruschetta (see page 53).*

## Broad Bean Soup

● *For a great soup, soak 450g (1 lb) dried broad beans overnight, drain, then pop the beans out of their skins.*
● *Combine with ½ tablespoon fennel seeds, 1 fennel bulb, very finely chopped, and 1 finely chopped onion and cook in 4 tablespoons good olive oil for 10 minutes.*
● *Add 1.2 litres (2 pints) chicken or vegetable stock and simmer until the beans are tender.*
● *Blend half of this mixture in a liquidiser and fold back into the soup.*
● *Season to taste and garnish with chopped fennel fronds.*

# White Bean and Butternut Squash Soup

Butternut squash and beans make a surprisingly good partnership, a lovely winter warmer.

**Preparation and cooking: overnight + 1½ hours**
**Serves: 4–6**

175g (6 oz) dried white beans (haricot, cannellini), soaked overnight

1½ tablespoons finely chopped sage

8 cloves garlic

2 bay leaves

2 sprigs thyme

1kg (2¼ lb) butternut squash, seeded, each half cut into 3 wedges

4 tablespoons good olive oil

2 onions, finely diced

2 carrots, cut into 1cm (½ in) dice

2 sticks celery, cut into 1cm (½ in) dice

1.2 litres (2 pints) vegetable stock

salt and ground black pepper

**Parsley purée**

2 cloves garlic

1 teaspoon Maldon sea salt

1 bunch flat-leaf parsley, finely chopped

4 tablespoons good olive oil

4 tablespoons freshly grated Parmesan

lemon juice to taste

**1** Pour off the bean soaking liquid and place the beans in a saucepan with half the sage, 2 garlic cloves, the bay leaves and thyme. Cover the beans by 2.5cm (1 in) with cold water, bring to the boil and simmer for 1 hour or until the beans are tender. Top up with extra water as required. Drain the beans, reserving the cooking liquor. Set the beans aside.

**2** Meanwhile, place your squash in a roasting tray and roast in the oven preheated to 180°C/350°F/Gas 4 with 1 tablespoon of the olive oil for about 45 minutes or until the squash has softened and caramelised. Remove the flesh from the skin; discard the skin.

**3** At the same time, heat the remaining olive oil in a large saucepan and cook the onion, carrot, celery, the remaining garlic and sage over a medium heat until the onion is soft but not brown. Add the stock and bean cooking liquor, bring to the boil and simmer for 20 minutes. Add the roasted squash and cook for a further 10 minutes.

**4** Place the soup in a liquidiser and blend until smooth. Return to the saucepan, add the beans and stir to combine. Season to taste.

**5** For the parsley purée, crush the garlic with the sea salt in a mortar and pestle until you have a fine paste. Add a little of the parsley and work together vigorously, then stir in the olive oil, the Parmesan and the remaining parsley. Add lemon juice and seasoning to taste.

**6** Serve a teaspoonful of parsley purée in each bowl of hot soup.

## Clams with Beans

- *Cook 450g (1 lb) soaked dried flageolet beans with 2 onions, 6 cloves garlic, 2 carrots, 2 sticks celery, 2 bay leaves and a pinch of saffron for 1½ hours until the beans are tender.*
- *Just before the beans are ready, in another pan cook 1 finely chopped onion and 1 teaspoon finely chopped garlic in 6 tablespoons olive oil until the onion has softened.*
- *Add 1kg (2¼ lb) clams and cook until the clams open (minutes only), then add 150ml (¼ pint) dry white wine, ½ teaspoon dried chilli flakes, ½ teaspoon paprika and 4 tablespoons roughly chopped flat-leaf parsley. Cook for a further 5 minutes.*
- *Stir the clams into the beans with all their liquid.*
- *Season to taste (serves 6–8).*

## Borlotti and Goat's Cheese Salad  Ⓥ

The use of tinned beans is fine here. Make sure you rinse the beans well and that you add the other ingredients while the beans are warm.

**Preparation and cooking: 15 minutes**
**Serves: 4**

1 x 400g (14 oz) tin borlotti beans, drained and rinsed
3 tablespoons extra virgin olive oil
1 tablespoon freshly squeezed lemon juice
1 teaspoon dried oregano
¼ teaspoon dried red chilli flakes, crushed
225g (8 oz) goat's cheese, cut in 1cm (½ in) cubes
sea salt and ground black pepper
3 tablespoons snipped flat-leaf parsley leaves

**1**  Place the beans and enough cold water to cover in a saucepan over a medium heat and warm through. Do not allow the beans to boil or become too soft.
**2**  Drain the beans well, and in a large mixing bowl toss to combine with all the remaining ingredients except for the parsley. The heat of the beans will allow the cheese to melt.
**3**  Just before serving, check the seasoning and adjust if necessary. Toss with the parsley and serve immediately.

## Spicy Broad Bean Purée

● *Purée 225g (8 oz) of cooked broad beans and combine with 4 cloves garlic, mashed with a little rock salt, ½ teaspoon toasted and ground cumin seeds, 3 tablespoons chopped fresh coriander, 4 chopped spring onions, ¼ teaspoon ground black pepper, ¼ teaspoon cayenne pepper and 6 tablespoons Greek yogurt.*
● *Serve as a purée to go on* crostini *or* bruschetta *(see page 53).*
● *Add ½ teaspoon baking powder and omit yogurt if you want to shape into patties for deep-frying.*

## Broad Bean and Rosemary Purée  Ⓥ

A delicious dip or spread for *crostini* or *bruschetta*. You could substitute any other form of dried beans for those used here (see page 33).

**Preparation and cooking: 25 minutes**
**Serves: 4**

6 tablespoons extra virgin olive oil
5 cloves garlic, mashed to a paste with a little salt
1 tablespoon very finely chopped rosemary
½ onion, finely chopped
450g (1 lb) cooked broad beans, with some of their cooking liquor
juice of ½ lemon
¼ teaspoon ground black pepper

**1**  Combine 4 tablespoons of the olive oil in a deep saucepan with the garlic, rosemary and onion, and cook over a medium heat until the onion is soft but without colour.
**2**  Add the beans, lemon juice and pepper, and cook gently for 10 minutes. Drain the solids, retaining the oil. Pass the solids through a **vegetable mouli** or food mill
**3**  Fold back in the cooking oil, and stir to combine. Add some bean cooking liquor if the mixture is too dry. Season with more salt or lemon juice as necessary. Dribble with remaining olive oil.

## Beef and Bean Stew

● *Combine 3 litres (5¼ pints) chicken stock with 225g (8 oz) soaked dried flageolet beans, 225g (8 oz) salt pork, 115g (4 oz) pancetta, 225g (8 oz) beef chuck, 2 roughly diced onions, 3 crushed cloves of garlic, 2 bay leaves and 1 roughly chopped leek. Bring to the boil, and simmer for 2 hours or until the beans are tender.*
● *Add 4 halved new potatoes, 2 quartered carrots and 300g (10½ oz) spring greens or kale, and cook for a further 30 minutes.*
● *Season to taste (serves 6–8).*

# BEANS, FRESH

As a gardener, I look forward enormously to the bean season. There is a world of difference between buying string or runner beans in the shops, and the pleasure of picking your home-grown ones and getting them on the table within half an hour.

Green beans, by which I mean beans that are eaten pod and all, belong to the *Phaseolus* family, and originated in South America; the Spanish brought them to Europe in the sixteenth century, after Columbus's discovery of the New World, and they were originally grown as flowers! *Phaseolus vulgaris* is known variously as the common, French, green, haricot, kidney and string bean. (The Americans call them snap beans, because that is what should happen when you try and bend them; however, many will bend double before they break, revealing how old they are.) It is varieties of *P. vulgaris* that produce dried beans such as borlotti, haricot, red kidney, black and flageolet. On the Continent, freshly matured beans, *out* of their pods, and before they are dried, are a prized fresh vegetable. The other common green bean is the runner, *Phaseolus coccineus*.

The only bean the Europeans can call their own is the broad bean, *Vicia faba*, which is thought to have originated before the Bronze Age, some time after the other European pulses: peas, lentils and chickpeas. This is also known as the fava or faba, horse, field, tick and Windsor bean. It is the seeds that are eaten as a vegetable, not the pods – unless you grow your own as I do, and you can pick them when very small and tender. The seeds are dried (see Beans, Dried).

As with most vegetables, the seasons have gone awry, with all varieties of beans available at all times of the year, instead of just in the summer. Buy beans when they are crisp, fresh and smooth with slightly silky skins, never wrinkled or extra bendy. Where possible, buy the smallest pods you can find, those with no evidence of swelling where the seeds are (which means they will have been left too long on the vine).

French beans or *haricots verts* just need topping; don't bother tailing them as the tails are perfectly edible, and cook them whole. Runner beans will generally require stringing unless you grow them yourself and pick them young. They will also require cutting, either into chunks or by using a device which slices and strings lengthways. Most of the broad beans you can buy will require podding. You can cook the broad bean seeds and eat the whole thing, although many cooks prefer to slip each bean out of its rough greyish skin to reveal the wonderful emerald-green kernels.

When cooking the beans plain, always place them in lots of boiling salted water. Deep boiling water quickly returns to the boil after the beans have been added, therefore speeding up the cooking. Salting is equally important, vital for lifting the true flavour of the vegetable, and it raises the boiling temperature of the water, thereby once again speeding up the cooking process. Beans will take anything from 3 to 10 minutes to cook, depending on size. Most chefs plunge the beans into iced water once cooked to arrest the cooking and set the colour, but this is not recommended for households (unless you are preparing a large amount of vegetables) as it detracts from the flavour and makes the beans watery.

The nutritional values of fresh beans are good: they are loaded with potassium, calcium and phosphorus, and are rich in vitamins A and C. A slimmer's bonus is that there are only 30 calories in an average portion.

• • • • • • • • • • • • • • •

*Lightly cooked French beans make great salads. Mix them with red onions, a touch of balsamic vinegar, some extra virgin olive oil, and salt and pepper. For an Oriental flavour, toss with some mirin, soy sauce, sesame oil, chopped ginger, garlic and chilli, and some sesame seeds.*

• • • • • • • • • • • • • • •

• • • • • • • • • • • • • • • • • • • • •

## Bean Dip
*A great dip for raw vegetables.*
● *Add 1 teaspoon finely chopped garlic, 1 tablespoon chopped fresh oregano, 1 teaspoon ground cumin, 150 ml (¼ pint) extra virgin olive oil and some ground black pepper to 450g (1 lb) broad bean purée.*
● *Garnish with spring onions, chilli powder, ground cumin and olive oil.*

• • • • • • • • • • • • • • • • • • • • • • •

# Coconut Beans with Shredded Carrots

From time to time everyone gets a bit bored with plainly cooked vegetables, especially when you grow your own and have a seasonal glut. This recipe, influenced by Indian cooking, gives beans a definite zap. Serve it with roast meats.

**Preparation and cooking: 25 minutes**
**Serves: 4–6**

450g (1 lb) extra fine *haricots verts* (French beans), topped
sea salt
4 tablespoons peanut or vegetable oil
1 teaspoon mustard seeds
1 fresh green chilli, finely diced
2 small onions, thinly sliced
2 cloves garlic, finely chopped
2 teaspoons grated fresh ginger
1 teaspoon ground turmeric
¼ teaspoon ground cardamom
115g (4 oz) shredded carrot (available in supermarkets)
175ml (6 fl oz) vegetable stock
85g (3 oz) desiccated coconut
55g (2 oz) hazelnuts, chopped and roasted
2 tablespoons chopped coriander

**1** Cook the beans for 4 minutes in boiling salted water, drain and set aside.
**2** Heat the oil in a frying pan, add the mustard seeds, cover and cook for 2 minutes over a medium heat until the seeds start to pop. Add the chilli, onion, garlic, ginger, turmeric and cardamom. Cook, stirring, for 4 minutes until the onion starts to soften.
**3** Add the carrot, stock and coconut and cook for 5 minutes.
**4** Finally add the beans, hazelnuts and coriander and cook for 1–2 minutes to infuse the flavours and warm the beans. Season to taste.

• • • • • • • • • • • • • • • • • • • • • •

*Puréed broad beans make an excellent partner to grilled fish. The best way to purée is to use a **vegetable mouli** which will mash the bean flesh but leave the skins behind. Add cream, salt, pepper and a hint of sugar.*

• • • • • • • • • • • • • • • • • • • • • •

# Herby Runner Beans

Next to freshly picked beans, immediately cooked and just tossed in butter, this recipe must come second favourite. It complements lamb wonderfully.

**Preparation and cooking: 35 minutes**
**Serves: 4**

55g (2 oz) unsalted butter
2 tablespoons extra virgin olive oil
6 cloves garlic
1 teaspoon finely chopped sage
450g (1 lb) runner beans, stringed and sliced with a bean slicer
salt and ground black pepper
2 tablespoons finely chopped spring onion
1 tablespoon snipped chives
2 tablespoons chopped flat-leaf parsley
2 teaspoons lemon juice

**1** Over a low heat warm the butter and oil with the whole garlic cloves and the sage. Cover and cook very gently for 20–25 minutes until the garlic is pale golden, and cooked through. Do not allow the butter and oil to burn. Mash the garlic with the back of a fork to a smooth paste with the oil and sage.
**2** Some 10 minutes before the garlic has finished cooking, cook the sliced runner beans in boiling salted water until tender, about 8–10 minutes. Drain and add to the garlic.
**3** Add the remaining ingredients to the pan, season to taste, then toss all well together.

• • • • • • • • • • • • •

*Raw broad beans, popped out of their skins and tossed with a trustworthy raw egg yolk, grated Parmesan, extra virgin olive oil and a splash of fresh lemon juice make a delicious starter at the beginning of the broad bean season.*

• • • • • • • • • • • • •

# Broad Beans Stewed in their Pods

This is a recipe for gardeners, as you rarely find broad beans young enough for this dish in markets or shops. This is my interpretation of a dish I discovered in Spain. Serve it as part of a *tapas* buffet, or as an accompaniment to grilled fish.

**Preparation and cooking: 1¼ hours**

**Serves: 4–6**

| |
|---|
| 300ml (½ pint) extra virgin olive oil |
| 2 onions, roughly chopped |
| 4 cloves garlic, finely chopped |
| 1kg (2¼ lb) young broad bean pods, topped, tailed and strings removed, cut into sections between the swell of each bean |
| 225g (8 oz) *jamón serrano* or Parma ham, cut into thin strips |
| 3 bay leaves |
| 1 x 400g (14 oz) tin chopped tomatoes |
| 85g (3 oz) soft white breadcrumbs |
| 1 teaspoon cumin seeds, toasted |
| pinch of saffron stamens, soaked in 1 tbsp cold water |
| 2 teaspoons Spanish paprika |
| 3 tablespoons chopped flat-leaf parsley |
| salt and ground black pepper |

**1** Heat half the olive oil in a large saucepan, add the onion and garlic, and cook over a medium heat until the onion is soft but not brown.

**2** Add the broad bean pods, ham, bay leaves and tomatoes, and stir to combine. Top up with water so the beans are just covered. Raise the heat and bring to the boil. Reduce the heat so the liquid is barely simmering, cover with a lid, and cook for 1 hour or until the beans are completely tender.

**3** Meanwhile, heat the remaining oil in a frying pan, and add breadcrumbs, cumin seeds, saffron and paprika. Fry until the breadcrumbs are golden. Remove from the heat and set aside.

**4** If there is too much liquid in the beans, increase the heat and boil until the liquid is of coating consistency. Fold in the breadcrumbs and flat-leaf parsley. Season to taste.

· · · · · · · · · ·

*When making a green bean salad don't add the acid element (lemon juice or vinegar) until just before serving as the beans will lose their colour.*

· · · · · · · · ·

· · · · · · ·

*Make a bean salad by tossing cooked beans in hot double cream with seasoning, chervil and toasted hazelnuts.*

· · · · · · ·

· · · · · · · · · · ·

*Beans don't always have to be bright green. Cook some onions, garlic, bacon and cumin in olive oil until soft but not brown, then add a tin of chopped tomatoes and some French beans, cut in 1cm (½ in) pieces. Stew for 15 minutes until the beans are tender.*

· · · · · · · · · · ·

## Creamy Broad Beans

*Good with grilled meat or fish.*

● *Boil podded broad beans for 2 minutes, drain and pop them out of their skins.*

● *Put into a saucepan with some chopped chives, chervil and summer savory, moisten with 5 tablespoons of stock and add a touch of caster sugar, salt and black pepper.*

● *Boil until the liquor has almost disappeared.*

● *Beat an egg yolk with 150ml (¼ pint) double cream, add to the beans and warm through until the cream has slightly thickened. Do not re-boil.*

*Raw broad beans, young and tender, go well with diced avocado mixed with some double cream, lemon juice, chopped parsley and coriander, a few chopped spring onions and seasoning. Serve with paper-thin slices of Parma ham.*

# BEEF

What can I say about beef that hasn't already been said before? Our beef industry has suffered badly from intensive farming methods and the resulting horror of BSE (bovine spongiform encephalopathy). And it was all in order to rear beef cattle quicker and at a cheap cost.

It is important to realise that in order to eat a wonderful product like beef we have to pay more. Beef fed from grass is a different creature: it will have a yellowing fat, whereas cattle with very white fat will have had a diet of grain or other concentrated forms of food. It is up to the public to demand to know the source of their beef from their butchers or supermarkets. And if you go on demanding cheap beef, that's what you will get. From now on rather than have roast beef on a regular basis, I will treat myself from time to time to the best grass-fed beef I can find.

Now the lecture is off my chest, I can concentrate on the *cooking* of beef. Lean, lean, lean is the message we have had to endure for several years, and yet it is fat that gives the beef its flavour. Look for yellowing fat and, if buying grilling or roasting cuts, look for marbling (the small rivulets of fat that run through the meat). The topside joints sold for roasting by supermarkets are completely devoid of fat, and therefore can be very tough. Look for beef that has a darker, reddish brown flesh which will indicate beef that has been hung and aged, rather than the bright red, spanking-new-looking meat which will tell you it is a recent kill. If you can establish the breed of cattle, such as Angus, all the better.

## Steaming or Poaching

Not a very popular way of cooking beef, but a French classic, *boeuf à la ficelle*, is a fillet of beef lowered on a string into a pot of simmering stock. Cooked properly it is delicious. The trick is not to let the meat touch the bottom of the pan, to have a good stock, and not to let the liquid boil. Use a tender cut of meat and cook for 10–20 minutes per 450g (1 lb), depending on how rare you like your beef.

## Grilling

On domestic equipment I don't recommend this method of cooking as home grills are not hot enough to seal the meat properly. If you have a barbecue or indoor char-grill, that will be fine but, failing that, use a griddle or ridged pan to simulate grilling. Have the grill or pan very hot before you add the meat, leave it for a few moments before turning and cooking a few more minutes, then reduce the temperature and cook on until it meets your requirements. Cuts for grilling include sirloin, rump, T-bone (if it has its ban lifted), fillet and *onglet*. The latter is a French cut best represented by the English skirt cut, a piece of meat found on the inside of the ribs. Unless you request this cut from your butcher you are unlikely to find it, but if you do, cook it very rare, smother it in fried shallots, and be prepared for an explosion of beefy flavour (and also for a good chew; it can be very tough). If I'm grilling or frying a steak I like it to be at least 5cm (2 in) thick. Cook one steak of 500g (18 oz) for two and slice it on the diagonal.

## Frying

Follow similar rules to grilling using a very hot pan to seal the meat before reducing the temperature. Don't salt the meat until just prior to or during cooking as salt draws out the blood and toughens the meat.

## Boiling

I have a particular soft spot for that classic dish, boiled beef and carrots. Use silverside or brisket, salted if you want a red hue to the meat. Cook very slowly in water or stock with a bouquet of root vegetables, a few herbs and a pig's trotter for extra richness. Cook very slowly for up to 4 hours until the meat is tender.

## Roasting

This demands a quality cut of meat. Pre BSE I would have recommended rib of beef on the bone, but for the time being that is not allowed, so rolled rib off the bone will have to do. You can also roast fillet and sirloin, but avoid those lean favourites, silverside and brisket. I prefer to seal my joint in a hot pan before putting it into a hot oven. Season with salt, pepper and a fine film of Dijon mustard if desired. Place the meat on a rack above a pan of dripping, roast potatoes or Yorkshire pudding, allowing the meat to drip delicious juices on to whatever you cook below. If you prefer to cook the beef in a roasting pan, place on a layer of sliced carrots, onions and potatoes to keep the joint off the surface of the hot pan, preventing a thick crust forming. Baste the roast regularly during cooking. I prefer to roast for a shorter time in a hotter oven, 220°C/425°F/Gas 7. Always allow the meal to **rest** for 10–15 minutes before carving. If you carve straight from the oven, all the juices will end up in your dish.

### Braising and Pot-roasting

Some of the most delicious ways to cook beef. It is possible to use cheaper cuts of beef such as topside or silverside, ideally **larded** with pork fat. For both methods one piece of meat is used which is normally dusted in seasoned flour then browned in dripping or oil. For braising, the meat sits on a bed of root vegetables with enough wine or stock to come halfway up the meat. Long slow cooking makes for tender meat packed full of flavour; cook for between 2 and 5 hours at 150°C/300°F/Gas 2, depending on the size of the joint. Pot-roasting is similar except that you cut back on the liquor and add some butter, so that the meat steam-roasts in the minimum of buttery stock.

### Stewing

Very similar to braising except that the meat is cut into bite-sized pieces and this allows you to buy even cheaper cuts from the shin, leg, chuck, blade, neck, skirt and blade. Some of the most delicious dishes fall into this category – *boeuf bourguignon*, goulash, *estouffades* and *carbonnades*. It's time more people got back to this sort of cooking as bargains and delicious flavours can be enjoyed all round.

### Stir-frying

As Britain becomes a culinary magpie, so this form of cookery becomes more and more popular. Ideally suited to the more tender cuts of meat, such as sirloin, rump or tail end of fillet.

# Steak Tartare

You really have to love your beef to enjoy this dish. Raw beef combined with raw egg yolk, among other ingredients, is a dish to break all the rules. If you are a tartare fan you'll love this recipe. Eat it with the best chips as the Americans do, rather than the British slices of toast. It's equally good as a canapé on top of pumpernickel bread with a little soured cream and caviar, or as an appetiser or main course. Traditionally hand-chopped and using fillet steak, it can, in my opinion, be almost as good using minced rump or sirloin.

**Preparation: 15 minutes**
**Serves: 4–6 as an appetiser, 2–3 as a main course**

| |
|---|
| 450g (1 lb) well-trimmed fillet, sirloin or rump steak, all fat discarded |
| 2 large raw egg yolks |
| 2 tablespoons Worcestershire sauce |
| 1 tablespoon Dijon mustard |
| 1 tablespoon finely chopped capers |
| 1 tablespoon finely chopped red onion |
| 1 tablespoon finely chopped shallot |
| ½ tablespoon finely chopped anchovy |
| 1 tablespoon finely chopped gherkin |
| 3 tablespoons extra virgin olive oil |
| ½ tablespoon freshly squeezed lemon juice |
| 2 tablespoons finely chopped flat-leaf parsley |
| ½ teaspoon Tabasco sauce |
| ¼ teaspoon sea salt |
| ½ teaspoon ground black pepper |

**1** Mince or chop the beef just before you want to serve the dish, in order to retain the colour of the beef.
**2** Combine the remaining ingredients, ensuring the oil is well emulsified with the egg yolks and liquid ingredients. Some people like to fold in finely chopped hard-boiled egg whites and yolks, but I don't think it adds anything to the dish. Feel free to vary the amounts of Worcestershire sauce, mustard and Tabasco, according to your palate. I love anchovies but the quantity can be reduced to suit your taste.
**3** Just before serving, mix the meat with the combined ingredients. Adjust seasoning as necessary.
**4** Serve with a large pile of very hot chips or the thinner *frites*, some mayo if you desire (I do), and a simple dressed leaf salad.

# Steak with Pepper and Mustard

I could have called this *steak au poivre* but I try to avoid using mixed languages, and anyway the French classic doesn't use quite the same ingredients. To be on the safe side, I've given this dish its own title.

**Preparation and cooking: 20 minutes**

**Serves: 2**

450g (1 lb) rump or sirloin steak, in one piece, 4cm (1½ in) thick

1 tablespoon white peppercorns, crushed

1 tablespoon black peppercorns, crushed

½ tablespoon good olive oil

55g (2 oz) unsalted butter

2 shallots, finely diced

2 teaspoons Worcestershire sauce

2 tablespoons brandy

90ml (3 fl oz) beef stock

1 teaspoon green peppercorns

½ tablespoon Dijon mustard

3 tablespoons double cream

salt

**1** Make sure the steak is dry. Press the mixed peppercorns into both sides of the steak by pushing with your hands. If you have time, cover with foil or clingfilm and leave for the pepper flavour to infuse into the steak for 2–3 hours.

**2** Pour the oil into a heavy-based frying pan, and over a high heat, seal the steak for 2 minutes on each side. Reduce the heat, add half the butter to the pan, and cook the steak for a further 5 to 10 minutes, turning one more time, depending on how rare you like it. Remove the steak to a warm place and set aside.

**3** Pour away most of the fat in the pan, then add the remaining butter with the shallots. Over a medium heat cook the shallot until soft but not brown. Pour in the Worcestershire sauce, brandy and stock, and cook rapidly, scraping the bottom of the pan. Fold in the green peppercorns, mustard and cream, and season to taste with salt.

**4** Slice the steak on the diagonal and add to the sauce. Stir to combine the meat juices with the pepper sauce, and warm the meat through, but do not re-boil. Serve with chips or new potatoes and a watercress salad.

## Horseradish Sauce

*Make your own sauce for your roast beef by combining 150ml (¼ pint) of lightly whipped double cream, 150ml (¼ pint) mayonnaise, 55–85g (2–3 oz) freshly grated or prepared horseradish, 2 tablespoons Dijon mustard, 1 tablespoon lemon juice, a pinch of sugar and seasoning.*

## Carpaccio

*For raw meat lovers, one of the best dishes in the world is carpaccio, which generally uses fillet steak. The beef should be very thin and to achieve this at home is not particularly easy (restaurants use a meat slicer). The best method is to freeze the meat for 1 hour or so to firm it up and then slice it as thinly as possible. Another method is to place slices of meat between clingfilm and beat to the desired thinness with a meat mallet. Lay the slices on a plate in a single layer. Brush with extra virgin olive oil and top with a grinding of black pepper. I prefer it simply without any adornments but you may feel you want to serve it with rocket or watercress, a wedge of lemon and some shavings of Parmesan cheese.*

## Oriental Beef Salad

*Another way of serving raw beef is to spice it up after cutting into matchstick strips by mixing it with chopped garlic, chilli, sesame seeds, soy sauce, lime juice, sesame oil, nam pla (fish sauce), sugar, red onions, cucumber, chopped mint and coriander and some chopped roasted peanuts.*

*Grilled steak is beautiful served with an anchovy butter (see page 8), or Roquefort butter (see page 59).*

## Yorkshire Pudding

*If you have problems with your Yorkshire puddings, then try my mate Brian Turner's* Ready Steady Cook *recipe.*

- *Take equal volume, e.g. 300ml (½ pint) each of plain flour, beaten whole eggs and milk, and whisk to combine.*
- *Season and allow to rest for 30–60 minutes.*
- *Heat dripping (preferably) or oil in your Yorkshire pudding mould until very hot; this is very important because if you pour your mixture into cold fat, the pudding will not rise to the same height.*
- *Only pour the mixture halfway up the sides of the mould. Cook for 20–30 minutes in a hot oven, 200°C/400°F/Gas 6, depending on the size of your mould.*

*When making hamburgers, buy beef with 20 per cent fat, which helps flavour and keep the burger moist. If you want to use onions, cook them in butter before adding to the meat, as raw onions discolour the beef and taste sour very quickly. Adding breadcrumbs or a raw egg to your burger creates too tight a texture.*

*The original bubble and squeak consisted of leftover beef chopped up and fried in beef dripping with cabbage, onion and leftover mashed potato. Always allow the base of the mixture to get nice and crispy before turning over. Nowadays bubble has lost its squeak and tends to be just potato, onion and cabbage (see page 62). Take your pick.*

# Mainstay Mince

Mince dishes seem to have slipped out of favour which is a shame. This mince here is a perfect stand-by for converting into any of the dishes such as bolognaise, *Moussaka* (see page 218), cannelloni, *chilli con carne*, lasagne, cottage pie and for fillings for pancakes and jacket potatoes.

**Preparation and cooking: 2½ hours**
**Makes: 2kg (4½ lb), to be split into 9 parts (each to serve 2) and frozen**

225g (8 oz) streaky bacon, diced
180–200ml (6–7 fl oz) good olive oil
2 onions, finely diced
2 sticks celery, finely diced
2 carrots, finely diced
5 cloves garlic, crushed with a little salt
2 teaspoons soft thyme leaves
2 bay leaves
2 teaspoons dried oregano
2 x 400g (14 oz) tins chopped tomatoes
2 tablespoons tomato purée
1 tablespoon anchovy essence
2 tablespoons Worcestershire sauce
1.8kg (4 lb) minced beef
225g (8 oz) fresh chicken livers, finely chopped
2 bottles dry red wine
1.75 litres (3 pints) chicken, beef or lamb stock
salt and ground black pepper

**1**  In a large heavy-based saucepan, fry the bacon in 2 tablespoons of the olive oil. When the bacon is crisp and has released some natural fats, add the onion, celery, carrot, garlic, thyme, bay leaves and oregano, and cook over a medium heat until the vegetables have softened and taken on a little colour.

**2**  Add the tinned tomatoes, the tomato purée, anchovy essence and Worcestershire sauce. Stir to combine.

**3**  Meanwhile, in a large frying pan, heat a little of the olive oil and fry off the mince in small batches until browned. While the meat is frying, break up any lumps with the back of a wooden spoon. Repeat, using more oil each time if necessary, until all the meat is used up. After each batch, add the meat to the sauce mix.

**4**  In the same frying pan, fry the chicken livers until brown and crusty in a little more olive oil, then add the livers to the meat. Deglaze the frying pan with some of the red wine, scraping any crusty bits from the bottom, then pour this wine, the remaining wine and the stock into the meat pot.

**5**  Bring to the boil, reduce the heat and simmer, stirring from time to time, for about 2 hours. Season to taste. If the liquid reduces too much, top up with water.

**6**  When the meat is tender, allow to cool, then refrigerate. When cold, lift off the solidified fat and discard. Freeze mixture in small batches.

# Aromatic Beef Stir-fry

The beauty of stir-fries is that they are so quick to prepare, as long as you have all the ingredients at your fingertips. As with any good cooking the secret lies in the preparation, so make sure you have all the components of the dish ready before you start cooking. Serve with rice or noodles.

**Preparation and cooking: overnight + 20 minutes**
**Serves: 4**

450g (1 lb) fillet or sirloin steak, trimmed of all fat

4 tablespoons soy sauce

4 tablespoons cornflour

2 tablespoons dark soft brown sugar

1 tablespoon *Hot, Hot, Hot Chilli Oil* (see page 258)

1 teaspoon 'gloop' from chilli oil

1 tablespoon grated fresh ginger

2 tablespoons finely chopped garlic

½ teaspoon dried chilli flakes

8 spring onions, half cut into 5mm (¼ in) slices and half cut into 2.5cm (1 in) pieces

450ml (¾ pint) chicken stock

2 tablespoons rice wine or dry sherry

1 tablespoon rice vinegar

350g (12 oz) green vegetables (asparagus, sugar-snap peas, broccoli florets, Chinese leaves)

2 egg whites

600ml (1 pint) peanut or vegetable oil

115g (4 oz) baby spinach leaves, washed

6 sun-dried tomatoes, cut into strips

4 cherry tomatoes, halved

2 tablespoons ripped basil leaves

1 tablespoon chopped coriander leaves

**1** Cut the beef lengthways into 5cm (2 in) wide strips, then cut each strip into 5mm (¼ in) slices.

**2** Combine half the soy sauce with 1 tablespoon of the cornflour and half the sugar, the chilli oil and the chilli oil 'gloop'. Fold in the beef and make sure each slice is coated. Cover and refrigerate overnight. Toss from time to time.

**3** Combine the ginger, garlic, chilli flakes and the finely chopped half of the spring onions. Set aside.

**4** Combine the chicken stock, remaining soy sauce and sugar, the rice wine and rice vinegar, and set aside.

**5** Blanch all the vegetables, depending on your combination, in boiling salted water (asparagus 3 minutes, sugar-snaps 1 minute, broccoli 2 minutes, Chinese leaves, cut in 2.5cm/1 in pieces, 2 minutes). Drain and plunge into iced water, drain again, dry and set aside.

**6** Remove the meat from its marinade. The next stage is to 'velvet' it: mix the egg whites with 2 tablespoons cornflour and coat the meat with this.

**7** In a wok or deep saucepan heat the oil to 175°C/350°F (a cook's thermometer is useful). Slide the beef into the oil, and stir to separate the strips of meat. Cook, stirring continuously, for 30–45 seconds, then immediately scoop the meat out into a colander or metal sieve. Drain all but 2 tablespoons of the cooking oil from the wok into a bowl (it can be re-used).

**8** Over a high heat, add the ginger and garlic mix to the oil in the wok, and stir for 45 seconds. Add the spinach and the remaining larger spring onion pieces, and cook for 3 minutes, stirring until the spinach has wilted. Add all the tomatoes.

**9** Add the chicken stock mixture, raise the heat and bring the sauce to a simmer. Combine the remaining cornflour with 2 tablespoons of stock and fold into the simmering sauce. Cook until the sauce becomes glossy and starts to thicken, about 30 seconds. Fold in the drained meat, blanched vegetables and herbs. Cook until warmed through.

• • • • • • • • • • • • • • • • • • • • • • • • • •

## Carpetbag Steak

*Some of the older dishes are still some of the best, and I really enjoy a carpetbag steak.*

● *Shuck two oysters. Melt butter in a frying pan and cook the oysters with 1 teaspoon of anchovy essence for 30 seconds or until their apron starts to curl. Set aside and allow to cool completely.*

● *Make a slit in the side of a 5cm (2 in) thick fillet steak, and insert the oysters. Season the steak and cook for 4 minutes on each side for medium rare.*

• • • • • • • • • • • • • • • • • • • • • • • • • •

*For a quick marinade for barbecued beef, combine 300ml (½ pint) soy sauce, 1 teaspoon dried chilli or red chilli flakes, 1 teaspoon chopped garlic, 1 teaspoon sesame oil, 1 tablespoon chopped spring onion, 1 tablespoon soft dark brown sugar and 1 teaspoon grated fresh ginger. Allow your steak or kebabs to marinate for 3–4 hours or overnight.*

• • • • • • • • • • • • • • • • • • • • • • • • • •

# BEETROOT

Indigenous to Europe and western Asia, beetroot belongs to the same family as spinach-beet and seakale-beet (chard), sugar beet and mangel wurzel or mangold. All the root varieties are rich in the sugars for which they are grown commercially on a massive scale in Europe. (Interestingly, it was Napoleon who founded the sugar-beet industry in France, when supplies of sugar cane from the West Indies were blockaded by the British.)

Although always omnipresent in Britain, no one seemed to like beetroot very much, probably because we were too often reminded of childhood salads which contained red, bleeding cubes or slices of the sharp pickled vegetable. Fresh was rarer, and I remember greengrocers always used to boil their own beetroot, knowing full well they would never sell the raw product as it took so long to cook. Cooked beetroot was often sold still steaming wrapped in the *Daily Sketch* or some other tabloid. Nowadays beetroot has had a reversal of fortune with restaurants finding it rather trendy to serve it fresh in one form or another. I'm still not a fan of the commercial pickled stuff, but love fresh beetroot cooked, especially roasted. If you haven't eaten it for some time give it another try, you'll be quite surprised at how delicious it tastes.

As to varieties you'll rarely find anything more glamorous than the standard purple variety, but if you are a gardener grow Burpess Golden (lovely yellow flesh), Albina Vereduma (ice-white flesh), Barbietola di Chioggia (red variety with white rings, cooks pink) and Detroit 2 Spinel which produces baby 4cm (1½ in) beets.

When buying beetroot, look for a smooth-skinned globe with crisp red stalks and crisp green leaves. Never buy when the leaves have been cut level with the root, as you will lose the red colour into the water when cooking. The same applies to the whiskery roots which should be intact. And don't buy too far in advance. To prepare beets for cooking, cut the leaves off, leaving about 5cm (2 in) of the stem, and rinse them under cold water. If the earth is hard to dislodge, use a soft scrubbing brush, but be careful not to break the skin. Beetroot contains many nutrients, particularly potassium, calcium and iron; the leaves, which can also be eaten, contain vitamin C.

## Boiling
Cook from cold in salted water for 1¼–1¾ hours for medium to large, and 30–45 minutes for small. To remove skins don't peel with a knife but merely rub the skins off using your fingers (I suggest rubber or surgical gloves to avoid heavy staining) under cold water.

## Steaming or Roast-steaming
1 hour for large/medium beetroot, 15 minutes for small. You may not have heard of roast-steaming – nor had I before I wrote about this ingredient but it sums up the process of wrapping beetroot in foil and cooking them in the oven: it's roasting, but without the crisp outside; it's cooking in a steamy heat, rather than the dry heat of baking. Cook in the oven for 2 hours at 180°C/350°F/Gas 4, and peel as above.

## Roasting
Cut the washed beetroot in wedges, dribble with olive oil, sea salt and chopped thyme, cook for 1½ hours at 350°F/ 180°C/Gas 4, and eat skin and all.

## Sweet Beet
*Ever tried beetroot as a dessert? Nor have I, but I have my aunt's recipe.*
- *Boil 2kg (4½ lb) baby beets for 40 minutes, then add 2kg (4½ lb) caster sugar, the strained juice of 6 lemons with their shredded peel, ½ cinnamon stick, 1 split vanilla pod and 6 cloves.*
- *Boil until the beetroot is tender, then remove, cool and peel.*
- *Skim the cooking liquor and fast-boil until it has thickened and is syrupy. Strain the liquor over the beetroots and leave to cool. Serve with cream or ice-cream.*

# Chunky Beetroot Soup

Inspired by *borscht*, the classic Russian soup, I find this much more satisfying, especially in winter. It's real peasant food, a meal in itself.

**Preparation and cooking: 2½ hours**
**Serves: 6**

| |
|---|
| 55g (2 oz) unsalted butter |
| 1 tablespoon olive oil |
| 2 onions, roughly chopped |
| 3 cloves garlic, finely chopped |
| 1 teaspoon soft thyme leaves |
| 1 carrot, diced |
| 1 turnip, diced |
| 2 sticks celery, diced |
| 1 parsnip, diced |
| 2 leeks, sliced |
| 450g (1 lb) raw beetroot, peeled and grated, plus 1 large beetroot, unpeeled, washed |
| 2 litres (3½ pints) good chicken stock |
| 450g (1 lb) cooked ham, diced |
| ½ Savoy cabbage, shredded |
| 450g (1 lb) floury potatoes, diced |
| salt and ground black pepper |
| 1 tablespoon raspberry vinegar (optional) |
| beetroot leaves, shredded |
| soured cream to garnish |

**1** Heat the butter and oil in a heavy-based saucepan, add the onion, garlic and thyme, and cook over a medium heat for 4 minutes or until the onion starts to soften.
**2** Add the carrot, turnip, celery, parsnip, leek and grated beetroot, and stir to combine. Pour in the chicken stock, bring to the boil and simmer for 30 minutes.
**3** Add the ham, cabbage, potato, and 1 teaspoon ground black pepper, and simmer for a further hour.
**4** Grate or centrifugally extract the juice from the remaining beetroot and add just before serving along with the vinegar and beetroot leaves. This brings back some of the characteristic pink colour to the soup. Season to taste and offer your guests soured cream to garnish.

## Beetroot Salads
● Combine sliced cooked beets with lemon juice, sherry vinegar, olive oil, sea salt, black pepper and lots of chopped mint.
● Or slice beetroots, mix with blood orange segments, extra virgin olive oil and lemon juice, and sprinkle with chives.

## Beetroot Relish
● *A hearty beetroot relish for cheese or grilled meats involves grating cooked beetroot (1kg/2¼ lb), and mixing it with 3 tablespoons grated horseradish.*
● *Boil 300ml (½ pint) aged red wine vinegar with 1 garlic clove, ½ teaspoon ground black pepper, 3 tablespoons caster sugar, 4 cloves, 12 coriander seeds and 300ml (½ pint) beetroot cooking liquor for 10 minutes.*
● *Pour this over the beetroot mix in warm sterilised jars, and store.*
● *Use after 2 weeks.*

*For a quickie chilled soup, blend together 350g (12 oz) chopped cooked beetroot, 4 chopped spring onions, 1 teaspoon grated horseradish, 750g (1 lb 10 oz) Greek yogurt and seasoning. Garnish with chives and raw grated beetroot. Thin if necessary with a little chilled chicken stock.*

*For a starter, toss peeled roasted beetroots with lemon juice and olive oil, combine with **wilted** beetroot leaves or baby spinach, and mix with crumbled feta cheese and chopped walnuts.*

## Roast Beetroot

*This is a wonderful partner for roast beef or game.*

● *Place in your roasting tray half a dozen unpeeled beets with 3 medium unpeeled red onions, some whole unpeeled garlic cloves, sprigs of thyme and olive oil.*

● *Roast in a medium oven – 180°C/350°F/Gas 4 – for about 1½ hours, then remove the veg and* **deglaze** *the pan with a little chicken stock, some balsamic vinegar and a teaspoon of chopped thyme leaves.*

● *Boil and scrape the bottom of the pan, then reduce the liquid until syrupy.*

● *Pour over the vegetables which you have peeled and sliced.*

*Combine chopped cooked beetroot with butter, crisp bacon pieces, soured cream, horseradish and chopped dill, and use as an accompaniment to cold meats, or as part of a buffet salad.*

*Combine cold diced cooked beetroot with diced apple, diced cooked potato, chopped pickled herring, chopped red onion, a little horseradish and Dijon mustard and fold into soured cream. Great for a starter or a topping for crostini (see page 53).*

# BREAD

I'm not going to give you recipes to *make* bread as I don't think this is the purpose of the book. Sure enough, dedicated cooks *will* make bread, and very satisfying it is too, but where do you start, there are so many varieties nowadays?

Both specialist bakers and supermarkets are now providing interesting loaves, but I still own up to enjoying the occasional slice of mass-produced bread, usually in a sandwich, one of the prime purposes of bread as far as I am concerned. However, I'm not a fan of sandwiches in thick slices of trendy bread; to me a sandwich needs thin slices of bread and large amounts of filling.

Some of the recipes here use bread in a way that is traditional in Europe, especially in Italy – in soups and salads, as a means of using up slightly stale bread.

## French Toast

*Pain perdu*, French toast and eggy bread all appear to be different names for the same breakfast indulgence.

**Preparation and cooking: 10 minutes**
**Serves: 3**

2 free-range eggs
85ml (3 fl oz) milk
85ml (3 fl oz) single cream
1 teaspoon ground cinnamon
1 tablespoon orange juice
2 teaspoons caster sugar
knob of butter
6 slices of bread

**To serve**
strawberries

**1** Beat the eggs with the milk, single cream, half the cinnamon and the orange juice to a smooth batter.
**2** Combine the caster sugar with the remaining cinnamon and set aside.
**3** Melt some butter in a frying pan, dip slices of bread into the batter and fry on both sides until golden.
**4** Top with strawberries and sprinkle with the cinnamon sugar.

## Bread Sauce

Most of us love a good bread sauce, especially with poultry – so easy to make so, please, don't go out and buy a packet!

**Preparation and cooking: 45 minutes**
**Serves: 4**

1 small onion
1 bay leaf
1 clove
300ml (½ pint) **scalded** milk
55g (2 oz) fresh white breadcrumbs
freshly grated nutmeg
salt and ground white pepper
40g (1½ oz) unsalted butter
2 tablespoons double cream

**1** Spike the onion with the bay leaf and clove. Infuse in the hot **scalded** milk for 30 minutes before adding the fresh white breadcrumbs.
**2** Simmer over a low heat for 15 minutes, stirring regularly, before removing the onion, clove and bay leaf.
**3** Add a grating of nutmeg, salt and ground white pepper with the unsalted butter and double cream.
**4** Serve hot, don't make in advance.

# Tuscan Bread and Tomato Soup

I've enjoyed making this soup ever since I first ate it in London's River Café, which specialises in classic Italian food. I don't use fresh tomatoes, as tinned have much more flavour.

**Preparation and cooking: 40 minutes**
**Serves: 4–6**

125ml (4 fl oz) extra virgin olive oil
3 cloves garlic, finely diced
6 anchovy fillets, finely chopped
1 onion, finely diced
2 x 400g (14 oz) tins chopped tomatoes with basil
600ml (1 pint) vegetable stock or still mineral water
350g (12 oz) *ciabatta* bread, crusts removed
½ bunch basil, leaves only
salt and ground black pepper

**1** Heat half of the olive oil in a large saucepan, and add the garlic, anchovies and onion. Cook until soft but not brown, then add the tomatoes and stock or mineral water. Bring to the boil over a high heat and cook for 20 minutes, stirring from time to time.

**2** Break the bread into small chunks and fold into the soup. Combine until the bread has softened and is well mixed with the tomatoes, about 10 minutes. Add the basil leaves and season to taste with a little salt and plenty of ground black pepper.

**3** Finish the soup with a dribble of the remaining olive oil.

## Parmesan *Croûtons*

● *For a* croûton *with a difference, cut up some good bread into 1cm (½ in) cubes.*
● *Melt 115g (4 oz) unsalted butter and pour into a bowl.*
● *Toss 225g (8oz) bread* croûtons *in the butter, then combine with 55g (2 oz) freshly grated Parmesan and ¼ teaspoon ground black pepper.*
● *Spread* croûtons *on a baking sheet and cook in a 180ºC/350ºF/Gas 4 oven until crispy and brown, stirring occasionally, for about 15 minutes.*
● *Drain* croûtons *on kitchen paper.*

## Savoury Fritters

*An oldie but a goodie.*
● *Pour boiling water on to 225g (8 oz) crustless bread, allow to rest 1 hour, then whisk until smooth.*
● *Combine with 55g (2 oz) mixed chopped rocket, parsley, chives and 4 beaten eggs.*
● *Season and fry small amounts in clarified butter, turning once, to make the fritters.*

## Bruschetta

Bruschetta *welcomes a variety of toppings nowadays, but this was not its original intention. The purist would merely cook bread slices over a wood fire then dribble liberal quantities of extra virgin olive oil over it. A simple present-day Italian snack might include some* bruschetta, *chunks of sun-warmed tomato, slivers of aged Parmesan, slices of San Daniele ham and some olives.*

## Crostini

Crostini *are smaller than* bruschetta.
● *Cut a* baguette *into 5mm (¼ in) slices, dribble with olive oil and cook in a 160ºC/325ºF/Gas 3 oven until golden and brittle.*
● *Rub with garlic while warm, allow to cool and store in an airtight container.*
● *Use as a base for a variety of savoury toppings.*

*For a bread and butter pudding with a difference, see Fruit, Dried, page 173.*

*Cut your stale bread into cubes and store in a polythene bag in the freezer. A useful standby for bread sauce, breadcrumbs or a bread soup.*

# Panzanella

A delicious salad from Tuscany that traditionally makes use of up to three-day-old bread that is soaked in water and squeezed dry, but I prefer to use slices of *bruschetta*, rubbed with garlic.

**Preparation and cooking: 25 minutes**
**Serves: 4–6**

| |
|---|
| 3 x 1cm (½ in) slices Italian olive oil bread or *ciabatta* |
| 6 tablespoons extra virgin olive oil |
| 3 cloves garlic |
| 4 anchovy fillets |
| 1 tablespoon small capers, drained |
| sea salt and ground black pepper |
| 2 tablespoons aged red wine vinegar |
| 2 tablespoons chopped flat-leaf parsley |
| 6 plum tomatoes, seeded and cubed |
| 1 small red onion, finely sliced |
| ½ cucumber, seeded and cut into 1cm (½ in) chunks |
| 2 sticks celery, finely sliced |
| 55g (2 oz) stoned black olives, chopped (optional) |
| 12 basil leaves, ripped |

**1** Make the *bruschetta* by dribbling the slices of bread on both sides with some of the olive oil. Ideally grill on both sides on a barbecue but, failing that, toast both sides under a grill. Rub each side of the bread with one of the cloves of garlic. Rip the bread into 1cm (½ in) cubes. Set aside.

**2** In a food processor or mortar and pestle blend the remaining garlic, the anchovies and capers with ½ teaspoon sea salt. Add the remaining olive oil, vinegar and parsley and **pulse** the food processor until the ingredients are combined.

**3** Mix the bread into the remaining ingredients, and toss with the anchovy dressing. Season with a few turns of ground black pepper.

## Fattoush (Bread Salad)

*A traditional Lebanese salad made with pitta bread.*
● *Combine toasted and shredded pitta bread with loads of parsley, some chopped garlic, lemon juice, extra virgin olive oil, chopped mint, diced cucumber, chopped spring onions, chopped tomato, chopped roasted red peppers and some celery.*

*To make toasted breadcrumbs for coating chicken, veal, lamb or fish, place stale bread in a low oven and cook until the bread is brittle. Blend in a food processor then pass through a sieve. Freeze or store in an airtight container.*

## Bread *Gnocchi*

This would make a good, quick lunch dish for four or a starter for six.

**Preparation and cooking: 30 minutes**
**Serves: 4–6**

450g (1 lb) stale Italian bread

600ml (1 pint) milk

1 teaspoon salt

85g (3 oz) Parma ham, chopped

115g (4 oz) Parmesan, grated

1 teaspoon ground black pepper

1 large egg

2 tablespoons chopped basil

4 tablespoons chopped flat-leaf parsley

seasoned flour

**1** Cut the crusts off the stale Italian bread, and tear the white of the bread into bite-sized pieces.

**2** Cover with milk and leave to soak for 15 minutes.

**3** Squeeze dry and add the remaining ingredients except for the flour.

**4** Mix until combined. Shape into little balls and press down on the balls with a fork.

**5** Roll in seasoned flour and refrigerate for 30 minutes.

**6** Place in boiling salted water and cook uncovered until the *gnocchi* rise to the surface.

**7** Serve with a sage and lemon butter sauce (see page 215).

*Combine ripped* bruschetta *with pine kernels, sultanas soaked in Vin Santo, loads of ripped rocket leaves, some just cooked chicken, and some hot dripping from the roasting tray, finished with a squeeze of lemon juice and seasoning. This makes a good main-course chicken salad.*

## Salade en Chaponnade

Salade en chaponnade *is a simple bread salad.*

● *Make it by rubbing stale French bread with garlic, and dribbling over equal quantities of walnut and olive oil.*

● *Rip up and fry in chicken, duck or goose fat.*

● *Toss hot with ripped greens – rocket, chicory, escarole, sorrel, dandelion leaves and radicchio – any oils left in the bowl or fat left in the pan, and aged sherry vinegar.*

# BROCCOLI

Broccoli, along with cauliflower, is a member of the cabbage family, therefore is native to Europe. It is familiar as either the larger green calabrese or as sprouting broccoli. The latter is available in green, white and purple forms; loose stalk clusters of heads are formed, rather than the tight head of the more recently developed calabrese (which, as you can guess from the name, originated in Italy). Broccoli (*Brassica oleracea* spp) is available in many varieties to the gardener, and I've had particular success with Ramosco and Romanesco which have lime-green heads, and White Sprouting and White Star which are very pale.

Broccoli is a delicious vegetable which is packed full of vitamins. Select tight heads of calabrese, avoiding woody stems, flowers that have started to sprout, and any that is strong smelling. To prepare, separate the florets from the stems and soak in salted water to remove any bugs. Don't throw away the stems, but peel off the woody outside and slice the tender flesh (good in stir-fries). To cook, plunge sliced stalks and florets into large amounts of boiling salted water, bring back to the boil and cook for 2–3 minutes until tender. If you overcook broccoli, never fear, convert it to a broccoli salad (see opposite).

## Raw Broccoli Pesto

Something entirely different, and wonderful for your health as it contains mega amounts of vitamins A and C, potassium, iron and calcium.

**Preparation and cooking: 10 minutes**
**Serves: 4**

675g (1½ lb) raw broccoli florets

25g (1 oz) basil leaves

4 cloves garlic

55g (2 oz) pine kernels

½ teaspoon sea salt

1 teaspoon ground black pepper

225ml (8 fl oz) extra virgin olive oil

85g (3 oz) freshly grated Parmesan

**1** In a food processor blend together all the ingredients. Excellent for folding into pasta.

*Toss cooked broccoli florets with extra virgin olive oil, crisp bacon pieces and a pinch of dried chilli flakes.*

## Baked Broccoli

Good for a starter or as a partner to roast meats.

**Preparation and cooking: 1 hour**
**Serves: 4**

350g (12 oz) cooked broccoli, chopped

85g (3 oz) Cheddar and Parmesan, grated

3 eggs

350ml (12 fl oz) double cream

salt and ground black pepper

**1** Place the chopped cooked broccoli in a small baking dish, and sprinkle with the grated Cheddar and Parmesan.
**2** Beat the eggs with the double cream, salt and pepper, and pour over the broccoli.
**3** Bake in the oven in a **bain-marie** with water coming halfway up the sides of the baking dish at 180°C/350°F/Gas 4 for 45–60 minutes until the custard is set.

*Chop the broccoli and anchovy mix (see page 57) and add to pasta with mozzarella dice, some grated Parmesan and chopped flat-leaf parsley.*

# A Salad of Broccoli Stewed in White Wine

There are times when I get bored of 'just'-cooked vegetables, and yearn for a good stewy pulp. Here's one made with broccoli. It's excellent cold as a salad with extra virgin olive oil.

**Preparation and cooking: 35 minutes**

**Serves: 4**

| |
|---|
| 4 tablespoons good olive oil |
| 4 garlic cloves, finely chopped |
| 1 small onion, finely chopped |
| 675g (1½ lb) broccoli |
| ½ tablespoon chopped oregano |
| 225ml (8 fl oz) sweet white wine |
| 3 tablespoons sultanas |
| 2 tablespoons flaked almonds |
| gratcd rind of 1 lemon |
| juice of ½ lemon |
| extra virgin olive oil |
| salt and ground black pepper |

**1** Heat the oil in a large saucepan, add the garlic and onion, and cook over a medium heat until the onion has softened without colouring.

**2** Meanwhile, separate the broccoli florets from the stems. Peel the stems and chop finely. Add the broccoli heads and stems, oregano, wine, sultanas, almonds and lemon rind to the pan, cover and simmer for 30 minutes. Stir occasionally.

**3** Add extra wine if required to prevent sticking. Season to taste with lemon juice, extra virgin olive oil as necessary, salt and pepper. Serve hot or at room temperature.

*Instead of discarding the stems of the broccoli, wash them and push them through a centrifugal juicer with a peeled and cored pear to make a refreshing drink that tastes like bananas! The kids love it and it's full of vitamins and goodness – one way of getting them to eat their greens.*

*Serve broccoli with hollandaise sauce (see page 113) or crisp breadcrumbs fried in garlic and herb-infused extra virgin olive oil.*

## Broccoli with Anchovy

● *Fry 4 garlic cloves in 5 tablespoons extra virgin olive oil until golden, remove garlic and discard.*

● *Add a pinch of dried chilli flakes and 6 chopped anchovy fillets to the oil, cook until they break up, then fold in 450g (1 lb) cooked broccoli with a little of its cooking water.*

● *Cook for 10 minutes until the broccoli is very soft, season and add a squeeze of lemon juice.*

● *Roughly chop, then serve on bruschetta or crostini (see page 53).*

## Quick Broccoli Bake

● *Toss blanched broccoli florets into sweated onions, garlic and soft thyme leaves.*

● *Combine with crumbled goat's cheese, chives and basil.*

● *Dribble with olive oil and season.*

● *Bake in a preheated oven at 180°C/350°F/Gas 4 for 10 minutes.*

*A crunchy salad is made by combining peeled and sliced raw broccoli stalks with seeded and chopped tomatoes, garlic, lemon juice, olive oil, chives and grated Parmesan.*

# BUTTER

Life would be boring without butter. I know we are meant to reduce our consumption of saturated fat, but my policy of everything in moderation with a little excess now and then is how I've always lived my life.

In the nineteenth century good butter was deemed to be yellow, although it was often coloured with carrot juice or annatto dissolved in hemp oil. It was highly salted, often by as much as 7 per cent. Butter made from fresh milk had little or no flavour so the milk was allowed to ripen from 1–7 days to develop flavour before churning. At the end of the last century, a Dane, C. O. Jensen, applied pasteurisation to butter, realising he could kill dangerous bacteria and make better butter.

Butter must be at least 80 per cent fat, with farmhouse butters reaching levels as high as 88 per cent. The colour comes from the grazing pastures and the level of fat in the milk. The choice of butter must be down to you, with most of them very standardised. For my taste, on bread or toast I enjoy Lurpak, which is slightly salted, or if I'm feeling particularly flush, I buy the king of butters, Echiré, which is sold in distinctive wooden tubs, or Isigny from Normandy. For cooking I always use an unsalted butter of good quality, or I make my own clarified butter (see page 60). For those of you near an Indian food shop, *ghee* is their version of clarified.

Spreadable butters have been with us for a few years now, and the texture is achieved by extracting the hard fats from the butter, and using early summer milk which has a smaller concentration of these fats. Avoid butter substitutes and margarines for cooking.

## Brandy (or Rum) Butter

A quick brandy butter that saves you money, and that actually tastes of the alcohol, is always welcome to accompany Christmas pudding or mince pies.

**Preparation: 5 minutes**
**Serves: 4–6**

300g (10½ oz) unsalted butter, softened

500g (18 oz) icing sugar

1 tablespoon warm water

125ml (4 fl oz) brandy (or rum)

**1** Beat the unsalted butter with the icing sugar, warm water and brandy (or rum) until white and creamy.
**2** Refrigerate until ready to use.

**N.B.** For a different look, substitute soft dark brown sugar for half the icing sugar.

• • • • • • • • • • • •

*Don't use salted butter for cooking as it contains more milk solids than unsalted, and these can burn and spoil your cooking.*

• • • • • • • • • • • •

## Very Savoury Butter

Butter for snails or chicken Kiev is much more tasty when you add more than just garlic and parsley. Make a large amount at one time, and freeze so that you always have it handy.

**Preparation: 20 minutes**
**Makes: 1.25kg (2¾ lb)**

1kg (2¼ lb) unsalted butter, softened

2 shallots, finely chopped

115g (4 oz) chopped parsley

25g (1 oz) anchovy fillets

3 tablespoons Pernod

40g (1½ oz) powdered almonds

50g (2 oz) garlic, chopped

15g (½ oz) ground white pepper

**1** Combine all of the above ingredients in a food processor.
**2** Make into eight foil-wrapped rolls, each about 150g (5½ oz), and place in the freezer.
**3** Remove 1 hour before use. Slice to garnish, melt for snails, mould into a torpedo shape for the innards of chicken Kiev.

• • • • • • • • • • • •

*Blend together equal
parts of unsalted butter and
Roquefort cheese with chives
for a delicious butter to go
with steaks or burgers or
in sandwiches.*

• • • • • • • • • • • •

• • • • • • • • • • •

*For browned butter
(beurre noir) – great with
some fish – melt butter over
a medium heat and cook until
it takes on a light brown
hazelnut colour and starts to
smell nutty. At this point add
a little white wine vinegar or
lemon juice and some chopped
parsley. Large quantities
of browned butter can
be frozen.*

• • • • • • • • • • •

A medley of savoury butters: Roasted
Garlic and Rosemary, Roquefort with
chives and red chilli and ginger also
make a refreshing alternative to the
usual garlic bread.

# Roasted Garlic and Rosemary Butter

Delicious on grilled lamb, or smeared on a lamb joint before roasting.

**Preparation: 40 minutes**
**Makes: 500g (18 oz)**

| |
|---|
| 2 heads of garlic, 5mm (¼ in) top removed |
| 1 tablespoon olive oil |
| 450g (1 lb) unsalted butter |
| 1 large sprig rosemary |
| 3 tablespoons chopped parsley |
| 2 tablespoons chopped chives |
| salt and ground black pepper |

**1** Wrap the heads of garlic in foil with a dribble of olive oil and roast at 180°C/350°F/Gas 4 for 20–25 minutes until soft.
**2** Pop the garlic from its skins and place in a food processor with the unsalted butter.
**3** While the garlic is roasting, **blanch** the leaves from the sprig of rosemary, drain and dry. Add to the garlic and butter, with the chopped parsley and chives.
**4** Purée until smooth, and season to taste.

## Red Chilli and Ginger Butter
*Great for grilled fish or shellfish, either chilling and slicing to garnish, or melting and pouring over.*
● *Combine 225g (8 oz) softened unsalted butter, 1 tablespoon chopped red chilli, 1 tablespoon grated ginger, 1 tablespoon lime juice, ½ tablespoon grated lime zest, 1 teaspoon salt and 1 teaspoon ground white pepper.*

# *Béchamel* Sauce

The classic white sauce.
**Preparation: 40 minutes**
**Serves: 4**

| |
|---|
| 600ml (1 pint) milk |
| 1 onion |
| 1 bay leaf |
| 2 cloves |
| 6 black peppercorns |
| 55g (2 oz) butter |
| 55g (2 oz) plain flour |
| grated nutmeg (optional) |

**1** Bring the milk just to the boil with the onion pierced with the bay leaf and cloves, and the peppercorns. Remove from the heat, and leave to **infuse** for 20 minutes. Strain.
**2** Melt the butter in a non-stick pan, stir in the plain flour, and cook over a low heat for 5 minutes. When smooth, start adding some of the strained flavoured milk. Stir until smooth, then add more milk until the sauce is thickened. Cook for 10–15 minutes to ensure the flour is thoroughly cooked.
**3** You could sprinkle in some grated nutmeg at the end.

**N.B.** For a richer sauce replace 150ml (¼ pint) of the milk with cream. For a cheese sauce, see page 85.

## Clarified Butter
*For cooking at higher temperatures, butter must be clarified.*
● *Heat the butter gently until fully melted then lift the clear liquid butter off the milk solids that have fallen to the bottom, or chill overnight and lift off the solids the next day.*
● *It is possible to buy ghee, which is the Indian version of clarified butter.*

# CABBAGE

Those of my generation and beyond will undoubtedly recall those days of soggy watery cabbage, cabbage that appeared to have been cooked in a washing machine prior to the invention of the spin-drier. I hated cabbage as a kid, probably because I had to eat it at my grandmother's. She boiled it to death, then drank the cooking water (there may be something in this as she lived to a ripe old age). School was no better in the cabbage-cooking stakes, and the cabbage smell of school corridors (from the sulphur) is a ghastly memory for many of us.

Members of the Brassica family all descend from the European wild cabbage, and there are many varieties. There are loose-hearted spring cabbages (often sold and eaten as spring greens), and firm-hearted cabbages which are available at various times of the year, ranging from Primo, the Dutch white, through to the dark, curly-leaved Savoy, which is my favourite. Red cabbage simply contains a pigment in addition to the chlorophyll, which gives it its red colour. Curly kales, Brussels sprouts and their tops are also related, as are Chinese cabbages – the Chinese leaf or *pe-tsai*, *pak-choi* or *bok-choy*, or *choy sum* (a stemmed rather than hearted cabbage). Try to use Chinese cabbages in Oriental dishes.

White cabbage in my opinion is only good raw in a salad such as coleslaw. Red cabbage needs to be either eaten raw or braised slowly until meltingly soft with hints of redcurrant and juniper. Spring greens are delicious cooked as you would cabbage, and *cavolo nero* is the cabbage of the moment, a long dark Italian leaf vegetable which should also be treated as spring greens or Savoy cabbage.

Many cabbages can be eaten raw and are good for you because of their nutrients, including vitamins A, B and C, and magnesium, potassium and calcium.

Nowadays we tend not to overcook cabbage. Remove any tough outer leaves, then cut the cabbage into quarters, cutting away most of the hard centre core. If cutting the cabbage in wedges, leave a little core to hold the cabbage together. Cabbage cooks more quickly if shredded. Cook in boiling salted water until tender, about 8–10 minutes. If eating plain, drain well and toss with black pepper and melted butter, but I prefer to adorn with other flavours.

# Dill Cabbage

This sweet and sour dish, with its fresh dill flavour, is a lovely partner for grilled fish, especially salmon, and for scallops wrapped in bacon (see page 154).

**Preparation and cooking: 25 minutes**
**Serves: 4–6**

1 Savoy cabbage, cored and shredded
2 egg yolks
1 onion, grated
2 tablespoons caster sugar
90ml (3 fl oz) cider vinegar
85g (3 oz) unsalted butter
150ml (¼ pint) double cream
2 teaspoons Dijon mustard
4 tablespoons chopped dill
salt and ground black pepper

**1** Cook the cabbage in boiling salted water until tender, about 8–10 minutes, then drain and dry out over a low heat.
**2** Meanwhile, combine the egg yolks, onion, sugar and vinegar, and cook over a low heat until thickened. Do not boil.
**3** Fold the butter, cream, mustard and dill into the egg yolk sauce, and continue to cook without boiling. Fold in the cabbage and season to taste.

# Cabbage Bake

● *Cook some butter in a frying pan until brown (see page 59), add some sage, garlic, leek, chilli flakes and thyme leaves.*
● *Add a few tablespoons of chicken stock and some shredded Savoy cabbage, and cook until the cabbage and leek wilt down.*
● *Combine the cabbage with diced cooked potato, some grated Parmesan and Taleggio cheeses.*
● *Place in a baking dish, sprinkle with Parmesan and breadcrumbs, dot with butter, and bake in a hot oven until bubbling and golden.*

# Deep-fried 'Seaweed'

A popular choice in Chinese restaurants, but often it has nothing to do with the sea – in fact, it is usually deep-fried cabbage. Eat as a snack or a soup garnish.

**Preparation and cooking: 20 minutes**
**Serves: 4–6**

| |
|---|
| 1 Savoy cabbage |
| vegetable oil for deep-frying |
| salt and soft brown sugar |

**1** Separate the leaves of the cabbage, wash and dry well.
**2** Roll up several leaves at a time to a cigar shape and slice as thinly as possible.
**3** Heat the oil to 180°C/350°F and deep-fry a handful of cabbage shreds at a time – a few seconds at most, until they stop sizzling.
**4** Remove the cabbage from the oil with a slotted spon and drain very well on kitchen paper.
**5** Sprinkle with salt and sugar to taste and serve immediately.

# Savoy Salad

A delicious salad using raw Savoy cabbage or Brussels sprouts.

**Preparation and cooking: 25 minutes**
**Serves: 4**

| |
|---|
| 450g (1 lb) Savoy cabbage or Brussels sprouts, trimmed and shredded |
| ½ red onion, diced |
| 2 garlic cloves, crushed |
| 225g (8 oz) Jersey new potatoes, cooked and sliced |
| ½ teaspoon fresh root ginger, finely chopped |
| juice of 2 lemons |
| 75ml (2½ fl oz) extra virgin olive oil |
| 1 tablespoon fennel seeds |
| ¼ teaspoon ground black pepper |
| ¼ teaspoon Maldon sea salt |
| ¼ tablespoon chopped dill |

**1** Combine all of the above ingredients, check seasoning and serve immediately.

## Braised Red Cabbage

● *Cook red cabbage with onions, juniper berries, apple, red wine, red wine vinegar, redcurrant jelly and thyme for a delicious vegetable to accompany red meat, game or poultry.*
● *This mixture needs to be cooked very slowly until the cabbage is very soft, about 1½ hours.*

*Shred some Chinese cabbage and combine with grated orange zest, sesame seeds, spring onions, chopped mint and chopped coriander. Dress with peanut oil, sesame oil, soy sauce, rice wine vinegar, orange juice, grated ginger, chopped chilli, salt and pepper. A refreshing salad.*

*Bubble and squeak is one of the nation's favourite dishes, made by frying chopped onions until golden in dripping, butter or oil, then adding equal parts of mashed potato and cooked cabbage. Cook until golden and crisp, then turn over and repeat. Serve with eggs.*

## Red Cabbage Salad

● *Shred red cabbage and combine with some hot red wine vinegar.*
● *Allow to rest for up to 12 hours, tossing from time to time.*
● *Make a dressing by combining chopped anchovies (a small tin only), 4 chopped garlic cloves, some extra virgin olive oil and chopped flat-leaf parsley, and lemon juice to taste.*

# Garbure

A meal in itself, comprising various vegetables including cabbage, and finished off with *Duck Confit*.

**Preparation and cooking: overnight + 1¾ hours**
**Serves: 6–8**

225g (8 oz) white haricot beans, soaked in cold water overnight
225g (8 oz) salt belly of pork, in the piece
2 leeks, washed and shredded
225g (8 oz) new potatoes, scrubbed and halved
6 sticks celery, thinly sliced
6 baby turnips, washed
1 ham hock
6 cloves garlic, finely chopped
2 sprigs thyme
2 onions, thinly sliced
2 carrots, sliced
2 bay leaves
3 litres (5¼ pints) chicken stock
1 Savoy cabbage, shredded
4 legs *Duck Confit* (see page 111)
salt and ground black pepper
chopped flat-leaf parsley to garnish

**1** Drain the beans then cover with fresh unsalted water and cook for 40 minutes. Drain and discard the cooking water. Put the beans back in a large saucepan and add the pork, leek, potato, celery, turnip, ham hock, garlic, thyme, onion, carrot, bay leaves and stock, and cook for 45 minutes.

**2** Add the cabbage and duck *confit* and cook for a further 20 minutes. Remove the pork belly and ham hock. Place the pork in a food processor and blend until smooth. Add back to the soup. Remove the meat from the ham hock and shred. Fold back into the soup.

**3** Season to taste and garnish with parsley.

· · · · · · · · · · · · · · · · · ·

*Instead of simply boiling cabbage, **sweat** it. Heat some sunflower oil with several garlic cloves for a few minutes, then add a little chicken stock. Bring to the boil, add the cabbage, some fennel seeds and diced ham, and cook for 5–8 minutes.*

· · · · · · · · · · · · · · · · · ·

# Cabbage Griddle Cakes

Lovely on their own or served with fried or poached eggs and crispy smoked bacon.

**Preparation and cooking: 30 minutes**
**Serves: 4–6**

450g (1 lb) Savoy cabbage, shredded
salt and ground black pepper
2 eggs
1 egg yolk
½ onion, grated
175ml (6 fl oz) milk
225g (8 oz) plain flour
85g (3 oz) butter, melted
2 tablespoons snipped chives
olive oil for frying

**1** Cook the cabbage in boiling salted water until tender, about 8–10 minutes. Drain and, when cool enough to handle, dry.

**2** Combine the eggs, egg yolk, onion, milk, flour, melted butter and some seasoning in a food processor and blend until smooth. The mixture should be a batter consistency: if too thin, add more flour; too thick, a little more milk.

**3** Pour the batter into a bowl, and fold in the cabbage, chives and some more seasoning.

**4** Heat a tablespoon of oil in a frying pan and spoon in a dollop of cabbage batter. Cook a few cakes at a time until golden on both sides. Keep warm while cooking a further batch, adding more oil to the pan if necessary.

· · · · · · · · · ·

*Blanched cabbage leaves make great containers for all sorts of fillings.*

· · · · · · · · · ·

# Coleslaw

● *Mix two-thirds finely shredded hard white cabbage with one-third shredded carrot.*

● *Add a few chopped spring onions (and, for a difference in taste, some caraway seeds).*

● *Substitute Greek yogurt for mayonnaise for a healthier alternative.*

# Stuffed Cabbage Leaves

Delicious as a starter, or as a vegetable to go with roast or grilled pork.

**Preparation and cooking: 45 minutes**
**Serves: 4–6**

---

2 Savoy cabbages

salt and ground black pepper

115g (4 oz) streaky bacon, cut into 1cm (½ in) cubes

85g (3 oz) unsalted butter

1 onion, finely chopped

1 clove garlic, finely chopped

1 teaspoon soft thyme leaves

85g (3 oz) Roquefort cheese (or other blue cheese)

3 tablespoons mascarpone cheese

2 tablespoons pine kernels

12 slices Parma ham

plain flour for coating

---

**1** Remove 6 outer leaves from *each* of the cabbages. In a pan of boiling salted water, cook the leaves for 4 minutes, then drain and cool. Remove and discard the large central ribs, and set the leaves aside.

**2** Shred the remaining cabbage and cook in the cabbage water for 8 minutes. Drain and cool, then set aside.

**3** In a frying pan cook the bacon in 25g (1 oz) of the butter until the bacon is golden. Add another 25g (1 oz) of the butter, then the onion, garlic and thyme. Cook over a medium heat until the onion has softened, then add the shredded cabbage and stir to combine. Tip this mixture into a bowl and fold in the crumbled Roquefort, mascarpone and the pine kernels. Season to taste.

**4** Divide the mixture into 12. Lay out the blanched cabbage leaves and line the inside of each of them with a slice of ham. Put one portion of the stuffing on to the ham. Roll up, folding in the sides.

**5** Roll each package in seasoned flour and fry in the remaining butter until golden on all sides. Cook in batches if necessary, and keep warm.

# CARROT

I hated carrots as a kid – they were boiled without being peeled, served with no butter, and often we had to endure tinned. My own children, on the other hand, love carrots whether raw or lightly caramelised. Carrots may be a common or garden vegetable, but they are indispensable in so many dishes: where would stocks be without carrots?; can you imagine stews or braises without them?; and how many of us would miss that oh-so-moist carrot cake?

When researching, it's funny what you turn up. Did you know that the carrot, being an umbellifer, is related to parsnip, celery, parsley, caraway and even the poison hemlock? Would you believe that carrots used to be purple, were first introduced to Europe by the Moors, and that it wasn't until the green-fingered Dutch worked on them that they became orange? Carrots contain more natural sugar than any other vegetable apart from sugar beet, and yet an average carrot contains only 30 calories. They are also an incredibly high source of beta-carotene or vegetable vitamin A, and contain high levels of potassium, calcium and phosphorus. And there is even some evidence to back up the old wives' tale that carrots make you see in the dark – night blindness is caused by a deficiency of vitamin A.

We can buy carrots that are large or small, with or without green tops. Organic carrots taste infinitely better than those washed ones sweating in plastic. Choose carrots that are firm but with little or no bend; the darker the colour the more beta-carotene it contains. Don't peel baby carrots, just give them a wash and a scrape. Larger carrots should always be peeled, especially if they have not been organically grown.

In my opinion carrots should not be cooked **al dente**, they should either be eaten raw or cooked thoroughly without being mushy. Sliced or roughly diced carrots should take about 10 minutes to cook, while **julienne** or **batons** should take 5 minutes. Roast carrots will take 45–60 minutes. Carrots can be boiled, steamed, roasted or mashed.

# Mediterranean Carrot Rolls

I ate these rolls in a Moroccan restaurant, but was subsequently told they are Turkish. Who cares? All I can say is that they are probably one of the tastiest things I have eaten in a long time.

**Preparation and cooking: 45 minutes**
**Serves: 4–6**

10 medium carrots, cooked until soft and well drained
2 slices white bread, rubbed into crumbs
6 dried apricots, finely diced
2 teaspoons sultanas, chopped
4 spring onions, finely diced
3 tablespoons pine kernels
4 cloves garlic, finely chopped
1 teaspoon chilli flakes
2 teaspoons grated orange rind
1 egg
6 tablespoons mixed chopped parsley, mint and dill
salt and ground black pepper

**To cook and serve**

plain flour for coating
sunflower oil for frying
1 red onion, sliced
a handful of coriander leaves

**1** Mash the carrots, and place in a bowl. Add the remaining ingredients up to the salt and ground black pepper and knead well; if too wet add further breadcrumbs – the mixture should be soft and slightly damp.
**2** Mould the mix into about 12–14 x 5cm (2 in) cylinders, coating your hands with flour to stop sticking. Roll each cylinder in flour, then shallow-fry in oil until brown on all sides.
**3** Serve with a yogurt dip (see pages 304 and 307) and some finely sliced red onion and coriander leaves.

# A Simple Carrot Soup

Carrot soups have been popular with the dinner party set for many a year.

**Preparation and cooking: 30 minutes**
**Serves: 2**

85g (3 oz) unsalted butter
4 large carrots, sliced
1 small potato, sliced
1 onion, sliced
½ teaspoon soft thyme leaves
600ml (1 pint) vegetable stock
4 tablespoons double cream
salt and ground black pepper

**1** Melt the unsalted butter and cook the carrot, potato, onion and soft thyme leaves for 5 minutes, then add the vegetable stock.
**2** Cook until the vegetables are tender, then liquidise.
**3** Finish off with the double cream and season to taste.
**4** You can alter the flavours by adding 200ml (7 fl oz) orange juice instead of the same amount of stock, or folding in 2 tablespoons chopped coriander just before serving.

## Carrot Juice

*Breakfast for me often includes a carrot juice in one form or another.*
● *One is made by centrifugally juicing 4 peeled carrots, 2 cored but not peeled apples and a 50p-sized piece of peeled ginger.*
● *This is mixed and served over ice.*
● *Another substitutes 2 celery sticks for the apples.*

# Carrot Fritters

Carrot fritters are a favourite vegetable for children.

**Preparation and cooking: 15 minutes**
**Serves: 2–4**

4 carrots, grated
1 teaspoon ground cumin
1 clove garlic, crushed
1 teaspoon ground coriander
1 teaspoon ground turmeric
½ teaspoon cayenne pepper
3 tablespoons finely chopped spring onions
2 tablespoons chopped coriander
1 egg, beaten
150ml (¼ pint) milk
140g (5 oz) plain flour
oil for cooking

**1** Combine the grated carrots with all the remaining ingredients except for the oil.
**2** Mix well, drop spoonfuls of the mixture into hot oil, and cook for 2 minutes on each side.

## Roast Carrots

*Roasting is one of my favourite ways of cooking carrots.*
● *Blanch halved carrots in boiling salted water for 5 minutes.*
● *Drain, pat dry and add to the dish in which you are roasting your Sunday joint.*
● *Coat with the hot dripping or roasting juices and cook for about 45 minutes, turning from time to time.*

# Carrot Cake with Cream Cheese Frosting

I don't know many people who don't love a slice of carrot cake, and it's a good way of persuading kids to eat vegetables. The idea is originally American, and I love the frosting.

**Preparation and cooking: 1½ hours**
**Serves: 6–8**

450g (1 lb) self-raising flour
2 teaspoons baking powder
½ tablespoon powdered cinnamon
½ teaspoon grated nutmeg
½ teaspoon ground allspice
225g (8 oz) soft dark brown sugar
225ml (8 fl oz) olive oil
3 eggs, lightly beaten
225g (8 oz) cooked carrots, puréed
115g (4 oz) shredded raw carrot
115g (4 oz) chopped walnuts
115g (4 oz) raisins
55g (2 oz) desiccated coconut
55g (2 oz) tinned crushed pineapple, drained

**Cream cheese frosting**
125g (4½ oz) cream cheese or mascarpone cheese
250g (9 oz) icing sugar
90g (3¼ oz) unsalted butter
½ teaspoon vanilla essence
juice of ½ lemon

**1** Preheat the oven to 180°C/350°F/Gas 4. Line a 23cm (9 in) springform tin with buttered greaseproof paper.
**2** Sift together the flour, baking powder, cinnamon, nutmeg and allspice. Fold in the brown sugar and combine well.
**3** Add the oil, beaten egg, carrot purée, raw carrot, walnuts, raisins, coconut and pineapple. Mix well.
**4** Pour the mixture into the lined tin (some may prefer the more traditional loaf tin). Place in the preheated oven and bake until the edges pull away from the sides of the pan and a skewer inserted in the centre comes out clean.
**5** Cool the cake in the tin for 15 minutes, then unmould on to a cake rack; remove the paper and allow to cool.
**6** To make the cream cheese frosting, put all the ingredients into a food processor and blend until smooth. Smooth over the top and sides of the carrot cake.

# CAULIFLOWER

It is strange that a vegetable we tend to think of as so British was actually originally cultivated in the eastern Mediterranean, and it wasn't until the twelfth century that the Moors brought it to Spain. The name comes from *cavolo a fiore*, 'cabbage that blooms like a flower', for it is a member of the Brassica or cabbage family.

When buying a cauliflower let your nose and nails do the talking. It should smell fresh without a particularly strong odour (which older caulis will have). Scratch the surface of the curds (the white bit) and it should feel crisp. A cauliflower should also feel heavy for its size. The curds should be very white without any discoloration, and the greenery should show no signs of yellowing. Tiny caulis can now be bought which look sweet but cost the earth!

If you grow cauliflowers yourself, then you will almost certainly have a few insect friends to evict before cooking. Do this by soaking the whole cauliflower or florets in salted water for about 10 minutes. How you cook the cauliflower thereafter is up to you. Some cook it whole root downwards with the head above the water so that it steams rather than boils. I prefer to break it into smallish florets and cook in fast boiling salted water for about 6–8 minutes until tender but not mushy. Drain and drench in butter or cheese sauce (see page 85).

As with all brassicas, overcooking produces pretty grim smells, caused by the mustard oils that the vegetable contains breaking down the sulphur compounds.

I'll leave you with the story of how my grandmother kept her cauliflower fresh in India. With a sharp knife hollow out the centre of the root core, being careful not to split the sides. Hang the cauliflower root upwards in a tree and pour water into the hollowed-out cavity! I think, on reflection, that I prefer refrigeration . . .

*Cauliflower is rich in things that do us good, so have a nibble on a raw floret. It gives you healthy amounts of vitamins A and C, potassium and phosphorus. Unusually for a vegetable, it has very high levels of folic acid, a B vitamin, which helps prevent birth defects. Some old wives' tales say that if childless women eat cauliflower, it almost always results in pregnancy . . .*

*Cooked cauliflower puréed together with half the quantity of cooked turnip and combined with butter, a touch of chilli sauce, anchovy sauce and cream, goes well with a game casserole.*

## Choufleur Polonaise

*This was one of the dishes always on the menu at college.*
- *Spread cooked cauliflower with a topping comprising fried breadcrumbs, chopped hard-boiled egg, butter, seasoning and parsley.*

## Cauliflower Soup

*Feeling a little frugal? Then make this soup.*
- *Sweat cauliflower stalks in butter with a chopped onion, a couple of chopped potatoes and a shredded leek.*
- *Add stock, boil until all is tender, then liquidise.*
- *Finish with milk or cream, nutmeg and seasoning.*

*Fry cauliflower florets in olive oil for a few minutes, then add toasted breadcrumbs, thyme leaves, chopped anchovies and garlic, and flat-leaf parsley leaves.*

# Cauliflower and Potato Spice Soup

There are so many dull cauliflower recipes that I turned my attention to the Indian continent to come up with something a little different and, the deciding factor, delicious.

**Preparation and cooking: 40 minutes**
**Serves: 4**

125g (4½ oz) desiccated coconut, soaked in warm water

225g (8 oz) onions, thinly sliced

4 cloves garlic, finely chopped

85g (3 oz) unsalted butter

2 fresh red chillies, finely sliced

1 teaspoon coriander seeds

pinch of mustard seeds

pinch of fenugreek seeds (optional)

½ teaspoon each of cumin seeds and ground black pepper

1 teaspoon each of turmeric, paprika and grated fresh ginger

225g (8 oz) potatoes, cubed

850ml (1½ pints) vegetable stock

1 large cauliflower, cut into florets

1 x 400g (14 oz) tin coconut milk

300ml (½ pint) double cream

salt

coriander leaves to garnish

**1** Squeeze the coconut dry and retain the soaking water. Set both aside.

**2** In a **non-reactive** saucepan cook the onion and garlic gently in the butter until the onion has softened, about 6–8 minutes.

**3** Add the chilli, coriander, mustard, fenugreek and cumin seeds, black pepper, turmeric, paprika and ginger, and cook for 1 minute, stirring to combine.

**4** Add the potato dice and retained desiccated coconut, and cook until the potatoes start to stick to the bottom of the pan. Add the retained coconut water and the stock. Cook until the potatoes are nearly tender. Add the cauliflower and coconut milk, and cook for 12 minutes.

**5** Ladle the soup into a liquidiser and blend until smooth. Pass through a fine sieve and return to the saucepan.

**6** If too thick, thin with extra stock. Add the cream and season to taste, heat through and garnish with coriander leaves.

# Cauliflower and Pineapple Pickle

A great pickle, with similarities to piccalilli.

**Preparation and cooking: overnight + 30 minutes**
**Makes: 1.5 litres (2¾ pints)**

1 medium cauliflower, florets only

750g (1 lb 10 oz) onions, sliced

2 tablespoons salt

white vinegar

55g (2 oz) plain flour

2 teaspoons English mustard powder

1 tablespoon *garam masala*

4 tablespoons dark soft brown sugar

2 garlic cloves, crushed

1 small tin crushed pineapple

**1** Combine the cauliflower florets with the sliced onion. Sprinkle over the salt and leave overnight.

**2** Next day rinse, drain and dry, place in a saucepan and cover with the vinegar. Bring to the boil and then simmer for 8 minutes.

**3** Make a paste with the plain flour, English mustard powder, *garam masala*, sugar and garlic.

**4** Fold this paste into the cauliflower, then add the tin of crushed pineapple. Cook for 10 minutes, stirring until thickened.

**5** Pot in clean jars.

* * * *

*Dip cauliflower florets into a batter, deep-fry and eat with a chilli-tomato sauce.*

* * * *

*Instead of the usual cheese sauce, make a creamy Béchamel Sauce (see page 60) and add some Dijon mustard, chopped capers and parsley. Pour over the cooked cauliflower.*

# CAVIAR AND OTHER FISH EGGS

Caviar more than any other food epitomises wealth and status. When digging into a bucket of caviar with a mother-of-pearl spoon (I should be so lucky), I get this feeling of decadence and naughtiness, so much so that I tend to do my caviar-eating behind closed doors. But I've often wondered, if the price of caviar and potatoes were the same, which would be the most popular? Caviar, for me, is delicious but it is after all just a load of processed, lightly salted fish eggs. I guess, like anything else that is rare, there will always be someone who wants it.

The caviar names – Beluga, Oscietra and Sevruga – come from the fish type, so Beluga sturgeon, Oscietra sturgeon, and so on; there used to be a Sterlet sturgeon but that is all but extinct now. Beluga eggs come from the largest sturgeon, which grows up to 6m (15–20 ft) long and weighs 900kg (2,000 lb). Beluga eggs are the largest, with a colour ranging from light steel grey to dark grey. It can take 20 years for the female Beluga to produce eggs, hence the eggs' rarity and high cost. Oscietra sturgeon weigh in at between 90 and 270kg (200–600 lb) and grow to about 1.8m (6 ft) in length, producing eggs at ten years. The eggs are brownish grey with a golden tint, and have a slightly fruity flavour. Some vendors of caviar will try to sell you Oscietra caviar as 'golden caviar', the caviar of the Tsars, but in fact true golden (or white) caviar rarely hits the market place as it comes from albino sturgeon of any species. The Sevruga sturgeon is the smallest, weighing fully grown about 22.5kg (50 lb). It produces eggs in seven years. One should never call caviar common, but these eggs are the most commonly found, dark grey to black with the strongest flavour.

The most highly prized caviar of any variety is marked with the word *malossol*, which means 'little salt'. For *malossol*, 1.8–2.75kg (4–6 lb) salt is used per 45kg (100 lb) caviar. Some manufacturers reduce the salt, but add borax which results in a moister caviar as the more salt used, the more liquid is drawn off and the drier the product. While *malossol* is a Russian word, it can be used by other processing countries.

Where possible buy caviar in its 2kg (4½ lb) tin, which is very expensive but worth it for the connoisseur. Caviar packed in small jars is hermetically sealed under a vacuum, then heated, so it becomes pasteurised which affects taste, consistency and texture. Look for 'berries' (the trade name for the eggs) that are whole, firm and well oiled. The size and colour of the egg is a matter of preference, and does not affect the quality. The eggs are lightest when the sturgeon has just spawned, and blackest towards the end of her spawning.

It is only the processed roe of the sturgeon that is legally allowed to be called caviar, but many other fish roes – salmon, mullet, whitefish, lumpfish and cod – are processed in the same way. All have their uses, but are not a patch on the real thing.

Salmon roe or *keta*, which is Russian for roe, is a bright red orange egg. When you first eat it, it's a bit like biting into a cod liver oil capsule, but the flavour grows on you. If I'm eating *sushi* in a Japanese restaurant, I can devour half a dozen pieces topped with these eggs.

Grey mullet roe is used by the Greeks for their *tarama* or *taramasalata* (elsewhere the tendency is to use smoked cod's roe). An increasingly popular form of mullet roe (and nowadays, tuna roe) is *bottarga* or *boutargue*. This roe is soaked in brine, dried in the sun and pressed, then usually wrapped in a coating of beeswax, which is removed before eating. Not long ago it was reasonably cheap but, as with most things, once chefs get hold of it the price rises.

I'm not sure health is a priority to most people when eating caviar, but it is good for you and interestingly it can help prevent a hangover because it contains a cetylchlorine which is linked to an increased tolerance to alcohol. It contains 47 vitamins and minerals and for those on a diet it only contains 70 calories per 25g (1 oz) portion. If you care, the slight downside is that it contains in 25g (1 oz) one-third of your daily recommended salt intake.

# Taramasalata

Instead of buying *taramasalata* in your local supermarket, make your own; it is so simple and so much better.

**Preparation and cooking: 25 minutes**
**Serves: 4**

6 slices of white bread, crustless

85g (3 oz) *tarama* (salted roe of the grey mullet) or

175g (6 oz) smoked cod's roe

juice of 1 lemon

½ onion, grated

175ml (6fl oz) extra virgin olive oil

ground black pepper

**To serve**

black olives

**1** Soak the bread in cold water for 10 minutes. Then squeeze out the water without making it too dry.

**2** Combine the bread in a food processor with either *tarama* or smoked cod's roe, plus the lemon juice and onion.

**3** With the machine running add the extra virgin olive oil in a thin stream as you would for mayonnaise.

**4** Tip into a bowl, season with ground black pepper and refrigerate until ready for use. Covered, the purée will keep at least 5 days.

**5** Decorate with cayenne or paprika pepper and serve with pitta bread and a bowl of olives.

## Spaghetti with *Bottarga* and Rocket

- *Pan-fry some diced onions and mashed garlic in olive oil until soft, then add some grated orange peel, red chilli flakes and ripped rocket.*

- *Add a dash of anchovy essence then cooked spaghetti, toss to combine, season and finish with a healthy grating of* bottarga *and a sprinkle of flat-leaf parsley leaves.*

*Make savoury profiteroles, split, pipe in soured cream and chives then a dollop of caviar, for a culinary taste explosion.*

*When you fancy a naughty nibble, make an open sandwich with black bread topped with cream cheese and slices of smoked sturgeon and spread with caviar!*

*Grate* bottarga *over thin slices of raw fish, salmon and/or bass, then dribble over a little lemon juice, a few grindings of black pepper, and a splash of extra virgin olive oil. Serve with some cucumber slices.*

*When making an Eggs Benedict (see page 117), substitute smoked salmon for ham or Canadian bacon, and grate* bottarga *over the top.*

*Roast or boil baby new potatoes, make a cross split on the top, pinch to open up and top with soured cream and caviar.*

*Bake new potatoes, cut in half, and remove most of the potato flesh. Deep-fry the shells, and fill with crème fraîche and caviar to make mini potato skins.*

*In the relentless search for ultimate luxury, or so they think, some chefs have been known to use caviar in hot dishes, for instance spread on sea bass or folded into a sauce. Shame, such a waste.*

*Serve caviar with Steak Tartare (see page 43): the taste contrast is quite extraordinary.*

# CELERIAC

I have never quite understood why celeriac is not more popular in Great Britain. It may be because it is so odd looking, some might even say ugly, or perhaps because, due to that rugged appearance, there's too much wastage when peeled. It is well worth trying, though, as it has a wonderful celery-like taste, and is indeed a form of celery, developing a bulbous root instead of succulent stems. Wild celery has been around for thousands of years, but celeriac is thought to be a much more recent cultivar. Celeriac is well endowed with potassium, phosphorus and calcium.

Look for smaller bulbs of celeriac, as large ones tend to have woody centres. Celeriac should feel heavy for its size, and have a green tinge at the base. As the bulb has to be peeled, buy one with a smooth skin. When preparing, have a bowl of **acidulated water** at the ready as cut celeriac discolours quickly. Peel, quarter and plunge the pieces into the water. Then cut to the size required, returning to the water until ready to cook. Some chefs cook celeriac in a *blanc* made by whisking 25g (1 oz) of flour into 1 litre (1¾ pints) of water seasoned with salt, lemon juice and bay.

• • • • • • • • • • • •

*Substitute a **julienne** of celeriac for celery in a Waldorf salad mixed together with apple, walnuts and mayonnaise.*

• • • • • • • • • • • •

## Celeriac Bread Sauce

I make a delicious celeriac bread sauce to go with game or roast chicken.

**Preparation and cooking: 30 minutes**
**Serves: 4**

½ celeriac, chopped

1 onion, chopped

300ml (½ pint) milk

1 bay leaf

2 cloves

pinch of grated nutmeg

55g (2 oz) soft white breadcrumbs

55g (2 oz) unsalted butter

4 tablespoons double cream

salt and ground black pepper

**1** Boil the chopped celeriac and onion in the milk with the bay leaf, cloves and nutmeg until the celeriac is tender, about 15 minutes. Remove the bay and cloves.

**2** Add the soft white breadcrumbs, and mash.

**3** Add the unsalted butter and double cream, and season to taste.

**4** Cook out gently until you reach the consistency of bread sauce.

• • • • • • • • • • • • • • • • • • • • • • • • •

## Celeriac Bake

• *Layer cooked slices of celeriac with chopped anchovy, chopped olives, marjoram leaves, chopped onion, chopped garlic, melted butter and grated Parmesan in a gratin dish.*

• *Top with a home-made tomato pasta sauce (see page 296), breadcrumbs and Parmesan, and bake in the oven.*

• • • • • • • • • • • • • • • • • • • • • • • • •

## Pan-fried Celeriac

**Blanch** *cubes of celeriac then pan-fry until golden with cooked Brussels sprouts, cooked baby onions, a sprinkling of thyme leaves, a little grated orange rind, and chopped chestnuts in a little butter for a vegetable accompaniment to Christmas turkey.*

• • • • • • • • • • • • • • • • • • • • • • • • •

# Celeriac and Mushroom Hash

A brunch dish, the perfect partner to poached eggs or smoked salmon.

**Preparation and cooking: 35 minutes**
**Serves: 4**

350g (12 oz) celeriac, peeled and cubed
600ml (1 pint) milk
55g (2 oz) unsalted butter
1 tablespoon olive oil
115g (4 oz) smoked streaky bacon or *pancetta*, cut in strips
1 onion, finely chopped
2 cloves garlic, finely chopped
115g (4 oz) button mushrooms, sliced
chopped parsley to garnish
salt and ground black pepper

**1** Cook the celeriac in the milk until tender, about 10 minutes. Drain and roughly mash with a potato masher. The mash doesn't want to be very smooth.

**2** Meanwhile, heat the butter and oil in a frying pan. Add the bacon or *pancetta* and cook over a medium heat until golden, then add the onion and garlic and cook for about 8 minutes or until the onion has softened.

**3** Add the mushrooms and cook for a further 8–10 minutes until the mushrooms have released their liquor. Add the celeriac mash and combine with the ingredients in the pan. Smooth down to make a cake.

**4** Cook over a high heat until the bottom of the celeriac cake is golden. Turn over with a spatula or stir and break up the mixture. The finished dish should look similar to bubble and squeak, golden and delicious. Season to taste.

# Celeriac and Apple Purée Ⓥ

A delicious vegetable to go with roast chicken, game and grilled calf's liver.

**Preparation and cooking: 30 minutes**
**Serves: 4**

350g (12 oz) celeriac, peeled and cubed
1 litre (1¾ pints) milk
1 teaspoon soft thyme leaves
225g (8 oz) apple, peeled, cored and diced
55g (2 oz) unsalted butter, cut in small cubes
100ml (3½ fl oz) double cream
salt and ground white pepper

**1** Put the celeriac, milk and thyme in a saucepan. Bring to the boil, reduce the heat and simmer for 15 minutes.

**2** Add the apple and cook for a further 10 minutes. Drain the celeriac and apple, discarding the milk and thyme. Place the apple and celeriac in the bowl of a food processor and blend until smooth. If you want a very smooth purée, pass the mixture through a fine sieve.

**3** Return the purée to a saucepan and fold in the butter and cream. Heat through until the butter has melted and emulsified into the purée. Season to taste, and serve hot.

## Celeriac Crisps
*Excellent as a substitute for potato crisps.*
● *Slice celeriac very thinly and dip in clarified butter.*
● *Place on a roasting rack and cook in a medium oven for 15–20 minutes until golden and crisp.*

*When making* gratin dauphinoise *(see page 273), layer the potatoes with slices of celeriac for a change.*

# Celeriac Rémoulade

A classic salad found all over France in *traiteurs* or delis. Try it with Parma ham, a bowl of olives and some crusty bread.

**Preparation and cooking: 15 minutes**
**Serves: 4–6**

350g (12 oz) celeriac, peeled

**Dressing**

2 tablespoons Dijon mustard

1 tablespoon lemon juice

2 teaspoons chopped parsley

1 teaspoon chopped tarragon

125ml (4 fl oz) *Mayonnaise* (see page 239)

125ml (4 fl oz) soured cream

salt and ground black pepper

**1** Make the dressing by combining the mustard, lemon juice, parsley, tarragon, mayonnaise and soured cream. Season to taste.

**2** Using a **julienne** attachment or shredder on your food processor, shred the peeled celeriac. Fold in enough dressing to coat liberally.

• • • • • • • •

*Add peeled prawns and blanched French beans to* Celeriac Rémoulade, *as in the photograph, for a refreshing starter.*

• • • • • • • •

# CELERY

Wild celery is native to European salt marshes, and was highly esteemed by the Egyptians, Greeks and Romans. Celery stalks were thought to be a cure for many male dysfunctions as well as for constipation and hangovers. The modern garden celery, with its thick sweet stalks, only really became popular in the UK and US in the nineteenth century. Celery is an umbellifer, therefore is related to carrots, parsnips etc., and to many herbs, like parsley, and is generally found in a green form, which is very clean. The white variety, which has been earthed up to blanch the stalks, is less clean, but to my mind it has a milder, more pleasant flavour. The leaves, which were once so valued medicinally, can and should be used as a herb – they are in the East.

The British tend to use celery mainly as a salad vegetable, discarding the best part, the heart, which is a great vegetable for braising (often on old hotel dining-room menus and unfortunately often out of a tin). It's also good incorporated into many dishes where it adds incredible flavour – particularly to stocks, soups and stews. Celery isn't actually very rich in nutrients, but it is extremely low in calories, thus its inclusion, I presume, in so many diets, as a crudité etc.

Look for celery that has fresh and crisp stalks with tight heads, never with brown or cracked stalks. If you can find the earthy white celery I would recommend it; it will need a good wash, and usually the outside stalks will require de-stringing. There are several stringless varieties available nowadays but, as with much modernisation, the flavour tends to suffer. To remove strings, take a sharp knife and make a small incision at the wide end of the celery stalk without cutting more than a third through; pull the strings away and down the stalk.

*Celery goes well with an anchovy dressing. Pound anchovies with olive oil and a dash of lemon juice, then season with plenty of ground black pepper and pour over cooked celery.*

*Celery salt is great for a Bloody Mary (see page 298), and for dipping hard-boiled gulls' eggs (or quails' eggs) into. You could make your own by grinding together celery seeds and some good salt.*

*Mix sliced celery with cooked shredded chicken, diced apple and chopped walnuts in a bowl, then combine with chives, mayonnaise and soured cream. A great leftover chicken salad, similar to Waldorf.*

# Celery and Roquefort Sauce

The freshest, most vibrant celery and Roquefort sauce.
**Preparation and cooking: 15 minutes**
**Serves: 4**

1 head of celery, washed
4 tablespoons Roquefort butter (made by blending equal parts of Roquefort cheese and unsalted butter)
salt and ground black pepper

1  Centrifugally juice the celery.
2  Boil the juice in a **non-reactive** pan and, when boiling vigorously, add the Roquefort butter.
3  Season to taste.

*Fry cooked celery in butter, then fold in Béchamel Sauce (see page 60) and double cream. Serve with steamed fish or boiled chicken.*

# Braised Celery

A classic recipe that should be reintroduced to our cookery curriculum. I have made a few flavourful changes to the original, and cook it for far longer – the celery should be meltingly soft.

**Preparation and cooking: 2½ hours**
**Serves: 4**

2 heads of celery, washed and trimmed

salt and ground black pepper

55g (2 oz) unsalted butter

1 tablespoon olive oil

1 onion, finely chopped

1 carrot, sliced

2 cloves garlic, finely chopped

115g (4 oz) smoked streaky bacon, chopped

½ teaspoon soft thyme leaves

350g (12 oz) pork rind, in the piece (optional)

1 teaspoon anchovy essence

50ml (2 fl oz) dry red wine

850ml (1½ pints) chicken or beef stock

**1** Cut the leafy tops off the celery, leaving a 15cm (6 in) heart. Remove the strings from outside stalks. Plunge the celery into boiling salted water and cook for 10 minutes. Drain and set aside to cool slightly. Cut the celery in half lengthways.

**2** Meanwhile, heat the butter and olive oil in a casserole dish. Add the onion, carrot, garlic, bacon and thyme and cook for 8 minutes. Push the vegetables to one side and, if using it, place the pork rind fat side down on the bottom of the pan.

**3** Place the celery on top of the rind and surround with the vegetables and bacon. Add the anchovy essence, wine and stock, and season to taste.

**4** Bring slowly to the boil, cover with a lid, place in the oven preheated to 180°C/350°F/Gas 4 and cook for 2 hours. (Many recipes for braised celery suggest you cook the celery for about 30 minutes. I think this information is wrong as the celery will still be tough and stringy.)

**5** Remove the celery and keep warm. Place the casserole over a high heat, uncovered, and boil to reduce the cooking liquor by half. Strain the liquor and pour over the celery. You can either discard the carrots, bacon etc., or eat them with the celery.

## Celery and Lovage Soup

I grow lovage, a celery-flavoured herb, and often make a celery and lovage soup.
● Cook a chopped onion in some butter with some thyme, then add cubes of potato, sliced celery and some lovage leaves.
● Top with chicken or vegetable stock, and cook until tender.
● Liquidise, pass through a fine sieve and finish with double cream.

## Creamed Celery

Good with roasts.
● Cook the tops of celery you trimmed from the hearts in the braised celery recipe in boiling salted water until tender.
● Drain and add to 175ml (6 fl oz) double cream combined with 2 egg yolks.
● Heat through until thickened, do not boil.

## Celery Vinegar

This makes a nice addition to salads.
● Infuse 25g (1 oz) of crushed celery seeds with 2 pints (1.2 litres) of boiled cider vinegar.
● Bottle and leave for 3 weeks, then strain.
● Add a dash to salad dressings or when making a stew.

*Another less sharp essence can be made in the same way as the vinegar, but substituting dry sherry for cider vinegar and halving the amount of liquid.*

*Boil 2.5cm (1 in) pieces of celery with water, olive oil, lemon juice, salt, peppercorns, fennel seeds, coriander seeds, chopped shallots, parsley and dill until tender. Serve hot or cold as part of an antipasti buffet.*

# CHEESE

Cheese, as you all know, is made from the curds of cow, goat, sheep or buffalo milk, but I don't intend to get technical about the process, as there are plenty of books that will inform you. We have a great cheese industry in Britain, and there has been a huge increase in the number of cheese-makers over the last few years, who are producing marvellous individual cheeses to compete with the best in Europe. However, they have to battle constantly against European directives, knee-jerk reactions by government, and nervous supermarket cheese-buyers. Unless you know of a local specialist cheese shop — and there are a few around — it is very difficult to buy good cheeses these days. Our cheese industry is something British to be proud of, something the government should support.

Cheese can be split into various categories.

## Surface-ripened Washed Rind Cheese

Sounds a little technical, I know, but all it means is that the cheese has a crusty rind that has been toughened by regular washing with a brine. You will generally see this cheese with a swollen rind, as if the cheese is trying to burst out of its skin. Livarot, Pont l'Evêque, Bel Paese, Taleggio and the German Münster are all cheeses of this type.

## Goat's Cheese

A distinctive, often acquired, taste. Some are very soft and fresh, some very hard, some are pure white, some are brown (the Norwegian *gjetost*), others are covered in charcoal, spices or leaves. They are often used in cooking and salads. I find eating them *au naturel* a bit boring, but then maybe I haven't discovered the right one.

## Fresh Cheese

Cheeses that are uncured, unripened and not usually cooked, therefore have a limited shelf life. Cheeses in this category include cream cheese, cottage cheese, ricotta, mozzarella, mascarpone and *fromage blanc*. They are usually very mild in flavour, often needing flavour to be *added*, and are excellent used in salads, cooking and dressings.

## Sheep's Cheese

There is not a great selection in this category but it does boast the king of cheeses, Roquefort, a delicious creamy blue that sits proudly on any cheeseboard. Feta is also made from sheep's milk, an essential for a good Greek salad, as is the Italian Pecorino.

## Hard Cooked Cheese

The milk is heated to about 45°C/113°F, then the curd is pressed and matured. Cheeses in this category include Gruyère, Emmenthal and Parmesan. Cooked cheeses are usually excellent in cooking.

## Blue Cheese

These include famous names like Stilton, Beenleigh, Cashel, Dunsyre, Roquefort, Gorgonzola and Danish. Moulds are injected into the cheese and the cheese ripens from the inside out. Blue cheese can be smooth or rough, creamy or crumbly and very mild to mildly powerful.

## Processed Cheese

I call these supermarket cheeses. As they get older, they don't mature as they have been heat-treated to stop ripening. Often boring, very boring, slabs and triangles of blandness.

• • • • • • • • • • • • • • • •

*It may be a little passé but deep-fried Camembert is still delicious. Dip Camembert portions into flour then egg and breadcrumbs, deep-fry for 30 seconds to 1 minute, and serve with gooseberry compote or cranberry sauce.*

• • • • • • • • • • • • • • • •

• • • • • • • • • • • • • • • • • • • • • • • •

## Blue Cheese Dip

*Blend in a food processor 150ml (¼ pint) soured cream, 150ml (¼ pint) Mayonnaise (see page 239). 2 teaspoons lemon juice, 2 tablespoons chopped spring onion, 1 chopped garlic clove, 1 teaspoon Tabasco sauce, and 115g (4 oz) blue cheese such as Stilton or Roquefort.*

• • • • • • • • • • • • • • • • • • • • • • • •

## Semi-hard Cheese

The milk is heated to lower temperatures than the hard cooked cheeses. The cheeses mature from 4 months to over a year and include the British favourite, Cheddar. Many cheeses in this category are useful in cooking.

## Surface-ripened White Mould Cheese

These are the cheeses I yearn for when I want a little comfort food – ripe Bries, Camemberts and triple-cream cheeses such as Boursault. These cheeses ripen from the outside in. You will often see a Brie or Camembert with a chalky centre, showing that it is not fully ripe.

It is sad that with government interference you rarely see a good cheeseboard in restaurants nowadays. Cheese *should* be served at room temperature, but as it is only allowed to be displayed unrefrigerated for 4 hours, this makes providing a varied cheeseboard very uneconomical. (How many restaurants pay attention to the rules is another question.) At home, ideally you would store your cheese in a cellar at between 9–12°C/48–54°F, but most of us store cheese in the fridge, so make sure you take it out well before you want to serve it. Unwrapped cheese will dry out and become crusty, so wrap it in cheesecloth or clingfilm (although, as cheese needs to breathe, clingfilm has its disadvantages). A hard cheese such as Parmesan will last a lot longer than a creamy one.

If serving cheese with red wine, don't offer the traditional cluster of grapes as the acids in the grapes will fight with the tannins in the wine. I would advise serving one cheese in perfect condition rather than a whole assembly of different cheeses. You are likely to be left with a tired arrangement of small pieces after your entertaining has finished.

## Ricotta Coffee Pudding

• *For a quick pud, combine 450g (1 lb) ricotta cheese with 2 tablespoons freshly and finely ground coffee beans, 115g (4 oz) caster sugar and 4 tablespoons Kahlua, Tia Maria or rum.*
• *Serve with poached pears.*

## Truffled Camembert

The occasional luxury is a necessity in life. This cheese extravaganza will cost a fortune, but it's worth it for that special occasion.

**Preparation and cooking: 24 hours**
**Serves: 4**

1 whole ripe Camembert
2 tablespoons chopped white or black truffle
2 tablespoons snipped chives
1 tablespoon truffle oil
115g (4 oz) mascarpone cheese
salt and ground black pepper

**1** The day before you intend to serve the cheese, turn the Camembert on its side and cut the cheese in half horizontally with a hot knife, creating two complete circles of cheese.
**2** Combine the truffle and chives with the truffle oil and fold this mixture into the mascarpone. Season to taste.
**3** Spread the truffle mixture on to one of the cut sides of the cheese, and top with the other half of the cheese, cut side down, sandwiching the two halves together. Wrap in clingfilm and refrigerate overnight.
**4** Remove the clingfilm and leave the cheese at room temperature for at least 1 hour before eating. Serve with a rocket salad and some plain crackers.

*Make a cheese and onion soup by cooking a couple of chopped onions with a little chopped garlic, some thyme and a bay leaf in butter until the onion has softened. Add flour to create a **roux**, then some red wine and chicken stock. Cook for 15 minutes, then add some blue cheese and some Cheddar. Liquidise, return to the pan and add double cream. Season to taste.*

# Roquefort, Chicory, Apple and Walnut Salad

A well-balanced salad, perfect for light lunch or supper. The combination is a classic, but feel free to substitute Gorgonzola, Stilton or Fourme d'Ambert for the Roquefort.

**Preparation: 20 minutes**

**Serves: 4–6**

2 tablespoons freshly squeezed lemon juice

¼ teaspoon salt

1 teaspoon grain mustard

¼ teaspoon ground black pepper

60ml (2 fl oz) extra virgin olive oil

1 tablespoon walnut oil

1 tablespoon snipped chives

2 Cox's apples, peeled and cored

4 heads chicory (Belgian endive), split into separate leaves

115g (4 oz) broken walnuts

175g (6 oz) Roquefort cheese, crumbled

**1** Combine the lemon juice with the salt, mustard, pepper, oils and chives in a bowl. Whisk to combine.

**2** Slice the apples into thin wedges, and add these to the dressing to stop discoloration.

**3** Place the chicory leaves in a large salad bowl. Sprinkle with walnuts and cheese, then combine with the apples and dressing. Serve with warm crusty bread.

• • • • • • • • • • • •

*When a recipe demands Parmesan, buy a chunk labelled* Parmigiano Reggiano *and grate it yourself. The standard of grated Parmesan in cartons leaves a lot to be desired.*

• • • • • • • • • • • •

• • • • • • • • • • • •

*A good topping is made by blending equal amounts of blue cheese and butter with some Calvados. Spread on* crostini *or crackers and top with diced apple or celery.*

• • • • • • • • • • • •

# A Warm Salad of Grilled Ⓥ Goat's Cheese, Fresh Peas and Broad Beans

I look forward to the pea and broad bean season, especially since I grow them myself and can choose the vegetables when very young and tender. This is a lovely combination for late spring or early summer.

**Preparation and cooking: 30 minutes**
**Serves: 2**

2 Crottins de Chavignol or other variety of small goat's cheese
salt and ground black pepper
1 bunch watercress, leaves only
1 tablespoon tarragon leaves
1 tablespoon flat-leaf parsley leaves
2 spring onions, finely sliced
85g (3 oz) podded peas
85g (3 oz) podded broad beans, outer skins removed
2 tablespoons hazelnut or walnut oil
2 tablespoons olive oil
1 tablespoon lemon juice
1 tablespoon freshly grated Parmesan

**1** Preheat the grill. Season the cheeses and cook under the grill until the top starts to melt, about 3–4 minutes.
**2** Meanwhile, toss the herbs with the spring onion, raw peas, broad beans, oils, lemon juice and Parmesan. Season to taste with salt and ground black pepper.
**3** Divide the salad between two plates and top with the goat's cheese. Serve with wedges of crusty bread.

• • • • • • • • • • • • •

*Take 4 wedges of Camembert cheese, toss each piece in 1 tablespoon seasoned flour, then dip into a beaten egg. Repeat the process then finally roll in 55 g (2 oz) fresh breadcrumbs. Fry in hot corn oil until golden brown, drain well and serve with cranberry sauce.*

• • • • • • • • • • • • •

# Mascarpone Cream

Possibly one of the nicest toppings for raspberries, strawberries or, in fact, any fruit, and a wonderful alternative to whipped cream. Because of the soft cheese and raw egg yolks, it should probably be avoided by pregnant women, small children and the elderly.

**Preparation and cooking: 10 minutes**
**Serves: 6**

2 tablespoons caster sugar
3 egg yolks
4 teaspoons Kirsch
225g (8 oz) mascarpone cheese
150ml (¼ pint) double cream

**1** Beat the caster sugar with the egg yolks until thick and **ribboning** and very pale. Fold in the Kirsch, then the mascarpone, and whisk until very smooth.
**2** Whisk the cream to soft peaks and fold into the mascarpone mixture. Serve in a sauce boat or bowl with another bowl full of the fruit – a delicious combination.

• • • • • • • • • • • • •

*Combine 250g (9 oz) cream cheese with 250g (9 oz) mashed tinned sardines, 1 tablespoon creamed horseradish, 2 teaspoons lemon juice and seasoning, for one of my favourite sandwich fillings.*

• • • • • • • • • • • • •

• • • • • • • • • • • • •

*For a starter, cut mozzarella and bread into 2.5cm (1 in) cubes and thread them alternately on metal or wooden skewers. Season and place in a hot oven just long enough for the cheese to start melting and the bread to turn brown.*

• • • • • • • • • • • • •

# Ricotta Cake

I have to admit I'm not a great cake-maker, but this one is guaranteed to work for even the most wobbly of cooks. I've used upmarket dried fruits that are now available in many supermarkets, but feel free to use any dried fruit in the same measurements. You can also use alternative nuts.

**Preparation and cooking: 1½ hours**
**Serves: 8–12**

vegetable oil for greasing
250g (9 oz) unsalted butter, softened
250g (9 oz) caster sugar
8 eggs, separated
finely grated zest of 2 oranges and 3 lemons
200g (7 oz) mixed dried fruits (I use whole cranberries, cherries and blueberries, and chopped apricots)
85g (3 oz) roasted hazelnuts, roughly chopped
250g (9 oz) ricotta cheese
85g (3 oz) plain flour

**1** Preheat the oven to 180°C/350°F/Gas 4, and grease a 23 x 5cm (9 x 2 in) springform cake tin sparingly with vegetable oil.

**2** Cream the butter and sugar together until pale and fluffy. Add the egg yolks one by one, beating well between each addition.

**3** In a separate bowl fold the fruit zest, dried fruit and nuts into the ricotta. Fold the butter and egg mix into the ricotta and fruit. Sift the flour into this mix and combine.

**4** Beat the egg whites to soft peaks. Mix 1 tablespoon of the egg whites into the ricotta mix. Once this is amalgamated, fold in the remainder carefully, ensuring that you do not lose too much of the air.

**5** Pour the mixture into the prepared cake tin and bake for about 1 hour 10 minutes. The rule about inserting the tip of a knife into the centre and coming out clean does not apply to this cake as it is very moist. The best way to tell if it is cooked is to shake the tin gently; if the cake wobbles very slightly, it needs just a little while longer to finish cooking.

*An easy but extravagant dish I ate in the Savoie region of France was a whole Reblochon cheese with the rind removed, wrapped in smoked ham then in egg-washed puff pastry. It was baked in a hot oven for 25–35 minutes.*

## Cheese Sauce

*For cheese sauce, make 600ml (1 pint) Béchamel Sauce (see page 60), and fold in 175ml (6 fl oz) double cream, a pinch of grated nutmeg, 85g (3 oz) grated Gruyère or Cheddar and 25g (1 oz) grated Parmesan.*

## Liptauer

*A cheese I used to eat as a kid which one rarely sees nowadays.*
● *Combine 225g (8 oz) cream cheese or ricotta cheese with 125g (4½ oz) softened unsalted butter, 2 teaspoons paprika, 1 teaspoon English mustard, 1 teaspoon caraway seeds, 2 teaspoons chopped capers, 2 teaspoons snipped chives and 3 tablespoons soured cream.*
● *Season to taste.*

## Stewed Cheese

*This is similar to the mix for Welsh rarebit, and is a good way to use up any dry leftovers.*
● *Put 115g (4 oz) of chopped cheese in a saucepan with 25g (1 oz) unsalted butter and 150ml (¼ pint) double cream. Let it simmer gently, stirring until the cheese has melted.*
● *Take it off the heat and fold in 1 teaspoon English mustard, 2 well-beaten eggs, and a tablespoon of port or beer.*
● *Do not re-boil, but serve as hot as possible with toast soldiers or triangles (points).*

# CHICKEN

Many years ago when I was a boy it was a real treat to have a roast chicken, but now it is commonplace. Funny how life goes full circle. In those days the cheapest white meat was rabbit, now three times as expensive as chicken. In fact we get bored of chicken in restaurants, but look forward to an interesting rabbit dish . . .

Chickens can be broken down into a number of categories. CORN-FED have yellow flesh and are fed on a diet of at least 70 per cent corn, maize or cereal. Do not be fooled, however, as they will almost certainly have not seen the light of day, being barn-reared. They're not likely to have any more flavour than EXTENSIVE REARED birds which are, when all is said and done, battery chickens. A little better but still to be avoided are FREE-RANGE BARN, where the birds are free to move about inside barns, but are often so crowded they almost stand on each other, with regular fighting among the inmates which causes damage to individual birds. The average 1.5kg (3¼ lb) bird, battery or barn-reared, is about 40 days old when it reaches the supermarkets. TRADITIONAL FREE-RANGE are less intensively reared, are at least 81 days old, and have access to grass.

We must encourage the buying of free-range birds. In the feather they may look a little rough and ready, and in the eating they may be a little tougher, but this is more than made up by the flavour, plus the big bonus is 'they have had a life'.

• • • • • • • • • • • • • •

*If you are looking for a sandwich a little more exciting than the railway variety, try this one. Split a mini* baguette *and butter it; lay on some rocket leaves with Brie, some sliced smoked chicken and top with some* **julienne** *of roasted peppers (see page 254). Drizzle with extra virgin olive oil and a squeeze of lemon.*

• • • • • • • • • • • • • •

## Thai Green Chicken Curry

I am really into the smooth silky taste of this very easy curry. Green curry paste is now available in some supermarkets, but it can be found in most Asian stores. If you're really keen, make your own (see page 255).

**Preparation and cooking: 30 minutes**
**Serves: 4**

1–2 tablespoons green curry paste

2 tablespoons vegetable oil

2 large cloves garlic, mashed to a paste with a little salt

2 stems lemongrass, tender part only, finely chopped

2 lime leaves, shredded

750ml (1¼ pints) coconut milk

4 tablespoons chopped coriander, leaves and tender stalks

12 chicken thighs, skin removed

2–3 green chillies, seeded and finely chopped

4 tablespoons ripped basil leaves

2 tablespoons *nam pla* (fish sauce)

1 tablespoon freshly squeezed lime juice

**1** Fry the curry paste (the more you add, the hotter it will be) in the vegetable oil over a high heat for 3 minutes. Add the garlic, lemongrass, lime leaves and half the coconut milk and cook until the sauce starts to split, about 5 minutes.

**2** Add the coriander, chicken and chilli and simmer for 15 minutes. Add the remaining coconut milk and cook for a further 5 minutes.

**3** Just before serving fold in the basil leaves, fish sauce and lime juice. Serve with fragrant rice and garnish with extra coriander leaves.

# Southern Fried Chicken

I could not write a chicken chapter without including this recipe (Paul, my brother-in-law, this one's for you). It's deeply unfashionable, but who cares? Whenever I eat it, I love it. Very similar to Chicken Maryland, a blast from the 1960s that was served with corn fritters, bacon and fried bananas – believe it or not, a delicious combination.

**Marination and cooking: overnight + 1 hour**
**Serves: 4**

600ml (1 pint) buttermilk or single cream
6 tablespoons chopped coriander
6 cloves garlic, finely chopped
2 shallots, finely chopped
½ tablespoon dried chilli flakes
1 tablespoon salt
4 large chicken breasts, skin removed
6 tablespoons plain flour
½ teaspoon celery salt
½ teaspoon cayenne pepper
½ teaspoon ground black pepper
½ teaspoon paprika
600ml (1 pint) vegetable oil

**1** Combine the buttermilk or cream with the coriander, garlic, shallot, chilli flakes and salt in a suitable dish. Add the chicken, turn to coat, and cover. Leave to marinate overnight.

**2** Combine the flour with the celery salt, cayenne, black pepper and paprika. Lift the chicken from the marinade and dip in the spiced flour to coat. Place the chicken in the refrigerator for 45 minutes.

**3** Fry the chicken in hot oil for 10 minutes each side until thoroughly cooked and golden.

# Sweet and Spicy Chicken Wings

Delicious at any time whether served as a snack or as a main meal with fragrant rice.

**Marination and cooking: overnight + 15 minutes**
**Serves: 4–6**

1kg (2¼ lb) chicken wings, cut in half through the joint, tips discarded

## Marinade

1 tablespoon Szechwan peppercorns, toasted and ground (in coffee grinder)
1 tablespoon minced garlic
3 tablespoons minced fresh ginger
3 tablespoons finely grated orange zest
4 spring onions, cut into 2.5cm (1 in) pieces
1 fresh red chilli, finely chopped
2 tablespoons liquid honey
2 tablespoons soy sauce
450ml (16 fl oz) corn oil
125ml (4 fl oz) sesame oil
salt and ground black pepper

## Garnish

1 tablespoon finely grated orange zest
2 tablespoons chopped parsley
2 tablespoons snipped chives

**1** In a pestle and mortar blend together the peppercorns, garlic, ginger, orange zest, spring onions and chilli until you have a paste.

**2** In a large bowl combine the honey, soy sauce and oils with the paste. Season to taste. Add the chicken wings, turn to coat, then allow to marinate for at least 4 hours or preferably overnight.

**3** Cook the chicken wings in a hot griddle pan or on a hot barbecue for 7–8 minutes each side or until thoroughly cooked and golden brown.

**4** Garnish the chicken with a mixture of orange zest, chopped parsley and chives.

# Bang-bang Chicken

Made popular in western circles at Le Caprice restaurant in London, and now copied everywhere – surprisingly, in very few Oriental restaurants. Some cooks make it with sesame sauce, but I prefer a peanut one.

**Preparation and cooking: 30 minutes**
**Serves: 6**

1 x 1.5kg (3 lb 5 oz) chicken, poached (see page 91)
125g (4½ oz) Chinese glass noodles, broken into small pieces
6 cloves garlic, lightly smashed
1 bunch coriander, leaves only
175g (6 oz) smooth peanut butter
4 tablespoons light soy sauce
2 tablespoons runny honey
1 teaspoon chilli oil
1 tablespoon Japanese rice vinegar
1 teaspoon dry sherry

**Garnish**

2 cucumbers, peeled, seeded and cut in thin strips

**1** Remove the skin from the chicken and the flesh from the bones. Beat the flesh with a rolling pin to loosen the fibres. Shred the chicken with a knife or pull it apart with two forks. Set aside.

**2** Soak the noodles in very hot tap water for 5 minutes, then drain.

**3** Blend the garlic in a food processor until finely chopped, then add the coriander leaves and blend again until fairly smooth. Add the peanut butter, soy sauce, honey, chilli oil, vinegar and sherry and blend until smooth, adding a little water if too thick.

**4** Spread a pile of warm noodles in the centre of six plates, top with cucumber strips then the chicken, and dribble with the peanut sauce, do not smother it. Garnish with extra coriander leaves.

## Sweet and Sour Chicken Soup

● *Put 3 chopped shallots, 1 teaspoon crushed black peppercorns, 5 chopped cloves garlic and 1 tablespoon shrimp paste (available in Asian food stores) into a food processor, and blend to a paste.*

● *Fry this paste in vegetable oil for 1 minute, then add 1.7 litres (3 pints) chicken stock.*

● *Add 1kg (2¼ lb) thinly shredded raw chicken, 1 tablespoon chopped fresh ginger, 125ml (4 fl oz) tamarind water and 1 shredded unripe pawpaw. Cook for 5 minutes until the chicken is cooked.*

● *Season with a little honey and garnish with sliced chilli, lime juice and sliced spring onion.*

## Garlic Chicken Casserole

*If you are a lover of garlic, then cook this simple casserole.*

● *Brown some chicken pieces in butter and oil, then remove and set aside.*

● *Add 40, yes 40, peeled garlic cloves, and brown them all over in the fat, then add 150ml (¼ pint) sherry vinegar, 150ml (¼ pint) dry white wine and 150ml (¼ pint) chicken stock.*

● *Return the chicken to the pan and cook in a preheated oven at 180°C/350°F/Gas 4 for 30 minutes.*

● *Remove the chicken from the dish and liquidise the liquid and garlic; if the liquid is too thin, boil rapidly to reduce.*

# Tandoori-style Roast Chicken

I love making a tandoori-style roast chicken, but it needs a little pre-thought.

**Marination and cooking: 2 days + 1½ hours**
**Serves: 4**

300g (10½ oz) Greek yogurt

3 tablespoons garlic, chopped

5 tablespoons chopped fresh ginger

1 tablespoon chopped fresh chilli

1 teaspoon ground coriander

1 teaspoon *garam masala*

2 teaspoons ground cumin

a pinch each of powdered cinnamon, cardamom and fenugreek

2 teaspoons sea salt

1 teaspoon ground black pepper

1 x 1.5kg (3 lb 5 oz) chicken

2 onions, sliced

600ml (1 pint) chicken stock

**1**  Combine in a food processor the Greek yogurt with the garlic, ginger, chilli, coriander, *garam masala*, cumin, cinnamon, cardamom, fenugreek, sea salt and ground black pepper. Purée until smooth.

**2**  Use to coat the chicken inside and out, and leave to marinate for 2 days in the fridge.

**3**  Wipe the chicken clean and roast in a preheated oven at 200°C/400°F/Gas 6 with the sliced onions and chicken stock, basting from time to time, for 1 hour 10 minutes.

**4**  Serve with the caramelised onion and the roasting juices.

# Roast Free-range Chicken

There is nothing nicer than a good roast chicken. Mind you, the first thing you need is a good bird, ideally free-range or, better still, if you have the spare cash, a *poulet de Bresse* which is the king of French chickens. Serve with *frites* or roast potatoes, and some vegetables or a leaf salad.

**Preparation and cooking: 1½ hours**
**Serves: 4**

1 x 1.5kg (3 lb 5 oz) free-range chicken

100g (3½ oz) unsalted butter, softened

1 teaspoon sea salt

several grindings of black pepper

2 sprigs thyme

1 head garlic, broken into cloves

175ml (6 fl oz) dry white wine

**1**  Preheat the oven to 220°C/425°F/Gas 7. Spread the butter all over the chicken, and sprinkle with the sea salt and black pepper. Pop the thyme into the chicken's cavity. Put into a roasting tray with the unpeeled garlic cloves and the white wine. Roast in the oven for 20 minutes.

**2**  Reduce the temperature to 190°C/375°F/Gas 5 and roast for a further 45 minutes, basting from time to time. Turn off the oven, place the chicken on a carving dish and return to the oven to rest for 10–15 minutes before carving.

• • • • • • • • • • • • • • • • • • • • •

*When roasting a chicken, place a sprig of thyme and some lemons in the cavity. Carefully work your fingers between skin and flesh and insert a mixture of half butter and half cream cheese flavoured with lots of chopped herbs (parsley, tarragon, chervil, chives) and chopped shallot. This helps to self-baste the chicken during cooking, and keeps the bird very moist. Place some whole garlic cloves, chopped onion and white wine around the bird and roast in the normal way, basting from time to time and adding more liquid as necessary. This liquid acts as a base for your gravy.*

• • • • • • • • • • • • • • • • • • • • •

# The Really Useful Poached Chicken Recipe

This poached chicken recipe has a myriad of uses – chicken curries, sandwiches, salads, *Bang-bang Chicken* (see page 89) – or just as it is, served with a soy dip. The poaching stock will be delicious; use it in a soup.

**Preparation and cooking: 1½ hours**
**Serves: 4**

1 x 1.5kg (3 lb 5 oz) free-range chicken
4 spring onions, sliced
3 x 50p-sized discs of fresh ginger
6 cloves garlic, peeled
1 fresh red chilli
1 tablespoon sea salt
10 black peppercorns
2 tablespoons peanut or sesame oil

**1** Place the chicken in a suitable saucepan, one in which it is a tight fit, cover with water and add all the remaining ingredients, apart from the oil. Bring to the boil and simmer for 25 minutes, turning the chicken once during the cooking process.

**2** Cover with a lid and switch off the heat. Allow the chicken to **relax** in the liquor for 1 hour.

**3** Remove the chicken, drain well, and rub all over with the chosen oil. Allow to cool completely, then cut up and use as required.

*Place a skinned chicken breast on a piece of foil and top with 2 spring onions cut in half lengthways, 1 x 1cm (½ in) round disc of fresh peeled ginger and 2 tablespoons light soy sauce. Wrap in the foil, creating a parcel, and place on a baking tray in a preheated oven at 180°C/350°F/Gas 4, for 20–25 minutes until tender. Serve with rice or noodles.*

## Crunchy Chicken Topping

● *Combine 175g (6 oz) pecan nuts with 175g (6 oz) plain flour, 150g (5½ oz) polenta, 4 teaspoons paprika, 2 teaspoons celery salt, 2 teaspoons ground black pepper and 2 teaspoons cayenne pepper in a food processor.*

● **Pulse** *until the pecans still have texture but are not completely smooth.*

● *Keep the mix in an airtight container.*

● *Dip the chicken in flour, egg, then the coating and fry in the normal way.*

## Spicy Chicken Salad

*An excellent refreshing salad.*

● *Shred 375g (13 oz) cooked chicken (Really Useful Poached Chicken Recipe) and combine with 2 finely shredded stems lemongrass, 2 tablespoons shredded spring onion, 2 tablespoons finely sliced shallot, 2 tablespoons shredded fresh mint, 2 tablespoons chopped coriander, 2 tablespoons nam pla (fish sauce), 2 tablespoons lime juice, 1 teaspoon honey and 2 sliced seeded red chillies.*

*Take a chicken fillet, and flatten it out with a rolling pin. Mix together 2 tablespoons ricotta cheese, 3 dried apricots, coarsely chopped, 1 teaspoon snipped chives and 1 teaspoon lemon juice, and spread the mix in the centre of the chicken. Roll up into a cylinder shape, wrap in Parma ham or thinly sliced streaky bacon, drizzle with maple syrup and bake in a preheated oven at 180°C/350°F/Gas 4 for 20–25 minutes. Chop into bite-sized nuggets. Great for the kids.*

*. . . Or drizzle a piece of chicken with Nando's wild herb peri-peri sauce and place under a medium grill until cooked. Serve with a crunchy salad.*

# CHICKPEAS

The tropical pulse known as the chickpea (*Cicer arietinum*) is best-known in Britain in its Middle Eastern *hummus* form, made by blending cooked chickpeas with *tahina* or sesame paste. Why we don't use chickpeas here is a bit of a mystery, as elsewhere they are part of staple diets, especially in Spain, Italy and Greece. Chickpeas, also known as Bengal gram, *chana dhal* or garbanzo bean, originated in the Far East and are now an important food crop in India, being used in curries and *dhals* or made into flour, for savoury pancakes and breads. In Europe and North Africa, they are made into pastes and added to stews. Rich in protein and highly nutritious, they are well worth adding to your cooking curriculum.

They are found dried or tinned in Britain, and are unlike any of the other dried pulses, being hazelnut-like in appearance. It is almost impossible to buy fresh chickpeas, and even fresh they are like little bullets. (I wish I had known about the dried variety in my youth as a pea-shooting villain, they would have been deadly.) Dried chickpeas are more economical, but they will need soaking for between 24 and 48 hours. Tinned, chickpeas are one of the more acceptable form of tinned pulses. If you are using a recipe that states dried chickpeas, treble the weight in tinned, as the dried will increase in volume when soaked, then increase again when cooked.

After soaking dried chickpeas you will need to cook them in unsalted water for up to 2½ hours until tender. Too often you will eat them in restaurants still hard, not a particularly pleasant experience. You can shorten the soaking process by pouring boiling water over the dried chickpeas; leave for 4–5 hours before cooking.

## Chickpea and Cabbage Soup Ⓥ

A wonderful warming soup for cold winter days.
**Preparation and cooking: 1 hour**
**Serves: 4–6**

50ml (2 fl oz) extra virgin olive oil
1 onion, finely chopped
3 cloves garlic, finely chopped
2 bay leaves
1 teaspoon soft thyme leaves
1 fresh red chilli, finely diced
4 tablespoons roughly chopped flat-leaf parsley
1 tablespoon chopped marjoram
1 x 400g (14 oz) tin chopped tomatoes
450g (1 lb) cooked chickpeas and their liquor
1 litre (1¾ pints) vegetable stock
450g (1 lb) shredded greens (Savoy cabbage, *cavolo nero*, spring greens)
grated Parmesan
extra virgin olive oil
salt and ground black pepper

**1** In a large saucepan heat the olive oil over a medium heat, and add the onion, garlic, bay leaves, thyme and chilli. Cook for about 10 minutes or until the onion has softened without colour.
**2** Add the herbs and tomato, and cook for 3 minutes. Add the chickpeas, their liquor and the stock, and cook for 30 minutes at a steady simmer.
**3** Add the shredded greenery and cook for 10 minutes.
**4** Pour the soup into bowls, sprinkle with grated Parmesan and dribble with extra virgin olive oil. Season to taste.

*Fry cooked chickpeas with onions and garlic, then add chopped tomato and spinach and some diced chorizo sausage. Fold in toasted pine kernels and almonds and season to taste. This is a snack to accompany drinks (put in a little bowl), put on crostini, or serve as part of a tapas buffet.*

*For an alternative snack to the one on the left, replace the chorizo with flaked salt cod that has been soaked for 48 hours.*

*For a snack, fry some cooked chickpeas in oil, then dry in a 150°C/300°F/Gas 2 oven until shrivelled, about 40 minutes. Toss hot with finely chopped garlic, chilli and rock salt.*

# Chickpea Curry

Indians often eat a chickpea curry as an alternative to *dhal*. It is delicious and great as part of a vegetarian meal.

**Soaking and cooking: overnight + 2¼ hours**
**Serves: 6–8**

250g (9 oz) dried chickpeas, soaked in cold water overnight

2.5cm (1 in) piece fresh ginger, sliced

3 bay leaves

7.5cm (3 in) cinnamon stick

3 large onions, peeled and roughly chopped

4 tablespoons good olive oil

1 tablespoon each of finely chopped garlic and grated fresh ginger

1 teaspoon each of ground turmeric and *garam masala*

2 fresh red chillies, finely sliced

2 x 400g (14 oz) tins chopped tomatoes

2 black cardamoms, crushed (optional)

6 cloves

1 teaspoon each of black peppercorns and toasted cumin seeds

1 cauliflower, broken into florets

2 handfuls washed spinach

1 tablespoon chopped mint

2 tablespoons chopped coriander

salt and ground black pepper

**1** Cook the chickpeas with the sliced ginger, bay leaves, two-thirds of the cinnamon stick and about 2.5 litres (4½ pints) water until tender, about 2 hours. Drain and discard the ginger, bay and cinnamon.

**2** Meanwhile, 45 minutes before the chickpeas have finished cooking, blend half the onion in a food processor and set aside. Add the remaining chopped onion to the chickpeas. Cook the onion purée in a large saucepan in olive oil with the garlic and ginger until the onion has softened without colour.

**3** Add the turmeric, *garam masala* and chilli to the onion, and cook for a further 3 minutes. Add the canned tomato and bring to the boil.

**4** Tie the cardamoms, cloves, peppercorns and cumin seeds and remaining cinnamon in muslin or cheesecloth and add to the tomatoes. Cook until reduced by one-third, then add the cauliflower and cook for 6–8 minutes.

**5** Add the spinach, stir to combine, and cook until the spinach has wilted. Add the drained chickpeas (this is the point at which you would add drained and rinsed tinned chickpeas), and simmer for a further 15 minutes. Add extra vegetable stock if the mixture is too dry.

**6** Fold in the chopped fresh mint and coriander, and season to taste.

## Chickpea *Falafel*

*This is a Middle Eastern speciality, often made with dried broad beans, but just as nice with chickpeas.*

● *In a food processor blend together 450g (1 lb) soaked chickpeas, drained, 2 cloves garlic, 2 bunches parsley leaves, 2 bunches coriander leaves, 3 tablespoons chopped mint, 1 roughly chopped onion, ½ teaspoon cayenne pepper, 1 teaspoon ground cumin, 1 teaspoon ground black pepper, 1 tablespoon rock salt, 1 teaspoon baking powder and 1 teaspoon ground coriander.*

● *Remove from the blender and shape into small patties.*

● *Fry in hot oil on both sides, and serve with a yogurt dip (see pages 304 or 307).*

## Hummus

*Rather than buy hummus in a supermarket, make your own.*

● *Soak 250g (9 oz) dried chickpeas in triple their volume of water overnight.*

● *Cook until tender, then drain and place in a food processor.*

● *Blend until semi-smooth, then add 3 tablespoons lemon juice, 2 teaspoons ground cumin, 50ml (2 fl oz) extra virgin olive oil, 4 chopped cloves garlic, 200g (7 oz) tahina (sesame seed paste), and continue to blend until smooth. If too thick add a little vegetable stock.*

● *Place in a bowl and garnish with flat-leaf parsley, extra virgin olive oil and a dusting of cayenne or paprika.*

# CHOCOLATE

There is something about chocolate that is addictive, but I have so far resisted except when I'm driving. When I'm filling up with petrol I can't resist buying a bar, although British chocolate is in deep water with the European authorities. They are trying to tell us we can't call our bars *real* chocolate because theirs has got more cocoa solids in it and is therefore thought to be better . . .

Chocolate has been around since ancient times, cultivated by the Indians of tropical Central America, but it has only become familiar as slab chocolate or powdered chocolate (cocoa) since the nineteenth century. Cocoa pods, the fruit of a small evergreen tree (*Theobroma cacao*) are split to reveal seeds which are then fermented, dried and processed to give a cocoa 'mass'. The more cocoa solids and fats there are in a slab chocolate, the darker, more flavourful and more chocolatey it will be.

Chocolate is broken down into several categories — unsweetened, bitter-sweet, semi-sweet, milk and white. The more bitter it is, the better it is for cooking, with a more intense flavour. Unfortunately supermarkets tend to bracket their chocolate into the less helpful dark, milk and white. For cooking, generally use dark and, if you can find it, use *couverture* chocolate. I usually go for a rich Belgian chocolate, heavier in cocoa solids and fats than most British varieties.

Most recipes demand that a chocolate is melted, and this can be done in a double boiler, in a bowl set over hot water, or in a microwave. Chop or grate before melting over a low heat, never overboiling the water or the chocolate will become grainy. Don't stir while the chocolate is melting, and make sure the bowl is dry, as water will cause the chocolate to **seize**; if it does, add a little oil, and the chocolate should come back to a smooth, shiny texture. Don't melt chocolate over a direct heat unless in a liquid such as coffee, milk or water.

Chocolate fat — cocoa butter — is the third most highly saturated fat after coconut and palm kernel oils, so is, as you all know, very fattening! It contains several stimulants — among them caffeine — so it can give energy. I don't know where the addiction comes from — maybe the delicious taste?

# Chocolate and Prune Terrine

One of my all-time favourites, which was a great success when demonstrated on the BBC's *Food and Drink* programme. Substitute other fruits such as cherries or oranges if prunes are not to your liking.

**Cooking and freezing: 1½ hours + 4–6 hours**
**Serves: 8–10**

20 dried prunes, pitted

200ml (7 fl oz) freshly made tea

50ml (2 fl oz) brandy

175g (6 oz) dark chocolate, broken into pieces

85g (3 oz) unsalted butter

40g (1½ oz) caster sugar

3 eggs, separated

20g (¾ oz) cocoa powder

300ml (½ pint) double cream

**1** Soak the prunes in the tea and brandy overnight until they are plump. If you are using ready-to-eat prunes, then soak for at least an hour. Drain thoroughly and chop roughly.

**2** Line a 900g (2 lb) loaf tin with oiled clingfilm. Melt the chocolate with half the butter in a bowl set over a saucepan of simmering water. Leave to cool slightly.

**3** Beat the remaining butter and the sugar together until light and fluffy, then gradually add the egg yolks and cocoa, beating continuously. (Adding a little cocoa after each addition of egg yolk stops the mixture from splitting.) Fold in the melted chocolate and prunes.

**4** Whisk the cream until it forms soft peaks. Whisk the egg whites until they form soft peaks. Fold the cream and then the egg whites into the chocolate and prune mixture until evenly combined.

**5** Pour the mixture into the loaf tin. Cover with foil or clingfilm and freeze for 4–6 hours, preferably overnight, until solid. Cut in thin slices and serve with a sauce made with raspberries (see page 164).

## Real Drinking Chocolate

● *Real drinking chocolate can easily be made by first mixing 2 tablespoons cocoa powder with 2 tablespoons milk to a paste.*

● *Over a low heat, bring 150ml (¼ pint) single cream to just below boiling.*

● *Remove from the heat and add 125g (4½ oz) dark cooking chocolate, broken into little pieces, and stir until the chocolate has melted.*

● *Return the saucepan to the heat, add 500ml (18 fl oz) milk and bring to the boil, whisking from time to time.*

● *Fold in the cocoa paste and whisk to combine.*

● *Divide the hot chocolate between two or three mugs, and put 2 white marshmallows on top of each mug. Yummy!*

*For an adult hot chocolate, heat together 125g (4½ oz) caster sugar and 300ml (½ pint) water. Add 25g (1 oz) cocoa powder and 2 cinnamon sticks. Allow to infuse for half an hour then strain on to 300ml (½ pint) hot milk, bring to the boil and add 100ml (3½ fl oz) rum. Pour into mugs or glasses and top with whipped cream.*

# Classic Chocolate Mousse

Always popular, but too often made with cream, which ruins it for me. Pregnant women, young children and the elderly should avoid this as it includes raw eggs.

**Cooking and chilling: ½ hour + 2 hours**
**Serves: 4**

150g (5½ oz) dark chocolate, broken into small pieces
3 tablespoons espresso strength coffee
100g (3½ oz) unsalted butter, cut into small cubes
3 eggs, separated
2 tablespoons caster sugar

**1** Melt the chocolate in the coffee over a low heat in a bowl over hot water.

**2** Add the butter, a piece at a time, and stir until melted before adding the next piece. The bowl should only be warm so the butter softens and does not turn to oil; it should be the consistency of thick cream.

**3** Add the egg yolks one by one, beating them in until the mixture is very smooth.

**4** Whisk the egg whites until they form soft peaks, then add the sugar and beat to glossy stiff peaks. Fold into the chocolate delicately to retain as much air as possible, making sure no white spots from the eggs remain.

**5** Spoon into a serving bowl or four individual ramekins. Chill to set, about 2 hours.

*A delicious sauce for big kids involves chopping up 2 Mars bars and melting the pieces in 150ml (¼ pint) double cream. Pour hot over vanilla ice-cream. The sauce will be slightly chunky.*

# Simple Chocolate Soufflé

Soufflés have never been simpler.

**Preparation and cooking: 50 minutes**
**Serves: 4–6**

butter

55g (2 oz) nuts, finely chopped

cocoa powder

25g (1 oz) cornflour

225ml (8 fl oz) milk

115g (4 oz) dark chocolate, broken into pieces

1 tablespoon instant coffee granules

55g (2 oz) caster sugar + 1 tablespoon

3 egg yolks

5 egg whites, beaten

**1** Liberally butter a litre (1¾ pint) soufflé dish and sprinkle the butter with finely chopped nuts and cocoa powder.

**2** Mix the cornflour with a little milk to a smooth paste.

**3** Heat 200ml (7 fl oz) milk with the dark chocolate and instant coffee granules

**4** Add the 55g (2 oz) caster sugar, and when the chocolate has completely melted, pour in the cornflour paste and boil for 1 minute until thickened.

**5** Remove from the heat and stir in, one by one, the egg yolks. Leave to cool a little then fold in the beaten egg whites with the 1 tablespoon caster sugar.

**6** Pour into the prepared soufflé dish and cook in a 190°C/375°F/Gas 5 oven for 35 minutes. Serve immediately.

. . . . . . . . . . . . . . . .

*Melt some chocolate in the usual way. Take a handful of pecan nuts and toast lightly under a medium grill. Make a small incision in the centre of dried figs, place a pecan inside, and roll in the finely chopped zest of 1 lemon and 2 oranges. Dip in the melted chocolate. Great as an after-dinner treat.*

. . . . . . . . . . . . . . . .

## Quick Chocolate Sauce

● *Heat together 125g (4½ oz) dark chocolate, 150ml (¼ pint) double cream, 150ml (¼ pint) milk and 1 tablespoon caster sugar until melted.*
● *Serve hot.*

## Chocolate Pud

● *A quick and easy adult chocolate pud is made by stirring together 300ml (½ pint) each of Greek yogurt and double cream, then whipping until the mixture becomes quite thick.*
● *Fold in 55g (2 oz) grated dark chocolate, and spoon into six ramekins.*
● *Sprinkle each ramekin with 1 teaspoon dark soft brown sugar mixed with 1 teaspoon dark rum.*
● *Refrigerate overnight.*

## Choc Icing

● *For a simple chocolate icing, put 375g (13 oz) dark chocolate, broken into pieces, in a saucepan with 300ml (½ pint) double cream; stir until the chocolate has melted and the mixture is smooth.*
● *Place in an electric mixer and beat until cool and thick.*
● *Spread over cake or as required.*

. . . . . . . . . . . . . . . .

*Roll the above icing into balls and dip in melted chocolate. Allow to cool slightly, then roll in cocoa powder for a simple chocolate truffle.*

. . . . . . . . . . . . . . . .

*Make vanilla ice-cream and churn in the normal way. Just as it appears to be setting, fold in some broken-up chocolate flake.*

. . . . . . . . . . . . . . . .

# COURGETTE, MARROW AND SQUASH

It doesn't seem that long ago that courgettes were a rare, cherished vegetable; now the shelves of our supermarkets and greengrocers are never without them. Since courgettes have become familiar, we have also encountered patty pan squash, butternut squash, acorn squash, kabocha squash, spaghetti squash, turban squash and, of course, pumpkin. Marrow has been with us for many years, and there can't be many of us over forty who haven't experienced marrow in white sauce or marrow stuffed with mince and topped with cheese sauce. Courgettes in reality are just small marrows. All these vegetables belong to the Cucurbitaceae family, which also embraces cucumbers and melons. All the plants share similar characteristics – they climb and trail, and bear fruits which contain a huge proportion of water. They are indigenous to North America.

The British tend to be a bit odd about pumpkin; we'd rather carve odd faces in it at Hallowe'en than eat it, which is a shame because it eats really well. Now that we can buy butternut squash, pumpkin may well slip even further into obscurity as the butternut is far meatier, not so fibrous, less watery and can be cooked in exactly the same way.

If you grow any of these vegetables, the flowers are delicious to eat, either battered and deep-fried or stuffed, battered and deep-fried. The downside is if you buy them in a top food store you can pay a fortune for each for them!

Courgettes and patty pan squashes – the 'summer squashes' – do not require peeling, whereas marrow, pumpkin and most other 'winter' squashes do. Make sure the vegetables are shiny and firm and feel heavy for their size.

# Courgette Griddle Cakes

Delicious as finger food topped with soured cream and chives, or served as a vegetable to accompany grilled or roast meats. A great dish topped with smoked salmon and soured cream or poached eggs and crispy bacon.

**Preparation and cooking: 40 minutes**
**Serves: 4–6**

375g (13 oz) courgettes, trimmed and grated

salt

1 fresh red chilli, finely chopped

2 spring onions, finely chopped

1 clove garlic, finely chopped

½ teaspoon curry powder

½ teaspoon soft thyme leaves

½ teaspoon ground black pepper

1 egg, lightly beaten

75ml (2½ fl oz) milk

140g (5 oz) plain flour

1½ teaspoons baking powder

vegetable oil for frying

1 Place the courgettes in a colander, sprinkle with salt, and toss to combine. Leave for 20 minutes. Squeeze the courgettes between your hands to extract any water.

2 Combine the courgettes with the chilli, spring onion, garlic, curry powder, thyme leaves and pepper. Fold in the egg and milk.

3 Sift the flour and the baking powder into the mix and stir to combine.

4 Lightly oil a non-stick frying pan and fry tablespoonfuls of the batter for 3 minutes on one side then 1 minute on the other. Keep warm while using up the remaining batter. (Large cakes can be made for main-course portions.)

# Courgette Pickle 🅥

Great with cold meats or in a sandwich.

**Preparation and cooking: 2¼ hours**

**Makes: 2 litres (3½ pints)**

1kg (2¼ lb) courgettes, cut into 1cm (½ in) chunks

2 tablespoons salt

4 onions, thinly sliced

850ml (1½ pints) white wine vinegar

350g (12 oz) caster sugar

2 tablespoons mustard seeds

1 dried red chilli

1 teaspoon English mustard powder

3 teaspoons ground turmeric

**1** Mix the chunks of courgette with the salt and onions. Cover with cold water, leave for 2 hours, and drain.

**2** Combine the white wine vinegar with the caster sugar in a saucepan over a medium heat.

**3** Add the mustard seeds, red chilli, English mustard powder and ground turmeric. Bring to the boil, then pour over the courgette and onion.

**4** Allow to cool, then bottle in sterilised jars.

• • • • • • • • • • • • •

*Cook long slices of courgette on the barbie, then sprinkle with chopped garlic, chilli and thyme, and serve with shavings of fresh Parmesan and an extra virgin olive oil and fresh lemon dressing.*

• • • • • • • • • • • • •

# Fried Butternut Squash 🅥 with Herbs

A dish for an informal starter, or as a partner for grilled fish or poultry.

**Preparation and cooking: 25 minutes**

**Serves: 4**

1 x 675g (1½ lb) butternut squash, peeled

85g (3 oz) plain flour

¼ teaspoon celery salt

¼ teaspoon cayenne pepper

¼ teaspoon ground black pepper

pinch of salt

2 tablespoons clarified butter (see page 60)

2 tablespoons olive oil

6 sage leaves

3 cloves garlic

2 tablespoons chopped flat-leaf parsley

1 tablespoon chopped mint

150g (5½ oz) Greek yogurt

**1** Cut the butternut squash in half vertically, remove seeds, then cut each half in three lengthways. Cut each length in 5mm (¼ in) slices.

**2** Combine the flour with the spices and seasonings, then toss the squash in this. Set aside.

**3** Heat the butter and oil in a frying pan, add the sage and garlic and heat gently until the garlic is golden and the sage is brown. Remove sage and garlic and discard.

**4** Add the squash slices to the heated oil and butter in the frying pan in a single layer. Fry until the squash is golden, about 3 minutes, then turn over and cook until tender. Remove and keep warm and repeat to use up remaining squash.

**5** Serve sprinkled with the parsley and mint, accompanied by a dollop of seasoned Greek yogurt.

## Stuffed Marrow

● *Cut a peeled marrow in half lengthways, scoop out the seeds, and fill with Mainstay Mince (see page 46).*

● *Top with a béchamel-based cheese sauce (see page 85) and bake in a hot oven for 1 hour.*

*Cut courgettes into 5cm x 5mm x 5mm (2 x ¼ x ¼ in)* **batons***, soak in milk for 15 minutes and toss in seasoned flour. Deep-fry in oil and season with salt and cayenne for courgette chips.*

*Grate courgettes, blanch in boiling salted water for 2 minutes, and drain. Combine 150g (5½ oz) Greek yogurt with a garlic clove crushed with a little salt, 1 tablespoon chopped coriander, 1 teaspoon chopped mint, 1 tablespoon extra virgin olive oil and a teaspoon of fresh lemon juice. Fold in the courgette and season.*

# Coconut Butternut Stew

A delicious dish for vegetarians and meat-eaters alike, which is very easy to make.

**Preparation and cooking: 1 hour**

**Serves: 4–6**

| |
|---|
| 4 dried hot red chillies, cut in pieces, soaked in warm water for 10 minutes, drained |
| 6 spring onions, roughly chopped |
| 2 teaspoons chopped garlic |
| 2 stems lemongrass, outer leaves discarded, chopped |
| 1½ tablespoons peanut oil, extra if required |
| 2 teaspoons ground coriander |
| ½ teaspoon ground turmeric |
| 1 teaspoon paprika |
| 300ml (½ pint) tinned unsweetened coconut milk, well stirred |
| 150ml (¼ pint) vegetable stock or water |
| 2 medium butternut squashes, peeled, seeded and cut into 5cm (2 in) chunks |
| 2 green cardamom pods, crushed |
| 1 cinnamon stick |
| salt to taste |
| 1 red pepper, **julienned** |
| 1½ tablespoons soy sauce |
| 1½ teaspoons light brown sugar |
| 1½ teaspoons lemon juice |
| 2 tablespoons fresh coriander leaves |

**1** Grind the chilli, spring onion, garlic and lemongrass to a paste in a processor, adding a little oil if necessary.

**2** Heat 1½ tablespoons of oil in a heavy saucepan over a medium-low heat. Add the chilli paste and cook, stirring, until it is fragrant and no longer tastes raw. Add the coriander, turmeric and paprika, and stir for 1 minute. Add the coconut milk and simmer, stirring, for 5 minutes.

**3** Stir in the stock and bring to a simmer. Reduce the heat to low, and add the squash, cardamom, cinnamon stick and salt to taste. Simmer, partially covered, until the squash is tender and the sauce is reduced, about 20–25 minutes.

**4** Add the red pepper julienne, and cook for 3 minutes. Stir in the soy sauce, sugar and lemon juice and simmer for another 2 minutes. This is quite a wet stew. (It can be thickened with cornflour paste if required.)

**5** Serve with plain rice, garnished with coriander leaves.

# Stuffed Courgette Flowers

Makes a wonderful starter with a simple tomato sauce. Only for the gardeners among you. Remove the stamens by cutting out a little circle at the base. Or you can simply split open and remove the stamen. Look out for bugs!

**Preparation and cooking: 30 minutes**
**Serves: 4**

8 courgette flowers

light olive oil for frying

**Stuffing**

100g (3½ oz) ricotta cheese

100g (3½ oz) mozzarella cheese

30g (1¼ oz) Parmesan, freshly grated

25g (1 oz) Parma ham, finely chopped

6 basil leaves, ripped

pinch of freshly grated nutmeg

salt and ground black pepper

**Batter**

200g (7 oz) self-raising flour

pinch of salt

600ml (1 pint) iced water

**1** Mix all the cheeses, Parma ham, basil and seasonings together. Divide the mixture into eight.

**2** Fill each flower with the stuffing. Just above the stuffing twist the petals slightly to keep the stuffing in.

**3** The batter should be prepared just before you need it. Sift the flour into a bowl, then add the salt and iced water. The flour should be barely mixed with the water. The batter should look lumpy – do not worry if unmixed flour shows, this is correct.

**4** Dip each flower into the batter. Deep-fry the flowers until golden, in hot oil. Drain on absorbent kitchen paper, and serve very hot.

## Pumpkin *Gratin*

● Boil 1kg (2¼ lb) of cubed pumpkin and 250g (9 oz) of diced potato in salted water until tender.

● Mash the two vegetables and fold in 2 beaten raw eggs, 85g (3 oz) softened unsalted butter, 55g (2 oz) grated Parmesan and 55g grated Gruyère.

● Spoon into a buttered gratin dish, dot the top with 25g (1 oz) butter and 25g (1 oz) each of Parmesan and Gruyère, and bake in a hot oven for 30 minutes.

*Cut pumpkin into unpeeled wedges, remove seeds and fibrous centre, and roast with your Sunday roast, some sprigs of thyme, whole peeled garlic cloves, ground black pepper and olive oil.*

# CREAM

Cream, in any form, is one of the reasons why I have a fairly substantial girth. An essential for much home cooking or perfect for just pouring liberally over fruit. Unlike many of our European counterparts, we have a huge selection.

## Half Cream

12 per cent fat, a bit like the American half and half which is designed for pouring into coffee. It cannot be whipped.

## Single Cream

18 per cent fat, good for pouring but not for cooking as it tends to split. This cream will not whip.

## Whipping Cream

30–35 per cent fat, useful for a wide variety of dishes and puds where whipped cream is required.

## Double Cream

48 per cent fat, best for cooking as it withstands high temperatures. It comes as pouring, thick and extra thick, but all are the same when heated. For a similar effect, but with fewer health problems, you may feel like substituting Greek yogurt which only has 10 per cent fat and also withstands high temperatures unlike ordinary unstrained yogurt which tends to split.

## Soured Cream

18 per cent fat. Buy the thickened variety for brunch dishes or pop a dollop on a baked potato or a spot of goulash. Made from single cream so cannot be whipped.

## Clotted Cream

A massive 55 per cent fat, but for that special pud it is irresistible. An English tradition that should be maintained, for cream teas wouldn't be the same without it.

## Crème Fraîche

An import from France that serves the same purpose as double cream, with fat varying from 30 to 40 per cent. Good for cooking but I can't get used to its slightly sour taste when it comes to eating it with puds. It cannot be whipped.

*A swirl of lightly whipped double cream mixed with fresh herbs is a nice finishing touch on a bowl of soup, hot or cold.*

# Crème Brûlée

We've adopted the French name for the very British Cambridge Burnt Cream. A classic that can rarely be beaten. Many chefs add different flavours or fruits, but for me it's got to be the classic original.

**Cooking and cooling: 30 minutes + overnight**
**Serves: 4**

600ml (1 pint) double cream
1 vanilla pod, split lengthways
6 egg yolks
1 tablespoon caster sugar

**Glaze**
4 heaped teaspoons caster sugar

1 Pour the cream into a saucepan and scrape the seeds from the vanilla pod into it. Add the scraped pods as well. Bring to **scalding** point, just below boiling point, then remove from the heat and allow to infuse for 15 minutes. Remove the vanilla pods.
2 Beat together the egg yolks and the tablespoon of caster sugar. Pour in the cream and stir to combine. Pour the mixture back into the saucepan and cook over a low heat, stirring continuously, until the custard becomes quite thick (it should coat the back of a spoon), but *do not allow to boil.*
3 Pour immediately into four ice-cold ramekins and chill for at least 4 hours, preferably overnight.
4 Spread a thin even layer of caster sugar over the custards, and caramelise by either using a blow torch or placing very close to a hot grill (if grilling under a domestic grill, put the ramekins in an iced-water **bain-marie** to prevent the cream splitting). Do not replace in the refrigerator as the sugar crust will melt.

*Boil double cream until it has reduced by one-third, season with salt and pepper and a squeeze of lemon juice, add a handful of chopped herbs, and pour over cooked spring vegetables.*

# Calvados Ice-cream

A delicious ice-cream that goes very well with caramelised apples (see page 177).
**Cooking and freezing: 2 hours**
**Serves: 8–10**

14 egg yolks
350g (12 oz) caster sugar
pinch of salt
1 vanilla pod, split lengthways
1.2 litres (2 pints) whipping cream
5cm (2 in) cinnamon stick
90ml (3 fl oz) Calvados

**1** Beat the egg yolks, sugar and salt together until pale and frothy.
**2** Scrape the seeds from the vanilla pod into the cream in a saucepan. Place the scraped pods and the cinnamon stick in the cream, and simmer gently over a low heat for 10 minutes.
**3** Remove the cinnamon stick and vanilla pods and discard. Pour the hot cream on to the whipped egg, and whisk to combine. Return the mixture to the pan over a low heat and cook, stirring continuously until the custard coats the back of a spoon. *Do not allow to boil.*
**4** Pour the custard into a bowl and allow to cool, stirring from time to time. Cover and refrigerate for 1 hour.
**5** Add the Calvados and stir to combine. Pour the mixture into an ice-cream machine and freeze according to manufacturer's instructions. Or freeze in a suitable container, stirring every so often. Transfer to a bowl and store in the freezer, covered, until ready for use.

• • • • •
*Cream whips better if it has been chilled.*
• • • • •

# Panna Cotta

The Italian version of *crème brûlée* but without the *brûlée*. In this recipe I've added the Italian lemon liqueur, Limoncello, but if you find it difficult to buy, substitute an orange liqueur such as Grand Marnier or Cointreau.

**Cooking and cooling: 1½ hours**
**Serves: 6–8**

1.2 litres (2 pints) double cream
2 vanilla pods, split lengthways
thinly pared rind of 2 oranges
4 gelatine leaves
150ml (¼ pint) cold milk
150g (5½ oz) icing sugar
125ml (4 fl oz) lemon liqueur (Limoncello), plus extra to serve

**1** Pour 850ml (1½ pints) of the cream into a saucepan and add the vanilla pods and orange rinds. Bring to the boil and, once boiling, reduce the heat and simmer until reduced by one-third. Take out the rinds and pods, and scrape the inside of the pods into the cream.
**2** Meanwhile, soak the gelatine leaves in the milk until soft. Remove the gelatine. Heat the milk until boiling, then return the gelatine to it, and stir until completely dissolved. Pour the gelatine mix into the hot cream, stir and let cool.
**3** Whip the remaining cream with the icing sugar, and fold into the cooled cooked cream. Add the lemon liqueur, and pour into a bowl or individual glasses or dishes (perhaps with a little liqueur in the bottom). Place in the fridge and leave to set for approximately 1 hour.
**4** To serve, scoop into serving dishes, or into the individual dishes. You could offer some poached fruit as well. Dribble a little liqueur over the top if you like, or serve separately in a tiny glass.

*When making any hot fruit pie, pour some double cream through the hole in the pastry and return to the oven for 10 minutes.*

## Cream Toast

*Cream toast*, pain perdu, *French toast or eggy bread are in all but name the same dish (see page 52).*
● *The old-fashioned method involves laying slices of bread in a dish, pouring over 300ml (½ pint) single cream and 150ml (¼ pint) milk, followed by a sprinkle of caster sugar and a pinch of powdered cinnamon.*
● *When the bread slices have soaked up the cream, dip the slices in beaten raw egg then fry them until golden on both sides in clarified butter.*

## Horseradish Cream

*Instead of buying commercial horseradish cream, fold 55g (2 oz) of freshly grated horseradish into 150ml (¼ pint) double cream whipped to* **soft peaks** *or soured cream with a dash of Worcestershire sauce, seasoning, 1 teaspoon chopped dill and a teaspoon of Dijon mustard.*

*A lovely sauce for pork or veal is made by heating 150ml (¼ pint) soured cream then whisking in an egg yolk, ½ teaspoon caster sugar, seasoning and 1 teaspoon Dijon mustard. Heat but do not allow to boil.*

*Pour a little double cream over a freshly made omelette and flash briefly under the grill for a touch of luxury.*

*If you find that, despite following all the rules, including adding and stirring the sugar, and pouring it over the back of a spoon, that the cream still sinks into your Irish coffee making it cloudy, try whipping double cream to soft peaks before spooning it on to the coffee.*

# CUCUMBER

What can I say about a cucumber? Quite simply, it is probably the most boring, tasteless vegetable known to man, and yet most of us love it. Why? It does us little good, especially when peeled (there is some beta-carotene in the peel); it's also supposed to be less digestible when peeled. It must be the crunch, for it has a great texture, but then so has an apple, with far more taste. It is refreshing . . .

One of the oldest vegetables known to mankind, it has been revered for well over 4,000 years. It is thought that it originated in India. In the Middle East, people were under the impression that eating several cucumbers a day would protect them from the bite of insects; it is a fact that if you grow them you will notice gnats and mosquitoes avoid them like the plague.

Cucumber is a member of the Cucurbitaceae family, closely related to the squash, pumpkin, melon, marrow and courgette, and is the most watery of them all, containing some 96 per cent water. *Cucumis sativus* is easy to grow if you have a vegetable plot and, grown outside instead of in the usual hothouse, it even develops a little flavour (although most cucumbers require a lot of heat). They come in long straight or bent columns, or can be ridged or warty. (Gherkins are small ridge cucumbers.) I grow Apple Shaped Ridge, Burpless Tasty Green and the Hokus Gherkin varieties.

Most cucumbers you buy today have been waxed in order to preserve them so remember to wash. Look for a hard and stiff cucumber: test it by pushing the stalk end, and if it has any give or softness at all, don't buy. There should be no yellowing of the bright green skin. Cucumbers, as they contain so much water, do not like excess cold, which is why they are shrink-wrapped in plastic film. They should keep for up to one week in the salad drawer but, as with any vegetable, eat as fresh as possible. Whether you peel or not must be up to you. Personally I don't, unless I am buying the small continental variety which has a tougher skin.

## Cucumber and Sorrel Soup

I make this soup regularly as I grow sorrel. Some supermarkets are selling sorrel nowadays, but you tend to pay silly money for it. If you have a garden, grow it, pick the leaves as required, and it will continue to come back year after year.

**Preparation and cooking: 45 minutes**
**Serves: 4**

225g (8 oz) sorrel, picked and washed
300ml (½ pint) double cream
300g (10½ oz) Greek yogurt
1 x 400g (14 oz) tin beef consommé
1 cucumber, peeled, seeded and chopped into 5mm (¼ in) dice
2 dill pickles, chopped into 5mm (¼ in) dice
2 tablespoons snipped chives
3 hard-boiled eggs, shelled and chopped
4 spring onions, finely sliced
1 tablespoon lemon juice
salt and ground white pepper
2 tablespoons roughly chopped flat-leaf parsley

1  Chop the sorrel and place in a saucepan over a low heat with 1 tablespoon water. Cook until the sorrel breaks down and becomes an olive-coloured purée.
2  Place the sorrel in a bowl and allow to cool. Add the remaining ingredients and stir to combine. Season to taste, and chill until ready to serve.
3  Some of you may prefer to salt the cucumber to extract water from it. Sprinkle diced cucumber with salt, leave for 30 minutes, then rinse and squeeze dry. Proceed as above.

* * * * * * * * * * * * *

*For a salsa, combine a dice of seeded, unpeeled cucumber with diced seeded tomatoes, a dice of bulb fennel, some fresh oregano and basil, some black olives, extra virgin olive oil, grated lemon zest and lemon juice.*

* * * * * * * * * * * * *

# Thai Cucumber Salad

A wonderfully refreshing salad, delicious with *Thai Fish Cakes* (see page 133), grilled fish, or the *Marinated Duck Breast* on page 109.

**Preparation and marination: 1 hour**
**Serves: 6**

2 cucumbers, peeled, halved lengthways and seeded

35g (1¼ oz) caster sugar

50ml (2 fl oz) rice vinegar

2 hot red chillies, finely diced

2 shallots, finely diced

2 tablespoons chopped coriander leaves

40g (1½ oz) roasted peanuts, chopped

½ tablespoon *nam pla* (fish sauce)

**1** Cut the cucumber into 5mm (¼ in) slices.
**2** Dissolve the sugar in the vinegar, and toss the cucumber slices in this. Fold in the chilli, shallot and coriander.
**3** Sprinkle with the peanuts and add the fish sauce just before serving.

# Cucumber and Pepper Relish

A colourful relish, delicious as part of a sandwich filling.

**Marination and cooking: 3 hours + 30 minutes**
**Makes: about 2 litres (3½ pints)**

6 cucumbers, diced, seeded, unpeeled

salt

5 onions, chopped

4 red peppers, diced

750g (1 lb 10 oz) caster sugar

600ml (1 pint) cider vinegar

2 teaspoons mustard seeds

2 teaspoons celery seeds

3 tablespoons cornflour

**1** Salt and soak the cucumbers for 3 hours.
**2** Drain, rinse and place in a **non-reactive** saucepan with the onion, red pepper, caster sugar, cider vinegar, mustard and celery seeds.
**3** Bring to the boil, stirring constantly.
**4** Mix the cornflour with a little water, fold into the relish and stir to combine. Cook over a low heat for 12 minutes.
**5** Pour into hot sterilised jars and seal.

## Cucumber with Yogurt

*Greeks are keen on yogurt and cucumber in the form of* Tzatziki *(see page 304), but I prefer this recipe.*
● *Drain 450g (1 lb) natural yogurt in muslin or cheesecloth overnight.*
● *Combine the drained curd with 1 large peeled, seeded and diced cucumber which has been soaked for 1 hour with 1 tablespoon white wine vinegar, 1 teaspoon salt and ½ teaspoon caster sugar. Make sure the cucumber has been squeezed dry before adding.*
● *Fold in 1 minced clove garlic, 2 tablespoons chopped dill, 1 tablespoon extra virgin olive oil and 2 teaspoons tarragon vinegar. Season.*

# Cucumber Salad with Soured Cream and Dill

An excellent salad to partner smoked or grilled fish. I prefer to **julienne** the cucumber, but feel free to slice thinly or cut in chunks.

**Preparation and cooking: 40 minutes**
**Serves: 4**

2 cucumbers, peeled, seeded and **julienned**

1 teaspoon salt

3 tablespoons cider vinegar

1 tablespoon caster sugar

300ml (½ pint) thick soured cream

4 spring onions, thinly sliced

4 tablespoons snipped chives

½ teaspoon celery seeds

4 tablespoons snipped dill

paprika

**1** Sprinkle the cucumber with salt, 2 tablespoons of the vinegar and half the sugar. Let stand for half an hour, then drain and gently squeeze dry.

**2** Place the soured cream, remaining vinegar and sugar, spring onions, chives, celery seeds and dill into a serving bowl. Check the seasoning. Fold in the cucumber and garnish with a dusting of paprika.

## Cooked Cucumber

● *Not many of us eat cucumber hot but if you choose to do so, peel, halve lengthways and seed 2 large cucumbers.*

● *Cut these into 1cm (½ in) half moons and fry for 2 minutes in 55g (2 oz) hot butter.*

● *Add 1 tablespoon Dijon mustard, 90ml (3 fl oz) double cream, 3 tablespoons snipped chives and 3 tablespoons chopped flat-leaf parsley.*

● *Bring to the boil, season and serve with grilled fish.*

# Cucumber Pickle

This is probably the best use of a cucumber. It is similar to the old-fashioned bread and butter pickle. Why they call it this I'll never know, as it certainly doesn't contain any bread or butter! And I can't imagine it can be great between two slices of the same . . .

**Marination and cooking: 3 hours + 15 minutes**
**Makes: 4 litres (7 pints)**

8 large cucumbers, unpeeled and cut into 5mm (¼ in) rings

3 large onions, sliced

4 green peppers, cut into rings

175g (6 oz) salt

2.5 litres (4½ pints) water

1.7 litres (3 pints) cider vinegar

1.5kg (3 lb 5 oz) caster sugar

1 tablespoon ground turmeric

½ teaspoon ground cloves

1½ teaspoons yellow mustard seeds

1 tablespoon celery seeds

**1** Combine the vegetables in a large **non-reactive** bowl, toss with the salt and pour over the cold water. Allow to stand for 3 hours, then drain thoroughly, without rinsing.

**2** In a large non-reactive saucepan, combine the remaining ingredients, bring to the boil, then add the vegetables. Bring back to the boil, then remove from the heat immediately.

**3** Pack into hot, sterilised jars and seal. Leave for at least 1 week before serving.

# DUCK

I don't know the exact figures, but I would guess that duck is not a big seller in butchers or supermarkets. One reason may be that it is still perceived as a luxury, something you would eat in a restaurant but not normally at home. Another may be that it is not a generous bird in its percentage of meat to bone; one duck will really only feed two hungry adults.

World-wide there are well over 60 species of domestic duck. They used to be very fatty but, as with most forms of animal farming, the fat is now being bred out of them. The domesticated ducks we are likely to know and find are the Peking, which are small, about 1.5–2kg (3½–4½ lb); the Gressingham which is a British development (the once familiar Aylesbury is now almost extinct), bred for a good meat-to-bone ratio and very little fat; and the Barbary, which is French, and one many chefs use because of their larger breasts. Duck is available whole (rarely with head on), or in portions, fresh or frozen. Buy fresh where possible. Don't buy a duck smaller than about 2kg (4½ lb) as the meat-to-bone ratio will be poor.

## Roasting

This is simplicity itself. Just pour boiling water over the skin two or three times. Prick the breast all over with a fork and rub with cider vinegar. Place in the refrigerator overnight, uncovered. This helps tighten the skin so that, when cooked, it will become crisp. Place the duck on a rack over a roasting tray and rub the skin with rock salt and ground black pepper. Roast in a 180°C/350°F/Gas 4 oven for 1½–2 hours, depending on the size and variety. The duck will release a great deal of fat during the roasting, which can be used for sauté or roast potatoes. If you want to keep the fat, drain several times during cooking and place in a container. To roast legs on their own, prick the skin and roast for about 1 hour.

Many chefs roast whole ducks for much less time but I would advise that the meat on the legs will be very tough and too rare. If you want rare breast and crispy legs, then you may cook the whole bird for 40 minutes, cut off the breasts and serve them and continue to cook the remainder of the bird for a further 1 hour or so. Serve the crispy legs with a salad.

## Grilling

I don't advise using a grill at all for breasts, as the fat will spit, causing an awful mess in a part of the cooker which is difficult to clean. Use the highly fashionable ridged griddle pan for a similar effect. Score the skin side of the breast in a criss-cross pattern, just cutting through the skin and fat, as this helps release the fat. For medium rare, cook the breast on the griddle pan skin side down for 12–15 minutes over a low heat (draining the fat as it is released). Brush the flesh side with a little of the melted fat, increase the heat, and cook flesh side down for about 5 minutes. Season as required. Allow to rest for 5 minutes before carving or serving, to allow the juices to settle.

*Take a cold duck breast and slice thinly at an angle. Spread each slice with plum sauce and top with 1 shredded spring onion and some finely diced cucumber. Roll up and serve as a canapé.*

*For a delicious glaze, soak 55g (2 oz) currants in 250ml (9 fl oz) balsamic vinegar. When plumped up, combine with 2 tablespoons honey and ¼ teaspoon cayenne pepper. Boil this mix until it has **reduced** by half. Paint cooked duck breasts with this thick syrupy glaze (strained if you like).*

# Braised Duck Red Curry

I was taught this dish at the Oriental Thai Cookery school in Bangkok, which was brilliant (even if a little painful on the bank balance). You could use whole ducks and get your butcher to portion it, but I use duck legs because they are so much cheaper.

**Preparation and cooking: 1¼ hours**
**Serves: 4**

6 duck legs, cut in 2.5cm (1 in) pieces, bone in
2 tablespoons duck fat (see page 111) or vegetable oil
12 shallots, thinly sliced
6 cloves garlic, finely chopped
2 tablespoons grated fresh ginger
75g (2¾ oz) Thai red curry paste
2 x 400ml (14 fl oz) tins coconut milk
1 tablespoon soft brown sugar
3 lime leaves, thinly sliced
2 tablespoons lime juice
20 basil leaves, ripped
3 handfuls washed spinach
1 tablespoon *nam pla* (fish sauce)
1 bunch coriander, leaves only
1 bunch spring onions, thinly sliced
2 fresh green chillies, sliced

**1** Brown the duck pieces (with bone) in the duck fat, remove and set aside. Add the shallot and garlic to the fat and cook over a medium heat until the shallot starts to brown.
**2** Add the ginger and curry paste and cook for 3 minutes, stirring continuously. Return the duck to the pan, then add half the coconut milk, the sugar and the lime leaves. Cook for about 40 minutes over a low heat until the duck is tender. The sauce will have split, but don't worry, this is normal.
**3** Add the remaining coconut milk, the lime juice, basil leaves, spinach and *nam pla*, and cook for a further 5 minutes.
**4** Garnish with coriander, spring onion and chilli, and serve with fragrant rice.

# Marinated Duck Breast

This marinade gives the duck breast a fabulous, slightly Oriental flavour. It could equally be used for other poultry. The duck is lovely served hot or cold as a starter, especially with the *Thai Cucumber Salad* on page 106.

**Marination and cooking: 24 hours + 30 minutes**
**Serves: 4**

2 large duck breasts

**Marinade**
300ml (½ pint) good olive oil
2 cloves garlic, finely diced
1 tablespoon diced fresh ginger
1 carrot, finely diced
300ml (½ pint) dry white wine
150ml (¼ pint) water
1 tablespoon dried oregano
1 fresh red chilli, finely diced
2 tablespoons soy sauce
1 roasted red pepper (see page 254), skinned, seeded and diced
2 tablespoons clear honey
½ bunch spring onions, finely diced

**1** Heat the olive oil, garlic, ginger and carrot together over a medium heat for 5 minutes – do not brown.
**2** Add the wine, water, oregano, chilli, soy sauce, red pepper and honey and simmer for 15 minutes; add the spring onions for the last 5 minutes of cooking. Allow to cool.
**3** Cut the duck breasts in half. Marinate them in the cold marinade for 24 hours, before roasting or grilling as described opposite.

# Duck and Cabbage Rolls

A different way of using the cheaper duck legs. 'Food that comes in packages', such as ravioli, *dim sum* and vine leaves, has always been popular. This dish has a great combination of flavours.

**Preparation and cooking: 2½ hours**

**Serves: 4**

4 duck legs

salt and ground black pepper

5 sprigs thyme

1 head garlic

1 teaspoon olive oil

1 Savoy cabbage

1 onion, finely diced

115g (4 oz) *pancetta* or smoked streaky bacon, diced

½ teaspoon soft thyme leaves

½ teaspoon fennel seeds

2 tablespoons aged red wine vinegar

3 tablespoons red wine

8 slices Parma ham

55g (2 oz) unsalted butter

150ml (¼ pint) chicken stock

25g (1 oz) soft white breadcrumbs

25g (1 oz) Parmesan, freshly grated

**1** Season the duck legs with salt, pepper and the thyme sprigs. Place on a rack above a roasting tray. Cut 1cm (½ in) off the top of the garlic head and then drizzle the cut sides with the olive oil. Replace the garlic 'lid' and wrap the head in foil. Place it alongside the duck legs.

**2** Bake the duck and garlic in a preheated oven at 200°C/ 400°F/Gas 6 for 30 minutes, then remove the garlic. Continue to cook the duck for a further 25 minutes. Drain off the fat, and set the duck and fat aside.

**3** Meanwhile, remove 8 outside leaves from the Savoy cabbage and cook them in boiling, salted water for 4 minutes. Finely shred the remaining cabbage and set aside. Refresh the whole cabbage leaves in cold water, dry and set aside.

**4** Remove the meat and crispy duck skin from the bones and shred finely. Set aside. Break the cooked garlic into cloves and squeeze each clove to remove the now softened garlic.

**5** Heat 1 tablespoon of the retained duck fat in a frying pan and add the garlic, onion, *pancetta*, soft thyme leaves and fennel seeds. Cook over a medium heat until the onion has softened without colour. Add the shredded cabbage, stir to combine, reduce heat and cover with a lid. Cook slowly for 12–15 minutes until the cabbage is tender.

**6** Remove the lid, increase the heat and add the vinegar and red wine. Cook until the liquid has evaporated. Fold in the shredded duck and skin and stir to combine. Season to taste.

**7** Lay the cabbage leaves on a work surface, first having removed the central rib.

**8** Place a large tablespoon of the cabbage–duck mixture to the front of each cabbage leaf and roll up, tucking in the sides, creating neat packages. Wrap each parcel in a slice of Parma ham.

**9** Use a little of the butter to grease a *gratin* dish, and place any remaining cabbage mixture on the bottom. Place the cabbage parcels on top and pour in the chicken stock. The dish can be prepared ahead to this point.

**10** Combine the breadcrumbs with the Parmesan and scatter over the cabbage parcels. Dot with the remaining butter and bake in the oven, at the same temperature as above, for 25 minutes until bubbling and heated through.

# Duck *Confit*

A classic that is worth the effort. Save the duck fat after you have used the legs – it's great for pan-frying potatoes.

**Marination and cooking: 24 hours + 2 hours**
**Serves: 6**

| |
|---|
| 6 duck legs |
| 250g (9 oz) sea salt |
| 2 tablespoons dried thyme |
| 2 tablespoons garlic salt |
| 1 tablespoon black peppercorns, crushed |
| ½ tablespoon allspice berries |
| ½ tablespoon juniper berries, crushed |
| duck fat |
| lard |

**1** Put the duck legs in a dish. Mix together the sea salt with dried thyme, garlic salt, black peppercorns, allspice and juniper berries.

**2** Cover the legs with this mixture, and leave for 24 hours, turning the duck every 6–8 hours.

**3** Wipe the salt from the duck legs, then submerge them in barely simmering duck fat for about 1½ hours until very tender.

**4** Remove the legs very carefully, and turn off the heat under the fat, allowing it to settle.

**5** Put the duck legs in a crock or glass jar and strain the settled fat over them so they are completely submerged.

**6** Cool in a refrigerator and, when set, pour over a thin layer of melted lard. The *confit* will keep up to 2 months refrigerated.

*Combine shredded Duck Confit with mashed potato enhanced with truffle oil, and use this as a stuffing for ravioli or wonton skins.*

## Oriental Duck Salad

- *Toss shredded cooked duck with finely shredded fresh lime leaves, tender chopped lemongrass, crisp-fried shallots (you can buy these ready-prepared in Chinese shops), sliced spring onions and grated ginger.*
- *Combine with a dressing made with lime juice, Thai fish sauce, honey, chilli sauce and chopped coriander and mint.*
- *Serve with sliced fresh mango.*

## One-pot Lunch or Supper

- *Toss 1 shredded heart of radicchio with 250g (9 oz) shredded smoked duck, 55g (2 oz) broken walnuts, 1 teaspoon soft thyme leaves, 1 teaspoon very finely chopped rosemary and some seasoning.*
- *Combine with 1 small tin of chopped tomatoes and mix with 250g (9 oz) cooked penne.*
- *Place the whole lot in a gratin dish and top with slices of Taleggio or grated Gruyère cheese.*
- *Bake briefly in a hot oven or flash under the grill.*

## Duck Fat

*Duck fat has so much flavour, and is perfect for cooking sauté potatoes. It will keep in a refrigerator for 2 weeks.*

- *To render it, take the inner fat from a raw duck, or fat from a roast, and any skin, and put in a pan with five times its volume of water.*
- *Simmer until the fat has dissolved.*
- *Pour into a bowl, cool and refrigerate overnight.*
- *The next day, remove the cold set fat and discard the water (which will contain the impurities).*

*To make duck cracklings for sprinkling on to soups or salads, take the duck skin and rub with rock salt and place on a rack above a roasting tray. Bake in a 180°C/350°F/Gas 4 oven until the fat has rendered and the skin is crisp. Chop it into small pieces.*

# EGGS

What would we do without eggs? From the ever-popular boiled egg, through fried, poached, scrambled, baked and omelettes, then on to mayonnaise and hollandaise sauces, soufflés, cakes, pastas, breads, pastries and binding agents for mousses. Life would not be the same without them.

Where possible, buy fresh free-range eggs. It is not until you taste an egg freshly laid by a chicken with a free run of a farm that you will notice any difference between it and a battery egg. Unfortunately, many eggs in the UK nowadays contain salmonella. It is not present in all eggs, but as a safeguard the 'official' advice is not to eat them at all unless they are hard-boiled or the equivalent. This ridiculous situation deprives us of the pleasure of soft-boiled, poached or scrambled eggs, as well as home-made mayonnaise, hollandaise and chocolate mousse. Where eggs are to be beaten, there is the alternative of pasteurised eggs, but not many supermarkets have decided to sell them yet. Pregnant women, the elderly and very young should beware, but personally I still choose to run the gauntlet when cooking at home.

Chicken, quail and duck eggs are all available but usually supermarkets will only stock the first two. Quail eggs are a bit of a waste of space as you pay as much for them as you do for chickens', with a similar taste but only a third of the product. They do look cute, though, and are quite good for garnishes or pickling. Duck eggs are delicious but not widely available. If you do come across them you will find them larger, stronger in flavour and richer than chicken eggs. An interesting piece of research reveals that duck egg whites are deficient in globulin and so are not good at holding air, making them unsuitable for whipping.

Gulls' eggs, my favourite, are becoming rarer and rarer, although I'm not quite sure why. There still seem to be hundreds of gulls' nests on every coastline; maybe there are fewer volunteers climbing the cliffs for this bounty. If you choose gulls' eggs with celery salt in a restaurant, watch out for the price. A restaurant had gulls' eggs on the bar, and I was merrily eating away when the barman came up and asked, 'Are you sure you want all those?' It turned out they were charged at £3.95 each; I had eaten six and peeled them all myself.

How do you tell an old egg? Several methods are available, but none at the point of purchase, unless you believe the date stamp. Unfortunately, it's the packing stations that date the boxes, and it may have been a few days before the eggs reached the station. If an egg is very old, it will float when put in a bowl of water, or the yolk will be off centre and flat when frying. When you eat a boiled egg, the yolk will have floated to the blunt end.

It is advisable to keep eggs in the fridge, but as the shells are very porous, make sure they are stored in an airtight container or they will pick up any other flavours floating around. Store eggs sharp end down as this helps keep the yolks centred and preserves the air cell at the blunt end. If you are making meringues and have whole egg yolks left over, submerge them refrigerated in cold water and they will keep for a couple of days. Leftover egg whites will store in an airtight container refrigerated for up to a week.

## Some Useful Facts about Eggs

• I find the easiest way to separate whites from yolks is to break the whole egg into a bowl and carefully lift out the egg yolks with my hand; a fresh yolk is a very sturdy product.

• Egg whites will beat more easily when they are at room temperature.

• Egg whites beat better in a clean copper bowl.

• Egg whites won't beat properly if your bowl is slightly dirty or greasy. Wipe a slice of lemon over the bowl to remove every last trace of grease. Ensure there is no trace of egg yolk in the whites before beating.

• When boiling eggs, bring them to room temperature before cooking to avoid cracking. Times to cook when gently put into boiling water: 3½ minutes – very soft yolks, slightly soft egg whites; 4 minutes – hard whites, still runny yolks; 6 minutes for just set yolks (*mollet*). Hard-boiled are best put into cold water, brought to the boil and cooked for 7 minutes; drain and run under cold water until easy to handle. Tap the shell all over then roll the eggs over a hard surface to make peeling easier.

• To fry eggs, break eggs into barely hot, melted butter in a non-stick frying pan. Gradually increase the temperature and baste the yolk with melted butter. The bottom of the egg should not be brown or crispy. Some people deep-fry eggs where the whites enclose the yolk when slipped into deep hot oil and become puffy and crisp. The choice is yours, but I'm not a great fan of the deep-fried variety.

• To scramble eggs, I prefer to use the English method where the egg is lightly broken up with a fork rather than using the metal whisk popular with the French. Slip 3 beaten eggs per person into 30g (1¼ oz) of foaming butter. With a wooden spoon continually draw in the sides, producing creamy curds. Remove before the eggs totally set as they will continue to cook in the residual heat of the pan. The French whisk continuously during the cooking process, creating an egg purée.

• For some reason poaching eggs scares even the best cooks; follow these rules and, depending on the freshness of the eggs, you will have no problems. Fill a deep pan with water and bring to the boil; the water should be at least 12cm (4½ in) deep. Add 1½ tablespoons of white wine vinegar for every 1 litre (1¾ pints) of water. Crack each egg into a coffee cup (this will prevent the whites becoming straggly) and slide the egg into the water at the exact point where it has a rolling boil; repeat with more eggs as required. Do not salt the water as this will cause the whites to break down. Poached eggs are easily made in advance. After 3 minutes' cooking lift the eggs out with a slotted spoon and lower them into iced water. When the eggs are cold any straggly bits can be removed. When the eggs are required, reheat them in boiling salted water for 30–40 seconds.

• Shirred eggs seem to have disappeared from our diet. They are simply made by sliding eggs into 25g (1 oz) melted butter in a shallow fireproof dish. Splash the yolks with some more melted butter and place in a 180°C/350°F/Gas 4 oven for 4–5 minutes. The eggs are ready when the whites have set and the yolks have a fine film over them.

• Baked eggs or *oeufs en cocotte* are made by cracking eggs into lightly buttered, seasoned ovenproof ramekins. Place in a **bain-marie** with boiling water two-thirds the way up the sides of the ramekins. Bake in a 190°C/375°F/Gas 5 oven for 7–8 minutes. A delicious difference is to break the egg into 1 tablespoon of hot cream and dot with a little butter. Bake for 8–10 minutes in the same way.

• The omelette is another egg dish that seems to baffle people, and I've tried so many that have the texture of leather. Break up 2 or 3 eggs with a fork to mix the yolks and whites; don't over-beat or the eggs will become too liquid and the result will be a heavy omelette. Melt 25g (1 oz) butter in an omelette pan over a medium-high heat; when it foams pour in the eggs. Tip the eggs to coat the bottom of the pan, then draw the edges of the eggs to the centre. Work quickly and continuously, until the desired texture is reached – well-cooked but creamy in the centre. Add any filling at this point. Take the pan handle in your left hand (if right-handed) and tip the pan towards the burner. Holding the fork in the right hand fold the omelette with your fork into the shape of the curve of the omelette pan. Tip the omelette on to the plate. Ideally the omelette should not have coloured at all, but feel pleased with yourself if it is pale golden.

## Hollandaise Sauce

*This is a classic sauce that everyone should feel comfortable about making.*
• *In a small saucepan combine 1 tablespoon white wine vinegar with 1 tablespoon water and **reduce** to 1 teaspoon. Cool, then add 3 egg yolks beaten with 2 tablespoons water.*
• *Stir with a whisk over a low heat, beating continuously. If you are not an experienced cook use a **double-boiler** or a bowl set over, but not touching, barely simmering water. Once cooked, your egg yolks should be smooth and velvety rather than granular.*
• *When the eggs have reached the right texture, little by little start incorporating the butter (225g/8 oz), cut in tiny pieces or melted. (If melted, the butter should not be hot, but just warm, and the whipping should be done off the heat.)*
• *Whisk vigorously while adding the butter. If it gets too thick add a few drops of warm water. Correct seasonings and keep warm, but not hot as the sauce will split. If it does split, add the sauce little by little to 1 tablespoon warm water.*
• *Some cooks prefer to substitute lemon juice for vinegar.*

# Egg, Bacon and Parmesan Hollandaise

For the classic hollandaise, see page 113. This version is deliciously different, a great topping for Eggs Benedict or Florentine (see page 117), or as a sauce to fold into pasta for a different *carbonara*.

**Preparation and cooking: 35 minutes**
**Serves: 2–4**

115g (4 oz) unsalted butter

115g (4 oz) fatty *pancetta* or smoked streaky bacon, cut into **lardons**

4 large free-range egg yolks

1 tablespoon lemon juice

2 hard-boiled eggs, peeled and chopped

2 tablespoons chopped flat-leaf parsley

1 tablespoon snipped chives

3 tablespoons grated Parmesan

salt and ground black pepper

**1** In a heavy frying pan over a low heat melt the butter. Add the *pancetta* and cook slowly for about 15–20 minutes until the bacon releases its fats and the meat becomes slightly crispy. Drain the fat and set aside apart from the meat.

**2** Combine the egg yolks with the lemon juice in a double boiler or a bowl over, but not touching, simmering water. Beat with a whisk until the yolks thicken. Remove from the heat.

**3** Add the bacon fat and butter drop by drop to the egg mix, whisking continually. Keep adding more until all is incorporated and emulsified.

**4** Add the crispy bacon meat, the hard-boiled eggs, parsley, chives, Parmesan and seasoning. Keep warm until ready to use.

• • • • • • • • • • • • • • • •

*Grill some large field mushrooms with butter and salt and pepper. Top with peeled 5-minute-boiled eggs then coat with a sauce made by puréeing slow-cooked white onions and folding them into a creamy Béchamel Sauce (see page 60).*

• • • • • • • • • • • • • • • •

# Butter-crumbed Eggs with Ham

I don't recall who taught me this dish, but I now cook it on a regular basis as a way of making a poached egg more exciting. The trick is to *under*-poach the eggs, then handle them with kid gloves. These are great with asparagus and crispy bacon.

**Preparation and cooking: 15 minutes**
**Serves: 2**

3 tablespoons malt vinegar

4 very fresh large eggs

2 eggs, beaten

75g (2¾ oz) fresh breadcrumbs

25g (1 oz) unsalted butter

2 thick slices boiled ham

½ bag cleaned watercress

2 plum tomatoes, quartered

**1** Fill a medium-sized saucepan with water, leaving 2.5cm (1 in) at the top. The water should be quite deep. Bring to the boil and add the vinegar.

**2** Break the 4 eggs into 4 egg cups or 4 small coffee cups; this stops a lot of the eggy straggle that occurs if you break the eggs directly into the water. Pour the eggs separately into the roll of the boil. Cook for 2 minutes.

**3** Remove the eggs with a slotted spoon and plunge straight into iced or cold water. This arrests the cooking. You can prepare ahead to this stage.

**4** This is where you must don the kid gloves. Drain the eggs and dry on kitchen paper. Dip each of them in the beaten egg and then roll gently in the breadcrumbs.

**5** Heat the butter in a non-stick frying pan until foaming, then slide the eggs into the pan and fry on all sides until golden. The secret is to start with very soft poached eggs, so they don't overcook during the second process.

**6** Place a slice of ham on each plate, garnish with watercress sprigs and the quartered tomato, and top with 2 butter-crumbed eggs.

# Curly Herby '*Frittata*' Ⓥ

Most of us think of the *frittata* as akin to a Spanish omelette or *tortilla*, but this version is more like a pancake.

**Preparation and cooking: 25–30 minutes**

**Serves: 4**

100g (3½ oz) spinach leaves, stalks removed

handful of torn rocket leaves

handful of flat-leaf parsley leaves

8 large free-range eggs

salt and ground black pepper

butter for frying

4 tablespoons fresh double cream

4 tablespoons grated Parmesan

**1** Boil the spinach, rocket and parsley leaves in 1cm (½ in) water until tender. Drain and refresh under cold water. Squeeze dry, place in a food processor, and blend until smooth.

**2** Beat the eggs with salt and pepper to taste, then pour into the food processor with the spinach. Blend until smooth and a uniform green.

**3** Brush a non-stick pan with a little melted butter, and set over a medium heat. Pour in a little of the egg mix and swirl in the pan, coating the bottom as you would for a pancake. Cook for about 45 seconds, then turn over and cook for a further 10 seconds. The *frittata* should be paper thin.

**4** Remove this one from the pan and repeat until you have finished the mix. Depending on your cooking skills, you should produce 6–8 *frittatas*.

**5** Roll up the *frittatas* and cut into 1cm (½ in) strips that resemble green pasta.

**6** Pan-fry the *frittata* strips in a little more butter, then add the cream, Parmesan and some seasoning. Toss to combine. Serve with a tomato salad as a starter or as an accompaniment to a piece of grilled meat or fish.

# Spiced Pickled Eggs Ⓥ

I've tried the pickled eggs you buy in every fish and chip shop, but I can't get my head round them. These ones are mildly curried and are delicious with cold meats and home-made *Mayonnaise* (see page 239).

**Cooking and marination: 10 minutes + 1 week**

**Serves: 4–6**

600ml (1 pint) cider vinegar

2 dried red chillies, chopped

6 green cardamom pods, slightly crushed

2 tablespoons coriander seeds

½ teaspoon celery seeds

½ teaspoon yellow mustard seeds

1 teaspoon mild curry powder

4 cloves

½ teaspoon powdered turmeric

6 cloves garlic, lightly crushed

½ teaspoon sea salt

1 medium onion, sliced into rings

12 free-range eggs, hard-boiled and peeled

**1** In a **non-reactive** saucepan combine all the ingredients except the onion and eggs. Bring to the boil and simmer for 7 minutes. Allow to cool.

**2** Layer the onion rings and eggs in a large, clean glass jar. Strain the vinegar on to the eggs to cover completely. Top up with extra vinegar if necessary. Seal and allow to marinate for at least a week before eating.

# Favourite Omelette Fillings

● *Fried bacon pieces; sorrel cooked down to a purée with a little butter; onions cooked with herbs until soft and golden brown; cooked buttered asparagus tips; chicken livers fried pink with mushrooms and a touch of balsamic vinegar; pan-fried potatoes and onions.*

● *When feeling flash, I like to make an omelette made with eggs that have been sharing a basket with white truffles (or black if you're skimping on the budget). I chop up a medium-sized truffle, gently cook it in the 25g (1 oz) butter and then pour on the truffle-infused beaten eggs.*

# Pavlova

For the benefit of those who have never married an Australian, pavlova is different from a meringue – same idea but different texture. While a meringue should be brittle throughout, a 'pav' should be marshmallowy in the middle and crispy on the outside.

**Preparation and cooking: 2 hours**
**Serves: 4–6**

| |
|---|
| 5 large egg whites, at room temperature |
| pinch of salt |
| 250g (9 oz) caster sugar |
| 2 teaspoons cornflour |
| pinch of cream of tartar |
| 1 teaspoon white wine vinegar |
| 4 drops vanilla essence |

**To serve**

| |
|---|
| 300ml (½ pint) double cream, firmly whipped |
| pulp of 12 passionfruits |

**1** Preheat the oven to 180°C/350°F/Gas 4. Line a baking tray with greaseproof paper or a new product called 'Lift-off' which serves the same purpose but is re-usable. Draw a 20cm (8 in) circle on the paper.
**2** Beat the egg whites with the salt and half the sugar in a clean bowl until soft peaks form.
**3** Continue beating, while adding the remaining sugar, until stiff and shiny. Sprinkle over the cornflour, cream of tartar, vinegar and vanilla essence and fold in gently.
**4** Mould the egg white mix on to the paper within the circle. Flatten the top and smooth the sides.
**5** Place in the oven and immediately reduce the heat to 150°C/300°F/Gas 2 and cook for 1¼ hours. Turn off the oven, leave the door slightly ajar and allow to cool completely.
**6** Invert the 'pav' on to a plate, pile on the whipped cream and dress with the passionfruit pulp.

# Burnt Butter *Sabayon*

*Sabayon, zabaglione* – different language, similar dish. This version is interesting in that it is cold and can be served on its own as a sort of 'fool', or spread over red fruits or tropical fruits, sprinkled with caster sugar, then glazed under a hot grill.

**Preparation and cooking: 30 minutes**
**Makes: 450ml (16 fl oz), to serve 4–6**

| |
|---|
| 300ml (½ pint) fresh orange juice |
| 600ml (1 pint) sweet white wine |
| 5 egg yolks |
| juice of 1 orange |
| 3 tablespoons caster sugar |
| 55g (2 oz) unsalted butter |
| 300ml (½ pint) double cream |

**1** Combine the orange juice and wine in a saucepan and bring to the boil over a high heat. **Reduce** to about 3 tablespoons. The reduction should be thick and syrupy. Set aside to cool.
**2** Whisk the egg yolks with the juice of 1 orange and the sugar over a **bain-marie** until they are thick and foamy. Remove from the heat and whisk in the reduced juice and wine.
**3** In a small pan heat the butter carefully until it is brown, and add it to the egg yolk sauce. Whisk the sauce over ice until it has cooled. (You must whisk continuously otherwise there is a danger the sauce will split.)
**4** In a separate bowl whisk the cream until stiff, then fold it into the cooled sauce. It will keep in the fridge for a day or so.

• • • • • • • • • • • • • •

*Cut a beefsteak tomato in two, extract and discard seeds and core, and fry the tomato halves in butter on both sides. Turn cut side up, sprinkle with chives and a little* Pesto *(see page 210), break an egg into the cavity and bake in a 180°C/350°F/ Gas 4 oven for 8 minutes. Pour a little nut-brown butter over each egg and serve.*

• • • • • • • • • • • • • •

*Eggs Benedict and Eggs Florentine are two of my favourite brunch egg dishes. The first is made by placing grilled Canadian bacon or ham on halves of a toasted English muffin and then topping each with a poached egg which is coated with hollandaise sauce (see page 113). The second involves spreading cooked buttered spinach on the base of a gratin dish, topping it with very soft poached eggs, a cheese sauce, a sprinkling of Parmesan mixed with breadcrumbs, and a few drops of melted butter; grill or brown this in the oven.*

# FENNEL

Fennel is one of those vegetables that you either love or hate. It took me a long time to like it, but I think many youngsters have an initial aversion to liquorice or aniseed flavours. The name fennel covers the herb, the bulb and the spice. Fennel herb, *Foeniculum vulgare*, is an umbellifer, like dill and parsley; it produces the leaves and the seeds (the spice). The seeds, fronds and dried stalks of fennel herb are used regularly in fish cookery. And in Greece even the roots are boiled and dressed with olive oil and lemon juice.

The bulb fennel, *Foeniculum vulgare*, var. *dulce*, is grown for its leaf base stalks (like celery and angelica). It is sometimes called Florence fennel to set it apart from the herb, a name relating to the country in which it was developed. The leaves of bulb fennel are similar to fennel herb.

When buying Florence fennel, try to buy it with some of the stalks still attached, as you can tell how fresh it is from the fronds. Test for freshness by pressing the bulb, it should resist any pressure; ignore any that are soft or browning. I have even seen some that are wet and slimy, so beware.

In preparation cut any stalk down to the main bulb, trim the root end and you will almost certainly need to remove the outer leaves as they are usually very stringy. The bulb is either quartered, halved or finely sliced. I prefer to eat fennel that has been braised until very soft. You either need the wonderful crunch of raw fennel or a vegetable that has been thoroughly cooked.

Fennel is high in potassium, and 250g contains a mere 60 calories, probably because it consists of 95 per cent water!

# Slow-cooked Fennel with Tomatoes, Olives and Parmesan ⓥ

This dish is good as an accompaniment for grilled fish or served as part of an antipasti buffet.

**Preparation and cooking: 2 hours**
**Serves: 4–6**

| |
|---|
| 4 fennel bulbs, tough outside leaves removed |
| 175ml (6 fl oz) extra virgin olive oil |
| 1 head garlic, split into cloves, peeled |
| 2 tablespoons chopped soft oregano leaves |
| 125ml (4 fl oz) dry white wine |
| 1 x 400g (14 oz) tin good chopped tomatoes |
| 300ml (½ pint) water, boiling |
| salt and ground black pepper |
| 2 tablespoons balsamic vinegar |
| 55g (2 oz) Parmesan, grated |
| 12 basil leaves, ripped |
| 24 black olives, stoned and roughly chopped |

**1** Quarter the fennel lengthways then cook in the olive oil over a medium heat for 20 minutes until starting to brown.

**2** Add the garlic, oregano, wine, tomatoes and boiling water. Cook over a very low heat for 1½ hours. If there is still a lot of liquid, cook on a fast heat until very little water remains and the sauce has thickened. Season with salt, black pepper and balsamic vinegar.

**3** Finish with grated Parmesan, the basil and chopped black olives.

• • • • • • • • • • • • • • • • • • • •

*Create a paste for spreading over fish prior to grilling by blending together ½ chopped fennel bulb, 3 cloves garlic, 2 chillies, 3 tablespoons chopped parsley, 1 teaspoon anchovy essence, 2 teaspoons mixed orange and lemon rind, 4 tablespoons extra virgin olive oil and 1 teaspoon sherry vinegar.*

• • • • • • • • • • • • • • • • • • • •

*Cut fennel lengthways in 5mm (¼ in) slices leaving the root attached. Cook in boiling salted water for 10 minutes, drain and pat dry. Dip the fennel slices in seasoned flour, then into egg, then into a Parmesan/breadcrumb mix. Deep-fry until golden on both sides.*

• • • • • • • • • • • • • • • • • • • •

# Fennel and Bacon Soup

Like garlic, fennel tones down considerably when cooked, becoming much more delicate in flavour. Fennel and bacon go really well together, and this soup is delicious hot or cold.

**Preparation and cooking: 1½ hours**
**Serves: 4**

| | |
|---|---|
| 175g (6 oz) smoked streaky bacon, diced |
| 2 tablespoons extra virgin olive oil |
| 1 bulb fennel, trimmed and finely chopped |
| 25g (1 oz) unsalted butter |
| 2 onions, finely sliced |
| 2 cloves garlic, finely chopped |
| 1 potato, cubed |
| ½ teaspoon soft thyme leaves |
| 1 bay leaf |
| 850ml (1½ pints) vegetable or chicken stock |
| 2 tablespoons Pernod or Ricard (optional) |
| 150ml (¼ pint) double cream |
| salt and ground white pepper |

**1** In a heavy saucepan cook the bacon over a medium heat with 1 tablespoon of the olive oil until the bacon is crisp and has released its fats. Remove the bacon and set aside.
**2** Add the fennel, butter and remaining oil to the same saucepan, then stir to combine. Add the onion and garlic and cook over a medium heat for 15 minutes until the vegetables have softened without colour.
**3** Add the potato, thyme and bay leaf and cook until the potato starts to stick to the bottom of the pan. Add the stock and simmer gently until the fennel is tender, about 30 minutes.
**4** Purée the soup in batches in a blender and pass through a fine sieve to remove any tough fibres.
**5** Return the soup to the saucepan, add the Pernod and cream, and season to taste. Sprinkle the bacon over the soup when serving. (If serving the soup cold, omit the butter.)

* * * * * * * * * * * * * * * *

*A fennel mash for fish, pork or veal is made by boiling together 2 chopped fennel bulbs, 2 chopped sticks of celery and 2 chopped peeled potatoes in chicken stock. Purée in a food processor or pass through a* **mouli-légumes***. Return to a saucepan and season with Pernod, butter and cream.*

* * * * * * * * * * * * * * * *

## Caesar Fennel
● *Finely shred a fennel bulb (a* **mandoline** *or meat slicer is best), and serve raw combined with 2 tablespoons snipped chives, 1 raw egg yolk, 1 chopped anchovy, 2 tablespoons extra virgin olive oil and juice of ½ lemon.*
● *Fold in 3 tablespoons freshly grated Parmesan.*

## Raw Fennel *Salsa*
● *Combine a finely diced fennel bulb with 2 diced tomatoes, 2 teaspoons chopped capers, 2 teaspoons chopped black olives, 3 finely sliced spring onions, 2 tablespoons chopped flat-leaf parsley, 1 tablespoon snipped fennel herb and 4 tablespoons extra virgin olive oil.*
● *Season to taste and serve with grilled fish.*

## *Gravadlax*
Gravadlax *is traditionally a dill-cured salmon, but try this variation.*
● *Take 2 even-sized fillets of salmon.*
● *Make a seasoning paste by combining 2 tablespoons ouzo, 2 tablespoons fresh lemon juice, 8 tablespoons sea salt, 4 tablespoons caster sugar, 2 tablespoons fennel seeds, 85g (3 oz) crushed white peppercorns and 6 tablespoons chopped fennel herb (or dill).*
● *Spread the paste over the fish fillet, sandwich with the other fillet and spread the remainder over the top.*
● *Wrap in clingfilm and weigh down.*
● *Turn the fish every 12 hours for 48 hours.*
● *Unwrap, wipe away the paste, and slice the fish thinly at an angle. Dribble with extra virgin olive oil.*

# FISH: CEPHALOPODS

Cephalopod is the generic term for advanced marine molluscs without a shell, and the family includes squid, cuttlefish and octopus. In recent years cephalopods, squid especially, have taken off as major culinary hits. Gone are the squid or octopus dishes of the rubber-band variety, deep-fried in flour or batter; now we can't eat enough stuffed squid, octopus salad, or risotto cooked with squid or cuttlefish ink.

Squid, cuttlefish and tenderised octopus all need a minuscule amount of cooking – 1–5 minutes – or a lengthy time – 1–2 hours. There is no in-between, as this will make them very tough, something many squid haters will probably have experienced.

## SQUID

Squid come in various sizes, and have two long tentacles, a tube-like body, eight arms, two fins and an ink sac. They also contain a transparent, plastic-looking quill (bone) which is removed with the guts and eyes – everything else is edible. Squid range in colour in their raw state from pink to brown to greyish purple.

To clean, grab the head and tentacles and give a sharp yank to detach them from the body. Cut the tentacles just in front of the eyes and discard the remainder unless you want to use the ink sac which is a clearly visible dark bulge. Place the sac in a small bowl and set aside until you want to use. Rinse the tentacles. Pull the fins off the tube body and remove the purplish black skin or membrane; remove the same from the tube. Pull the transparent quill from the tube and discard. Push the pointed end of the tube in on itself with one of your fingers, then place the indent over a clean broom handle or the handle of a large wooden spoon and push down so the tube turns itself inside out. Clean off any internal remains. Rinse all parts in cold water, but do not allow to soak as squid absorbs a great deal of liquid and will make grilling or frying difficult.

## CUTTLEFISH

Like squid, cuttlefish have two tentacles and eight arms. The 'bone' in the middle is what you see on beaches and in budgies' cages! Cuttlefish are less fine to eat than squid, but good nonetheless. To prepare them, cut off the tentacles in front of the eyes and remove the beak-like mouth from the tentacles. Cut open the body and remove the cuttlebone. Slip your fingers under the membrane, detach it and throw it away. You will now have exposed the guts and the ink sac. Retain ink sac if required and discard the guts. Rinse the body and tentacles and strip off the coloured membrane. Rinse again, dry, and set aside until ready for use.

## OCTOPUS

Unlike their relatives, octopus do not have any form of bone at all and, unless pre-tenderised by your fishmonger, can be very tough. Greek fishermen usually bash them 40 to 50 times against the sides of rocks, but at home you'll need a meat mallet. If sufficiently tenderised, octopus can be grilled in much the same way as squid or cuttlefish, otherwise it will need to be stewed for a very long time. Cut the tentacles away from the head below the hard central beak. Cut away the beak and the anal parts, turn the body inside out and remove any guts. Pull off the strips sticking to the side of the body. Strip away the skin if you are going to grill. Some cooks cut the suckers and tips from each of the tentacles, but I have not found that necessary.

## Char-grilled Squid

- *Slit each squid body along one side and with a sharp knife score the inside with a tiny criss-cross hatched effect by cutting diagonally in two directions.*
- *Marinate in olive oil, chilli, garlic and chopped oregano.*
- *Char-grill on both sides for 45 seconds on a very hot grill.*
- *Serve with a Salsa Verde (see page 215), dressed rocket leaves and frites.*

*Follow the same cutting procedure as for char-grilled squid. Rub dark soft brown sugar into the cuts and cut the body into 6 pieces. Dress with soy sauce and olive oil and grill for the same amount of time. Serve with spring onions and stir-fried pak-choi*

*A quick stir-fry. Cut squid in bite-sized portions. Pan-fry chopped garlic in olive oil, add squid and fry over a fast heat for 30 seconds. Add lemon juice, 2 chopped tomatoes, some chopped olives, some wine-soaked raisins, a handful of washed spinach and some toasted pine kernels, and cook until the spinach has wilted. Season to taste.*

121

# Squid Stuffed with Oriental Pork and Prawns

A delicious stuffing that normally fills *dim sum* wrappers, but which I find works even better for squid.

**Preparation and cooking: 1½ hours**
**Serves: 6**

| | |
|---|---|
| 6 medium-sized squid, cleaned, tentacles reserved | |
| 2 tablespoons olive oil | |
| 1 onion, finely chopped | |
| 3 cloves garlic, finely chopped | |
| 2 fresh red chillies, finely chopped | |
| 375ml (13 fl oz) dry white wine | |
| 1 x 400g (14 oz) tin chopped tomatoes | |
| 3 tablespoons chopped coriander | |
| salt and ground black pepper | |

**Stuffing**

the squid tentacles, finely chopped
225g (8 oz) shelled raw prawns, finely chopped
175g (6 oz) minced pork
4 tablespoons chopped bamboo shoots
6 tablespoons finely chopped spring onion
2 cloves garlic, finely chopped
1 fresh red chilli, finely chopped
3 tablespoons chicken stock
1 tablespoon light soy sauce
1 teaspoon sesame oil
1 teaspoon caster sugar
½ tablespoon cornflour
8 dried Chinese wood-ear mushrooms, soaked in hot water for 1 hour, then finely chopped (discard water)

**1** For the stuffing, combine all the ingredients in a large bowl. Season with 2 teaspoons salt.

**2** Preheat the oven to 180°C/350°F/Gas 4.

**3** Push the stuffing into the squid tubes. Fill only two-thirds full, then stitch up the ends with thread or secure with wooden cocktail sticks.

**4** In a saucepan heat half the olive oil and add the onion, garlic and chilli and cook over a medium heat for 5 minutes. Add the white wine and tomatoes, increase the heat and bring to the boil. Fold in the coriander and season to taste.

**5** Meanwhile, as the sauce cooks, heat the remaining olive oil in a frying pan and seal the stuffed squid tubes on all sides for 2 minutes.

**6** Place the squid in a shallow casserole dish in one layer and pour over the sauce. Bake in the oven for 45–60 minutes, or until the squid can easily be pierced with a fork. Serve with rice.

## Deep-fried Squid

● *For the classic deep-fried squid, marinate squid rings and tentacles in half cream and half milk for 3 hours, preferably overnight.*

● *Drain and massage the squid with seasoned flour which includes celery salt, cayenne pepper, black pepper and garlic powder.*

● *Deep-fry until golden, and serve with lemon wedges.*

## Roast Squid

*A delicious way of using up your tentacles.*

● *Preheat the oven to 230°C/450°F/Gas 8.*

● *Marinate squid or octopus with chopped rosemary, garlic, chilli, salt and pepper.*

● *Roast in the oven for about 25 minutes or until tender, basting regularly with the juices.*

● *Garnish with chopped flat-leaf parsley and lemon wedges.*

# Greek Octopus Stew

Go on, be brave, find yourself an octopus in a specialist fishmonger, and have it prepared for you. You'll enjoy this satisfying fish stew with a leaf salad and chunks of crusty bread.

**Preparation and cooking: up to 5 hours**
**Serves: 6**

1kg (2¼ lb) octopus, cleaned
3 tablespoons olive oil
3 large Spanish onions, roughly chopped
6 cloves garlic, finely chopped
2 bay leaves
1 teaspoon chopped oregano
1 cinnamon stick
4 cloves
1 tablespoon tomato purée
1 tablespoon anchovy essence
salt and ground black pepper
175ml (6 fl oz) dry red wine
90ml (3 fl oz) Punt e Mes
3 tablespoons extra virgin olive oil

1   Put the octopus in a saucepan and cover with water. Bring to the boil and simmer for 30 minutes. Drain and wash thoroughly in cold water.

2   Cut the octopus into small pieces and set aside.

3   In a saucepan warm the olive oil over a medium heat, then add the onion, garlic, bay leaves and oregano and cook for 10 minutes. Add the octopus, cinnamon, cloves, tomato purée, anchovy essence, season with 6 turns of black pepper, and stir to combine. Add enough water to cover, then the red wine and Punt e Mes. Bring to the boil.

4   Reduce the heat until the stew is barely simmering. Add the extra virgin olive oil and cook for 3–4 hours, covered, until most of the liquid has evaporated and the octopus is tender. Season to taste.

# Squid, Olive and Celery Salad

One of the most refreshing seafood salads I have tasted. A big seller at Woz, my London restaurant.

**Preparation and cooking: 1¼ hours**
**Serves: 6–8**

900g (2 lb) squid, cleaned
100ml (3½ fl oz) extra virgin olive oil
3 tablespoons red wine vinegar
1 garlic clove, finely chopped
½ teaspoon dried oregano
½ teaspoon salt
¼ teaspoon crushed hot chilli flakes
2 tender sticks celery, thinly sliced
85g (3 oz) pitted green olives, sliced
2 tablespoons chopped flat-leaf parsley
ground black pepper

1   Cut the squid sacs into 1cm (½ in) rings. Cut the tentacles in half through the base.

2   Bring a large saucepan of water to a boil over high heat. Add the squid and cook just until opaque, about 1 minute. Drain and rinse under cold running water.

3   In a large bowl, whisk together the oil, vinegar, garlic, oregano, salt and chilli. Stir in the squid, celery, olives and parsley. Cover and chill for 1 hour or overnight.

4   Just before serving, taste and correct the seasoning.

## Vegetable and Squid Stir-fry

● *Blanch a selection of green vegetables – pak-choi, broccoli, sugar-snap peas, asparagus – in boiling salted water for 2 minutes, drain and refresh.*

● *Blanch prepared squid in the same water for 45 seconds, and set aside.*

● *Heat some sesame oil and vegetable oil in a wok with some sliced garlic, spring onions, chillies and ginger. Cook for 1 minute then add soy sauce, caster sugar, the vegetables and squid. Toss to warm through. Check seasoning.*

# FISH: FRESHWATER

Freshwater fish have become rather unfashionable. It wasn't that long ago that every restaurant menu included trout, but where has the trout gone? The question should actually be, where has the *flavour* gone? Since the introduction of farmed trout, the brown trout and true rainbow trout have disappeared from local rivers, much of it to do with the amount of pollution.

In Britain there's not much choice of freshwater fish in a culinary sense. In a nation where fishing is a major hobby it is rare to see perch, carp and roach finding their way on to our plates, and yet other European countries have recipes for all of them. If you are ever in Switzerland or France, try *omble-chevalier* which is the lake char or Arctic char, truly delicious. We are really limited to trout, salmon, crayfish, pike and eel. And it is disputable as to whether salmon is a river fish, as most of it is farmed and kept in natural tanks out at sea. Even wild salmon are often trapped at estuaries as they attempt to make their way up their home rivers to spawn.

With the demise of the fishmonger one will rarely, if ever, see eel or pike on the slab. I have seen 'golden trout' in the supermarkets, something that didn't really impress me for flavour.

Fish of any kind has to be really fresh to fully reveal its delicious flavour. Look for glossy shiny skin, bright full eyes and bright red gills. Ask your fishmonger to clean and fillet any fish for you – he's the expert, and will be delighted to do so.

## Trout in Red Pepper Blanket

Ask your fishmonger to 'spatchcock' the trout by cutting a slit through the belly and removing the back bone. The trout is then opened out to create a large flat area which is spread with a purée of roasted peppers.

**Preparation and cooking: 1 hour**
**Serves: 4**

3 roasted red peppers (see page 254), quartered, seeded and skinned

85g (3 oz) pine kernels, toasted

85g (3 oz) fresh breadcrumbs

3 cloves garlic, finely chopped

3 tablespoons extra virgin olive oil

salt and ground black pepper

olive oil for grilling

4 trout, 'spatchcocked' as above

**1** Place the peppers in the bowl of a food processor and blend until smooth.

**2** Add the pine kernels, breadcrumbs and garlic and blend again to a smooth purée. With the machine running, add the olive oil in a thin stream. Season with salt and pepper.

**3** Slash the skin of the trout. Rub the trout on the flesh side with the red pepper purée, and push some purée into the slashes as well. Refrigerate for half an hour.

**4** Heat a ridged griddle pan, large frying pan or barbie until very hot. Oil the pan.

**5** Cook the trout flesh side down for 3 minutes, then turn the fish carefully and repeat.

**6** Transfer to a serving platter and serve with buttered noodles, rice or new potatoes.

# Pickled Dill Trout

This recipe is based on the Scandinavian *gravadlax*, fish fillets marinated with sugar, salt and dill. It makes an easy starter.

**Preparation and marination: 10 minutes + overnight**
**Serves: 4**

| |
|---|
| 175g (6 oz) Maldon salt flakes |
| 175g (6 oz) caster sugar |
| 55g (2 oz) white peppercorns, crushed |
| 6 tablespoons chopped dill |
| 2 tablespoons vodka |
| 1 x 1kg (2¼ lb) sea trout, filleted |

**1** Mix together the salt, sugar, crushed peppercorns, dill and vodka. Lay a third of this mixture on the bottom of a shallow ceramic dish. Place 1 fillet on top of the marinade, skin-side down.

**2** Place another third of the marinade over the trout flesh. Place the other fillet, flesh-side down on top, and cover with the remaining marinade. Cover with clingfilm and weigh down with a heavy weight. Allow to marinate for 36 hours, turning the trout over every 12 hours.

**3** Scrape off the marinade, remove the skin, and serve a half fillet per person with brown bread and a dill and mustard sauce (see page 213).

# Pickled Trout

Someone in the nineteenth century obviously thought trout didn't have great flavour either, because I found this recipe for pickled trout and it tastes great.

**Preparation and cooking: 20 minutes + overnight**
**Serves: 6–8**

| |
|---|
| 1kg (2¼ lb) fillets of trout (or carp) |
| maize meal or polenta, to coat the fillets |
| olive oil |
| 6 onions, sliced |
| 25g (1 oz) turmeric |
| 2 teaspoons grated fresh ginger |
| 1 teaspoon ground coriander |
| 1 teaspoon ground cumin |
| 1 teaspoon English mustard powder |
| 3 tablespoons mango chutney, finely chopped |
| 1.2 litres (2 pints) cider vinegar |
| a sprinkling of fresh chillies |

**1** Coat the trout (or carp) fillets in maize meal (sometimes available in health-food shops) or polenta then fry in olive oil on both sides for 5 minutes. Remove from the pan.

**2** Fry the onions in oil for 10 minutes without colouring them.

**3** Combine the turmeric with the ginger, ground coriander and cumin, English mustard powder and mango chutney. Add the cider vinegar and bring to the boil, simmer for 5 minutes then cool.

**4** Lay the fish fillets in a dish, cover with half the onions, a sprinkling of fresh chillies and some of the spiced vinegar. Repeat with another layer and so on. Leave overnight.

**5** Eat cold with brown bread and warm potato salad.

# Trout *Saltimbocca*

*Saltimbocca* is a title the Italians give to a veal dish topped with sage and Parma ham. Trout takes to this method of cooking exceptionally well. Now that most of the trout we buy are farmed, the addition of the ham and sage gives it the zap it needs. Serve with buttered spinach and new potatoes.

**Preparation and cooking: 30 minutes**
**Serves: 4**

8 large slices Parma ham
150g (5½ oz) cold butter, cut in thin slices
4 large trout, skinned and filleted
10 sage leaves, 2 shredded
salt and ground black pepper
2 tablespoons olive oil
juice of 1 lemon

**1** Preheat the oven to 190°C/375°F/Gas 5.
**2** Lay the slices of Parma ham lengthways on a flat surface. Place a thin slice of butter on top of each slice (this should leave you with about 55g/2 oz butter).
**3** Top the butter and ham with the trout fillets. Place a sage leaf in the middle of each trout fillet. Season the fish with salt and ground black pepper.
**4** Roll up each fish fillet in the ham, creating a fish roll, and secure with a wooden cocktail stick.
**5** Oil a baking dish and place the 8 fish rolls in the bottom. Ensure they are not touching. Place in the oven and bake for 15 minutes.
**6** Heat a frying pan. Tip the juices from the roasting tray into the frying pan. Add the remaining butter and the 2 shredded remaining sage leaves. Cook over a high heat until the butter starts to froth and go a nutty brown. Add the lemon juice and some salt and pepper and pour over the trout. Serve immediately.

# Thai Steamed Salmon

Farmed salmon tends to be a bit bland so this recipe packs it full of flavour. Serve with new potatoes or rice and a leaf salad.

**Marination and cooking: 30 minutes**
**Serves: 4**

1 bunch coriander, washed
12 mint leaves, washed
1 teaspoon salt
3 cloves garlic, crushed
2 green chillies
3 tablespoons fresh lime juice
1 tablespoon caster sugar
1 teaspoon chopped fresh ginger
1 tablespoon *nam pla* (fish sauce)
4 x 175g (6 oz) salmon fillets

**1** In a food processor blend together the coriander leaves and stalks, the mint leaves, salt, garlic and chillies to make a paste. Add the lime juice, caster sugar, ginger and fish sauce and process until smooth.
**2** Spoon the sauce into a bowl and combine with the salmon. Marinate for 20 minutes.
**3** Boil water in the bottom half of a steamer. Place the bowl with the marinated salmon in the top half, and steam for 6–8 minutes. Serve immediately.

## Poached Salmon

*Simple poached salmon is a delight but too often when you encounter it at a wedding or in a restaurant, it is overcooked.*

- *Place a 2.5–3kg (5½–6½ lb) salmon in a pot of cold water, just enough to cover, add 4 tablespoons sea salt, bring to the boil, reduce heat and simmer for 5 minutes.*
- *Turn off the heat and allow the salmon to cool in the water.*
- *If you are eating it hot, take the salmon out after 20 minutes.*
- *Many chefs will throw in the whole garden when poaching, but I prefer the clean taste of the fish and the sea, so only add salt.*

# Salad of Salmon and Jersey Royals

Salmon is very cheap nowadays because the majority is farmed, so I have selected this dish as a quickie you can knock up for supper or brunch. Farmed salmon is a good product, but think of it as you would cod, no longer an indulgence (such as *wild* salmon), more a way of life.

**Preparation and cooking: 1 hour**
**Serves: 4**

| |
|---|
| 55g (2 oz) Maldon sea salt |
| 55g (2 oz) caster sugar |
| 1 tablespoon lemon juice |
| ½ teaspoon white peppercorns, crushed |
| 450g (1 lb) salmon fillet, cut into 8 x 1cm (½ in) slices, skinned |
| 450g (1 lb) Jersey Royal new potatoes, washed, scraped and halved |
| 225g (8 oz) smoked streaky bacon, rindless |
| 4 tablespoons extra virgin olive oil |
| 2 tablespoons finely chopped shallot |
| 2 tablespoons snipped chives |
| 1 tablespoon balsamic vinegar |
| sea salt and ground black pepper |
| handful of cleaned watercress |

**1** Mix together the salt, sugar, lemon juice and crushed white peppercorns. Add the salmon slices and toss to combine. Leave to rest and 'cook' for 1 hour.

**2** About 20 minutes before serving, cook the new potatoes in salted water until tender, about 12–15 minutes.

**3** At the same time, cut the bacon into 5mm (¼ in) strips and fry in a hot, dry frying pan, until the bacon crisps and releases some of its fats. Add 1 tablespoon of the olive oil and the shallot, and fry over a gentle heat until the shallot has softened, about 5 minutes.

**4** Drain the potatoes well, and add them to the bacon pan. Toss to combine, adding the chives, the remaining olive oil and the balsamic vinegar. Season to taste.

**5** Remove the salmon from the marinade, and brush off any salt mix.

**6** Divide the potatoes between four plates. Arrange the watercress around the potatoes and place two slices of salmon astride the potatoes. Dribble the remaining dressing from the potatoes over the salmon.

# Salmon and Smoked Haddock Fish Cakes

A perennial British favourite, these are served at my London restaurant, Woz, and they walk out the door. I usually serve a 225–250g (8–9 oz) cake on a bed of buttered spinach surrounded by parsley sauce. Most customers usually want chips . . . good for them.

**Preparation, chilling and cooking: 2½ hours**

**Serves: 4**

250g (9 oz) smoked haddock fillets (undyed)

250g (9 oz) salmon

600ml (1 pint) milk seasoned with a little onion and carrot, 1 bay leaf, 6 black peppercorns and 2 cloves

250g (9 oz) dry mashed potatoes

55g (2 oz) butter, melted

1 small onion, finely diced and **sweated** in butter

2 teaspoons anchovy essence

2 hard-boiled eggs, chopped

2 tablespoons chopped parsley

1 tablespoon chopped dill

salt and ground black pepper

plain flour for coating

beaten egg for dipping

fresh breadcrumbs

55g (2 oz) butter for frying

**1** Poach the haddock and salmon in the seasoned milk in a deepish pan until cooked, about 6–8 minutes, depending on the thickness of the fillet. Retain the poaching milk.

**2** Remove the fish from the milk and, when cool enough to handle, flake each fish separately, discarding any skin or bone.

**3** Combine the haddock with the mashed potato, melted butter, sweated onion and anchovy essence in a mixer with a dough hook, then fold in the salmon, hard-boiled egg, parsley and dill by hand until well combined. Do not overmix.

**4** Season to taste. If the mixture is too dry at this point, add some of the poaching milk.

**5** Divide the mixture up into 4 equal amounts, then shape into patties. Dip in the flour, egg and finally breadcrumbs. Refrigerate for 2 hours before use.

**6** Pan-fry the fish cakes in butter for 5 minutes on each side, and keep warm in the oven until you wish to serve.

## Eel Stew

*Eel can be delicious, but not jellied eels for me. Try this simple stew with mashed potatoes.*
- *Heat 3 tablespoons olive oil, add 2 finely sliced onions and 4 chopped garlic cloves, 1 teaspoon soft thyme leaves, 1 sprig rosemary and 2 bay leaves.*
- *Cook until the onions are soft but not brown.*
- *Add 300ml (½ pint) red wine and 1 tablespoon sherry vinegar.*
- *Pop in 1kg (2¼ lb) sliced eel and cook over a low heat for 20–30 minutes until tender.*
- *Season to taste and sprinkle with parsley.*

*If perchance you have leftover cooked salmon, make yourself this hash. Fry onions and sliced potatoes in butter until golden. Add flaked cooked salmon, and cook until heated through. Add cayenne, salt, chives and dill and serve with poached eggs and hollandaise sauce (see page 113).*

# FISH: SEAWATER

Fish consumption, despite advice to eat more, has been on the decline in the UK for many years. The majority of fish eaten is in the form of fish fingers or frozen fillets in sauce. It seems as though we are prepared to eat fish if it doesn't look like fish, and our biggest take-away trade is still fish and chips. I would love to lead a campaign to teach the British that given a fresh fish fillet, a little oil or butter and a squeeze of lemon, you can have a superlative meal in 8–12 minutes. Consumers must be taught that fish fillets, which have no bones, and little or no smell, are one of the simplest foods to cook.

It is amazing that in the British Isles, we are surrounded by water and yet seem to care so little for our fish. The majority of the catch around our shores is snapped up by France, Spain and Japan. Our coastal waters produce some of the finest fish in the world, and yet it appears we are captivated by anything foreign. Supermarkets constantly try and sell us the pleasures of parrot fish, swordfish, trevally and the like, and yet cold-water fish taste so much more delicious than fish from warmer waters.

Take a look at this list of our fish, and ask yourself why we should want any foreign stuff. We have cod, coley, haddock, hake, ling, whiting, herring, mackerel, pilchard, sardine, bream, grey mullet, red mullet, John Dory, monkfish, sea bass, skate, plaice, brill, dab, flounder, halibut, sole and turbot, all of them fabulous foods with so many recipe possibilities.

With the demise of local fishmongers' shops, supermarkets have taken over our fish sales, which is not necessarily a good thing. It should have been a great move forward, but they have missed out on the message they should be selling to the public: how easy fish is to cook, how versatile it is, and how it will improve your health. Instead we are often faced with a load of lifeless fish, with dry skins and dull eyes, which smell a little suspect. Too often the only message displayed is 'This product has previously been frozen'.

When buying fresh fish, the key word must be 'fresh'. To tell whether a fish is fresh, *smell* it: a fresh fish shouldn't really smell, whereas older fish will be slightly ammoniacal. The eyes should be clear, the skin shiny and taut. The eyes should be slightly protruding rather than sunken. If you get a chance to look at the gills, they should be pinky-red rather than brown. When possible, buy fish on the day you want to eat it.

Never buy fish then place it in the boot of the car and go off for a long lunch unless you possess an insulated chill bag.

As far as filleting, gutting and cleaning, I could write about it, but to do it well needs time and practice. My best advice would be to use your fishmonger; as I said before, he's the expert.

Not all fish can be cooked by all methods, as different fish suit different cooking.

## Steaming

Buy yourself a stainless-steel steamer or a bamboo basket that will fit over one of your saucepans (these are available in Chinese supermarkets). Normally the fish is placed on an oiled plate which stops the fish sticking. Steaming is a fast method of cooking, think of about 5 minutes per 2.5cm (1 in) thickness of fish. Steaming doesn't have to be boring, as all sorts of flavours can be added to the fish, especially Oriental ones such as ginger, garlic, chilli, soy and coriander.

## Grilling

You could buy yourself a hinged fish basket which allows you to turn the fish on a barbecue without damaging it. This is suitable for oily fish, especially if you're using a barbecue. Grill with the skin on as quite often the fish can fall apart, especially the more flaky fish such as cod. Ridged griddle pans work very well as a grill substitute. If using an overhead grill make sure you turn on the grill well in advance as you want a fairly fierce heat to give the fish that wonderful crusty look. Lightly oil the fish before cooking. You can flavour the oil with garlic, chilli or herbs. Grill fish for 3–5 minutes each side, depending on the thickness of the fish.

## Roasting

An excellent method of cooking for whole fish or cutlets on the bone. Rub the fish with salt and pepper, and you can fill the cavity with herbs, onions or lemon. Place a film of olive oil in a baking dish, make a couple of slashes in the deepest part of the fish, about 5mm (¼ in) deep. Pour a glass of white wine or vermouth into the bottom of the baking dish, and cook in a 180°C/350°F/Gas 4 oven, for about 20–25 minutes per kg (2¼ lb). Baste the fish from time to time with the cooking juices. Various vegetables and flavourings can be added to the fish if required (see *Roast Cod with Anchovy and Garlic,* page 132).

## Poaching

An excellent method of cooking fish you want to eat cold. I explain how to poach salmon in Freshwater Fish, where I just use salt, but you can add other flavourings. Generally larger fish start cooking in cold water and smaller fish or fillets in simmering water. For eating cold, follow the salmon method of allowing fish to cool in the water; it will produce a much moister texture. For serving hot, simmer the fish for 20 minutes for every 2.5cm (1 in) of thickness, then remove the fish immediately and drain well. Season after cooking.

## Deep-frying

The most popular method of cooking fish in Britain. Cod or haddock are my favourite. To make a good batter, whisk together 15g (½ oz) fresh yeast with 3 tablespoons from a 330ml bottle of lager to make a smooth cream, then stir in the remainder of the lager. Place 175g (6 oz) plain flour in a bowl with 2 teaspoons salt, make a well in the flour and add the lager/yeast mix slowly, whisking constantly until smooth. Allow to rest in a warm place for at least 1 hour. Use plenty of oil for cooking – vegetable, sunflower or groundnut – at 170°C/340°F. If using a domestic deep-fryer, remove the basket otherwise you may find the batter sticks to the holes in the basket. Cook until golden, holding the fish under the hot oil with tongs. Lift out, drain on kitchen paper and keep warm in a low oven, while cooking more fish or the chips.

## Pan-frying

*Sole meunière*, sole pan-fried in butter with lemon and parsley, used to be a 1960s and 1970s classic. Pan-frying is a quick and flavoursome way of cooking fish, especially fillets, as you get an immediate hit of searing heat, creating a light crust to seal in the fish's natural juices. Use a heavy-based non-stick pan, good quality unsalted butter, perhaps mixed with a little olive oil to raise the burning temperature. Heat the butter to foaming point, add the fish, floured or not as you prefer, then seal presentation side down for 4 minutes, then turn and cook for a further 2–3 minutes. If you want to serve the fish with lemon butter, remove from the pan and tip away the cooking fat; wipe the pan with kitchen paper and add further butter, and cook it until turning nutty brown. Add lemon juice and parsley and pour over the fish.

## Marinated Sardines

*Sardines are a great cheap fish, and a source of lots of healthy and natural oils. Here is an unusual recipe that makes a delicious starter.*
- *Make a marinade by bringing a bottle of red wine to the boil with 150ml (¼ pint) red wine vinegar, 2 sliced onions, 2 sliced carrots, 2 bay leaves, a few peppercorns, a sprig of thyme and 1 sliced clove garlic, and then simmering until reduced by one-third.*
- *Allow to cool, then immerse 16 cleaned sardines in the marinade overnight.*
- *Place the pan on top of the hob, sprinkle with lemon juice, bring to the boil and cook for 1 minute.*
- *Remove the sardines and set aside. Boil the marinade to reduce by half, pour it over the sardines, and allow to cool.*

## Skate with Black Butter

*Skate is a delicious fish that is under-used. I love the classic skate with black butter.*
- *Get your fishmonger to skin the wings. Place them in salty water and bring to the boil, simmer for 10 minutes, remove and keep warm.*
- *In a frying pan heat unsalted butter to a nutty colour, then add capers, lemon juice and parsley.*
- *Pour the butter over the skate, then **deglaze** the pan with 2 tablespoons of wine vinegar, boil and pour over the skate as well.*

## Fried Herring Roes

- *Fry ½ finely diced onion in 55g (2 oz) unsalted butter with 3 chopped anchovy fillets until the onion is soft and the anchovies have broken down.*
- *Fold in 1 tablespoon anchovy essence and ½ teaspoon soft thyme leaves.*
- *Add 250g (9 oz) soft herring roes and fry for 3 minutes on each side. Remove the roes and set aside.*
- *To the pan, add 300ml (½ pint) each of fish stock and double cream. Boil and reduce by one-third.*
- *Return the roes, warm through, and serve on grilled bread.*

# Roast Cod with Anchovy and Garlic

Cod is an excellent fish, which can take on many guises. In this dish I have been heavily influenced by Spanish cooking, although the Spanish would probably use hake. The end result is a delicious herby stew, which could be partnered by rice or boiled potatoes.

**Preparation and cooking: 30 minutes**
**Serves: 4**

175ml (6 fl oz) extra virgin olive oil
4 cloves garlic, crushed with a little salt
1kg (2¼ lb) cod fillet, cut into 5cm (2 in) cubes
4 tablespoons chopped parsley
1 tablespoon chopped capers
1 tablespoon chopped anchovies
2 fresh green chillies, finely chopped
1 tablespoon lemon juice
salt and ground black pepper

**1** Heat the oil in a deep frying pan, add the garlic and cook over a moderate heat for 5 minutes or until it begins to colour.
**2** Add the pieces of cod with half the parsley, the capers, anchovies and chilli, and continue to cook until the oil begins to boil. Reduce the heat to low, and begin to swirl the pan so the pieces of fish move around in the sauce. This allows the fish to release its gelatine and the oil to begin to emulsify, forming a sauce, about 6 minutes.
**3** Finally add the remaining parsley and season with lemon juice, salt and black pepper according to taste.

* * * * * * * * *

*Spread very fresh mackerel with Dijon mustard and grill until the fish is crispy on both sides. Serve with new potatoes.*

* * * * * * * * *

# Grilled Tuna *Niçoise*

*Salade Niçoise* in a sea-front restaurant in Nice is a wonderful experience. Why doesn't the same salad taste the same in London or Manchester? I guess it's the sun, the sea and a relaxed frame of mind. A dish that does well and is exceptionally trendy is based on the traditional salad, but using fresh tuna instead of tinned. I encourage my restaurant customers to think of fresh tuna as a healthy alternative to fillet steak, and to try it rare, but the option is yours.

**Marination and cooking: 4 hours + 20 minutes**
**Serves: 4**

3 tablespoons balsamic vinegar
135ml (4½ fl oz) extra virgin olive oil
2 tablespoons chopped parsley
2 tablespoons snipped chives
2 garlic cloves, finely chopped
½ teaspoon salt
½ teaspoon ground black pepper
4 tuna steaks, 2.5cm (1 in) thick
2 Little Gem lettuce hearts
16 black olives in oil, halved
3 plum tomatoes, quartered
115g (4 oz) extra fine French beans, topped
1 red onion, finely sliced
6 anchovy fillets, roughly chopped
8 cooked new potatoes, halved
3 hard-boiled eggs, quartered
8 basil leaves, ripped

**1** Make a marinade for the tuna by whisking together the vinegar, 7 tablespoons of the olive oil, the parsley, chives, garlic, salt and pepper. Pour half of this over the tuna in a **non-reactive** bowl, and chill for 2–4 hours.
**2** Heat a ridged griddle pan on the hob for 5 minutes. Drain the tuna. Cook the tuna steaks for between 1–3 minutes each side, depending on how rare you like your fish.
**3** Toss together the lettuce, olives, tomato, beans (cooked for 4 minutes and refreshed in cold water), onion, anchovy and potato, and add the remaining marinade plus the remaining extra virgin olive oil. Toss to combine.
**4** Arrange the salad on a platter, place the tuna on top and garnish with the hard-boiled eggs and ripped basil.

# Thai Fish Cakes

There's something magical about the flavours of the East, and when these flavours can be transposed into a western-style product, you have a winner on your hands. Most ingredients are now readily available so don't panic when you see the list. Included in the recipe is a seasoning paste which is made ahead; use what you need and keep the rest in the fridge. Serve with a *Thai Cucumber Salad* (see page 106).

**Preparation and cooking: 30 minutes**
**Serves: 4**

| |
|---|
| 675g (1½ lb) cod fillet, skinless |
| 2 tablespoons seasoning paste (see below) |
| 4 tablespoons chopped coriander |
| 2 tablespoons fresh lime juice |
| 2 fresh red chillies, finely diced |
| 4 spring onions, finely diced |
| 175ml (6 fl oz) peanut oil *fish sauce* |

**Seasoning paste**

| |
|---|
| 2 stems lemongrass, tender middle finely chopped |
| 3 fresh red chillies, sliced |
| 2 teaspoons chopped fresh ginger (or galangal) |
| 4 shallots, finely chopped |
| 6 cloves garlic, sliced |
| 4 teaspoons coriander seeds, toasted and crushed |
| 2 teaspoons cumin seeds, toasted and crushed |
| 4 fresh kaffir lime leaves, shredded |
| 1 teaspoon chilli powder |

**1** First make the seasoning paste. Place all the ingredients in a food processor and blend to a smooth paste.
**2** Place the cod, 2 tablespoons of the seasoning paste, the coriander, lime juice and chilli in the food processor and blend until smooth.
**3** Place the mixture in a bowl and fold in the spring onions.
**4** Form the mixture into 8 'patties' and refrigerate until ready to cook.
**5** Heat the oil in a deep frying pan, and cook the fish cakes for 3 minutes on each side or until golden.

# Classic Fish Soup

One of the nicest soups in the world is that thin fish soup you get all over France but especially in the Mediterranean. Ideally it is made with Mediterranean fish (gurnard, rascasse and grey mullet), but these are rarely available in our fishmongers.

**Preparation and cooking: 1 hour**
**Serves: 6–8**

4 tablespoons good olive oil

3 teaspoons chopped garlic

2 onions, roughly chopped

1 carrot, roughly chopped

2 sticks celery, roughly chopped

1 leek, roughly chopped

1 bulb fennel, roughly chopped

1kg (2 lb) non-oily fish, bones and all, roughly chopped

1 teaspoon soft thyme leaves

2 bay leaves

2 x 5cm (2 in) strips orange rind

½ teaspoon cayenne pepper

1 roasted red pepper (see page 254), skinned, seeded and chopped

1 x 400g (14 oz) tin chopped tomatoes

½ tablespoon tomato purée

1 teaspoon fennel seeds

1 tablespoon anchovy essence

350ml (12 fl oz) dry white wine

2 litres (3½ pints) water

large pinch of saffron stamens, soaked in cold water

2 tablespoons Pastis or Pernod

salt and ground black pepper

**1** In a large saucepan heat the olive oil, and add the garlic, onion, carrot, celery, leek and fennel. Cook over a medium heat until the vegetables have softened and lightly browned, about 15 minutes.

**2** Add the fish and its bones, thyme, bay leaves, orange rind, cayenne, roasted pepper, tomato, tomato purée, fennel seeds and anchovy essence. Stir to combine, and cook for 10 minutes.

**3** Add the white wine and water, bring to the boil, reduce the heat, and simmer for 20 minutes.

**4** Pass the soup through the coarse mill of a **mouli-légumes** in small batches, discarding the pulp. Repeat this procedure through the fine mill disc.

**5** Return the liquid to the saucepan, add the saffron, and cook for 10 minutes. Add the Pastis and cook for a further 3 minutes. Season to taste.

**6** Serve with small dishes of French bread *croûtons*, grated Gruyère cheese and *Rouille* (see right).

# Rouille

My recipe is adapted from that of Michel Guérard, which I think is packed with flavour. Feel free to use your own, though!

**Preparation: 20–25 minutes**
**Serves: 6–8**

3 hard-boiled egg yolks

3 tinned anchovy fillets

2 cloves garlic

1 teaspoon tomato purée

2 raw egg yolks

1 teaspoon English mustard

salt and ground black pepper

300ml (½ pint) extra virgin olive oil

2 teaspoons lemon juice

1 teaspoon *Harissa* or chilli paste (see page 259)

good pinch of saffron stamens, soaked in a little cold water

**1** In a food processor blend the hard-boiled egg yolks with the anchovy, garlic and tomato purée. Remove and set aside.

**2** Place the raw egg yolks in the food processor with the mustard, a little salt and several grindings of black pepper.

**3** With the machine running, add the oil, a few drops at a time to start, then in a thin stream, thinning down every so often with the lemon juice.

**4** Add the *harissa*, saffron and remaining lemon juice. Pulse briefly, then add back the hard-boiled egg mix. Pulse and check seasoning.

# Poached Haddock with Poached Eggs and a Cheesy Egg Sauce

A real nursery dish that is forever satisfying, and which is easy to prepare ahead. Use undyed smoked haddock where possible.

**Preparation and cooking: 45 minutes**
**Serves: 4**

| | |
|---|---|
| 100g (3½ oz) unsalted butter | 1kg (2¼ lb) undyed smoked haddock fillets |
| 1 onion, finely diced | 600ml (1 pint) milk |
| 1 stick celery, finely sliced | 200ml (7 fl oz) double cream |
| ½ leek, finely sliced | 3 hard-boiled eggs, chopped |
| 1 carrot, finely diced | 2 tablespoons chopped flat-leaf parsley |
| ½ teaspoon soft thyme leaves | 1 tablespoon snipped chives |
| 1 bay leaf | 85g (3 oz) Gruyère cheese, grated |
| 1 clove | salt and ground white pepper |
| 55g (2 oz) plain flour | 4 poached eggs (see page 113) |

**1** Heat half the butter in a non-stick saucepan over a medium heat, then add the onion, celery, leek, carrot, thyme, bay leaf and clove and cook for about 12–15 minutes until the vegetables have softened and started to colour.

**2** Add the flour, lower the heat and cook for 7–8 minutes, stirring regularly.

**3** Meanwhile, place the haddock fillet and milk in a saucepan. Bring to the boil, reduce the heat, and cook for 6 minutes. Remove the haddock and set aside. Allow to cool slightly.

**4** Strain the haddock poaching milk on to the floured vegetables little by little, stirring, until the sauce is velvety and the correct thickness (like single cream).

**5** Fold in the cream and stir to combine. Pass the sauce through a sieve to remove the vegetables and herbs. Discard the vegetables.

**6** Return the sauce to a clean saucepan. Fold in the remaining butter, the hard-boiled egg, parsley, chives and half the cheese. Heat until the cheese has melted. Check the seasoning.

**7** Remove the skin and any bone from the cooked haddock fillets. Flake the fish into a lightly buttered shallow *gratin* dish. Place the 4 poached eggs on top of the fish and pour over the sauce.

**8** Sprinkle with the remaining cheese and place under a hot grill until golden and bubbling. (If you like your poached eggs very soft, warm them through separately for 30 seconds in boiling salted water and spoon the browned haddock and sauce over the eggs just prior to eating. Likewise the haddock does not have to be flaked, but can be left in individual portion fillets and the sauce poured over at the last minute.)

## *Prosciutto*-wrapped Monkfish

*A different way with monkfish.*
- *Buy a small monkfish tail, remove the cartilaginous bone, but leave 5cm (2 in) attached to the flesh at the end of the tails.*
- *Lay 2 strips of* prosciutto *or Parma ham on a flat surface, side by side (the same length as the fish).*
- *Season the tail inside and out.*
- *Arrange a herb mix (see page 215) along the length of the tail and bring the two halves of the tail together sandwiching the herbs.*
- *Lay the tail on the ham and wrap it around the fish. Allow to rest in the fridge for about 1 hour.*
- ***Seal** the fish in a hot pan with a little olive oil and then transfer to a preheated oven at 190°C/375°F/ Gas 5, and roast for 10–15 minutes per 450g (1 lb).*

## Pickled Herrings

- *Make your own by spreading herring fillets with Dijon mustard and rolling them around strips of pickled sweet gherkins and sliced onion.*
- *Boil together 300ml (½ pint) each of water and dry white wine, 1 teaspoon crushed black peppercorns, 1 sprig thyme and 3 bay leaves.*
- *Cook for 5 minutes then allow to cool.*
- *Pour over the herrings.*
- *Serve after 4 days' marination.*

# FISH: SHELLFISH

Why are shellfish so appealing? There are several attractions. Visually, they ooze sensuality. One can only marvel at their make-up, tender morsels of flesh surrounded by armour-plated housing. They look challenging, and the eating is always a great adventure, often using implements designed especially for each type. And in the eating of shellfish there is a distinct sweetness, a real taste of the sea. All shellfish, from the most expensive lobster to the humble mussel, have their own quality and distinct taste.

There are two principal sub-divisions of shellfish – crustaceans and molluscs. Crustaceans are animals with a hard external skeleton or shell, and include lobsters, shrimps, prawns and crabs. (*Ecrevisses*, or freshwater crayfish, are the only shellfish not to live in salt water.) Molluscs can be further sub-divided. Gastropods are snail-like, with one shell (whelks, winkles etc.), and bivalves have two shells hinged together and which are closed by strong muscles (clams, cockles, mussels, oysters and scallops). The cephalopods – octopus, squid and cuttlefish – are the most advanced of the molluscs (see page 120).

## CLAMS

The British are only just getting to grips with clams. Not that long ago a clam was just a clam, and wasn't marketed under any specific name. The Americans, on the contrary, identify several varieties, and these include littlenecks (the smallest), cherrystones (medium sized), and chowder clams or quahogs (the largest and toughest). Occasionally one finds the very tiny or Manila clams, and also excellent are the razor and the soft-shell or steamer clams which have long siphons or necks.

When buying clams make sure the shells are tightly closed. They often contain sand so should be soaked for an hour in fresh water before using. Always scrub the shells as sand can get stuck in the ridges. The small littlenecks or cherrystones are usually eaten raw, and are opened with a blade similar to an oyster knife. Larger clams are usually steamed open, chopped up and used in a chowder, or minced and combined with a stuffing to return to the shells. If planning to open clams with a knife, place the clams in a freezer for 45 minutes which makes their muscles relax, enabling you to open them more easily.

Other clams available in British waters but more often than not eaten by the French, Spanish or Portuguese, are the warty Venus, carpet-shell, Venus shell and surf clam, all of which are thoroughly delicious.

## CRABS

For my taste, these are the most flavourful of the shellfish, although they require a lot more work than lobster, and for that reason are cheap in the shell but relatively expensive in the fresh-picked alternative. Varieties available in the UK worth bothering with include the edible or common crab, the largest and most frequently eaten. The rock crab is imported from the USA, and is much smaller, with very sweet flesh, the biggest catch coming from Chesapeake Bay in the USA. The blue crab is native to and highly prized in America, and has now set up home in the Mediterranean in small quantities (soft-shell crabs are blue crabs). The shore or green crab is our most common species, seen in rock pools all around our coastlines; it is rarely used in anything but crab soups as it is so small. If in France or elsewhere on the European coast, you may encounter spider crabs, which make good eating.

Crabs may be sold live or cooked, as cooked claws, shelled or picked, fresh or frozen. When buying live crabs, make sure they are quite lively. If you are squeamish about killing the crab, get your fishmonger to do it for you. If you are not, then you need to use an awl or sharp-pointed tool to pierce the crab in two places. Point 1 is revealed by folding back the tail flap on the underneath and piercing the central nervous system. Point 2 is also on the underneath just below the mouth and above the brain. Don't plunge the crab into boiling water alive as it is likely to shed its claws. When cooking crab, unless you follow the American method of heavily spiking the water with spices, just add a fair quantity of salt to the boiling water and cook the crab for between 15 and 25 minutes, depending on size. Remove the crab and run it under cold water for 1 minute, then leave to cool at room temperature before refrigerating. The yield of crabs is poor, with a 1.8kg (4 lb) crab producing about 450g (1 lb) of meat.

During its lifetime, especially in the first two growing years, the crab will shed its protective housing to enable it to 'grow' into a new home. During this shedding period, soft-shell crabs, which are completely edible, legs, claws and all, are a great delicacy. In the UK it is rare to find fresh soft-shell crabs, but they can be bought ready-prepared and frozen, imported from the USA (the blues). Well worth a taste.

## LOBSTERS

Lobster is now the most luxurious shellfish, but this wasn't always the case. At one time lobsters had not been over-fished and were so abundant that fishermen used them for bait. Two types of lobster are available in the UK, the European and the American. Surprisingly the American is the cheapest, although it is generally the larger. (Although we call it the American, in fact Canada has twice the catch.) These lobsters are a dark greeny-brown, turning dull red mahogany when cooked. The European lobster is found from Scotland down to the Mediterranean, and is dark bluey-black, turning bright pillar-box red when cooked. Other close relatives are the spiny lobster, crayfish or crawfish (*langouste* in French), and the Dublin Bay prawn, scampi or Norway lobster (*langoustine* in French). *Langoustines* are native to northern Europe, especially Scotland. Most used to be exported and, until recently, we had the ridiculous situation in Britain of having to import Scottish *langoustines* from France!

The RSPCA recommend that a live lobster be put in the freezer for 1–1½ hours before cooking. Chefs tend to plunge a sharp knife into the natural cross on the back of the head. Some put the lobster alive into boiling water. Unless I want to grill, I tend to place the lobster in heavily salted cold water then bring it gently to the boil and cook it for 5–15 minutes after boiling depending on the size of the lobster. This makes for a more tender cooked dish. If you plunge a live lobster into boiling water, the muscles seize, making it tough.

Once you have cooked the lobster, place it on a board stomach side down and, with a large knife, cut it down the length from head to tail. Remove the dark gut which runs the length of the tail section and discard the gritty sand sac which will be in two parts in the top section of the head. Crack each of the large claws. Everything edible is now on show. Some people just eat the white/red flesh, but the best taste for me comes from the creamy substance and tomalley (or liver) lying in the head. Female lobsters also have a creamy red roe. To tell which is which, turn the lobster on its back and look at the pair of small fins: the female's are rounded and hairy, whereas the male's are smooth and pointed.

## MUSSELS

These are another favourite shellfish. Their gleaming blue-black shells look attractive, but they also have a wonderful briny taste. You can still buy wild mussels, but more and more are being cultivated. The latter tend to have much cleaner shells, and are not so gritty, but for me the meat is not so sweet. (The meat is possibly safer, however, as mussels from polluted water can cause poisoning.)

When buying mussels, look for closed shells, which should feel heavy for their size. Place the mussels in a bucket of water with a handful of flour or pinhead oatmeal for a couple of hours. This will self-clean the inside of the mussels. Rinse then scrub the outsides, removing any barnacles and the 'beard'. To remove the beard, the 'hairs' which stick out of the side of the mussel (and by means of which it attaches itself to rocks etc.), pull it with the side of a knife towards the sharp end. Discard any that gape open or do not close when tapped – they could be dead.

When cooking mussels, discard any that don't open – they too could have been dead to start with (and any which, in the shell, look a bit shrivelled). Cooking takes very little time, just long enough to open the shells, 2–5 minutes depending on how hot the cooking liquor is and how many mussels are in the pan. Allow 500g (18 oz) per person for a starter and 1kg (2¼ lb) for a main course.

## OYSTERS

Everyone would love to love these shellfish, but many people can't face them partly because of their unusual texture, partly because of the fear of poisoning (the bodies of those who suffer this will almost certainly not be able to tolerate oysters again for several years). With waters increasingly polluted around our coastlines, it is probably safer to buy cultivated oysters, and these have improved dramatically in quality over the years. In their earlier development, cultivated or farmed oysters tended to be very limp and sometimes quite milky, but now they are comparable to the wild.

Two varieties are available generally: the natives or *Ostrea edulis*; and the Pacific or Japanese, *Crassostrea gigas*. You should eat native oysters only when there is an 'r' in the month as, being hermaphroditic, they fertilise and incubate their young (spat) inside their bodies in the warmer months of the year, and tend to become very milky. They won't do you any harm if eaten, but the flavour is very odd as they develop an unnatural warmness and lose their characteristic taste of the sea. The larger Pacific oysters emit milt and eggs separately into the sea to be fertilised, so are non-incubatory and can be eaten all year round.

Ideally buy unopened oysters on the day you want to eat them, but if you have fears about opening them, get your fishmonger to do it for you. Use as soon as possible. Oysters bought unopened will keep for 3–4 days in a cool place with a wodge of wet newspaper over them. Describing the oyster-opening isn't easy without a demonstration, but here goes. Place the oyster on a flat surface or rest it on a tea towel to stop it slipping. Wrap the non-opening hand in a tea towel, or wear a leather gardening glove. Insert the oyster knife into the hinge and work it in like a lever, gently forcing it between the two shells. When you feel the knife going in, twist it to break the hinge, then slide the knife along the top shell until you feel you have cut the muscle. Lift off the top shell and discard it. Place the oysters on to ice or rock salt so they have a secure base, which will prevent any juices escaping.

Oyster purists will only eat them raw with perhaps a squeeze of lemon (none of your Worcestershire sauce or Tabasco for them), but oysters do take well to cooking too. Preparation is minimal. Open them over a bowl to catch the juices, but don't separate the oyster muscle from the bottom shell as this will kill them. Don't rinse them, as the juices are delicious and briny. Remove any fragments of shell that may have broken off during the opening process. If cooking, do so for a brief time only, just until the edges curl.

## SCALLOPS

These shellfish have beautiful fluted shells, and two varieties are available in Britain: the one known as great scallop, which is up to 15cm (6 in) in diameter, and the queen scallop, or queenie, which is usually about 6–10cm (2–4 in). The edible parts are the creamy, slightly grey adductor muscle in the centre, and the orange coral, although I have seen foreign gentlemen eating some of the other parts (the gills and the mantle).

More often than not you will find scallops that are ready shucked, which is not a good way of buying them, as too often the fish will have been soaked in water (this increases their weight and size, an unacceptable practice). Soaked scallops are very white, so look for those with a much darker colour and which have a slightly sticky texture. Scallops that have been soaked tend to 'boil' when grilled or fried, rather than producing the wonderfully crusty exterior they should. So, where possible, buy scallops in the shell, and ask the fishmonger to clean them for you. Scallops have a delicious sweet taste, and can be enjoyed raw or cooked. They can vary greatly in price depending on whether they have been dredged or diver caught. Dredged scallops can quite often be very muddy and *appear* heavy for their size (because of the mud),

whereas scallops caught by hand, literally by a diver, are pure, clean and a good weight.

## PRAWNS AND SHRIMPS

These small crustaceans are enjoyed the world over, from the ubiquitous prawn cocktail through to some of the more exotic Asian dishes. There are several varieties and sizes available in the northern waters around Europe, the most common of which are the brown shrimp or shrimp (grey-green and translucent when alive, brown when cooked), and the prawn or common prawn (also grey-green and translucent when alive, but orange-pink when cooked). When buying the British favourites, cooked pink prawns, buy cold-water ones from the North Atlantic or Norway, as they have far more flavour than those fished from warmer Asian waters. Larger prawns or king prawns are available from cold deep waters, but many imports – jumbo prawns and the like – are from Asian waters as well, and suffer from a similar lack of flavour.

You are unlikely to find raw prawns fresh out of the water as they deteriorate very quickly, but what are called 'green' prawns are becoming more popular in their frozen state, and quite often in their defrosted state, on supermarket slabs. Look out for the sign that will tell you that they have been previously frozen. These are the ones with grey-green shells.

When a recipe states raw or green prawns, never be tempted to use jumbo *cooked* prawns, as the re-cooking will leave them tough and rubbery. And when defrosting frozen prawns, do not leave them out at room temperature or sitting under a running tap. In the first instance you may well poison yourself, and in the second instance, you will render the prawns tasteless. When preparing raw prawns with their heads still on, don't cut off the heads as you will lose some of the tail; instead, twist and pull off the heads.

Prawns take very little time to cook. If you are going to boil them cook them in boiling water that has been salted to the tune of 175g (6 oz) salt to every 2 litres (3½ pints) of water. Cook in deep water so the water regains its boil very quickly. Boil until they change colour, 1–3 minutes depending on their size. Allow the prawns to cool at room temperature, but do not run under cold water or they will lose flavour. When grilling or barbecuing prawns it is advisable not to remove the shells as the flesh it protects toughens quickly.

The Americans call prawns *and* shrimps 'shrimp', whereas to us shrimps are usually the little ones associated with potted shrimps. When eating in America, be prepared for 'shrimp' to be gynormous (everything is bigger over there).

# New England Clam Chowder

This chowder is creamy white, whereas the Manhattan variety is red, because it is tomato based. A delicious meal in itself.

**Preparation and cooking: 45 minutes**

**Serves: 6–8**

600ml (1 pint) milk

600ml (1 pint) double cream

64 cherrystone clams (or any other variety), washed

1.7 litres (3 pints) light fish stock

55g (2 oz) unsalted butter

1 tablespoon olive oil

175g (6 oz) smoked streaky bacon, cut into dice

2 onions, chopped

1 clove garlic, finely chopped

1 teaspoon soft thyme leaves

3 sticks celery, cut into fine dice

25g (1 oz) plain flour

¼ teaspoon cayenne pepper

salt and ground black pepper

3 large potatoes, cut into 1cm (½ in) dice

4 tablespoons chopped flat-leaf parsley

**1** Combine the milk and cream in a large saucepan. Bring to just under boiling and simmer very gently for about 25 minutes, to reduce by about half.

**2** Place the clams in a large saucepan with the fish stock. Cover and bring to the boil, shaking the pan from time to time. Cook for about 3 minutes. Remove from the heat and take out all the clams that have opened. Return the pan to the heat and cook for a further 1–2 minutes. Discard any clams that have still failed to open. Strain the cooking liquor and set aside.

**3** Meanwhile, in another saucepan heat the butter and oil, add the bacon and cook until golden over a medium heat. Add the onion, garlic, thyme and celery. Reduce the heat and cook for a further 8 minutes, stirring from time to time.

**4** Add the flour, cayenne and 1 teaspoon ground black pepper and stir to combine. Cook for a further 3 minutes. Add the potato and clam cooking juices, increase the heat, bring to the boil and simmer for 10 minutes.

**5** Strain the reduced milk and cream into the soup, and simmer for a further 5 minutes.

**6** Meanwhile, shell the clams, discarding the shells. Chop the clams.

**7** Just before serving, fold the parsley and clams into the soup, and season to taste. Serve with hot crusty bread.

## Hake with Clams

● *A delicious Spanish dish of hake (or cod) with clams is made by frying 4 hake steaks, which have been seasoned and floured, in 4 tablespoons extra virgin olive oil with 4 chopped garlic cloves and 2 chopped fresh red chillies for 5 minutes.*

● *Turn the hake over, and add 125ml (4 fl oz) each of fish stock and dry white wine. Simmer for 2 minutes then add 24 clams, cover with a lid and cook until the clams have opened (discard any that haven't).*

● *Add 2 tablespoons Salsa Verde (see page 215) and swirl to combine.*

● *Fold in 55g (2 oz) chopped unsalted butter and stir to combine.*

● *Serve with new potatoes and salad.*

## Moroccan Spiced Clams

*These are delicious.*

● *Pan-fry ¼ teaspoon cayenne pepper, ½ teaspoon paprika and 2 tablespoons chopped garlic in 3 tablespoons extra virgin olive oil for 3 minutes.*

● *Add 150ml (¼ pint) dry white wine and bring to the boil. Add 1kg (2¼ lb) of clams and cook in the normal way.*

● *When they have opened, fold in 2 tablespoons chopped coriander, 2 tablespoons chopped flat-leaf parsley and the juice of ½ lemon. Season to taste. Discard any clams that remain closed.*

# *Crostini* of Citrus Clams

A deliciously refreshing snackette or starter, in which I've combined two cultures – Italian clams with Oriental flavours. If clams aren't available, you could use cockles instead.

**Preparation and cooking: 45 minutes**
**Serves: 4**

| | |
|---|---|
| 2 tablespoons good olive oil | 1 teaspoon grated lemon rind |
| 1 tablespoon sesame oil | 1 teaspoon fresh lime juice |
| 1 teaspoon chilli oil | 2 spring onions, finely chopped |
| 2 shallots, finely diced | 2 teaspoons chopped mint |
| 2 cloves garlic, finely diced | salt and ground black pepper |
| 3 tablespoons chopped coriander | |
| 1 tablespoon grated fresh ginger | **To serve** |
| 2 fresh red chillies, finely diced | 8 thin slices of French bread |
| 150ml (¼ pint) dry white wine | olive oil |
| 2 bay leaves | 2 handfuls rocket leaves |
| 1kg (2¼ lb) fresh clams, washed | |
| 1 tablespoon grated orange rind | |

**1** Preheat the oven to 180°C/350°F/Gas 4. To make *crostini*, lightly sprinkle the French bread on both sides with olive oil and place in the oven on a baking sheet. Bake until golden and brittle, about 20 minutes, keeping an eye on them in case they burn. Set aside to cool.

**2** Heat the three oils in a large saucepan. Add the shallot, garlic, half the coriander, half the ginger and half the chilli, and cook over a medium heat until the shallot has softened without colour.

**3** Add the wine and bay leaves and increase the heat, bring to the boil and add the clams. Cover with a lid and cook over a brisk heat, shaking the pan from time to time for between 3 and 5 minutes or until the clams have opened.

**4** Remove the opened clams and set aside. Return the unopened clams to the heat and cook for a further 2 minutes. Discard any that fail to open.

**5** Strain the cooking juices into another saucepan and boil until they have reduced to about 4 tablespoons. Set aside to cool.

**6** Remove the clams from their shells, discarding the shells. Chop the clam flesh into small pieces and combine with the remaining coriander, ginger and chilli. Add the citrus rinds, the lime juice, spring onion and mint. Season to taste. Finally fold in the cooled cooking juices. Refrigerate until ready to serve.

**7** Arrange the clam mixture on the cooled *crostini*, and serve with a rocket salad.

*For a great aniseedy taste, cook clams with chopped garlic, finely chopped fennel, fennel seeds, a small amount of chopped rosemary, white wine and olive oil. Discard any clams that remain closed.*

## Crab Salad

● *Combine 450g (1 lb) white crabmeat with 2 tablespoons chopped radishes, ½ cucumber, seeded and chopped, 2 tablespoons snipped chives, 2 tablespoons chopped spring onion, 1 tablespoon lemon juice, ¼ teaspoon cayenne pepper, 100ml (3½ fl oz) Mayonnaise (see page 239) and 100ml (3½ fl oz) soured cream.*

● *Season to taste.*

## Quickie Crab Soup

● *Melt 55g (2 oz) butter in a saucepan and cook 1 chopped onion, 1 teaspoon thyme and 1 chopped chilli in it over a medium heat until the onion has softened.*

● *Add 35g (1¼ oz) flour and stir to combine, cook for 3 minutes, then add 425ml (¾ pint) fish stock, 225ml (8 fl oz) milk and 225ml (8 fl oz) double cream.*

● *Cook until the liquor thickens then add 225g (8 oz) brown crabmeat, 225g (8 oz) white crabmeat, 1 tablespoon tomato purée and 2 tablespoons brandy. Stir to combine and cook for 5 minutes. Season to taste.*

# Crab *Blinis*

Great brunch food served with poached eggs and hollandaise sauce (see page 113). Make small ones and serve them topped with soured cream as part of a canapé menu.

**Preparation and cooking: 1½ hours**
**Serves: 4**

115g (4 oz) polenta or fine cornmeal
½ teaspoon baking powder
55g (2 oz) plain flour
½ teaspoon chilli oil
1 teaspoon sesame oil
2 egg yolks
2 tablespoons freshly squeezed lime juice
approx. 200ml (7 fl oz) milk
225g (8 oz) white crabmeat
½ teaspoon finely diced pickled Japanese ginger (optional)
2 tablespoons finely chopped coriander leaves
2 tablespoons finely chopped mint leaves
2 tablespoons finely chopped basil leaves
2 tablespoons finely chopped spring onion
1 small fresh red chilli, finely chopped
2 egg whites
salt and ground black pepper
115g (4 oz) unsalted butter

**1** Combine the polenta, baking powder and flour in the bowl of the food processor.
**2** Add the oils, egg yolks, lime juice and milk; **pulse** to mix well, adding extra milk if necessary to make a smooth batter.
**3** Add all the remaining ingredients except for the egg whites, seasoning and butter. Allow to rest for an hour.
**4** Just before cooking, beat the egg whites to soft peaks. Fold them into the mixture, and season it to taste.
**5** Heat the butter in a frying pan. If feeling perfectionist use a *blini* ring or *blini* pan. They're normally about 10cm (4 in) across. Otherwise use a tablespoon of the batter (or a teaspoon for mini *blinis*). Cook on the first side until the mixture starts to bubble on the top, then turn and cook for a minute or so longer. Keep warm while cooking the remainder.

# Spicy Crab Cakes

I could give you four or five different versions of crab cakes, all of which are delicious. An upmarket alternative to fish cakes, they are great for brunch.

**Preparation and cooking: 3–12 hours + 1 hour**
**Serves: 4**

1 large egg, beaten
375g (13 oz) white crabmeat
250g (9 oz) diced cooked potatoes
2 roasted red peppers (see page 254), skinned, seeded and diced
2 spring onions, finely chopped
½ teaspoon paprika
½ teaspoon cayenne pepper
2 tablespoons chopped coriander
¼ teaspoon celery salt
1 tablespoon Worcestershire sauce
2 tablespoons soured cream
2 tablespoons lime juice
3–4 drops Tabasco sauce
½ teaspoon English mustard powder
½ teaspoon ground black pepper
½ teaspoon sea salt
fresh white breadcrumbs
150ml (¼ pint) groundnut oil

**1** Combine all the ingredients down to and including the sea salt. Add enough breadcrumbs to bind and absorb excess moisture.
**2** Shape the mixture into 4 large or 8 small patties, and place on waxed or greaseproof paper in a refrigerator to firm up for 3 hours or preferably overnight.
**3** Heat the oil in a large frying pan over a medium heat and add the crab cakes. Do not overcrowd. Cook in batches if required. Cook for about 5 minutes on each side, depending on the size of the crab cake, or until golden and heated through.
**4** Serve brunch style with poached eggs (see page 113), or accompanied by a leaf salad.

# Crab and Asparagus Fettuccine

Flavour-packed, the crab adds a wonderful zap to this fresh pasta dish. The dish works as a starter or main course, perfect for a quick supper on a cold winter's night. Adding the browned butter at the end may sound fattening, and you'd be correct, but it is essential for that touch of magic.

**Preparation and cooking: 20 minutes**
**Serves: 4–6**

2 tablespoons extra virgin olive oil

1 shallot, finely diced

1 teaspoon soft thyme leaves

2 teaspoons anchovy essence

150ml (¼ pint) dry white wine

150ml (¼ pint) fish stock

salt and ground black pepper

450g (1 lb) asparagus, trimmed and cut into 2.5cm (1 in) pieces

350g (12 oz) white crabmeat

675g (1½ lb) fresh fettuccine

55g (2 oz) unsalted butter

juice of ½ lemon

2 tablespoons chopped parsley

**1** Heat the olive oil in a heavy-bottomed frying pan, add the shallot and cook gently until soft but not brown. Add the thyme, anchovy essence, wine and fish stock and bring to the boil. Cook until the liquid has reduced by half.

**2** Meanwhile, bring a large pot of salted water to the boil. Add the asparagus and cook for 6 minutes. Drain, retaining the water, and add to the reduced shallot liquid with the crab.

**3** Cook the fettuccine in the asparagus water for about 3–4 minutes, depending on its freshness. Drain and add to the crab sauce.

**4** To finish, heat the butter in a frying pan until nutty and golden, add the lemon juice and parsley, and pour over the pasta. Toss to combine. Season to taste with plenty of black pepper.

# Soft-shell Crab Sandwich

All the rage in America, there's nothing quite like the taste of soft-shell crabs. Unfortunately in England you can only buy them frozen, but they're good nonetheless.

**Preparation and cooking: 20 minutes**
**Serves: 4**

115g (4 oz) plain flour
2 large eggs, beaten
115g (4 oz) polenta or cornmeal
salt and ground black pepper
4 soft-shell crabs, defrosted
2 tablespoons corn oil
25g (1 oz) unsalted butter

**To serve**

4 large wholegrain rolls
*Mayonnaise* (optional, see page 239)
85g (3 oz) rocket leaves
2 plum tomatoes, sliced
1 red onion, finely sliced
juice of 1 lime

**1** Place the flour, eggs and polenta separately in three bowls and season each with salt and pepper.
**2** Dip each crab into the flour, shake off any excess, then dip in the egg, immersing them completely. Then dip in the polenta to cover, shake off any excess, and set aside.
**3** Heat the oil and butter in a large frying pan over a medium heat. When hot add the crabs and fry until crisp, about 2–3 minutes on each side.
**4** Cut the rolls in half and spread both sides with mayonnaise. Top the bottom half with rocket leaves, tomato slices, red onions and then a crab. Season and drizzle with some lime juice, and top with the other roll half.

# Singapore Chilli Crab

This is not a dish for the faint-hearted as you have to munch, crunch, lick and suck, real back-to-basics stuff. You might find that, unless you are an Oriental, this dish is better eaten in the bath, as it can be incredibly messy.

**Preparation and cooking: 40 minutes**
**Serves: 2–4**

1 x 2kg (4½ lb) crab, alive if possible
3 teaspoons groundnut oil
3 cloves garlic, crushed with a little salt
5cm (2 in) piece fresh ginger, grated
4 fresh red chillies, finely chopped
2 tablespoons sweet chilli sauce
4 tablespoons Heinz tomato ketchup
300ml (½ pint) chicken stock
1 teaspoon caster sugar
1 teaspoon cornflour, blended with a little water
4 spring onions, sliced in 2.5cm (1 in) pieces
3 tablespoons chopped coriander
1 egg, beaten
salt

**1** Kill the crab as described on page 136.
**2** Use a knife to lever the top flat shell away from the body. Remove fronds or dead men's fingers. Remove claws and crack lightly without cutting through. Cut the body in half from front to back then in half again, crossways, keeping small legs attached.
**3** Heat the oil in a wok, and fry the crab pieces for 5 minutes, turning regularly. Remove and set aside.
**4** Drain most of the oil from the wok, and place it back over a medium heat. Add the garlic, ginger and chilli and stir-fry for 2 minutes, then add the chilli sauce, ketchup, chicken stock and sugar. Stir to combine.
**5** Fold in the cornflour mix, bring to the boil and stir to thicken. Return the crab to the sauce with the spring onion and coriander. Add the raw egg and stir to thicken; do not re-boil at this stage. Season to taste and serve with jasmine rice.

# Lobster with Wine, Tomato, Garlic and Herbs

A great lobster classic, usually called Lobster American, and it is delicious when made well. I've changed the original slightly.

**Preparation and cooking: 50 minutes**
**Serves: 4**

| |
|---|
| 2 x 1kg (2¼ lb) live lobsters, frozen for 1½ hours just prior to preparation |
| 4 tablespoons extra virgin olive oil |
| 1 large onion, roughly chopped |
| 2 cloves garlic, finely chopped |
| 1 teaspoon soft thyme leaves |
| 350ml (12 fl oz) dry white wine |
| 125ml (4 fl oz) fish stock |
| 50ml (2 fl oz) brandy |
| 1 x 400g (14 oz) tin chopped tomatoes |
| 1 tablespoon tomato purée |
| 1 teaspoon anchovy essence |
| ¼ teaspoon cayenne pepper |
| ¼ teaspoon ground black pepper |
| 55g (2 oz) unsalted butter, softened |
| 1 tablespoon chopped fresh oregano |
| 2 tablespoons chopped flat-leaf parsley |

**1** Stretch the lobsters out lengthways, twist off the heads and remove the large claws. Chop each claw into three. Cut each tail into four. Split the heads in two lengthways, remove the gritty sacs and discard. Scrape the remaining head innards – the creamy substance and tomalley – into a bowl and set aside.

**2** Heat the oil in a large saucepan or frying pan and fry the lobster pieces, including the head shells, until the shells become red. (Frying the head shells gives additional flavour.) Remove and set aside to keep warm. Discard the head shells.

**3** Add the onion, garlic and thyme to the oil and cook until the onion has softened without colour. Drain off the oil and discard.

**4** Add the white wine, stock and brandy to the onion mix. Bring to the boil and add the tomato, tomato purée, anchovy essence, cayenne and black pepper and cook over a medium heat until the sauce has reduced by half, about 10–12 minutes.

**5** Meanwhile, mash the butter with the retained lobster tomalley and creamy substance. This can be done in a food processor. Set aside in the refrigerator.

**6** Return the lobster to the sauce and cook for 5 minutes. Add the herbs and the lobster butter and bring to the boil. Remove immediately from the heat and serve with rice pilaff.

## Lobster Thermidor

*Another of my favourite classic oldie lobster dishes.*

● *Split a humanely killed lobster (see page 137) in half lengthways, remove the gritty sac and discard.*

● *Crack the claws. Season the lobster with salt and pepper and roast in a 220°C/425°F/Gas 7 oven for 10 minutes, basting with melted butter.*

● *Remove the lobster meat from the shells and slice it, mix it with Béchamel Sauce (see page 60) to which you have added some strong mustard, a little brandy, a raw egg yolk, some cheese and cream.*

● *Replace meat in the shells and top with more sauce, sprinkled with cheese. Brown in the oven.*

*Avoid cooked lobsters from supermarkets as they tend to be dry, overcooked and expensive. Where possible, boil your own raw lobsters for dishes such as lobster salad.*

F

*Make a dressed lobster salad by removing cooked lobster from the claws and body. Cut in thin slices and toss with a small amount of Mayonnaise (see page 239). Fill the cavity of the lobster tail and head with dressed shredded lettuce hearts. Top with the lobster slices and dress with strips of anchovy fillets, quartered hard-boiled eggs, a few drained capers and a dusting of cayenne pepper.*

# Thai Lobster and Noodle Salad

A wonderful way to spice up lobster and make its expensive flesh go further.

**Preparation and cooking: 50 minutes**
**Serves: 4**

2 tablespoons vegetable oil
1 fresh red chilli, finely diced
2 teaspoons chopped garlic
4 large *shiitake* mushrooms, sliced
4 small heads *pak-choi*, roughly chopped
55g (2 oz) roasted peanuts, chopped
4 spring onions, sliced in 5mm (¼ in) pieces
4 x 450g (1 lb) cooked lobsters, meat removed
4 teaspoons chilli oil
2 tablespoons chopped mint
1 tablespoon chopped coriander
1 teaspoon grated fresh ginger
150ml (¼ pint) good olive oil
50ml (2 fl oz) fresh lime juice
2 tablespoons *nam pla* (fish sauce)
¼ teaspoon ground black pepper
grated rind of 1 lime
55g (2 oz) Chinese egg noodles, cooked, cooled and drained

**1** Heat the vegetable oil in a frying pan, add the chilli, garlic and mushrooms and cook over a medium heat for 5 minutes.
**2** Add the *pak-choi* and stir-fry for a further 3 minutes until the greens wilt. Fold in the peanuts, spring onion, lobster flesh and 1 teaspoon chilli oil. Toss to combine, then allow to cool.
**3** Combine the remaining chilli oil with the herbs, ginger, olive oil, lime juice, *nam pla*, pepper and lime rind, then toss with the noodles.
**4** Combine the noodles with the lobster mixture and allow to rest in the refrigerator for 30 minutes before serving.

# Lobster Club Sandwich

A delicious way of treating lobster with irreverence, a snack for the good times.

**Preparation and cooking: 15 minutes**
**Serves: 2**

6 slices streaky bacon
2 tablespoons olive oil
6 slices country bread
4 tablespoons good *Mayonnaise* (see page 239)
1 head Belgian chicory, broken into bite-sized pieces
2 x 450g (1 lb) cooked lobsters, meat removed
juice of ½ lemon
2 hard-boiled eggs, sliced
salt and ground black pepper
18 slices cucumber
2 plum tomatoes, sliced

**1** Cook the bacon in a dry frying pan until crispy and set aside. Add the olive oil to the bacon fat in the pan, and in the combination of hot fats, fry 4 slices of the bread on one side only until golden.
**2** Lay the 4 fried slices (crispy side down) and 2 fresh slices of bread on the work surface. Spread the uncooked sides with mayonnaise. Top 2 of the fried slices with chicory followed by lobster, lemon juice, more mayo and the sliced egg. Season.
**3** Top this combo with the uncooked bread then cucumber, bacon and tomato. Season.
**4** Top with the remaining bread slices fried-face up. Secure each sandwich with two cocktail sticks and slice in half. Serve with *frites* or crisps.

# Warm Mussel and Potato Salad

The simple things are best, and this salad is a winner every time.

**Preparation and cooking: 40 minutes**

**Serves: 4**

675g (1½ lb) waxy new or Pink Fir Apple potatoes, sliced

4 rashers smoked streaky bacon, diced

100ml (3½ fl oz) extra virgin olive oil

1 tablespoon lemon juice

1 tablespoon sherry vinegar

2 teaspoons Dijon mustard

1 clove garlic, finely chopped

¼ teaspoon ground black pepper

4 spring onions, finely sliced

2 tablespoons chopped flat-leaf parsley

1 tablespoon finely chopped capers

2kg (4½ lb) just cooked mussels, shucked

**1** Cook the potatoes in boiling salted water until tender, remove from the heat and leave in the water until ready to use.

**2** Meanwhile, cook the bacon in 1 tablespoon of the olive oil until crisp. Mix with the remaining ingredients, apart from the mussels, to make the dressing.

**3** Drain the potatoes and toss with the dressing and the mussels. Serve warm or at room temperature.

· · · · · · · · · · · · · · · · ·

*Cook large mussels, remove the top shell and use the base shell with its mussel for all sorts of fillings: breadcrumbs, garlic and herbs; chopped mushrooms and reduced red wine; diced onion, sun-dried tomato, chilli, olives and Parma ham; diced crispy bacon, garlicky breadcrumbs and Worcestershire sauce.*

· · · · · · · · · · · · · · · · ·

# Thai-inspired Mussels

A great combination for a spicy mussel dish.

**Preparation and cooking: 40 minutes**

**Serves: 2 as a main course, 4 as a starter**

1 tablespoon vegetable oil

1 x 400g (14 oz) tin coconut milk

2 teaspoons Thai green curry paste

1 stem lemongrass, outer leaves removed, finely chopped

5cm (2 in) piece fresh ginger, grated

2 fresh red chillies, finely chopped

850ml (1½ pints) chicken stock

2kg (4½ lb) mussels, cleaned

2 tablespoons fresh lime juice

2 lime leaves, finely sliced

2 handfuls baby spinach

2 tablespoons *nam pla* (fish sauce)

12 basil leaves, ripped

**1** Heat the oil in a large heavy-based saucepan, add half the coconut milk and over a medium heat cook until the milk starts to split.

**2** Add the curry paste and stir to combine. Add the lemongrass, ginger and chilli and cook for 3 minutes. Add the chicken stock and cook until the liquid has reduced by half, about 10 minutes.

**3** Add the mussels, cover with a lid, and cook over a medium heat for 3 minutes. Fold in the remainder of the coconut milk, the lime juice, lime leaves, spinach and fish sauce and cook for a further 3 minutes.

**4** Finally fold in the basil and discard any mussels that have not opened. Serve immediately with plain rice. (The sauce may appear split but this is normal when coconut milk is used.)

# Mussel and Saffron Soup

One of the nicest combinations I know, and it's a recipe I have been cooking and people have been enjoying, since my days at *Ménage à Trois*, my first London restaurant.

**Preparation and cooking: 50 minutes**

**Serves: 4**

75g (2¾ oz) unsalted clarified butter (see page 60)

2 shallots, finely chopped

2 cloves garlic, finely chopped

2 teaspoons finely chopped fresh ginger

500ml (18 fl oz) dry white wine

1 tablespoon soy sauce

2kg (4½ lb) mussels, cleaned

1 stick celery, diced

½ small bulb fennel, diced

white of 1 leek, diced

1 small potato, diced

1 small carrot, diced

500ml (18 fl oz) fish stock

1 bay leaf

1 sprig thyme

1 pinch saffron stamens, soaked in 1 tablespoon warm water

300ml (½ pint) double cream

salt, white pepper and grated nutmeg

**1** Heat the clarified butter in a large saucepan. Add the shallot, garlic and ginger and cook over a low heat until soft but not brown.

**2** Remove half the ginger mixture to a second saucepan. Add the wine and soy sauce to the first pan and bring to the boil. Add the mussels and cook, covered, for about 5 minutes, shaking the pan at regular intervals. When the mussels have opened, shell them, discarding any that remain firmly closed, and set aside. Strain their stock into the second saucepan.

**3** Add the vegetables, the fish stock, bay leaf and thyme to the mussel stock and reserved **sweated** shallot mixture. Bring to the boil and simmer for about 20 minutes or until the vegetables are soft.

**4** Remove the bay leaf and thyme. Liquidise the soup and pass through a fine sieve. Return to the heat. Add the saffron stamens to turn the soup pale yellow. Add the cream, and season with nutmeg, salt and pepper. Do not allow to re-boil.

**5** Pop the mussels into the soup, and gently heat through. Serve the soup in warm bowls.

## Moules à la Marinière

Moules à la marinière *is the simplest basic method for cooking mussels.*

● *Heat 55g (2 oz) unsalted butter in a large saucepan and cook 1 chopped onion in it until soft. Add 75ml (2½ fl oz) dry white wine and bring to the boil.*

● *Add 1kg (2¼ lb) cleaned mussels, cover the saucepan, and cook over a high heat, shaking the pan from time to time until the mussels open.*

● *Remove mussels (discarding any that have not opened), and add another 55g (2 oz) butter, some black pepper and 4 tablespoons chopped parsley.*

● *Boil to emulsify, then pour over the mussels.*

*Cream may be added at the end of cooking* moules à la marinière *for a smoother, less rustic dish.*

*Remove the top shell from cooled cooked mussels, and fill the cavity and top of the mussel with garlic butter. Sprinkle with breadcrumbs and flash under the grill when you want to serve.*

# Individual Oyster Stew

One of those little indulgences for when you are on your own. Go out and buy yourself some oysters, and whip this dish up in an instant.

**Preparation and cooking: 10 minutes**

**Serves: 1**

25g (1 oz) unsalted butter

pinch of celery salt

dash of Tabasco sauce

dash of Worcestershire sauce

1 teaspoon anchovy essence

150ml (¼ pint) milk

150ml (¼ pint) double cream

9 freshly opened oysters, juices retained

**1**  Place all the ingredients except the oysters in a saucepan and whisk together until nearly boiling.

**2**  Add the oysters and their juices and cook until the edge of the oysters just start to curl. Do not boil. Serve with hot crusty bread.

• • • • • • • • • • • •

*Make some chive butter by mixing softened butter with lots of snipped chives. Put a knob in the centre of an open oyster shell. Sprinkle over a mixture of fresh breadcrumbs and a little grated lemon zest, place under a hot grill and cook until golden and bubbling.*

• • • • • • • • • • • •

# Oysters Stuffed with Crabmeat

A delicious brunch recipe I found when visiting New Orleans. Serve with crispy bacon and a leaf salad.

**Preparation and cooking: 30 minutes**

**Serves: 4**

rock salt

24 oysters in the half shell, freshly opened and juices retained

1 free-range egg, lightly beaten

2 tablespoons *Mayonnaise* (see page 239)

2 tablespoons soured cream

¼ teaspoon ground black pepper

¼ teaspoon curry powder

¼ teaspoon Tabasco sauce

1 teaspoon Worcestershire sauce

1 tablespoon lemon juice

½ teaspoon anchovy essence

¼ teaspoon garlic powder

¼ teaspoon celery seeds

¼ teaspoon English mustard powder

225g (8 oz) white crabmeat

soft white breadcrumbs to bind

**1**  Preheat the oven to 230°C/450°F/Gas 8.

**2**  Place a pile of rock salt on four ovenproof plates, and heat in the oven 5 minutes before you need to cook the oysters.

**3**  Combine the egg, mayonnaise, cream, oyster juices and all the seasonings. Fold in the crabmeat and enough breadcrumbs to bind. The mixture should not be too wet.

**4**  Place 1 dessertspoon of the crabmeat mixture on top of each oyster. Remove the plates from the oven and place 6 oysters on each, standing them in the hot salt. Bake in the oven for 5–8 minutes until hot and lightly golden.

# Oysters Rockefeller

A dish created over 100 years ago in New Orleans. Originally made with 18 ingredients, over the years the dish has diminished to oysters on spinach with a cheese sauce and a dash of Pernod. This recipe is an attempt to bring it back to its former glories.

**Preparation and cooking: 40 minutes**

**Serves: 4**

rock salt

24 oysters in the half shell, opened and juices retained

4 shallots, finely diced

1 stick celery, finely diced

250g (9 oz) unsalted butter

1 teaspoon chopped chervil

1 teaspoon chopped tarragon

2 tablespoons chopped flat-leaf parsley

450g (1 lb) spinach, picked and washed

1 bunch watercress, leaves only

115g (4 oz) soft breadcrumbs

1 teaspoon Worcestershire sauce

1 teaspoon anchovy essence

½ teaspoon ground black pepper

1 tablespoon Pernod

85g (3 oz) Parmesan, grated (optional)

**1** Preheat the oven to 230°C/450°F/Gas 8.

**2** Place a pile of rock salt on four ovenproof plates, and heat in the oven 5 minutes before you need to cook the oysters.

**3** Pan-fry the shallot and celery in 55g (2 oz) of the butter until softened, about 8–10 minutes over a medium heat.

**4** Add the oyster juices, herbs, spinach and watercress leaves, and cook until the greens have wilted, about 5 minutes. Increase the heat to boil away any liquid that has come out of the greens.

**5** Place the spinach mixture in the bowl of a food processor with the remaining butter, half the breadcrumbs, the Worcestershire sauce, anchovy essence, pepper and Pernod. Blend until smooth.

**6** Top each oyster with about 1 dessertspoon of the spinach mix. Remove the plates from the oven and place 6 oysters on each, positioning them in the hot salt.

**7** Combine the remaining breadcrumbs with the Parmesan and sprinkle a little on top of each oyster. (The recipe may be prepared in advance up to this stage.)

**8** Bake in the hot oven for 5–8 minutes until lightly golden and the oysters are bubbling.

• • • • • • • • • • • • •

*Bake oysters briefly in a hot oven or under the grill with a little anchovy butter and a sprinkling of crispy bacon until hot.*

• • • • • • • • • • • • •

*In America you often find a dish called 'hangtown fry' which involves flouring, egging and coating oysters in cracker crumbs or breadcrumbs, pan-frying them in butter, then folding in beaten eggs to make a folded omelette. It's served with crispy bacon and oven-roasted tomatoes.*

• • • • • • • • • • • • •

# Tom Yam Gung

One of the most delicious, refreshing, healthy soups you will find, originating in Thailand.

**Preparation and cooking: 30 minutes**
**Serves: 4**

| |
|---|
| 16 large raw prawns, peeled (heads, if available, and shells reserved) |
| 1 tablespoon peanut or vegetable oil |
| 2 litres (3½ pints) chicken stock |
| 1 tablespoon *nam prik pow* (chilli jam, optional) |
| 1 teaspoon grated lime rind |
| 1 shallot, finely sliced |
| 1 clove garlic, finely chopped |
| 3 lime leaves, finely shredded |
| 3 fresh red chillies, finely shredded |
| 1 stem lemongrass, outside leaves removed, finely shredded |
| 12 *shiitake* mushrooms, thinly sliced |
| 4 spring onions, finely sliced |
| 3 tablespoons *nam pla* (fish sauce) |
| 3 tablespoons lime juice |
| 1 teaspoon caster sugar |
| 3 tablespoons coarsely chopped coriander |

**1** Fry the prawn shells and heads in the oil for 6–8 minutes.

**2** Add the stock, chilli jam, lime rind, shallot, garlic, lime leaves, 2 of the chillies and the lemongrass. Simmer gently for 20 minutes. Strain the liquid into a new saucepan.

**3** Add the remaining chilli, the mushroom, spring onion, fish sauce, lime juice and sugar, and simmer for 3 minutes. Add the prawns and cook just until they change colour, about a minute. Add the coriander leaves and serve immediately.

## Thai Prawns

● *Combine 2 tablespoons* nam pla *(fish sauce) with the juice of 1 lime, 3 tablespoons coconut milk, 1 teaspoon honey, 1 crushed clove garlic, 1 teaspoon grated ginger, 1 chopped fresh red chilli, 2 tablespoons chopped mint and 1 tablespoon chopped coriander.*
● *Toss 4 jumbo raw prawns per person with this mixture and allow to 'cook' in the marinade for 1 hour. Serve on salad leaves.*

## Prawn Barbie Marinade

*An excellent marinade for jumbo raw prawns to go on the barbie.*
● *Combine 4 tablespoons extra virgin olive oil with 4 tablespoons lemon juice, 2 tablespoons chopped parsley, 1 teaspoon garlic crushed with a little salt, 1 teaspoon chopped oregano, ½ teaspoon grated lemon rind, ½ teaspoon salt and ¼ teaspoon ground black pepper.*
● *Marinate 4 raw prawns per person in this for 1 hour before cooking.*

# American Prawn Cocktail

When we talk about prawn cocktail, we British tend to think of tiny prawns sitting on a bed of shredded iceberg lettuce topped with a pink gloop and a dusting of paprika. The Americans, on the other hand, buy jumbo cooked 'shrimp', their name for prawns, and dip them in a red-hot cocktail sauce. They use fingers to do the feeding, and mayonnaise doesn't feature at all.

**Preparation and cooking: 25 minutes**
**Serves: 6**

36 cooked jumbo prawns, shelled and de-veined

3 lemons, halved

**Sauce**

150ml (¼ pint) chilli sauce

150ml (¼ pint) tomato ketchup

1 tablespoon fresh lemon juice

2 tablespoons grated horseradish (not creamed)

1 teaspoon Worcestershire sauce

1 stick celery, very finely diced

dash of Tabasco sauce

**1** Combine all the sauce ingredients and chill ready for use.
**2** Arrange the prawns on crushed ice on 6 plates with a ½ lemon per person. Serve with the cocktail sauce.

• • • • • • • • • • • • •

*Split the back and de-vein raw prawns in the shell, sprinkle with chilli, garlic, olive oil and lemon juice, then cook, shell-side down only, for 3 minutes until the flesh is opaque. Sprinkle with sea salt and chopped coriander.*

• • • • • • • • • • • • •

# Scallop and Green Mango Salad

Scallops in their freshest state are delicious raw, so sweet and tender. This recipe has always been a huge success when we serve it in the restaurants. Use only fresh scallops.

**Preparation and marination: 45 minutes**
**Serves: 3–4**

6 large raw diver-caught scallops, thinly sliced horizontally as many times as you can

1 tablespoon liquid honey

1 tablespoon *nam pla* (fish sauce)

2 tablespoons lime juice

1 unripe green mango, diced

2 tomatoes, seeded and diced

4 spring onions, finely diced

1 tablespoon chopped coriander

1 teaspoon chopped mint

1 teaspoon finely chopped lemongrass

1 clove garlic, finely diced

1 fresh red chilli, finely chopped

2 Little Gem lettuces, leaves picked

**1** Combine all the ingredients except the lettuce and allow to marinate for 30 minutes.
**2** Arrange the salad on the lettuce leaves, and serve.

• • • • • • • • • • • • •

*Using 1 lettuce leaf, 1 large cooked tiger prawn and 1 dollop of prawn cocktail sauce (see above left), make a mini prawn cocktail in a shot glass for a canapé . . . Down in one!*

• • • • • • • • • • • • •

# Steamed Scallops with Soy, Ginger, Sesame and Spring Onions

I've always enjoyed steamed scallops in Chinese restaurants, so simple and so delicious. So here is the recipe, give or take an ingredient or two.

**Marination and cooking: 12 hours + 20 minutes**
**Serves: 3–4**

| |
|---|
| 1 teaspoon grated ginger |
| ½ fresh red chilli, finely chopped |
| 1 clove garlic, finely chopped |
| 2 tablespoons sesame oil |
| 2 tablespoons soy sauce |
| 1 teaspoon lemon juice |
| ½ teaspoon clear honey |
| 1 tablespoon chopped coriander |
| 2 spring onions, finely chopped |
| 16 scallops in the half shell |

**1** Mix together all the ingredients except the scallops in a screw-top jar, shake everything together and leave to rest for up to 12 hours to allow the flavours to infuse.
**2** Place the scallops flat in a large steamer basket over a wok of boiling water. Spoon a little of the mixture over each scallop and steam for about 3 minutes. Eat immediately.

• • • • • • • •

*Serve grilled scallops with a little* Avocado and Charred Corn Salsa *(see page 26) on tortilla crisps for a pleasant mouthful.*

• • • • • • • •

• • • • • • • • • • • •

*Wrap whole scallops in pancetta or smoked streaky bacon, and thread a wooden thyme skewer through the parcel. Char-grill or grill for 2 minutes on each side until the bacon is crispy.*

• • • • • • • • • • • •

# FISH: SMOKED

Virtually everything that is edible seems to get smoked – fish, meat, game, poultry, tomatoes, garlic, even butter. Certain fish come into their own when smoked, especially salmon, eel, haddock, cod, trout, mackerel, herring and some roes. The quality of the smoked product depends on a few things, however: on the quality of the raw ingredient, on the type of wood used for the smoking method, and on the smoker himself or herself. Some salmon you get has been over-smoked or over-salted prior to smoking. I prefer a moist smoked salmon with not too strong a smoke, but unfortunately it doesn't have such lasting qualities. Mackerel smokes very well, as the oiliness of the fish prevents it from drying out. And of course a good kipper (a smoked herring) is hard to beat. Most smoked fish are salted first in dry salt or a brine, then are either hot smoked (when they do not need further cooking) or cold smoked (when some cooking is called for). Smoked salmon is cold smoked, but is the exception to the rule and is eaten raw.

Avoid smoked haddock and cod which have been dyed with tartrazine – easy to spot as the fish will be golden yellow; smoked mackerel and kippers can be artificially coloured as well. You must be the judge of which smoked fish you enjoy, but for those of you who want a good salmon, my butcher (Machin Butchers in Henley on Thames, see page 28) does mail-order of an excellent product. (I'll let you into a secret: his salmon is used regularly on Concorde.)

• • • • • • • • • • • • • •

*Line a timbale mould with smoked salmon and fill with creamy scrambled eggs. Turn out on to a plate of curly endive for a different way of presenting smoked salmon and scrambled eggs.*

• • • • • • • • • • • • • •

• • • • • • • • • • • • • •

*Lay fillets of smoked eel on a plate, place under the grill to warm through and dribble over a dill butter sauce (see page 213) and crispy bacon. Serve with dressed Belgian endive.*

• • • • • • • • • • • • • •

# Smoked Haddock, Kipper and Egg Mousse

This is one of those starters you get at dinner parties that has probably been handed down through generations of families. You eat it and think 'Wow, that was really great.' It's simple, it's delicious, and beats most other smoked fish appetisers. For a special treat, serve it with dollops of genuine caviar.

**Preparation and cooking: 30 minutes**
**Serves: 4**

6 hard-boiled eggs
½ x 400g (14 oz) tin Campbell's beef consommé
2 teaspoons anchovy essence
1 teaspoon Worcestershire sauce
250g (9 oz) Finnan haddock, cooked and flaked
2 kipper fillets, poached and roughly chopped
300ml (½ pint) double cream
2 teaspoons snipped chives
salt and ground black pepper
lemon juice

**1** Place 4 of the eggs in a food processor and blend until smooth. Add the consommé, anchovy essence, Worcestershire sauce and cooked flaked haddock. Blend until smooth.
**2** Tip the mixture into a bowl and fold in the chopped kipper fillet. Chop the remaining eggs and fold into the fish mousse mixture. Set aside.
**3** Beat the cream to stiff peaks and fold into the mousse. Add the chives and season with salt, pepper and lemon juice.
**4** Serve with hot toast.

• • • • • • • • • • • • • • • • • • • •

*Serve thin slices of smoked cod's roe with crusty wholemeal bread and country butter, plus a home-made horseradish cream (see page 104).*

• • • • • • • • • • • • • • • • • • • •

*For a great sandwich filling, fold flakes of smoked salmon, trout or mackerel into soft scrambled eggs. Fold in a little soured cream flavoured with horseradish and a little Mayonnaise (see page 239). Allow to cool and mix in snipped chives.*

• • • • • • • • • • • • • • • • • • • •

# My Favourite Sandwich

Everyone has probably got an eccentric, slightly quirky, favourite sandwich . . . this is mine. I like it as an open sandwich, but you can top it with more bread if you like.

**Preparation and cooking: 10 minutes**
**Serves: 2**

2 slices wholemeal bread
55g (2 oz) cream cheese
2 teaspoons diced red onion
55g (2 oz) smoked salmon, sliced
2 tablespoons mango chutney, puréed
4 slices streaky bacon, cooked until crispy
1 teaspoon small capers, drained
1 teaspoon snipped chives
ground black pepper

**1** Spread both slices of bread with the cream cheese, top with red onion and smoked salmon, then add a dribble of mango chutney.
**2** Top this with crispy bacon and capers.
**3** Finish with a dusting of snipped chives and ground black pepper.

## Kipper Toast

● *Mash some cooked kipper fillets with a little butter, cayenne pepper, double cream and grated Cheddar cheese.*
● *Toast a slice of bread on one side and spread the untoasted side with mango chutney.*
● *Top with the kipper mix, and pop under the grill until hot and bubbling.*

## Smoked Haddock *Gratin*

● *Place a fillet of smoked haddock in a gratin* dish *and pour in half milk and half double cream, leaving the top of the fish showing.*
● *Place under a hot grill and cook for 10 minutes.*
● *Serve with boiled new potatoes and salad.*

*Substitute smoked salmon for the bacon in Eggs Benedict (see page 117).*

# FRUIT: BERRIES AND CURRANTS

When one thinks of berries one thinks of Great Britain, sunny days, Pimms by the river, Wimbledon, Henley and Ascot and forgotten times; of PYO strawberries, and picking blackberries, coming home looking like we had been covered in gentian violet and finishing the day smothered with scratches covered with Germolene.

Enough of the clichés. What we are confronted with today is a vast array of out-of-season berries available all year round. Supermarkets today are reluctant to sell British strawberries as apparently they deteriorate much more quickly than imported varieties. Shame, as you really can't beat the flavour of the British variety. The same applies to Scottish raspberries and wild blackberries.

## BLACKBERRIES (*Rubus ulmifolius*)

A member of the Rosaceae family (that of the rose), and known traditionally as the moreish fruit of the thorny bramble. Various hybrids have been created, such as the loganberry (thought to be a cross between a blackberry and a raspberry), and the American boysenberry, just making an entry on to the British market. The traditional season is early autumn. When making a jam, either add a percentage of red unripe fruit or one-third apples to two-thirds blackberries which will help the setting qualities. Only wash if cultivated (you never know what they've been sprayed with) or if muddy. They are high in manganese, and in vitamins A, E, B₂ and folic acid.

## BLUEBERRIES (*Vaccinium angustifolium*)

Along with close relatives cranberries and huckleberries, they are native to North America, but are part of the same family – the Ericaceae – as European bilberries and lingonberries. Another variety (*V. corymbosum*), or highbush blueberry (as opposed to lowbush), is now being grown in Britain. Widely available in supermarkets but at a price. To me they are a bit overstated, and quite often can be a bit chewy and tasteless. Make your own mind up about them. They can be used in any recipe that suggests blackcurrants or bilberries. They contain vitamins A and C.

## CURRANTS (*Ribes* spp)

Black, red and white members of the Grossulariaceae family are often used by chefs on the stem for decorating puddings or game dishes. They are a bit fiddly to remove from the stalk but the best way I have found is to place the stem through the prongs of a fork and in one sweeping movement push the prongs from top to bottom, popping off all the berries into a bowl. If life is not too short add a combination of the berries to a summer pudding. Don't bother making redcurrant jelly because, apart from the satisfaction, the flavour won't impress

you any more than buying a good quality commercial brand, and it will actually end up costing you a lot more. Blackcurrants are worth a little more effort, but only just. Whitecurrants, forget it! The red and white are very sour unless very ripe. Currants, however, are rich in vitamins A and C, the latter especially in blackcurrants.

Something that grows wild and is free, although not related, is the elderberry (*Sambucus nigra*). Now here we're talking flavour, whether it is infusing the flowers in a syrup, or using the berries in jellies. This is worth a country stroll, but avoid trees and shrubs near to main roads.

## GOOSEBERRIES (*Ribes grossularia*)

This fruit, a close relative of the currants, is really only popular in Britain, and the rest of the world doesn't know what it's missing. The French don't even have an individual name for it, calling it *groseille*, the name for redcurrant; more recently it has become *groseille à maquereau*, probably because of the happy combination of the oily mackerel with the tartness of the gooseberry (one that is traditional in Britain too). Never mind, we like them in Britain, and have developed over 100 varieties ranging from green through to yellow and red.

For preparation, just wash them, don't bother topping and tailing unless you are using them whole in a pie. Many recipes demand that you sieve them, and I see no value in extra work for the sake of it. Gooseberries have good supplies of phosphorus, vitamins A, E, B₂ and C.

## MULBERRIES (*Morus nigra*)

These belong to the same family as figs, but are not a fruit to spend too long on; not because of the quality of the fruit, but because they are almost impossible to find unless you grow a tree yourself. Treat them exactly as you would a blackberry or raspberry, and beware, they deteriorate extremely quickly and their stains are almost impossible to remove. By the way, mulberries contain a good amount of potassium and some vitamin C. They also make a good laxative and they may be eaten by those with gout and rheumatism. (That latter piece of information came from my gran!) White mulberries (*Morus alba*) can be eaten, but the trees are cultivated principally because the leaves feed the common silkworm.

## RASPBERRIES (*Rubus idaeus*)

Another member of the Rosaceae family, and of all the red fruits this is the king. British or Scottish fruit taste phenomenal; ignore raspberries from the USA as their taste is poor to average and their price is high to gross. Pick your own as they deteriorate quickly in the punnet (check the punnet for stains at the bottom), and eat within 2 days of purchase. As they grow well off the ground they shouldn't need washing. When making raspberry jam or any dish where you cook the raspberries, add a third of the weight of raspberries in redcurrants, which help to intensify the flavour of the raspberries. The fruits contain vitamins B and C, and manganese, phosphorus, iron and zinc.

## STRAWBERRIES (*Fragaria* spp)

Probably the best loved of the red summer fruits, and they contain minerals and a good amount of vitamin C. There is no need to say much more, but I should just like to ask a couple of questions. Why can't we pull the hulls out of strawberries any more? And why do foreign strawberries last much longer than British strawberries? I'm deeply suspicious. Buy British in season and enjoy real flavour.

Treat yourself occasionally to *fraises des bois*, wild strawberries (*F. vesca or moschata*) which are exquisite but very expensive (or grow them yourself, it's easy).

# Blackberry Pickle

A blackberry pickle is a nice combo with a strong cheese or cold meats.

**Preparation and cooking: overnight + 30 minutes**
**Makes: 1.3kg (3 lb)**

| |
|---|
| 900g (2 lb) blackberries |
| 675g (1½ lb) caster sugar |
| 2 teaspoons ground allspice |
| 2 tablespoons ground ginger |
| 600ml (1 pint) white vinegar |

**1** In a bowl add to the blackberries the caster sugar, ground allspice, and ground ginger. Toss to combine. Allow to rest overnight.
**2** Bring the white vinegar to the boil, add the berries, reduce the heat and cook gently for 20 minutes.
**3** Allow to cool and spoon into sterilised jars.

# Blackberry Chutney

Blackberry chutney is also a winner.
**Preparation and cooking: about 1¼ hours**
**Makes: 4.5kg (10 lb)**

| |
|---|
| 2.7kg (6 lb) blackberries |
| 900g (2 lb) apples, peeled, cored and chopped |
| 450g (1 lb) onions, finely chopped |
| 2 teaspoons ground ginger |
| 2 teaspoons English mustard powder |
| ½ teaspoon grated nutmeg |
| ½ teaspoon ground mace |
| ½ tablespoon crushed black pepper |
| 2 teaspoons sea salt |
| 900g (2 lb) soft dark brown sugar |
| 1.2 litres (2 pints) white vinegar |

**1** Boil together all of the ingredients.
**2** Cook for about 1 hour for desired consistency, remembering it will be thicker when cold.
**3** Spoon into hot sterilised jars and seal.

# Blackberry and Red Wine *Compote*

An excellent adult sauce-cum-pud that can be either eaten as is with some cream, poured over ice-cream or served with apple pie.
**Preparation and cooking: 30 minutes**
**Serves: 4**

675g (1½ lb) ripe, undamaged blackberries

juice of 2 lemons

juice of 1 orange

175g (6 oz) caster sugar

1 bottle red wine

85ml (3 fl oz) *Crème de Mûre* (blackberry liqueur)

1 tablespoon finely chopped mint

1  In a food processor blend half the blackberries with the two citrus juices until smooth. Strain the resulting purée through a fine sieve into a **non-reactive** saucepan. Discard the pips.
2  Add the sugar and red wine and over a medium heat bring to the boil. Reduce the heat and simmer, skimming off any scum that may come to the surface, until the purée is reduced to about 450ml (16 fl oz). Allow to cool.
3  Just before serving fold in the remaining blackberries, the liqueur and the chopped mint.

• • • • • • • • • • • • • • • • • •

*Make a stack of* crêpes. *Sift 115g (4 oz) plain flour and a pinch of salt into a bowl, and make a well in the centre. Pour 1 egg and 1 egg yolk with a little milk into the well. Whisk well, drawing in the flour. When thick and creamy, beat in 1 tablespoon olive oil. Add 300ml (½ pint) milk and water mixed, and stir to combine. Chill, then cook as for normal pancakes. Layer the* crêpes *with* Mascarpone Cream *(see page 84) and blackberries, like a sandwich.*

• • • • • • • • • • • • • • • • • •

# Blackberry Jam

For blackberry jam you may find you prefer to add apples in the proportion of one-third apples to two-thirds blackberries.
**Preparation and cooking: 45 minutes**
**Makes: 3 litres (5¼ pints)**

900g (2 lb) apples

300ml (½ pint) water

2.7kg (6 lb) blackberries

1.5kg (3 lb 5 oz) sugar

1  Peel, core and roughly chop the apples then wrap peel, seeds and core in muslin.
2  Stew the apples in the water until soft, then pass through a sieve.
3  Place the purée, blackberries, sugar and the muslin bag into a **non-reactive** saucepan and boil for 15 minutes, skimming regularly, until setting point is reached. Remove the bag, squeezing it into the jam, and discard.
4  Pour the jam into sterilised jars.

• • • • • • • • • • • • • • • • • • • • • • • • • •

## Blackberry 'Wine'
*My gran used to make this rather lethal blackberry 'wine'. At the age of eight, I would sneak a slurp only a week after it had been bottled!*
● *Cover blackberries with boiling water, and then leave them in a cool oven (120°C/250°F/Gas ½) overnight.*
● *The next day, mash or liquidise the berries with their liquid, pass them through a sieve and allow the juice to ferment for 2 weeks in a crock in a dark room.*
● *After this process, for every 4.8 litres (8 pints) of liquid add 450g (1 lb) sugar and 300ml (½ pint) gin.*
● *Bottle and leave for up to a year.*

• • • • • • • • • • • • • • • • • • • • • • • • • •

# Blackberry Sorbet

Blackberries make a lovely sorbet.

**Preparation and cooking: 40 minutes**
**Makes: 600ml (1 pint)**

675g (1½ lb) blackberries

4 sweet geranium leaves

100g (3½ oz) sugar

150ml (¼ pint) water

90ml (3 fl oz) lime juice

125ml (4 fl oz) vodka

2 tablespoons *Crème de Mûre* (blackberry liqueur)

**1** Purée and sieve the blackberries.

**2** Make a syrup by boiling the geranium leaves with the sugar and water, then allow to cool.

**3** Combine the purée with the strained syrup, lime juice, vodka and *Crème de Mûre*.

**4** Freeze in an ice-cream machine according to manufacturer's instructions.

# Blackberry Syrup

*A nice alcoholic syrup to serve in champagne or for zapping up a gravy for a game bird.*

● *Liquidise blackberries, pass through a sieve and for every 600ml (1 pint) of liquid add 450g (1 lb) soft brown sugar*

● *Boil for 15–20 minutes then add 300ml (½ pint) vodka or brandy for every 1.2 litres (2 pints) syrup.*

● *Bottle when cold.*

# Blueberry Chutney

Serve this with cold duck, pork or chicken.

**Preparation and cooking: 45 minutes**
**Makes: 1.5 litres (2¾ pints)**

900g (2 lb) blueberries

1 Bramley apple, cored, peeled and chopped

675g (1½ lb) soft dark brown sugar

350ml (12 fl oz) white vinegar

150g (5½ oz) mixed dried cranberries, cherries and blueberries

1 teaspoon salt

1 teaspoon ground ginger

12 cloves

½ teaspoon allspice

1 teaspoon English mustard powder

**1** Bring all of the ingredients to the boil in a **non-reactive** pan.

**2** Simmer for 20–30 minutes or until the desired consistency.

**3** Spoon into hot sterilised jars and seal.

# Blueberry Sauce

*For a blueberry sauce excellent for ice-cream or pancakes, mix together 55g (2 oz) caster sugar, ¼ teaspoon each of ground nutmeg and cinnamon, 2 level teaspoons cornflour and 150ml (¼ pint) water. Stir to a smooth paste, then add 2 bay leaves and 450g (1 lb) blueberries. Simmer until the liquid thickens and the sauce is glossy. Adjust taste by adding lime zest, lime juice and sugar.*

*Fresh blueberries with a sprinkling of caster sugar and a squeeze of lime juice served with Greek yogurt make me a semi-healthy breakfast.*

# Cumberland Sauce

An often forgotten sauce that is served cold with baked ham or game. Make a decent quantity and bottle in small jars.
**Preparation and cooking: 45 minutes**
**Makes: 850ml (1½ pints)**

4 blood oranges or oranges
2 lemons
3 shallots, finely diced
450g (1 lb) redcurrant jelly
90ml (3 fl oz) port
90ml (3 fl oz) red wine
1 tablespoon Dijon mustard
½ cinnamon stick
½ teaspoon ground ginger
salt and ground black pepper

**1** Peel the oranges and lemons with a potato peeler, and cut the peel into **julienne**. **Blanch** the peel and shallot in boiling water for 5 minutes, drain and set aside. Juice the oranges and lemons.
**2** Melt the redcurrant jelly with the port and wine over a medium heat.
**3** Put the juices, citrus peel, shallot, mustard, cinnamon and ground ginger into the liquid and stir to combine. Cook over a medium heat for 15–20 minutes. Season to taste.
**4** Pour into sterilised jars and seal. This will keep for a few weeks.

# Redcurrant Ketchup

This old redcurrant ketchup I discovered in an antique cookbook is a useful condiment added to stews or gravies or served on its own with cold meats or grilled mackerel.
**Preparation and cooking: 40 minutes**
**Makes: 2 litres (3½ pints)**

1 litre (1¾ pints) redcurrant juice
750ml (a good 1¼ pints) white vinegar
900g (2 lb) caster sugar
1 tablespoon powdered cinnamon
1 teaspoon Tabasco sauce
½ teaspoon ground ginger
½ teaspoon ground allspice
1 teaspoon salt

**1** To make redcurrant juice, either use a centrifugal juicer or cover redcurrants with boiling water, cook for 5 minutes, then pass through a fine sieve or jelly bag.
**2** Combine the juice with the white vinegar, caster sugar, powdered cinnamon, Tabasco sauce, ground ginger, ground allspice and salt.
**3** Cook for 20 minutes then pour into hot bottles and seal.

· · · · · · · · · ·
*Add a little redcurrant jelly*
*to your gravy for a hint of*
*sweetness and richness.*
· · · · · · · · · ·

## Blackcurrant 'Cheese'
*This recipe for blackcurrant 'cheese' comes from my great aunt. It is excellent served with a strong blue cheese.*
● *Take equal weights of the currants (without stems) and caster sugar.*
● *Place in a preserving pan over a low heat and bring gradually to the boil, stirring continuously.*
● *Remove any scum that rises to the surface.*
● *Simmer for 1 hour then pass through a sieve into a mould. Leave to set.*

## Blackcurrant Gin
*You'll know by now that my gran was partial to a drink or two, but she was ahead of her time. Here's her recipe for blackcurrant gin.*
● *Combine 900g (2 lb) sugar with 2.4 litres (4 pints) blackcurrants, a cinnamon stick, 4 cloves and 1.7 litres (3 pints) gin.*
● *If possible place it in a stone jar with a corked mouth and shake it regularly for the first month.*
● *It will be ready to drink in a couple of months, when it should be strained. Eat the berries if you dare!*

# Gooseberry and Mint Jelly

Wonderful with lamb and makes a pleasant change from the standard mint jelly we usually eat.

**Preparation and cooking: overnight + 30 minutes**
**Makes: 1 litre (1¾ pints)**

1.8kg (4 lb) gooseberries, topped and tailed

juice of 1 lemon

preserving sugar

a large bunch of mint

**1** Cover the gooseberries with water and the lemon juice.

**2** Simmer gently to a pulp and pass through a jelly bag overnight into a bowl.

**3** Measure the liquid and weigh out 450g (1 lb) preserving sugar for every 600ml (1 pint).

**4** Combine and return to the heat with the mint. Remove the mint when the flavour is strong enough for your palate.

**5** Pour into hot sterilised jars when it reaches setting point.

## Gooseberry 'Cheese'

*Don't discard the pulp from the* Gooseberry and Mint Jelly.

● *Weigh the gooseberry pulp, return to a saucepan, and boil until the pulp starts to come away from the side. For every 450g (1 lb) pulp add 225g (8 oz) caster sugar and cook over a medium heat for a further 15 minutes, stirring constantly or it will burn and stick.*

● *Pour into an oiled mould, cool and refrigerate.*

● *Slice and eat with cheese. It's similar to the quince 'cheese' known in France as* pâte de coings, *and as* marmelada *in Spain.*

# Gooseberry and Prune Chutney

One of my favourite chutneys, perfect with cheese or cold meats.

**Preparation and cooking: 1½ hours**
**Makes: 2.7kg (6 lb)**

900g (2 lb) gooseberries, topped and tailed

450g (1 lb) pitted prunes, chopped

2 cloves garlic, finely chopped

450g (1 lb) onions, halved and sliced

450g (1 lb) sultanas

100g (3½ oz) flaked almonds

1 tablespoon ground ginger

½ teaspoon cayenne pepper

1 teaspoon salt

1.2 litres (2 pints) malt vinegar

500g (18 oz) soft brown sugar

**1** Place all the ingredients except the sugar in a **non-reactive** saucepan and, over a medium heat, bring slowly to the boil.

**2** Simmer for 1 hour, stirring regularly until the fruit has broken down and the ingredients are well combined.

**3** Add the brown sugar and cook for a further 5 minutes.

**4** Pour into hot sterilised jars and seal.

## Gooseberry Sauce

*A classic sauce to accompany oily fish such as mackerel.*

● *Boil 450g (1 lb) gooseberries with a splash of water until tender, pass them through a sieve and fold in 300ml (½ pint) clarified butter (see page 60).*

● *Simmer over a low heat with ½ teaspoon ground ginger, ½ teaspoon grated lemon rind, a pinch of grated nutmeg and 2 tablespoons caster sugar for 15 minutes then fold in 2 handfuls of chopped sorrel.*

● *Cook until the sorrel has broken down, about 5 minutes.*

# Summer Pudding

No summer is complete without at least one tasting of summer pudding served with clotted cream. As the name suggests, you can use any combination of summer fruits – excluding strawberries. My favourite combination is raspberries and redcurrants with a few blackcurrants thrown in for good measure.

**Preparation and cooking: overnight + 2½ hours**
**Serves: 6–8**

900g (2 lb) raspberries

225g (8 oz) redcurrants, picked

55g (2 oz) blackcurrants, picked

225g (8 oz) caster sugar

½ loaf of day-old bread, crusts removed, sliced

125ml (4 fl oz) Framboise liqueur or Kirsch

**1** Sprinkle the fruit with the sugar and toss gently to combine. Cover and leave to macerate for 2 hours. They will start to give out copious juices.

**2** Meanwhile, line a 1.2 litre (2 pint) pudding basin with clingfilm then with slices of bread which you have dipped in the juices from the fruit. Make sure the bread overlaps slightly and covers the sides and bottom completely.

**3** Tip the fruit and juices into a **non-reactive** saucepan with the Framboise and cook over a medium heat for 4 minutes to release some more juices.

**4** Using a slotted spoon, fill up the bread-lined basin with fruit. Pour over half the juices, then cover the fruit completely with more bread slices. Cover with clingfilm, then top with a plate which fits into the rim of the basin. Place a heavy weight on top of the plate and refrigerate overnight.

**5** When ready to serve, invert the basin on to a shallow but not flat dish, then remove the bowl and clingfilm. Serve wedges with clotted cream, a few loose berries of your choice, and a little of the reserved juices.

• • • • • • • • • • •

*For a quick and easy*
*raspberry sauce or coulis,*
*blend raspberries with a little*
*lime juice and icing sugar to*
*taste. Pass through a fine*
*sieve to remove seeds.*

• • • • • • • • • • •

## Raspberry Sweets

When I was a kid my great aunt used to give me some amazing raspberry sweets. Put 600ml (1 pint) raspberries in a saucepan with 2 tablespoons sugar, and heat gently until the juices start to flow. Pass the juice and pulp through a sieve. Mix the raw weight of fruit purée with the same weight of sugar and boil, stirring continuously, until it forms a dry paste. Pour the mix into shallow moulds and place in a low oven (140°C/275°F/Gas 1) overnight. Cool and cut into cubes and store in an airtight container until required.

## Raspberry Custard

Another old-fashioned recipe is raspberry custard. Bruise raspberries, sprinkle with sugar, and heat to bring out the juices. Pour the juice off and for every 600ml (1 pint) beat in 4 egg yolks. Heat over a low flame, stirring continuously; do not boil. Allow to cool and then fold in 150ml (¼ pint) double cream whipped to **soft peaks**. Pour into glasses.

## Raspberry Pie

Occasionally I eat a fab raspberry pie made by filling a pie dish with raspberries, sprinkling over sugar and covering with puff pastry. Bake in a 180°C/350°F/Gas 4 oven until the pastry is cooked, about 35 minutes. Beat together 300ml (½ pint) double cream with 2 egg yolks. Carefully lift the crust off the pastry, and pour in the cream mix. Replace the pastry and return to the oven for 8 minutes. Serve hot or cold.

For a summer breakfast treat, top pancakes, waffles or eggy bread (see page 52) with mashed raspberries folded into thick double cream.

For a truly adult pud, mix 1kg (2¼ lb) fresh raspberries with 150ml (¼ pint) ruby port, 2 tablespoons caster sugar, 2 tablespoons brandy and 2 tablespoons lime juice. Chill and serve with cold custard or thick double cream.

# Strawberry Floater

For the kiddie in all of us, an adult ice-cream floater.
**Preparation: 10 minutes**
**Serves: 4**

450g (1 lb) strawberries

175g (6 oz) caster sugar

150ml (¼ pint) water

150ml (¼ pint) Laurent-Perrier *rosé* champagne

**To serve**

a scoop of strawberry ice-cream per serving

**1** Combine the strawberries with the caster sugar and water in a liquidiser.
**2** Pass through a fine sieve.
**3** Pour the champagne into a glass, and combine with 4 tablespoons of the strawberry purée.
**4** Float a scoop of strawberry ice-cream on the top.

• • • • • • • • • • • •

*For something a little different, combine 2 punnets of hulled strawberries with 2 tablespoons sugar and 2 tablespoons balsamic vinegar 1 hour before eating. This does wonders for the flavour, and also produces delicious juices.*

• • • • • • • • • • • •

• • • • • • • • • • • •

*Mash strawberries in Sauternes and add grated lemon rind. Mix in a couple of tablespoons of strawberry* eau-de-vie *or brandy. Pour into glasses and float whipped double cream on the surface.*

• • • • • • • • • • • •

# Strawberry Squash

If you are bored with everyday soft drinks, try this refreshing little recipe.
**Preparation: 15 minutes**
**Makes:  about 450ml (16 fl oz)**

225g (8 oz) hulled strawberries

4 tablespoons caster sugar

450ml (¾ pint) water

½ lemon

**To serve**

iced water

**1** Take the strawberries and combine with the caster sugar and 150ml (¼ pint) of the water.
**2** Purée in a food processor, pass through a fine sieve, then place in a jelly bag over a bowl.
**3** When the pulp is dry, add another 300ml (½ pint) water and allow to drip through.
**4** Mix with the strained lemon juice.
**5** Dilute with iced water when ready to drink.

• • • • • • • • • • • •

*Most of the recipes for raspberries and blackberries can be used for strawberries.*

• • • • • • • • • • • •

• • • • • • • • • • • •

*Mash strawberries with a little sugar and port, and fold in broken meringues and softly whipped double cream.*

• • • • • • • • • • • •

• • • • • • • • • • • •

*Serve sliced strawberries with mascarpone or ricotta cheese, offering sugar and double cream on the side*

• • • • • • • • • • • •

# FRUIT: CITRUS FRUITS

Where would we be without orange juice in the mornings, fresh limes in Oriental food and *margaritas*, marmalades, lemon with fish or in drinks, and grapefruit for all those wonderful diets?

The Citrus genus belongs to the rue or Rutaceae family, and originated in China. The original forebear of all today's varieties of orange and other citrus fruit was probably *Citrus aurantium*, the bitter, sour or Seville orange. Oranges were brought to Europe from China by the Arabs, and at one time a large part of southern Spain was covered in orange groves (thus the name Seville). Christopher Columbus took oranges to the New World.

All citrus fruit are high in vitamin C (both flesh *and* peel).

## GRAPEFRUIT (*Citrus paradisi*)

These used to be very sour, but they've sweetened their act up and I think the pink Florida grapefruit is great. The pomelo is a close relative; it's not found widely over here, but if you can get it, try it, especially in Asian salads – each individual droplet of juice can be separated so causing a miniature juice explosion when you bite into one.

The grapefruit was probably a cross between a pomelo and an orange and was first developed in Florida in the late 1800s. The pomelo has been known since the seventeenth century in Europe, and originated in Malaysia and Java. The ugli fruit (a grapefruit/orange/tangerine hybrid) is a more recent arrival, popular for a time probably because it was sweeter than the grapefruit.

## LEMON AND LIME (*Citrus limon, C. aurantifolia*)

The trees from which these fruit come grow in different parts of the world: the lemon likes Mediterranean countries, whereas the lime prefers the tropics. The Kaffir lime is grown extensively in the East and is used a great deal in Thai cooking, as are its leaves. The Mexican lime, also known as Key lime, is considered to be *the* authentic fruit, and if ever you are in America, especially the Florida Keys, you will see Key Lime Pie on many menus. The Meyer lemon is greatly valued and is a lemon-orange hybrid, making it sweeter and less acid than a regular lemon.

The lemon starts green and turns yellow on the tree, whereas the lime is ripe when it is very green. The lime will turn a muddy yellow colour as it gets older, but this dehydration increases the juice content, so if I want lime juice in large quantities I slip down to the market and kindly take their old stock off their hands.

## ORANGE (*Citrus sinensis*)

The orange has many offspring – tangerines, mandarins, satsumas, clementines and kumquats. I prefer the navel orange which has that sharp point at the top. You must be the ultimate judge, but beware of the larger glossy-looking orange which has very thick skin and a poor juice ratio. I remember well the Christmas tangerine in my stocking, which had a delicious flavour but was full of pips. Now every year they seem to invent a new hybrid, mainly to eliminate the pips, and the clementine is my favourite of these. (What I can't understand is that if these fruits are seedless, how do they continue to grow the strain?)

### A Few Useful Tips on Citrus Fruits

• Most citrus fruit is waxed nowadays, so if you want to use the rind, soak the fruit in hot water for 10 minutes before using.

• Soak the whole fruit in hot water for 30 minutes before juicing to produce the best juice yield.

• When using lemon juice for lime juice in a recipe double the quantity as lime juice is much stronger. Do the same in reverse, halving lime juice if used in a lemon recipe.

• To remove the rind without the pith use a thin-bladed sharp knife, a grater or zester.

• Lemon and lime juice are useful stored in ice-cube trays in the freezer. Once frozen the juice cubes can be removed and kept frozen in freezer bags and used as required.

• Dried orange peel is a useful addition to stews and soups. Don't waste your peelings, dry them in an airy space, an airing cupboard, or a very low oven overnight.

• To remove segments from any citrus fruit, remove the peel and pith. Cut between the internal sides of the two membranes on either side of each segment. This will free each segment. Try to retain all the juices, and squeeze the core and pulp too.

• To candy citrus peel, cut the peel in strips 5mm (¼ in) wide and boil in two or three changes of water for 5 minutes each time to remove excess bitterness. Drain and weigh the fruit peel and add the same weight in sugar with a small amount of water. Simmer very gently for the best part of an hour until the peel is translucent. Drain the peel on cake racks in a dry place; this could take a couple of days. Roll in sugar and store in an airtight container. Add to cakes and biscuits, dip in chocolate or serve as they are with coffee after dinner.

• To test the set on citrus marmalade (or indeed any preserve), chill a couple of saucers in the freezer. When cool put a spoonful of the marmalade on to one of the saucers. It is ready, or at setting point, when you draw your finger or spoon through the cool marmalade and the two stay apart, the channel in the middle staying open. (Always take the marmalade off the heat while doing the test!)

## Technicolour Marmalade

Ordinary marmalades tend to be an adult affair, especially if you make your own. This marmalade adds other ingredients that make it more attractive for kids.

**Preparation and cooking: 2 days + 2 hours**
**Fills: 6 x 600ml (1 pint) jars**

6 grapefruit

6 oranges

6 lemons

water

preserving sugar

675g (1½ lb) glacé cherries, halved

450g (1 lb) candied pineapple, cut in small cubes

225g (8 oz) preserved ginger, cut in small cubes

**1** Peel the rinds from the grapefruit, oranges and lemons. Mince or finely chop the grapefruit rind, and thinly slice the orange and lemon rind.

**2** Slice the fruits thinly, then cut each slice in quarters. Reserve the pips and tie them in muslin.

**3** Measure the fruit and rind by volume then put in a preserving pan and add the pips and the equivalent amount of water. Allow to stand overnight.

**4** The next morning cook the rinds, fruit pips and water together until the rinds are tender, about 20 minutes. Allow to stand overnight again.

**5** The next day measure the fruits and liquids by volume and add the same volume of preserving sugar. Cook for 1–1½ hours, stirring regularly. Remove and discard the pips.

**6** Add the candied fruits and continue to cook until the marmalade reaches setting point, approximately 104°C/220°F, or after 20 minutes. Use the saucer method to test the set (see above). Pour into hot jars and seal.

## *Crêpes* Suzette

This pud appears to have gone out of fashion, yet it deserves to make a comeback because it is so delicious.

**Preparation and cooking: 25 minutes**
**Serves: 4–6**

8 sugar lumps

4 large juicy oranges, unwaxed if possible

55g (2 oz) caster sugar

85g (3 oz) unsalted butter, cut in small cubes

juice of 1 lemon

12 pancakes (buy them in the supermarket)

3 tablespoons Cointreau

2 tablespoons Cognac

**1** Rub the sugar lumps over the skin of the oranges until they absorb the orange oil. Put the lumps into a frying pan once they are saturated. Squeeze the juice of the oranges through a sieve into a bowl and set aside.

**2** Add the caster sugar to the frying pan with the sugar lumps and set over a medium heat. Once the sugar begins to caramelise, pour in the orange juice. Add the butter, cube by cube, then the lemon juice, and bring to a gentle simmer.

**3** Take one pancake, pop it in the sauce and turn it over. Fold it in half and then half again to form a triangle. Push to the side of the frying pan and repeat with the remaining pancakes.

**4** By now the sauce should be nicely concentrated. Add the Cointreau and stir to combine.

**5** Pour the Cognac into a ladle and hold over a flame. When warm, it will ignite. Pour it over the pancakes and serve immediately with cream if you are a piggy like me.

# Elizabeth David's Everlasting Syllabub

No section on citrus fruits should be without this recipe.

**Preparation and cooking: overnight + 20 minutes**
**Serves: 4–6**

| |
|---|
| 125ml (4 fl oz) white wine or sherry |
| 2 tablespoons brandy |
| pared rind and juice of 1 lemon |
| 55g (2 oz) caster sugar |
| 300ml (½ pint) double cream |
| freshly grated nutmeg |

**1** Put the first three ingredients into a bowl and leave overnight.

**2** Next day strain the liquid into a bowl and stir in the sugar until it has dissolved. Pour in the cream with a pinch of nutmeg.

**3** Beat the syllabub with a wire whisk until it holds its shape – do not go on too long, or do it too vigorously, or the cream will split.

**4** Spoon the syllabub into small glasses and refrigerate until ready to serve. Sprinkle with nutmeg and serve with citrus biscuits.

## Citrus Biscuits

*These citrus biscuits are a great hit with kids, and are also good served with a syllabub.*

- *In a bowl combine 115g (4 oz) plain flour with 75g (2¾ oz) powdered almonds and a pinch of salt.*
- *In a saucepan combine 150g (5½ oz) light soft brown sugar with 150g (5½ oz) golden syrup and 115g (4 oz) unsalted butter. Stir over a medium heat until the mixture comes to the boil.*
- *Remove from the heat and fold in the flour mixture along with 2 tablespoons lemon juice and the grated zest of 2 oranges.*
- *Drop teaspoonfuls of the mixture on to a lightly greased baking tray about 10cm (4 in) apart.*
- *Cook for about 12 minutes or until golden in a preheated oven at 180°C/350°F/Gas 4.*
- *Allow to cool for a few minutes, then cool completely on a wire rack.*

## Lemon Oil Pickle

*Makes a pleasant change from salted lemons, a current vogue.*

● *Slice lemons, remove pips, put them in a bowl, sprinkle with salt, and leave overnight.*

● *Drain them and layer them in Kilner jars, sprinkling each layer with a little paprika and a few green peppercorns.*

● *When full add a few stamens of saffron and then fill the jar with a decent olive oil.*

● *Screw or clip lids on tightly, then place in a saucepan on some folded newspaper or a rack with cold water to the neck.*

● *Bring to the boil and simmer for 30 minutes.*

● *Keep for 1 month before using.*

● *Delicious folded into curries or with grilled fish. Use the oil in salad dressings or for frying or grilling fish.*

*Try Buck's Fizz made with blood orange juice for a nice change – they're available in December/January.*

*Lemon, lime or orange curd is always a favourite. Remove the rind and juice from 3 lemons, 4 limes or 2 oranges and chop finely. Put into the top of a **double-boiler** with 90g (3¼ oz) unsalted butter and 175g (6 oz) caster sugar. Stir over simmering water until the sugar has dissolved. Add 3 beaten large eggs and stir continuously until the mixture is thick; do not allow to boil. Pour into small pots and cover. Keeps for a month in a refrigerator.*

## *Avgolemono*

*This Greek lemon and egg soup is one of my wife's favourites. It's a great soup to give you a lift if you're feeling under the weather.*

● *Bring 1.2 litres (2 pints) really good chicken stock to the boil.*

● *Whisk 4 large eggs with the juice of 2 large lemons.*

● *Allow the stock to cool slightly, add a little to the lemon mixture, and whisk well.*

● *Pour the lemon mix back into the stock, stirring continuously over a low heat until thickened. Do not allow to boil.*

● *Season to taste.*

*Sea Breeze is a refreshing cocktail. Pour 2 measures of vodka over ice and top with two-thirds cranberry juice and one-third fresh grapefruit juice.*

*The old ones can often be the best ones. Cut a grapefruit in half, sprinkle with ground cinnamon and brown sugar and glaze under the grill.*

*For fresh lemonade make this lasting base. Remove the zest of 6 lemons with a potato peeler and place in a saucepan with 1 litre (1¾ pints) water, 1.5kg (3 lb 5 oz) caster sugar, 25g (1 oz) citric acid, 25g (1 oz) tartaric acid and the juice of the lemons. Stir until the sugar has dissolved. Strain into bottles, allow to cool, then refrigerate. When required, dilute a little as required with water, soda or lemonade.*

# FRUIT: DRIED FRUIT

We're used to regular dried fruits – prunes (dried plums), apricots, raisins and sultanas (dried grapes), figs, apples and pears – but now so many other varieties have started to appear in the shops – mangoes, blueberries, cherries and cranberries to name but a few. The new varieties are expensive but occasionally they add something a little special to a cake or pudding. I use them in my *Ricotta Cake* (see page 85) and Christmas cake or pudding.

When fruit are dried, their nutrients become concentrated. For instance, an 84g plum contains 1.6g fibre, 240mg potassium and 13mg calcium; a 22g prune contains 6.5g fibre, 860mg potassium and 38mg calcium.

## AWT's Christmas Pudding

A fruit-rich pud that can be eaten by vegetarians as it has no suet.

**Preparation and cooking: 2 days + 9 hours**
**Makes: 2 x 1.3kg (3 lb) puddings, to serve 12**

### Fruit mix

juice and grated rind of 2 oranges
juice and grated rind of 1 lemon
350g (12 oz) pitted prunes, diced
115g (4 oz) *marrons glacés*, quartered
175g (6 oz) dried apricots, diced
225g (8 oz) candied peel, diced
225g (8 oz) sultanas
280g (10 oz) whole glacé cherries, halved
115g (4 oz) flaked almonds
55g (2 oz) ground almonds
55g (2 oz) toasted hazelnuts, chopped
55g (2 oz) stem ginger, diced
280g (10 oz) apples, cored and grated
225g (8 oz) dark soft brown sugar
300ml (½ pint) barley wine
6 tablespoons brandy
6 tablespoons Bénédictine
3 tablespoons walnut oil

*Pack the kids off to school with a few raisins or sultanas in their lunch box.*

### Dry ingredients

225g (8 oz) wholemeal breadcrumbs
115g (4 oz) self-raising flour
½ teaspoon each of ground cinnamon, nutmeg, mace, cloves, allspice and cardamom
175g (6 oz) cold unsalted butter, grated

### Mixing medium

2 tablespoons clear honey
2 tablespoons rough-cut marmalade
6 eggs

**1** Combine the fruit mix ingredients and leave at least overnight, preferably for 48 hours.
**2** On day 2, combine the dry ingredients, then fold into the fruit mix.
**3** Beat the mixing medium ingredients until fluffy, and fold into the other ingredients.
**4** Prepare the basins and their covers. Butter the 2 pudding basins well and cut small greaseproof rounds to fit the bottom of the bowls. Butter the greaseproof rounds and fit them in place. Cut out double rounds of greaseproof paper 7.5cm (3 in) larger than the tops of the basins. Butter well on the side to be placed on top of the mixture.
**5** Divide the mixture between the pudding basins, filling them four-fifths full. Smooth over the tops, making a small indentation in the middle. Cover with the prepared greaseproof rounds and wrap the complete basin in baking foil or muslin (rinsed and floured on the inside), tying firmly at the top.
**6** Stand the basins on a rack in a large saucepan and pour in boiling water to come three-quarters of the way up the sides of the basins. Cover the pan tightly and steam for three periods of 2 hours. Allow to cool between each period and top up the pan with extra *boiling water* often during each cooking period.
**7** Cool then store in a cool, dark place until ready to use. On Christmas Day, steam for a further 2½ hours. Serve with *Brandy (or Rum) Butter* (see page 58).

# Breakfast Dried Fruit *Compote*

This is a great way of getting kids – big and little alike – to eat their vitamins. A very healthy and nutritious breakfast.

**Preparation and cooking: 40 minutes**
**Serves: 4–6**

| |
|---|
| 115g (4 oz) dried apricots |
| 55g (2 oz) dried cherries |
| 55g (2 oz) dried blueberries |
| 55g (2 oz) dried figs |
| 55g (2 oz) dried pears |
| 55g (2 oz) dried mango |
| ½ stick cinnamon |
| 2 tablespoons clear honey |
| 2 cloves |
| ½ vanilla pod, split |
| zest of ½ lemon |
| pinch of saffron stamens, soaked in 1 tablespoon cold water |
| 15g (½ oz) flaked almonds, toasted |
| 15g (½ oz) pine kernels |
| few drops of orange or rose water (optional) |

**1** Place all the ingredients down to and including the saffron in a **non-reactive** saucepan and just cover with cold water. Bring to the boil, reduce the heat and simmer for 25 minutes.
**2** Allow to cool then add the remaining ingredients. Serve with cereal, wheatgerm or Greek yogurt.

. . . . . . . . . . . . . . . . . . . .

## Spicy Apricot and Chilli Chutney
*Great with cold meats and cheese.*
● *Cook 1kg (2¼ lb) dried apricots that have soaked overnight with their soaking liquor until soft.*
● *Add 12 chopped chillies, 1kg (2¼ lb) soft brown sugar, 1 tablespoon salt, 1 tablespoon grated fresh ginger, 1 teaspoon ground mace, and 2 litres (3½ pints) white vinegar.*
● *Simmer gently for 45–60 minutes until thick.*
● *Pot in sterilised jars.*

. . . . . . . . . . . . . . . . . . . .

# Cherry Bread and Butter Pudding

Make this delicious cherry bread and butter pudding, a change from the norm.

**Preparation and cooking: 2 hours + 1 hour**
**Serves: 4–6**

| |
|---|
| 250ml (9 fl oz) milk |
| 250ml (9 fl oz) double cream |
| 1 vanilla pod, split |
| 3 large eggs |
| 115g (4 oz) caster sugar |
| 12 slices crustless bread |
| butter |
| cherry jam |
| dried cherries |
| Kirsch |

**1** Bring the milk to the boil with the double cream and a vanilla pod.
**2** Beat the eggs, strain on the hot cream and milk, add the caster sugar, and stir until the sugar dissolves.
**3** Thinly butter the crustless bread and spread with a thin layer of cherry jam. Arrange the slices in a buttered baking dish, sprinkling each layer with a few dried cherries.
**4** Pour a couple of measures of Kirsch into the milk mixture and pour over the bread slices; if you have time, allow to sit for a couple of hours.
**5** Cook in a **bain-marie** for 50 minutes in a preheated oven at 160°C/325°F/Gas 3.
**6** Remove from the oven and brown the top under the grill.

. . . . . . . . . . .

*Give young children dried apricots, mangoes and prunes instead of sweets. Before they know they're meant to hate them, you've given them a good start in life.*

. . . . . . . . . . .

# FRUIT: ORCHARD FRUIT

I always imagine this category of fruits to be quintessentially British but, as in so many areas of farming, we seem to have lost the plot. Dessert apples now come from everywhere but Britain; even Cox's Orange Pippins, first grown in Slough in 1825 by Richard Cox, seem to be imported. When did you last eat an English cherry, or for that matter a plum or greengage? And whatever has happened to damsons? I've just planted over 150 varieties of old apples, pears, plums and cherries at home in an attempt to discover what real fruit should taste like.

All the orchard fruit here are members of the Rosaceae family (along with the rose and many berry fruits). A number are plants of temperate regions (apples, cherries, pears and the plum family), others prefer some warmth (apricots, peaches and nectarines). All contain good vitamin C and potassium levels. The apricot, peach and nectarine are rich in vitamin A, particularly the apricot.

## APPLE (*Malus* spp)

Apples are native to Europe and Asia, and the many thousands of varieties (sadly, so few of which are now grown) have developed from the wild crab apple.

Please don't buy those thick red-skinned apples with collapsed cotton-wool flesh, they seem to be produced just for film sets or photo shoots. As with most farming there is much emphasis on uniformity of size and the perfect shape. The larger the apple the more often it seems to suffer in flavour. Without access to the older varieties, a newcomer developed in New Zealand, the Braeburn, has the best crunch now, with lots of juice and flavour. Of the cooking variety, choose Bramley (if you want a 'fluff'), although the dessert apple Granny Smith cooks well and holds its shape.

With the wide use of pesticides it is advisable to peel or certainly wash the apple before eating. Remember when peeling apples that they discolour quickly, so if you are preparing a decent quantity, pop them in a bowl of water to which you have added some lemon juice.

Special varieties of apples are grown which go to make cider or apple brandy.

## APRICOT (*Prunus armeniaca*)

This stone fruit of the same genus as cherries, peaches and plums, originated in China about 4,000 years ago. Although apricots grow quite successfully in sheltered positions in the UK, most varieties we buy are imported from California, Turkey or Australia. Much of the apricot harvest goes to producing dried fruits, which go through a sulphur process which acts as a preservative and helps to set the colour. Personally I prefer the unsulphured varieties, such as Hunza.

(These come from a valley in Kashmir where the people live to a great age, due in part, it is thought, to the high vitamin A content of the apricots, fresh *and* dried.)

Unfortunately many imported fresh apricots look wonderful but are often woody, dry and disappointing. For that reason you won't find many people who eat them raw, using them mainly for cooking. Apricots are used regularly in savoury cooking in the Middle East and North Africa.

Apricots have very thin skins so are rarely peeled, but are usually stoned for cooking. Cut along the natural seam of the apricot all the way round, twist the fruit and remove the stone. When making jam, the kernel inside the stone can be used. Crack the stone with a mallet or nutcracker. The kernel will impart a slight almond flavour.

## CHERRY (*Prunus* spp)

There are two principal types of cherry, the sweet dessert cherry (*P. avium*) and the bitter cooking cherry (*P. cerasus*); there are a number of hybrid varieties which tend to be a cross between the two. They are native to temperate Europe and Asia. Most people are tempted by rich dark cherries for their looks, but in reality dark cherries can be sweet or sour, whereas the lighter coloured yellow/pink ones are always sweet. Bitter cherry types are Morello or, if you are in France, Montmorency, and are used in the making of liqueurs such as Kirsch and Maraschino.

Buy cherries that are plump and shiny-skinned with stalks; check for bruising and tell-tale brown markings around the stalks. Store them in the fridge as cherries deteriorate quickly at room temperature. Wash the cherries just before eating. If cooking bitter cherries use a **non-reactive** pan which will help to preserve the colour. If making jam, stone the cherries using an olive stoner, and crack some of the stones, using a hammer, and tie them in muslin to submerge in the jam. Bitter cherries have more pectin for making jam, but you will almost certainly need to add apple juice or commercial pectin to achieve a set.

## PEACH AND NECTARINE (*Prunus persica* spp)

These fruit originated in the Far East but can grow in the warmer parts of temperate regions. They are often considered luxury fruits, but nowadays are flown from everywhere and anywhere and at any time. This means, however, that it is rare to find much flavour. When you are visiting Italy, South Africa or Australia and choose a wonderfully ripe peach or nectarine from a market stall, the flavour is incomparable.

The peach has a downy skin, and the nectarine is a peach variety with a smooth skin. Both fruits are available in gold, pink and white; the nectarine is usually richer in colour. The white peach is thought to be superior, but find a gold peach at its peak of ripeness, warmed by the sun, and it is a wonder. If you can find the blood or red-fleshed peach, buy one, it's delicious.

When buying peaches or nectarines, like many fruit, smell them; they should have a sweet perfume, indicating ripeness. Don't be fooled by the colour; the redness of the peach skin does not indicate ripeness, as the setting of the colour occurs before the fruit is mature on the tree. What you want is a fruit that, when you bite into it, oozes so much juice that it will undoubtedly dribble down your chin. Too often for the export market the fruit is picked unripe, and these fruits do not become sweeter as, once picked, the sugar content will not increase. For this reason, late-season peaches and nectarines, when the fruit has had time to sweeten, are best. There are clingstone and freestone varieties of peaches and nectarines. In clingstones the stone clings to the flesh, making it very difficult to remove it without ripping the flesh; freestone stones are easily detachable.

Peeling nectarines is a very difficult task, so I wouldn't bother. The freestone variety of peach peels more easily. Run a knife down the natural seam of the peach, just cutting through the skin. Plunge into boiling water for 1 minute, then into a bowl of cold water. Lift the peel off with the edge of a spoon rather than a knife as you are less likely to damage the flesh.

## PEAR (*Pyrus communis*)

Like apples, pears are native to temperate Europe and Asia, and have been cultivated, particularly in China, for thousands of years. Many varieties were developed by the French from the seventeenth century. Standards vary in current varieties, and as the more edible Williams and Doyenné de Comice tend to bruise and deteriorate very quickly, so supermarkets often play safe by stocking the harder varieties such as Conference, which I feel is more suitable for cooking.

Pears should be bought or picked firm and ripened at home; unusually, they ripen from the inside out so when ripe to the touch they will deteriorate quickly. When you buy pears from the supermarket or greengrocer you will almost certainly have to ripen them at home. As with apples, pears discolour very quickly once peeled, so rub them with lemon juice or, if using for a savoury dish, rub them with a little olive oil. Softer pears such as Williams don't like being kept in **acidulated water** as they tend to become soggy and spongy. When cutting pears, always use a stainless-steel knife as other metals hasten discoloration.

## PLUM, DAMSON AND GREENGAGE (*Prunus domestica* spp)

These are considered to be very British fruits, but they are native to temperate Europe and Asia, and once again many of the ones we buy in supermarkets tend to be imported. Green plums or gages are considered to be the sweetest, but personally I am a fan of the Victoria plum.

Choose plums that still have a white bloom and no sign of wrinkling skin. Buy them firm as they will continue to ripen at home; once ripe, though, they do not take very long to become squashy and inedible. Generally plums do not need peeling. If preparing plums for cooking, cut the plums through their natural seam, twist and remove the stone. The inside of the stone, the kernel, can be used in jam. Some stones are hard to remove, so you may need to gouge them out with a knife.

*Make a covered apple pie in the normal way then, when cool, remove a circle from the pastry, leaving a rim of pastry. Pour thick hot custard over the top of the fruit and allow to cool. Then you can put the pastry lid back on again if you desire.*

## Deep-fried Apple Rings

- *Beat together 300ml (½ pint) double cream, 125ml (4 fl oz) port, 90ml (3 fl oz) cider and the yolks of 2 eggs, then add enough plain flour to make a light batter.*
- *Pass through a fine sieve, then fold in 2 whipped egg whites.*
- *Dip apple rings in the batter and deep-fry until golden.*
- *Dust with caster sugar and serve immediately.*

# Apple and Calvados Risotto

Sounds like a strange combination but I ate it in California (where else?) and really enjoyed it.

**Preparation and cooking: 30 minutes**
**Serves: 4–6**

## Apples

25g (1 oz) unsalted butter

2 small (275–350g/9½–12 oz) Granny Smith apples, peeled, cored and cut into 5mm (¼ in) dice

3 tablespoons caster sugar

grating of nutmeg

pinch of powdered cinnamon

1 tablespoon Calvados

1 teaspoon vanilla extract

## Risotto

1.2 litres (2 pints) unsweetened apple juice

25g (1 oz) unsalted butter

225g (8 oz) arborio rice

1 teaspoon soft thyme leaves

1 bay leaf

85g (3 oz) mascarpone cheese

## To serve

25g (1 oz) mascarpone cheese

55g (2 oz) almonds or walnuts, toasted and coarsely chopped

**1** For the apples, melt the butter in a small, heavy, non-stick frying pan over a medium heat. Add the apple, sugar, nutmeg and cinnamon and cook until the apples are just tender, about 6 minutes. Pour the Calvados into the corner of the frying pan. Heat briefly, ignite carefully and shake the pan until the flames go out. Stir in the vanilla.

**2** Meanwhile, bring the apple juice to a simmer in a medium saucepan. Melt the butter in a separate large, heavy, non-stick saucepan over a medium-low heat. Add the rice, thyme and bay leaf and stir for 2 minutes. Add the apple juice, ladle by ladle until the liquid is absorbed by the rice and the rice is cooked, about 20 minutes. Stir in the cooked apple mixture and fold in the mascarpone.

**3** To serve, divide the risotto between four plates. Top with the mascarpone, and sprinkle with nuts. Serve immediately.

# Baked Apples with Fruit and Nuts

This brings back memories of childhood, albeit a little more sophisticated. Baked apples always seem to be popular, especially when served with thick cream.

**Preparation and cooking: 1¼ hours**
**Serves: 4**

| |
|---|
| 4 large Bramley cooking apples |
| 115g (4 oz) soft dark brown sugar |
| 4 tablespoons sweet mincemeat |
| 55g (2 oz) flaked almonds or chopped pecans |
| 1 teaspoon powdered cinnamon |
| 2 tablespoons raisins |
| 25g (1 oz) unsalted butter |
| apple juice for basting |

**1** Preheat the oven to 190°C/375°F/Gas 5.

**2** Remove the centre core of the apples, leaving 5mm (¼ in) uncut at the bottom. Run the tip of a sharp knife round the circumference of the apple, just to pierce the skin. This stops the apples bursting in the oven.

**3** Combine all the remaining ingredients except for the butter and juice, and spoon it into the cavities of the apples, place the excess in the bottom of a buttered baking dish. Place the apples on the fruit in the dish, dot the top with butter and pop in the oven for 45–60 minutes. Every 10 minutes, add 2 tablespoons of apple juice to the bottom of the dish, and spoon the juices over the apples.

**4** Serve piping hot with double or clotted cream.

• • • • • • • • • • • • • • •

*Slice half a dozen apples and cook until soft with a touch of cinnamon and enough sugar to sweeten, then pass through a sieve and allow to cool. Fold in 125ml (4 fl oz) double cream whipped to* **soft peaks** *and 3 egg whites, beaten to* **stiff peaks** *with a little sugar. This makes a great apple snow.*

• • • • • • • • • • • • • • •

*Cut chunks of apple and marinate with garlic, thyme and olive oil. Cook on a griddle pan or barbecue until deep golden brown. Turn over, repeat, and serve alongside pork or duck.*

## Simple Apple Sauce

• *Place 450g (1 lb) peeled, cored and diced apple in a saucepan with the grated rind of ½ lemon, 4 tablespoons water and 2 teaspoons caster sugar.*
• *Cook until the apples soften, then beat in 25g (1 oz) unsalted butter with a whisk (this will also break down the apple).*

## Caramelised Apples

• *Heat 55g (2 oz) butter until frothing in a small frying pan.*
• *Peel and core 4 small Granny Smith apples and cut into 1cm (½ in) dice. Add to the butter along with 4 tablespoons caster sugar.*
• *Cook fast until the apple is tender and a rich golden brown colour, about 10 minutes.*
• *Stir in 2 tablespoons Calvados, and serve with Calvados Ice-cream (see page 103).*

# Poached Apricots with Honeycomb and Greek Yogurt

Very Mediterranean, very delicious. You could use dried apricots, but only half the weight and soak them for a few hours in cold water first to plump up. When removing the stones from fresh apricots, do not cut the apricots all the way through.

**Preparation and cooking: 1½ hours**
**Serves: 4–6**

| |
|---|
| 600ml (1 pint) water |
| 115g (4 oz) caster sugar |
| 4 cardamom pods, crushed |
| 2 teaspoons fresh lemon juice |
| 1kg (2¼ lb) apricots, split but not halved, stone removed |
| 225g (8 oz) honeycomb |
| 300g (10½ oz) very thick Greek yogurt |
| 55g (2 oz) flaked almonds, toasted |
| pomegranate seeds (optional) |

**1** Preheat the oven to 180°C/350°F/Gas 4.

**2** Put the water in a medium ovenproof dish or pan with the sugar, cardamom and lemon juice and bring to the boil. When boiling, add the apricots. Cover the apricots with wet parchment paper, put the lid on the pan and place in the preheated oven. Cook for 1 hour. Remove from the oven and allow to cool in the syrup.

**3** To serve, remove the apricots and drain. Open each one out and put in 1 small piece of honeycomb, 1 teaspoon Greek yogurt and top with flaked toasted almonds and pomegranate seeds. Pour some of the syrup over the apricots.

## Apricot and Orange Chutney

*Wonderful with cheese and cold meats.*

● *Chop up 4 oranges and quarter 1.5kg (3 lb 5 oz) apricots.*

● *Mix with 450g (1 lb) sliced onions, 450g (1 lb) caster sugar and 1 teaspoon sea salt, ½ teaspoon ground cloves, 1 teaspoon ground black pepper, ½ teaspoon chilli flakes, ½ teaspoon ground mace, 1 teaspoon curry powder, 1 tablespoon mustard seeds, 1 teaspoon turmeric and 1 litre (1¾ pints) of cider vinegar.*

● *Bring to the boil, reduce the heat and simmer for 1–1½ hours until thick, stirring from time to time, especially nearer the end of cooking time.*

## Apricot Ratafia

● *Cover some apricots by 2.5cm (1 in) with white wine and simmer for about 45 minutes until the apricots have been reduced to a pulp.*

● *Pass the apricots through a sieve into an earthenware jar.*

● *For every litre (1¾ pints) of pulp add 175ml (6 fl oz) brandy and 100g (3½ oz) caster sugar. Add ½ teaspoon mace, a pinch each of ground cloves and cinnamon.*

● *Let the mixture macerate for 1 month, then strain through a jelly bag. Bottle and drink as a liqueur or chilled as an aperitif.*

● *Fold the pulp into whipped cream for an alcoholic pud.*

## Spiced Cherries ⓥ

A delicious partner for a country *terrine* or for cold meats.

**Preparation and marination: 30 minutes + 1 month**

**Fills: 2 x 1 litre (1¾ pint) jars**

1kg (2¼ lb) Morello cherries

1 litre (1¾ pints) cider vinegar

750g (1 lb 10 oz) caster sugar

1 tablespoon black peppercorns

6 juniper berries

12 cloves

1 cinnamon stick, broken in two

6 bay leaves

2 cloves garlic

**1**  Place all the washed cherries in 2 sterilised 1 litre (1¾ pint) jars.

**2**  Place the remaining ingredients in a **non-reactive** saucepan, bring to the boil and simmer for 3 minutes. Pour the hot vinegar over the cherries, distributing the spices evenly between the jars.

**3**  Cover when cool, then allow to pickle for 1 month before eating.

• • • • • • • • • • • • •

*Make a syrup by simmering together 300ml (½ pint) water and 115g (4 oz) caster sugar with 1 tablespoon redcurrant jelly until slightly thickened. Add 450g (1 lb) cherries and cook for 10 minutes. Add 175ml (6 fl oz) brandy, and thicken with a cornflour paste. Pour hot over ice-cream, a great sauce.*

• • • • • • • • • • • • •

## Baked Peaches with *Amaretti*

The almond flavour of the Amaretto and the *amaretti* biscuits makes for a great partnership with the peaches. Serve warm or at room temperature with cream or ice-cream. A popular dish in Italy.

**Preparation and cooking: 40 minutes**

**Serves: 6**

70g (2½ oz) unsalted butter

6 ripe freestone peaches

12 *amaretti* biscuits

2 tablespoons sliced almonds, toasted

2 tablespoons soft brown sugar

1 teaspoon ground ginger

50ml (2 fl oz) Amaretto

200ml (7 fl oz) orange juice

**1**  Lightly butter a baking dish using 15g (½ oz) of the butter, and preheat the oven to 190°C/375°F/Gas 5.

**2**  Bring a saucepan of water to the boil. Drop in the peaches, simmer for 1 minute, then remove with a slotted spoon to a bowl of iced water; the skins should peel off easily. Cut the peaches in half and remove the stones. Place the peach halves, cut-side up, in the prepared baking dish.

**3**  Combine the *amaretti*, almonds, sugar and ginger in a food processor and pulse until crumbled. Add the remaining butter and the Amaretto and **pulse** to make a paste.

**4**  Place a teaspoon of the mixture into the centres of the peach halves and bake for 25 minutes, basting with a little orange juice from time to time.

• • • • • • • • • • • • • • • • • • • • • • • •

## Peach Melba

*This classic dish is wonderful when made correctly.*

● *Peel and halve the peaches.*

● *Make a raspberry sauce by blending fresh raspberries with a little icing sugar and a squirt of lime juice. Pass through a fine sieve to remove the seeds.*

● *Cup 2 halves of peaches around a scoop of good vanilla ice-cream, dress with the raspberry sauce, and sprinkle with a few toasted flaked almonds.*

• • • • • • • • • • • • • • • • • • • • • • • •

# Pear Crisp

The American equivalent of a crumble, perfect for cold winter days.

**Preparation and cooking: 1¼ hours**
**Serves: 4–6**

6 Conference pears, peeled, cored and cubed

juice of 2 oranges

2 tablespoons caster sugar

pinch of grated nutmeg

pinch of powdered cinnamon

25g (1 oz) powdered milk

55g (2 oz) ground almonds

25g (1 oz) rolled oats

175g (6 oz) unsalted butter, cut in cubes

55g (2 oz) desiccated coconut

175g (6 oz) plain flour

175g (6 oz) soft dark brown sugar

½ teaspoon salt

55g (2 oz) flaked almonds, toasted

**1** Preheat the oven to 200°C/400°F/Gas 6. Grease the bottom of a deep baking dish with extra butter.

**2** Combine the pears with the orange juice, sugar, nutmeg and cinnamon, and place in the bottom of the baking dish.

**3** In a food processor blend together the powdered milk, almonds and rolled oats on a **pulse** action. Add the butter, coconut, flour, sugar and salt, and continue to pulse until the mixture resembles a crumble. Fold in the toasted almonds.

**4** Pop this mixture on top of the pears and place in the oven to bake for 45–60 minutes, or until the top is golden. Serve hot with thick double cream or clotted cream.

*Substitute peeled and quartered peaches for the pears in the Pear Crisp.*

*Serve raw pears with shards of Parmesan.*

## Pear Sauce

*A great sauce for game.*

● *Fry 4 thinly sliced button mushrooms in 1 tablespoon groundnut oil with 3 finely chopped shallots until the shallots have softened.*

● *Add 6 peeled and chopped pears, 1 teaspoon soft thyme leaves, ½ tablespoon ground black pepper, 2 chopped chillies and 1 tablespoon green peppercorns, and cook for 5 minutes.*

● *Add 125ml (4 fl oz) port and 600ml (1 pint) good beef or chicken stock, cook for 15 minutes then strain.*

● *Finish with a little melted redcurrant jelly and 25g (1 oz) cold unsalted butter.*

*Spice pears with rosemary by boiling together 300ml (½ pint) cider vinegar with 150ml (¼ pint) water, 225g (8 oz) caster sugar, 1 teaspoon dried chilli flakes and 3 sprigs rosemary for 5 minutes. Add 8 peeled and halved pears, and cook gently until the pears are tender. Allow to cool in the liquor and serve the pears with blue cheese.*

## Sloe Gin

*Best to leave for a year, but it doesn't taste bad that first Christmas!*

● *Gather sloes (a sour, wild relative of the plum) from the countryside in autumn and pierce them in several places after washing well.*

● *Macerate in gin with sugar to taste to make a wonderful liqueur fruit gin.*

*Peel and dice raw pears and combine with watercress and escarole leaves, chopped walnuts and crumbled Gorgonzola cheese. Toss with a walnut or extra virgin olive oil dressing.*

# FRUIT: TROPICAL FRUIT

Regular supplies of recognisable and unrecognisable tropical fruits are available year round. We have known about bananas, pineapples, passionfruit, mangoes and kiwis for many years but now we can buy many other varieties. I'll give you a quick run through.

## BANANA (*Musa sapientum*)

These grow in bunches on tropical trees, and consist mainly of starch. They must be fully ripe for the best flavour, for the starch to convert into sugar, and then are easily digestible. They can be cooked, when the sweetness intensifies. Plantains (*Musa paradisiaca*) grow in the same way and in the same climates, but are not sweet; the starch does not convert into sugars and so they must be cooked before eating.

## CARAMBOLA (*Averrhoa carambola*)

The fruits of a small Malaysian tree are also known as star fruit, and to my mind are a waste of space. They are often used as a garnish in their sliced form because of their attractive star shape, but unless you get them ripe, they are pretty tasteless. If you feel you must eat them, buy the yellow ones as the green are unripe with a taste a little less exciting than a cucumber.

## GUAVA (*Psidium guajava*)

These fruits are native to Central America, and are rarely seen fresh in the UK except in specialist shops. (We used to get them regularly in tins.) If you find a fresh one you'll experience a wonderful perfume and discover a creamy to pinky-orangey flesh. The fruit is peeled and can be eaten raw, seeds and all. When cooking guava, take care as the flesh breaks down very quickly. It's excellent for mousses and water ices. Guavas are exceptionally high in vitamin C.

## KIWI (*Actinidia chinensis*)

The Chinese gooseberry originated, not surprisingly, in China, but was made popular by the farmers of New Zealand. The fruit made a brief impact in the 1980s during our *nouvelle cuisine* period, garnishing everything from meat to fish dishes, and got rather a bad name as a result. However, they are actually quite pleasant when eaten as the Lord intended, as a fruit. Peel the fruit and slice, or halve and eat straight from the skin. They should still be quite hard, as soft they are pretty unpleasant. They are very high in vitamins C and E, twice that of a medium orange and an avocado respectively.

## LYCHEE (*Litchi chinensis*)

Lychees are one of the better tinned fruits, regularly seen on Chinese restaurant menus. The fresh fruit, which originates in South China, has a brittle shell casing, and is imported into the UK in its unripe brown form. Wait until the shell turns a bright scarlet before enjoying its delicious taste. Peel back the shell, then suck the pearly white flesh away from the large brown date-like seed. Don't swallow the seed as it is mildly poisonous.

## MANGO (*Mangifera indica*)

One of my favourite tropical fruits. Several varieties are available, ranging from the large red-green Asian variety to the smaller sweeter Indian ones. Unripe mangoes and the green varieties available in Indian and West Indian shops are used in cooking and for making chutneys. Unless you know the technique you will find removing the large flat mango stone difficult and wasteful. Stand the mango on its narrow side and make downward cuts 1cm (½ in) to the left and right of the centre; this should clear the stone leaving you with two neat halves, or 'cheeks'. It will also leave you with a central slice containing the stone; peel off the skin and treat yourself to sucking the stone to release the flesh! Mangoes are a major source of vitamin A.

## MANGOSTEEN (*Garcinia mangostana*)

Not related to the mango, despite the name. In flavour it is closest to the lychee, and is one of my all-time favourites (except for its price). It is a small round fruit with a thick brown-purple skin which needs to be cut skin deep in quarters. Peel back the leathery petals and you will find half a dozen highly perfumed, translucent white segments. Delicious.

## PAPAYA (*Carica papaya*)

Also known as pawpaw, this fruit looks similar in shape to the avocado, and has a skin varying from green through yellow to rosy pink. Unripe green papaya is used in Asian salads and has a lovely melony texture. Ripe papaya has a bright orange flesh which is soft and slightly oily. It has almost no acidity, so benefits from a good squeeze of lime juice. When you cut a papaya in half you are greeted with a luscious looking flesh and a mass of dark grey-brown seeds, which are discarded. Meat marinated in puréed papaya tenderises very quickly (due to the digestive enzyme, papain). Papaya has good amounts of vitamin A and C.

## PASSIONFRUIT (*Passiflora edulis*)
These fruit are native to Brazil, but are now grown commercially in the USA and Hawaii especially. The British, and even some of their chefs, don't always understand them. They tend to buy them with perfectly smooth skins, eat them and then wonder why they are still slightly sour. You should leave them until their skin becomes dimpled, as only then will you discover the wonderful sweetness of the flesh and seeds and experience the magnificent perfume. Cut the passionfruit in half, and scoop out the flesh and seeds, both of which are eaten. Australians use them in Pavlova, the French make sorbels, sauces and glazes for cakes, and the British have yet to fully appreciate their beauty.

## PINEAPPLE (*Ananas comosus*)
This fruit is a great favourite of the British. In the past it came in tins (and is one of the better tinned fruits), but now pineapple in its fresh form has come down in price and is relatively good value compared to other tropical fruit. The skin of a ripe pineapple will be golden orange, so avoid an all-green one unless you ripen it at home. If ripe enough the fruit should smell sweet, and you should be able to pull out one of the leaves from the plume. Either slice the pineapple, cut off the skin and remove the central core; or, if you want to leave the pineapple whole, cut away the peel in downward strips, then cut diagonal grooves either side of the 'eyes' with a sharp small knife. For those wanting to make a mousse or jelly with gelatine, raw pineapple will not set because of the digestive enzyme, bromelin. It must be cooked first to allow the gelatine to work (or you could use the vegetarian alternative, agar-agar).

## RAMBUTAN (*Nephelium lapaceum*)
This small reddish hairy fruit, which looks rather like a sweet chestnut, is very similar to the lychee and should be treated in the same way.

# Sexy Banana and *Panettone* Toffee Pudding

A recipe I created on *Ready Steady Cook* and have subsequently reproduced on *Food and Drink*. It always gets rave reviews wherever I serve it, but don't eat it on a diet!
**Preparation and cooking: 40 minutes**
**Serves: 4**

115g (4 oz) unsalted butter
4 tablespoons golden syrup
125g (4 oz) soft dark brown sugar
4 bananas, peeled and sliced in 2.5cm (1 in) pieces
150ml (¼ pint) double cream
150ml (¼ pint) milk
6 slices *panettone* (or raisin bread)

1 Preheat the oven to 190°C/375°F/Gas 5.
2 Place the butter, golden syrup and sugar in a saucepan and combine over a medium heat until the butter and sugar have melted and the mix has become a bubbling toffee sauce. Add the banana and cook for 5–8 minutes, depending on the ripeness of the banana.
3 Mix together the cream and milk and warm over a low heat.
4 Place three slices of *panettone* (or raisin bread) in the bottom of a baking dish, and pour over half the cream mix. Next ladle in half the toffee and banana mix, then repeat, finishing with the toffee and banana. Place in the oven and bake for 20 minutes. Serve with thickened double cream if you dare, or vanilla ice-cream for a cooling sensation.

*Wrap bananas in smoked streaky bacon and grill until the bacon is crispy.*

*Cook bananas in their skins on a barbecue until the skins blacken and they feel very soft. When you cut back the skin you will discover this natural banana soufflé, delicious.*

*One of my favourite secret comfort foods (it does nothing for my waistline) is mashed banana mixed with thickened double cream and soft dark brown sugar.*

# Mango Chutney

This chutney is always a welcome addition to an Indian curry, and it is also great in a cheese sandwich.

**Preparation and cooking: 4 hours + 2¼ hours**
**Fills: 4 x 1 litre (1¾ pint) jars**

1.5kg (3 lb 5 oz) soft brown sugar

1.3 litres (2¼ pints) white wine vinegar

24 green, hard mangoes, peeled and sliced

2 tablespoons salt

500g (18 oz) sultanas, chopped

125g (4½ oz) chopped garlic

100g (3½ oz) grated fresh ginger

100g (3½ oz) chopped crystallised ginger

12 small dried red chillies, finely chopped

1 tablespoon ground allspice

**1** Boil the sugar and vinegar together until the sugar has dissolved. Allow to cool.

**2** Salt the mango and leave to macerate for 4 hours.

**3** Drain the mango and add to the vinegar syrup along with the remaining ingredients.

**4** Bring to the boil and cook slowly for about 2 hours, stirring regularly, especially in the latter stages of cooking.

**5** Spoon into sterilised jars and seal.

- - - - - - - - - - - - - - - - - - - -

## Mango Smoothie

*In a food processor, blend the flesh of 1 mango, 1 banana, 2 teaspoons honey, ½ cup crushed ice, 425ml (¾ pint) milk and 175ml (6 fl oz) single cream for a tropical smoothie.*

- - - - - - - - - - - - - - - - - - - -

# Thai Papaya Salad

A refreshing oriental salad to which you can add prawns and crabmeat.

**Preparation and cooking: 30 minutes**
**Serves: 4–6**

2 hard green papayas, peeled, seeded and grated

2 cloves garlic, finely chopped

2 small fresh red chillies, finely sliced

4 tomatoes, seeded and diced

4 tablespoons chopped mint

55g (2 oz) peanuts, chopped

2 tablespoons chopped coriander

grated zest and juice of 2 limes

1½ tablespoons clear honey

1 tablespoon dried shrimp powder (available in ethnic shops)

**1** Combine all the ingredients and allow the flavours to develop for 15 minutes before serving.

- - - - - - - - - - - - - - - - - - - -

## Mango 'Hedgehogs'

● *Cut the 'cheeks' off the mangoes as described on page 182.*
● *Make a criss-cross hatched pattern in the flesh, cutting in 5mm (¼ in) wide on the diagonal and then the reverse diagonal, without cutting through the skin. Fold the skin back to create the hedgehog shape.*
● *Sprinkle with fresh lime juice.*

- - - - - - - - - - - - - - - - - - - -

# Passionfruit Curd

This makes a pleasant change from lemon curd.

**Preparation and cooking: 30 minutes**

**Makes: 300ml (½ pint)**

| |
|---|
| 115g (4 oz) caster sugar |
| 60g (2¼ oz) unsalted butter |
| 2 eggs, beaten |
| 6 passionfruit, pulp and seeds |

**1** Stir the caster sugar with the unsalted butter over a moderate heat until the sugar has dissolved.

**2** Add the eggs and the passionfruit pulp and seeds, stirring continuously until thickened. Do not allow to boil.

**3** Pour into sterilised jars and refrigerate for up to 2 months.

# Passionfruit Liqueur

*Jane Grigson tells us how the Guadaloupians make a passionfruit liqueur.*

● *Fill a bottle a third full of passionfruit pulp and seeds, add 4 parts light rum with 1 part sugar syrup to fill the bottle.*

● *After 6 weeks strain the liquor and re-bottle.*

● *Drink neat or with ice.*

*Place a kiwi in an egg cup, slice off the top and eat as you would an egg, scooping the flesh out of the skin.*

# Pineapple Chutney

A good chutney to go with ham or pork.

**Preparation and cooking: 3½ hours**

**Makes: 1 litre (1¾ pints)**

| |
|---|
| 1 large pineapple, peeled and cored |
| 1 tablespoon salt |
| 2 garlic cloves, chopped |
| 175g (6 oz) raisins, chopped |
| 350g (12 oz) soft dark brown sugar |
| 300ml (½ pint) cider vinegar |
| 2 x 5cm (2 in) pieces of cinnamon stick |
| 1 teaspoon mustard seeds |
| 3 cloves |

**1** Chop up the pineapple and sprinkle it with the salt. Drain after 2 hours.

**2** Add the garlic, raisins, soft dark brown sugar, cider vinegar, cinnamon stick, mustard seeds and cloves.

**3** Cook over a low heat for 1 hour until thick.

**4** Spoon into sterilised jars and seal.

# Pineapple *Sambal*

● *Char-grill peeled and cored slices of pineapple, and sprinkle with black pepper.*

● *Chop up the pineapple and mix with 1 chopped roasted pepper (see page 254), 2 tablespoons sambal oelek (an Indonesian chilli paste), 2 teaspoons chopped mint, 2 tablespoons lime juice, 1 teaspoon clear honey and 1 tablespoon chopped coriander.*

● *Serve this sambal with grilled fish or curry.*

*Slice pineapple thinly, arrange the slices on plates, and sprinkle with ground black pepper or Kirsch.*

# GAME

The term game used to apply to anything that wasn't bred on a farm. Our ancestors would kill and eat anything that moved, and nothing was sacred – swan, peacock, thrush, blackbird, wild pig . . . Nowadays we are limited as to what we can kill and eat, and much of what used to be wild is now reared on farms: quail, guinea fowl, venison, partridge, rabbit and wild (or not) boar.

While shooting is not popular with many people, you can't deny that any bird or animal from the wild has a much better flavour. It is to do with what they eat, burrowing for real food, and the fact that they have had a real life. Some game is becoming popular because it is such lean meat, containing very much less fat than domesticated food animals, with very little cholesterol. However, because of that leanness, most game animals require *added* fat to ensure they do not become too dry in cooking: most game birds, for instance, need to be protected by fatty bacon over their breasts when roasting.

The *age* of game too is very important to the cook, dictating the method of cooking – roasting for young, braising for older, for instance. I give individual guidelines as to what to look for, but you should find a game supplier whose word and expertise you can trust. I list here game that you are likely to find in the shops.

## GROUSE (*Lagopus lagopus scoticus*)
Season 12 August–10 December

The red or Scottish grouse is possibly the UK's finest game bird, probably because it is the one bird that is native only to the British Isles. French attempts to rear grouse have been unsuccessful, probably because the birds feed almost entirely on young heather shoots on the moors of Scotland, Ireland, Yorkshire and Derbyshire. Buy the birds at the beginning of the season when they are young and tender. The spur at the back of the leg should be soft and rounded. Hang for a short while if fresh. These are one-man birds, weighing approximately 500g (18 oz) each. A wild bird that is such a treat should be respected by cooking it as simply as possible. Roast preferably in a 200°C/400°F/Gas 6 oven for 15–25 minutes, depending on how rare you enjoy it. If perchance you happen upon an older bird, braise it or, failing that, and you have some other game hanging around, make a game pie.

## HARE (*Lepus europaeus*)
No fixed season, but it is not sold fresh between 1 March and 31 July

Not popular, for no apparent reason other than the fact that it is gamey and possibly (the Brits being animal lovers) because it is lovable and furry. Personally I find it delicious. A young hare will feed four people and should be hung for about 6 days before skinning. One usually roasts the saddle and jugs or casseroles the legs. Hare is better marinated before cooking.

## MALLARD OR WILD DUCK (*Anas* spp)
Season 1 September–31 January (inland) or 20 February (foreshore)

At 1–1.5kg (2¼–3¼ lb), these are a perfect size for two, although the smaller varieties, widgeon and teal, are really one-man birds. Wild duck should not be hung for long as it is fattier than most wild birds, and the fat could turn rancid. As it feeds on water life, there is a chance of it being a little fishy in flavour. To safeguard against this, pop a ½ lemon, some thyme sprigs and a ½ onion into its cavity when cooking. The flesh is dark and has a tendency toward dryness. A medium-sized bird will cook in a 200°C/400°F/Gas 6 oven in about 30 minutes; allow 10 minutes for it to rest after roasting. You won't get much pleasure from the legs, so eat the breasts only, then use the carcass for soup, or mince the leg meat for a sauce to accompany pasta.

## PARTRIDGE
Season 1 September–1 February

One of my favourite game birds, as it is generally tender without being overpowering. Two varieties are found in Britain: the grey (*Perdix perdix*) and the red-legged (*Alectoris rufis*). The former is the more highly prized. Young birds should have soft feet and pointed flight feathers. Another one-portion bird, the young should be roasted (20–25 minutes in a 200°C/400°F/Gas 6 oven), and the older bird braised with cabbage or in casseroles, terrines or soups.

## PHEASANT (*Phasianus colchicus*)
Season 1 October–1 February

Originally native to the Far East, the pheasant is now a fairly common sight in the English countryside. Many are reared in shooting parks so they have, to some degree, lost their gaminess. One bird will produce two to four portions, depending on appetite. A little hanging does do the birds a flavour favour. Roast pheasants for 15–20 minutes per 450g (1 lb), then remove the breasts and thighs, and chop up the carcasses to make soup or sauce.

## PIGEON (*Columba palumbus*)
No close season, so fire away

Don't bother with townie pigeons, you need plump country wood pigeons, preferably young. The breast is for eating and the legs can be potted or made into soup or meatballs. A good pigeon is surprisingly good, considering its cheap price, and the breasts can be really tender, especially if cooked rare and sliced thin. Roasting times: 15–25 minutes at 200°C/400°F/Gas 6.

## RABBIT (*Oryctolagus cuniculus*)
No close season

Rabbit can be bought wild or farmed. Frozen rabbit is often imported from China. Farmed rabbit has become quite expensive recently, although it doesn't seem that long since rabbit was cheaper than chicken. Rabbit can be cooked in many recipes that use chicken or veal. As with hare, the rabbit saddle is often roasted, or it can be boned and stuffed. The legs can be casseroled or braised, and the forequarter meat can be minced and made into meatballs. Wild rabbit tends to be a lot tougher than farmed, but it has more flavour, and is a lot cheaper.

## VENISON
Season for wild venison varies according to breed, sex and locality

Venison – the meat of deer (roe, fallow, red or Sika) – can be bought wild or farmed, although most of what we buy is farmed. Venison was touted as the meat to replace our 'so-called unhealthy diet of beef', but so far it hasn't really taken off. Europe imports much of our venison as they rate it very highly. Buy young venison where possible, and treat it much as you would beef. Grill or roast the loin or saddle and braise the legs. The forequarter can be stewed or cooked in mince form. The meat from venison is very lean, dark and dense textured, high in protein and low in saturated fat. When roasting or braising venison, it is advisable to **lard** the meat, inserting strips of pork fat into the flesh with a larding needle.

# Pot-roasted Pheasant

*A delicious way of keeping pheasant moist and full of flavour.*
**Preparation and cooking: 1½ hours**
**Serves 4–6**

| |
|---|
| 2 x 1kg (2¼ lb) pheasants |
| 2 sprigs each of fresh rosemary and thyme |
| salt and ground black pepper |
| 55g (2 oz) unsalted butter |
| 1 tablespoon olive oil |
| 6 slices streaky bacon, diced |
| 1 large carrot, sliced |
| 1 large onion, chopped |
| 1 stick celery, sliced |
| ½ teaspoon soft thyme leaves |
| 8 cloves garlic, crushed |
| ½ tablespoon tomato purée |
| 250ml (9 fl oz) dry red wine |
| 425ml (¾ pint) chicken stock |
| 1 tablespoon redcurrant jelly |

**1** Preheat the oven to 220°C/425°F/Gas 7. Place the rosemary and thyme in the cavities of the pheasants. Season the birds. In a deep casserole brown the pheasants in half the butter and the olive oil until golden all over. Remove and set aside.

**2** To the same casserole add the bacon, carrot, onion, celery, thyme and garlic. Cook until the vegetables have softened and started to brown.

**3** Add the tomato purée and red wine, scraping any coagulated parts on the bottom of the pan.

**4** Return the pheasant to the casserole, pour in the chicken stock and bring to the boil. Cover with a lid, place in the oven and cook for 35 minutes.

**5** Remove the pheasants from the casserole. Cool a little, then remove the breasts and thighs. Set aside.

**6** Chop up the rest of the carcasses and add to the casserole. Simmer for 20 minutes. Strain through a fine sieve, pushing down hard to extract all the juices.

**7** Add the redcurrant jelly and remaining butter to the sauce, and boil until the jelly has melted and the butter emulsified. Check the seasoning.

**8** Cut the pheasant breasts in two and add to the sauce with the thighs to warm through. Serve with creamy mashed potatoes and braised red cabbage.

# Roast Partridge with Sausage Stuffing

This recipe, using a classic game bird, was inspired by the Italians, and has lots of Mediterranean flavours. A real gutsy dish.

**Preparation and cooking: 1¾ hours**

**Serves: 4**

| | Stuffing |
|---|---|
| 4 partridges | 1 red onion, finely chopped |
| 4 slices Parma ham | 4 cloves garlic, finely chopped |
| olive oil | 2 sticks celery, finely chopped |
| 55g (2 oz) dried ceps or *porcini*, soaked for half an hour in | 1 carrot, finely chopped |
| 450ml (16 fl oz) hot water, drained, squeezed and chopped | ½ teaspoon fennel seeds |
| (reserve soaking liquor) | ½ teaspoon soft thyme leaves |
| 3 cloves garlic, finely chopped | 3 tablespoons good olive oil |
| 1 onion, finely diced | 350g (12 oz) pork sausagemeat |
| 115g (4 oz) chicken livers, chopped | 12 dried sage leaves, crumbled |
| 1 teaspoon soft thyme leaves | 115g (4 oz) chicken livers, diced |
| salt and freshly ground black pepper | 250ml (9 fl oz) dry red wine |
| 350ml (12 fl oz) dry red wine | about 85g (3 oz) soft white breadcrumbs |
| 25g (1 oz) unsalted butter | |

**1**  Make the stuffing first. Cook the onion, garlic, celery, carrot, fennel seeds and thyme in the oil until soft but not brown. Crumble the sausagemeat into the onion mix with the sage and fry for 10 minutes. Add the chicken livers and cook for a further 2 minutes. Add the wine and boil to reduce by half. Season with salt and pepper, allow to cool, then fold in enough breadcrumbs to bind. Allow the stuffing to cool.

**2**  Stuff the birds, then wrap each in a slice of Parma ham.

**3**  Heat 3 tablespoons olive oil in a pan and cook the chopped *porcini*, garlic, onion, chicken livers and thyme, until the onion is softening. Add the *porcini* juices and cook until about 4 tablespoons liquid remain.

**4**  Preheat the oven to its hottest setting. In a roasting pan heat 2 tablespoons olive oil. Season the birds then brown them on each side. Roast in the oven for 10 minutes, then turn the birds and roast for a further 10 minutes. Remove the birds from the oven and keep warm.

**5**  Add the wine to the roasting pan, scraping the bottom of the pan, and boil until the liquid has **reduced** by half. Stir the mushrooms and juices into the pan, add the butter to enrich the sauce, and boil until emulsified. Serve the birds with the mushrooms and juices.

## Pigeon Salad

*Rare pigeon breasts are excellent in a warm salad.*

- *Cook pigeons for 12–15 minutes in a hot oven, allow to cool, remove breasts and slice lengthways into very thin strips.*
- *Heat 2 tablespoons walnut oil and fry 2 tablespoons chopped bacon until golden.*
- *Add 3 tablespoons of tiny bread croûtons and fry until the bread is golden; remove from the heat and set aside.*
- *Meanwhile in a separate pan, fry 1 chopped shallot in 55g (2 oz) unsalted butter with 1 chopped clove garlic and 4 sliced oyster mushrooms until the mushrooms are cooked.*
- *Combine the two pans and add the juice of ½ lemon.*
- *Place a couple of handfuls of your favourite salad leaves in a bowl, pour over the mushroom mix and toss to combine.*
- *Arrange on plates and top with slices of pigeon and orange segments.*

# Hare Soup

Another of Gran's recipes, which is a little long-winded, but as it tastes so good, if you've got the odd hare lying around, it is well worth creating. Whoever is cleaning the beast should save you the blood if you want to use it in the soup.

**Preparation and cooking: 4 hours**
**Serves: 6–8**

| | |
|---|---|
| 1 hare, jointed | ½ teaspoon mustard seeds |
| 1kg (2¼ lb) shin of beef, cut in small pieces | 6 juniper berries, crushed |
| 3.7 litres (6½ pints) game or beef stock | 55g (2 oz) unsalted butter |
| or water | 2 cloves garlic, finely chopped |
| 5 onions, peeled, 2 chopped | 35g (1¼ oz) plain flour |
| 6 bay leaves | 150ml (¼ pint) dry red wine |
| 6 cloves | 150ml (¼ pint) port |
| 2 pieces dried orange peel | 2 tablespoons redcurrant jelly |
| 2 carrots, sliced | blood of the hare (optional) |
| 2 leeks, sliced | salt and ground black pepper |
| 2 sticks celery, sliced | |
| ½ tablespoon black peppercorns | **To serve** |
| 1 tablespoon soft thyme leaves | 100–125ml (3½–4 fl oz) soured cream |
| ½ teaspoon celery seeds | handful of chives, snipped |

**1** Place the hare and the shin of beef in a large saucepan with the stock or water. Bring to the boil.

**2** When boiling add the 3 whole onions, each stuck with 2 bay leaves and 2 cloves, the orange peel, carrot, leek, celery, peppercorns, thyme, celery and mustard seeds and juniper berries. Continue to simmer over a low heat for 2 hours, skimming off any impurities that float to the top from time to time

**3** Take out the best joints of the hare, remove the meat, and return the bones to the stock. Chop the meat and set aside. Cook the soup for a further 1 hour.

**4** Fry the chopped onion in the butter with the garlic until the onion has softened and taken on a little colour. Add the flour and stir to combine. Cook over a low heat for 10 minutes, stirring from time to time. Add some of the soup liquid to the onion **roux** and stir until smooth. Fold this mixture into the soup and cook the soup for a further 15 minutes.

**5** Strain the soup through a sieve into a new saucepan. Pick off any meat from the remaining meaty carcasses. Pass this meat and the cooked shin through the fine blade of the **mouli-légumes** and fold into the soup with the retained hare meat, the red wine, port and redcurrant jelly. Allow to cook until the jelly dissolves.

**6** *Optional.* Instead of making a flour *roux* to thicken the soup, mix a little of the soup with the hare's blood and fold back into the soup. Cook for 5 minutes, but do not allow to boil or the blood will curdle. (When you originally receive the blood, stir in a little vinegar to stop it clotting.)

**7** Season to taste and serve with soured cream and chives.

## Smoked Quail

*Quail are fairly useless, I think, except as a starter. They become quite expensive as a main course, because you need at least two to satisfy a healthy appetite. However, smoking your own quail is fun, and not difficult. This idea is equally good with pieces of chicken.*

● *Make a smoking mixture by combining 200g (7 oz) each of jasmine tea leaves, demerara sugar and rice.*

● *Cut a circle of foil that will fit the bottom of a wok, and scrunch the sides until you have made a container about 12cm (4½ in) in diameter. Place it in the bottom of the wok and put 5 tablespoons of the smoking mixture in the bottom.*

● *Turn up the heat to full and once the mixture starts to smoke place in the quail (which have been rubbed with sesame oil) on a circular metal rack. Cover with a tight-fitting lid and smoke for 5 minutes.*

● *Remove from the heat but allow the quail to continue to smoke without lifting the lid.*

● *Once cool the quail can be chopped up and cooked with chilli, garlic, spring onion, sesame and peanut oils and honey. The smoking process will only partially cook the quail.*

● *Store remaining smoking ingredients for future use.*

*Serve traditional roast game birds with Bread Sauce (see page 52), fried breadcrumbs, sprigs of watercress, game chips and redcurrant gravy.*

# Rabbit with Fennel, Peppers and Chicory

An adaptation of a Mediterranean recipe, which imparts wonderful earthy flavours.

**Preparation and cooking: 1¼ hours**
**Serves: 4–6**

4 tablespoons extra virgin olive oil
1 medium onion, finely chopped
1 teaspoon chopped rosemary
1 fresh red chilli, finely diced
2 cloves garlic, finely diced
1 bay leaf
2 heads fennel, quartered
2 heads chicory, halved lengthways
1.5kg (3 lb 5 oz) tinned chopped tomatoes
2 large red peppers, roasted (see page 254), peeled and each cut into 4
375ml (13 fl oz) chicken stock
8 rabbit saddle fillets
salt and ground black pepper
2 tablespoons coarsely chopped flat-leaf parsley
1 tablespoon chopped fresh basil
10 pitted black olives, chopped

**1** Heat 3 tablespoons of the oil in a saucepan and fry the onion, rosemary, chilli, garlic and bay leaf until the onion is soft and translucent. Add the fennel quarters, the chicory and tomatoes. Cover the pan and adjust the heat to a gentle simmer.

**2** When the fennel is cooked (after about 45 minutes), add the peppers, along with half the stock, and increase the heat to **reduce** the sauce by half. Reserve until needed.

**3** Trim the rabbit fillets of any fat, or silver skin. Season with salt and ground black pepper. Cook the fillets in the remaining oil for 5–8 minutes until brown on all sides. Transfer the rabbit to the vegetable stew, add a little more stock if necessary, and simmer to reheat.

**4** Slice the fillets on to serving plates and spoon the vegetables around. Sprinkle with parsley, basil and olives, and serve with new potatoes.

# Rabbit *Rillettes*

A popular starter at my London restaurant, Woz, served with *cornichons* (continental gherkins), chutney and grilled country bread.

**Preparation and cooking: 3½ hours + overnight**
**Makes: 2kg (4½ lb)**

1 rabbit, jointed
1kg (2¼ lb) salt belly of pork, soaked overnight and chopped
500g (18 oz) pork dripping
600ml (1 pint) water
1 teaspoon soft thyme leaves
6 cloves garlic
2 bay leaves
salt and ground black pepper

**1** Place all the ingredients in a large saucepan. Cover, bring to the boil, then reduce the heat so that the fat merely 'burps' on the surface. Cook for 3 hours, stirring occasionally.

**2** Lift out the meat, discarding the bay leaves and garlic; remove the rabbit meat from the bone and shred it and the pork meat with two forks.

**3** Boil the liquid fat until no water remains. Pour the fat over the shredded meat and pack in small stoneware pots. Refrigerate at least overnight.

**4** Allow to come to room temperature before serving.

# Venison and Stout Crumble

A delicious way of cooking the cheaper cuts of stewing venison. If the crumble's not for you, then replace with a puff pastry topping.

**Preparation and cooking: 2½–3 hours**

**Serves: 4–6**

1kg (2¼ lb) lean venison, cut in 4cm (1½ in) cubes

seasoned plain flour for cooking

55g (2 oz) lard or dripping

1 large onion, roughly chopped

1 teaspoon chopped garlic

12 small onions

75g (2¾ oz) button mushrooms

1 teaspoon grated orange rind

1 teaspoon thyme leaves

salt and ground black pepper

1 tablespoon Dijon mustard

6 juniper berries, roasted and crushed

2 bay leaves

300ml (½ pint) Guinness

150ml (¼ pint) beef stock

1 tablespoon soft dark brown sugar

### Crumble topping

¼ teaspoon ground nutmeg

175g (6 oz) plain flour

1 teaspoon chopped fresh marjoram

115g (4 oz) unsalted butter

**1** Toss the venison in the seasoned flour, and shake off any excess. Heat the lard in a heavy-based casserole and brown the meat all over. Remove and set aside.

**2** Add the chopped onion to the casserole with the garlic and small peeled onions. Cook until the onions have softened and browned.

**3** Add the mushrooms, orange rind, thyme, 1 teaspoon black pepper, mustard, juniper and bay leaves, and cook over a medium heat for 8 minutes. Add the Guinness and scrape off any coagulated patches that have stuck to the bottom of the casserole.

**4** Add the stock and brown sugar and return the venison to the casserole. Simmer over a low heat until the meat is tender, about 1½–2 hours. Season to taste. (Ideally you can make it to this point the day before and allow it to cool, so that you can remove any solidified fat from the surface.)

**5** Transfer the stew to a shallow dish, leaving 1cm (½ in) space at the top for the topping. Preheat the oven to 200°C/400°F/Gas 6.

**6** For the topping, sift together ½ teaspoon salt, the nutmeg, flour and marjoram. Rub the butter into the flour, using cool hands, until it resembles coarse breadcrumbs. Spoon over the meat and bake in the oven for 25 minutes until bubbling and golden. If the crumble starts to burn, reduce the heat of the oven and cover loosely with foil.

*Combine 1 tablespoon finely chopped cucumber, 1 tablespoon chopped red peppers, 1 tablespoon salted capers, rinsed, drained and chopped, 1 tablespoon salted anchovies, rinsed, drained and chopped, 1 teaspoon chopped flat-leaf parsley, 1 teaspoon snipped garlic chives, 1 teaspoon coarsely chopped fresh mint and 1 teaspoon lime juice. Mix well and use as a dressing to pour over leftover cold roast venison.*

*Substitute venison steaks for the beef in the Steak with Pepper and Mustard recipe on page 45.*

# Venison Chilli for a Crowd

If venison mince is hard to find (use a reputable butcher rather than a supermarket), you can substitute a mixture of coarsely ground pork and beef.

**Preparation and cooking: 3¼ hours**

**Serves: 10–12**

55g (2 oz) lard or 2 tablespoons olive oil

2kg (4½ lb) venison, coarsely minced

500g (18 oz) streaky bacon, cut into 1cm (½ in) cubes

1kg (2¼ lb) onions, finely diced

1 tablespoon finely diced garlic

3 sticks celery, finely diced

4 fresh red chillies, finely diced

1 bay leaf

2 tablespoons ground cumin

1 tablespoon ground coriander

2 tablespoons oregano leaves

1½ tablespoons paprika

1 tablespoon fennel seeds

1 tablespoon cayenne pepper or to taste

1 tablespoon unsweetened cocoa powder

1 teaspoon powdered cinnamon

2 x 400g (14 oz) tins chopped tomatoes

stock as required

2 tablespoons tomato purée

1 tablespoon ground black pepper

500g (18 oz) dried red kidney beans, soaked overnight

handful of coriander leaves

● ● ● ●

*If you enjoy beef carpaccio, try your favourite method using venison for a change.*

● ● ● ●

## Venison Steaks

● *For a quick venison dish, pepper a couple of venison steaks, pan-fry until cooked to your taste, then keep warm.*

● *Pour a glassful of claret into the pan with 1 tablespoon redcurrant jelly, a glassful of stock, a teaspoon of Dijon mustard, a teaspoon of Worcestershire sauce and seasoning.*

● *Boil until **reduced** by half.*

● *Fold in 25g (1 oz) unsalted butter and swirl the pan to combine.*

● *Strain over the steaks.*

**1** Heat the lard in a large saucepan, and brown the ground venison. Work in batches if necessary, and set aside.

**2** Fry the bacon until golden, then add the onion, garlic, celery, chilli, herbs and spices (down to the cayenne). Sweat until softened and brown.

**3** Return the meat to the pan and add all the remaining ingredients except for the beans and coriander leaves. Cover and simmer for 1½ hours over a low heat.

**4** Add the drained beans, and cook for a further 1–1½ hours or until the beans are tender, keeping them covered with juices. (Alternatively, after 2½ hours, add 3 drained 400g/14 oz tins of red kidney beans and cook for 15 minutes or until hot.)

**5** Fold in the coriander leaves just before serving. Serve with chopped red onions, a *guacamole* (see my version on page 26), soured cream and *taco* chips.

# GARLIC

Garlic is becoming more and more popular. Nowadays I don't know many people who are totally opposed to it, as used to be the case. There was a huge prejudice against its anti-social qualities, but I think as more cooks learn to cook with it, rather than using it raw, they discover that those lingering garlic odours are a thing of the past. When garlic is used in long slow cooking, the smell (due to the sulphur content) is almost undetectable.

Garlic probably originated in Asia. *Allium sativum* is a member of the lily family, along with onions, leeks, chives and shallots. It is very easy to grow, but don't buy it at your garden centre, because you will pay twice as much. Buy a couple of good healthy heads from the supermarket or greengrocer, store them in a dark place and wait for the cloves to start sprouting; then separate the cloves and plant them pre-Christmas. By midsummer you will be able to harvest your own garlic. Young, new-season garlic is delicious, as are the green leaves that grow above the ground. Wait until these leaves start to wilt and turn yellow before you dig up the garlic.

Jacinta, my wife, tells a story of when she first started to cook, when she was following a recipe that specified 1 clove of garlic. Thinking a head of garlic was what was required, she gave her guests a nasty surprise! I too suffered a few divorce situations from my customers when I used to make my *Garlic Terrine* (opposite) without blanching the garlic first in several changes of water. A head of garlic is made up of several cloves, each set in its own wrapping of a paper-thin pinky skin, then the whole head is encased in its own layers of wrapping.

There are many truths and myths concerning garlic: it keeps vampires away, aids digestion, keeps colds away, improves the memory, gives you the gift of the gab, helps prevent cancer, relieves high blood pressure and prevents heart disease. Even if it only does half of these, it is quite obviously very good for you. It actually contains vitamins $B_1$, $B_6$ and C, as well as iron, iodine and phosphorus.

New-season garlic is still juicy, and has a much milder flavour; the overwhelming pungency develops as the garlic dries. When choosing garlic in a shop, feel it to make sure it is firm all the way round. Store it in an airy larder rather than the fridge as the dampness of the fridge encourages mould.

## *Useful Facts about Garlic*

• To separate cloves, place the garlic head on a hard surface and lean on it heavily or crack with the base of a saucepan.

• To peel garlic for chopping, place the garlic clove on its flattest side on a chopping board and smash it with the flat side of a large knife. This will release the skin, which can be picked off and the garlic then chopped.

• If garlic has a green inner germ, cut the clove and ease the germ out with the point of a sharp knife. The germ can be bitter.

• To peel garlic cloves for using whole, cut away the blunt end of the clove and drop into a bowl of boiling water for 5 minutes, then peel off the skin.

• To make a smooth garlic paste, chop garlic then sprinkle a few flakes of sea salt on to it. Mash the garlic on the surface of a chopping board with the flat of the knife. The salt acts as an abrasive and makes the garlic easy to work into a paste.

• To preserve raw (or cooked) garlic paste for a few days, place it in a small glass or china container and cover with an airtight bath of olive oil.

• Roast a whole head of garlic to produce roast garlic paste. Cut 1cm (½ in) off the pointed end of the head. This exposes the cloves which should be dribbled with olive oil. Wrap the garlic in foil and bake in a 180°C/350°F/Gas 4 oven for 35 minutes. Allow to cool a little before separating the cloves. Squeeze or push the cloves with the back of a knife for the soft flesh to pop out of its skin. Store in the same way as raw garlic paste.

• To make garlic-flavoured oil, heat 300ml (½ pint) olive oil in a frying pan, add 6 cloves garlic, and cook until the garlic turns golden. Discard the garlic and when cool bottle the oil.

• To make a simple garlic butter, mix softened butter with raw (or cooked) garlic paste to taste.

• To make garlic powder, slice garlic thinly and cook in a low oven at 150°C/300°F/Gas 2 until dry and brittle. Blend to a powder in an electric coffee grinder and pass through a fine sieve into an airtight container.

# Garlic Terrine

There is a 'chefy' element to this dish which will probably shock your guests, so choose them carefully. After the initial surprise you should get murmurs of satisfaction.

**Preparation and cooking: 1½ hours + chilling**
**Serves: 10–12**

10 heads garlic, cloves peeled, cut in half and green inner germ removed
salt
600ml (1 pint) clear vegetable stock
10 leaves gelatine, softened in cold water
2 red peppers, roasted (see page 254), peeled, seeded and finely diced
6 tomatoes, skinned, seeded and diced
3 shallots, finely diced
18 black olives, pitted and chopped
2 tablespoons chopped parsley
2 tablespoons snipped chives

**To serve**
few dressed rocket leaves
slices of toast
extra virgin olive oil

**1** Cook the garlic in boiling salted water for 5 minutes, remove from the heat then plunge into cold water and drain. Meanwhile, heat another pan of salted water to boiling point and plunge the garlic into this water; cook for another 5 minutes. Repeat this process eight to ten times, treating the garlic more gently each time to retain the shape. Rather boring I know, but essential I'm afraid.

**2** While this process is being completed, bring the vegetable stock to the boil. Remove from the heat, and melt the gelatine in this liquor. Set aside.

**3** Using a conventional terrine mould 30 x 7.5cm (12 x 3 in), scatter some of the garlic cloves over the bottom in one layer, then sprinkle with a little of each of the other vegetable and herb constituents, repeating each layer until the terrine is full. When full, pour over the warm, well-stirred vegetable and gelatine stock. Tap the mould lightly on a surface to remove any air bubbles, and leave to cool at room temperature. Refrigerate for several hours.

**4** To remove the terrine from the mould, dip the bottom and sides of the mould in hot water for a few seconds, then invert the terrine on to a plate.

**5** Cut the terrine into 2cm (¾ in) slices and place a slice on each of ten to twelve plates. Garnish with a few dressed rocket leaves and serve with toasted country bread dribbled with a little olive oil.

THE ABC OF AWT

## Skordalia

A cross between a garlicky mash and a garlic potato sauce, which is excellent with grilled fish.

**Preparation and cooking: 15 minutes**
**Serves: 4–6**

| |
|---|
| 8 cloves garlic, crushed to a paste with 1 teaspoon rock salt |
| 350g (12 oz) cooked warm mashed potato |
| 6 tablespoons hot water |
| 115g (4 oz) ground almonds |
| 350ml (12 fl oz) extra virgin olive oil, warmed |
| 125ml (4 fl oz) double cream, warmed |
| 125ml (4 fl oz) fresh lemon juice |
| freshly ground white pepper |

**1** Blend and pulverise the garlic and salt in a mortar and pestle or food processor. (A pestle and mortar give the best results.) Add the potato, water and ground almonds.

**2** Gradually mix in the olive oil and cream as you would for mayonnaise.

**3** Add lemon juice to taste, less than specified here, if you like. Season with ground white pepper.

### Garlic Bread

● To make garlic bread, cut a French stick at 2cm (¾ in) intervals four-fifths of the way through and spread with garlic butter (see page 194).
● Wrap loosely in foil and bake in a 180°C/350°F/Gas 4 oven for 20 minutes.

*Spike legs of lamb with slivers of garlic, chopped anchovy and rosemary sprigs before roasting.*

## Aïoli

A fabulous mayonnaise-type sauce that can be used as a dip for raw vegetables, for folding into sauces (do not boil after adding *aïoli*) or making salads. It's very potent, so prepare yourself for abusive phone calls the next day.

**Preparation and cooking: 15 minutes**
**Serves: 12**

| |
|---|
| 2 heads garlic, cloves finely chopped |
| 2 teaspoons salt |
| 600ml (1 pint) extra virgin olive oil |
| 4 egg yolks |
| 2 teaspoons Dijon mustard (optional) |
| juice of 3 lemons |
| pinch of saffron stamens, soaked in 1 tablespoon warm water (optional) |
| ½ teaspoon ground white pepper |

**1** Place the garlic cloves in a mortar and pestle, and crush with the salt and 1 tablespoon of olive oil until a smooth paste. (The whole process can be carried out in a food processor but the mortar method is more genuine.)

**2** Add the egg yolks and mustard, if using, and combine thoroughly. Add the remaining oil drop by drop to start with, and then in a slow continuous flow, until the consistency is thick.

**3** Add the lemon juice and the saffron water (if using). Season with pepper and extra salt if necessary.

*Throw some whole cloves of peeled garlic with a few sprigs of thyme and a bay leaf or two around your Sunday roast with some red or white wine. Add some water from time to time and when the roast is cooked you will have a lovely garlicky gravy.*

# Garlic Ketchup

This dressing, like a brown garlic ketchup, is great with sausages, especially garlicky ones.

**Preparation and cooking: 1¼ hours**
**Makes: 2.5 litres (4½ pints)**

500g (18 oz) apples

250g (9 oz) garlic cloves, unpeeled

1.5 litres (2¾ pints) malt vinegar

1 tablespoon ginger, sliced

3 dried chillies, chopped

1 tablespoon cloves

3 teaspoons salt

4 tablespoons black peppercorns

500g (18 oz) black treacle

**1**  Chop up the apples, cores, peels and all, and combine with the unpeeled garlic cloves.

**2**  Place in a **non-reactive** saucepan with the malt vinegar, sliced ginger, dried chopped chillies, cloves, salt and black peppercorns.

**3**  Bring to the boil and simmer gently for 1 hour. Push through a **mouli-légumes** into a clean saucepan.

**4**  Add the black treacle and boil for a further 5 minutes. Funnel into hot sterilised bottles, seal and store in a dark cupboard.

**5**  Store for 4 months, shaking the bottles from time to time.

*Add dried chilli flakes to roast garlic paste (see page 194) for a punchy pureé that you can fold into mashed potatoes or a sauce, or spread over chicken pre roasting, or on toast.*

*Spoon roast garlic paste and extra virgin olive oil into mashed potato instead of butter and cream.*

## Garlic Salt

● *Blend together in a food processor 115g (4 oz) sea salt flakes with 115g (4 oz) peeled garlic cloves to a smooth paste.*

● *Spread on a sheet of greaseproof paper on a baking tray and place in a very low oven (pilot light low) for between 2 and 3 hours until very dry.*

● *Grind in an electric coffee grinder until a fine powder.*

● *Store in an airtight container.*

## Garlic Mustard

● *Blend 175g (6 oz) English mustard powder with 2 teaspoons salt, 1 tablespoon clear honey, 125ml (4 fl oz) white wine vinegar, 125ml (4 fl oz) water, 2 teaspoons garlic paste, 2 teaspoons paprika and 125ml (4 fl oz) light olive oil.*

● *Pour into small jars and seal.*

## Garlic and Lemon Oil

*Lovely in salad dressings or with grilled fish.*

● *Alternate 3 garlic cloves and 3 slices of lemon on a long wooden skewer, place the skewer in a clear glass bottle and top up with olive oil.*

● *Place the oil in sunlight to help release the flavours.*

● *Leave for 1 week before using.*

*Add peeled cloves of garlic to 2cm (¾ in) cubes of raw potato, with rosemary leaves and olive oil. Roast in a hot oven for 45 minutes for a classic Italian potato dish.*

# GRAINS

When talking grains one tends to think 'boring', and yet every newspaper, magazine and nutritionist touts them as life-preserving foods that fight against cancer, digestive problems and heart disease. Why is it then that when you find these grains in restaurants, vegetarian or not, they all seem to be utilised in dishes with less imagination than a frozen pea? Grains can taste really good, but only if they are prepared with flair.

Most grains are indeed good for us, being major sources of many vital nutrients. The grain seed, which is what we eat, is the storehouse of food and life for the next generation of plants; as a result, grains are a major source of energy (carbohydrate) and thus a major food for many populations throughout the world. Grains also provide protein (although this is incomplete due to the lack of the essential amino acid, lysine), and minerals and vitamins (most have good quantities of B vitamins, potassium, magnesium and phosphorus). They are also low in fat. However, some people suffer an intolerance to the wheat protein, gluten, known as coeliac disease. Wheat products such as bulgur, semolina and couscous, and rye, oats and barley also contain gluten.

Grain seeds are made up of an outer seed coat or husk and the kernel. The husks are inedible in rice, barley and oats, and must be removed to render the grain edible. The kernel is divided into three parts: the outer layer which is the bran (a good source of dietary fibre), the embryo or seed (the germ, which is rich in oil and nutrients), and the endosperm (high in protein, carbohydrate and other nutrients). Too often, though, grains are over-refined and processed and many of their nutrients are lost (white flour uses only the endosperm, for instance).

I have included here a selection of grains and grain products which I use regularly, and which I think are the most popular – it would take a whole book to cover every aspect of this category!

## BARLEY (*Hordium distichon*)

Most of us perceive this as belonging to soups, but recently it has become quite fashionable as an alternative base for risotto. It is used in cereals, flour, and in the making of malt spirits (like whisky) and beer. Scotch or pot barley has only had the husks removed; pearl barley is the more common, refined barley, having lost the husk, bran and embryo, leaving only the endosperm. This refining means a loss of protein, fibre and B vitamins, but all the same, 225g (8 oz) of cooked pearl barley offers the same protein content as a glass of milk. Pearl barley has a good shelf life: 6–9 months in an airtight container. To cook barley, simmer three parts liquid (water or stock) to one part barley for 1 hour for pot barley, 30–40 minutes for pearl. If you pre-soak barley overnight, the cooking time can be as quick as 15 minutes.

## BRAN, OAT AND WHEAT

Bran is the tough outer covering of any seed. It contains nutrients, and because it cannot be digested by the human gut, it has proven value in relieving constipation (and an unproven value in regulating cholesterol and lowering blood sugar levels).

Both oat and wheat brans can be bought; wheat should be kept for no more than 6 months as it loses its nutrients. Oat bran makes a good substitute for breadcrumbs when you want to coat foods such as fish or chicken.

## BUCKWHEAT (*Fagopyrum esculentum*)

Not a true cereal or grain but the fruit of a member of the rhubarb family, Polygonaceae. Buckwheat contains complex carbohydrates, as well as a high count of essential amino acids, the basic components of protein (including lysine).

You can purchase two types of buckwheat – plain whole buckwheat or roasted buckwheat (*kasha*). Plain buckwheat is available as hulled groats (the husk is inedible) and stone ground; *kasha* is available whole, or coarse, medium and fine ground. *Kasha* is usually served as a side dish to stews, or as a stuffing; its nutty flavour is popular in Continental Europe. Plain groats are used as a cereal or pilaff. Buckwheat flour is used to make *blinis* and pancakes or *crêpes*; it is made into *soba* noodles in Japan.

## BULGUR

Bulgur, bulgar or burghul is a wheat product thought to be interchangeable with cracked wheat, but they are in fact different. They both come from whole wheat berries, but cracked wheat is uncooked wheat that has been dried and cracked apart by milling, while bulgur is wheat that has been steamed then dried before being cracked. Bulgur is high in nutrients.

Bulgur merely requires pre-soaking when used for salads such as *Tabbouleh* (see page 211), whereas cracked wheat requires a lengthier period of cooking. Bulgur is best stored in an airtight jar out of sunlight. When soaking bulgur add four times the volume in boiling liquid, leave to soak for 20–30 minutes, then squeeze dry. If using it like rice, pour bulgur into three to four times the volume of boiling liquid, and cook for about 20 minutes.

## CORNMEAL

Maize or corn – *Zea mays* – comes in two principal forms – the sweetcorn eaten as a vegetable, and field corn. The latter, which is harder and starchier, is ground to cornmeal. In the UK, we know this better as polenta, the Italian name. Corn is high in nutrients, and is also processed for cornflour and oils.

## OATS (*Avena sativa*)

Whole oats are rich in nutrients. They are easily digested, and higher in protein and fat than other cereals (so go rancid quite quickly).

There are a number of ways of milling oats. Steel-cut oats are organic unrefined oats which are dried, roughly sliced and processed with little or no heat, and so retain most of their B vitamins. They tend to be on the chewy side and require longer cooking. Rolled oats are seeds which are steamed then cut into thin flakes and then dried; these are the porridge oats which take about 5 minutes to cook. Quick oats are cut thinner, are slightly pre-cooked, and take about 3 minutes' cooking. Instant oats, many varieties of which are sugared and flavoured for children, only need boiling water to reconstitute them. There are also various textures of oatmeal.

## RICE (*Oryza sativa*)

Rice consists mainly of carbohydrate, comprising 80 per cent starch and 12 per cent water, and there are three classifications: long-grain, medium-grain and short-grain. All rice starts life as brown, then in the processing it is stripped of its husk, bran and germ to achieve its whiteness; brown rice still has its bran and germ. The main varieties found in the UK include:

WHITE LONG-GRAIN, rices such as Texmati, Carolina and Patna. Not a glutinous rice, used for savoury cooking, and absorbs twice its volume in liquid.

WHITE LONG-GRAIN EASY-COOK, which has been steam-treated. This rice never sticks, but needs extra cooking time (some 20–25 minutes whereas ordinary long-grain needs 12–15 minutes).

BROWN LONG-GRAIN and EASY-COOK absorb three to four times their volume of liquid, and the former needs 45 minutes to cook, easy-cook 50–60.

ITALIAN RISOTTO RICE is short-grain, and includes arborio and carnaroli. The higher the quality, the more liquid it absorbs, about four to five times in volume. A risotto, after the initial buttering and flavouring, will take about 20 minutes.

WHITE and EASY-COOK BASMATI RICE, used mainly to accompany curries, are long-grain separate-grain rices. White takes 10–12 minutes' cooking, easy-cook, 18–20 minutes.

SPANISH *CALASPARRA*, a medium-grain Valencia rice, is used for *paella* and cooks a little sticky but dry; an excellent rice, but if you have difficulty finding it, substitute risotto rice. Takes 15–18 minutes to cook.

GLUTINOUS RICES are very starchy, so are sticky when cooked – popular in the East, as easy to pick up with chopsticks! FRAGRANT or JASMINE RICE is indeed fragrant, and cooks very quickly.

WILD RICE is not actually a rice but the seed of a North American grass, and is now cultivated. When cooked, the long and dark brown kernel bursts open to display its pale interior. It is chewy with a wonderful earthy flavour. If cooked in a pilaff, it will need about 1 hour.

Store rice in airtight containers in a cool, dry and, if possible, dark place. White rice in those conditions should keep indefinitely. Brown rice on the other hand lasts at best six months because oxidation of oil in the bran can cause rancidity.

## SEMOLINA

This is another wheat product, prepared from the roughly milled endosperm of durum wheat, a hard high-protein wheat used almost exclusively in the manufacture of dried pasta. An average portion of semolina contains 10–12g of protein, 40g of carbohydrate and 1g of dietary fibre, less than 1 per cent fat and no cholesterol. Semolina flour is not durum wheat flour, but flour which is the residue left after the processing of semolina. The two flours, however, are interchangeable in recipes. Couscous is in turn a product of semolina, a sort of 'pasta' made from a combination of fine and coarse semolinas and water. Ready-prepared and quick-cook couscous is available. Semolina stored in an airtight glass container will keep for up to 6 months. It is a useful store-cupboard ingredient as it will thicken soups or stews when mixed with stock, milk or water, and flavoured with vegetables or herbs it can be delicious and a lot less calorific than a plate of mashed potato. Leftovers may be sliced like polenta and grilled or fried. Semolina is also often used instead of potato in making *gnocchi*.

. . . . . . . . .

*Barley is excellent added to many old-fashioned stews and soups, making them more nourishing.*

. . . . . . . .

## Barley Stuffing

*Makes an excellent stuffing for poultry.*

- *Fry 55g (2 oz) diced pancetta (or bacon) with ½ diced red onion, ½ teaspoon soft thyme leaves and 1 chopped clove garlic in 55g (2 oz) unsalted butter until the onion has softened, about 8 minutes.*
- *Add 2 seeded and diced tomatoes and 1 teaspoon chopped basil, and cook for a further 5 minutes.*
- *Add 350g (12 oz) cooked pearl barley, 1 teaspoon Nando's peri-peri sauce, and the grated rind of ½ lemon.*
- *Stir to combine and set aside to cool.*

# Barley with Greens, Sausage and Ham

A bowl of this Mediterranean-inspired soup/stew will nourish you in every way.

**Preparation and cooking: 1 hour**
**Serves: 4–6**

| |
|---|
| 115g (4 oz) unsalted butter |
| 2 onions, finely chopped |
| 2 cloves garlic, finely chopped |
| ½ teaspoon soft thyme leaves |
| 2 handfuls mixed spinach and rocket leaves, roughly chopped |
| 225g (8 oz) pearl barley |
| ½ teaspoon cayenne pepper |
| 55g (2 oz) Parma ham, chopped |
| 900ml (1½ pints) chicken stock |
| 115g (4 oz) *chorizo* sausage, diced |
| 55g (2 oz) Parmesan, freshly grated |
| 4 tablespoons chopped flat-leaf parsley |
| 2 tablespoons snipped chives |
| 2 tablespoons pine kernels, toasted |
| salt and ground black pepper |

**1** Melt half the butter in a saucepan over a medium heat. Add the onion, garlic and thyme, and cook for 8 minutes until the onion has started to soften.

**2** Stir in the chopped greens, then fold in the barley, cayenne, Parma ham and chicken stock. Bring to the boil, reduce the heat and simmer, covered, until the liquid has evaporated and the barley is tender, about 35–40 minutes.

**3** Add the *chorizo*, Parmesan, parsley, chives, pine kernels and remaining butter. Stir to combine and season to taste.

. . . . . . . . .

*Replace rice with pearl barley when making risotto. You may need to cook it for 30–40 minutes instead of the usual 20, but it is much more nutritious and, unlike many dishes that are good for you, it tastes great.*

. . . . . . . . . . .

## Buckwheat Noodles

- *Place 3 large free-range eggs in the food processor and blend.*
- *With the machine running, add 225g (8 oz) buckwheat flour, 115g (4 oz) durum flour (hard wheat flour), 115g (4 oz) plain flour and 1 teaspoon coarse rock salt in a fine stream. Add enough water to make a firm dough.*
- *Let the machine run until the dough comes away from the side of the bowl and forms a ball.*
- *Place the dough ball on a floured surface and knead for 5 minutes.*
- *Roll the dough out by hand or use a pasta machine to roll very thin. Cut into noodles.*

# Buckwheat *Blinis*

A recipe given by an Australian who purloined it from an Englishman, who got it from . . . Perfect for brunch with smoked salmon and soured cream or caviar, melted butter and chopped shallots.

**Preparation and cooking: 1 hour**
**Makes: 8 *blinis***

1 dessertspoon caster sugar

15g (½ oz) dried yeast

1 tablespoon lemon juice, strained

125ml (4 fl oz) warm water

140g (5 oz) buckwheat flour

¼ teaspoon salt

2 free-range eggs, separated

75g (2¾ oz) plain flour

150ml (¼ pint) warm double cream

150ml (¼ pint) double cream, whipped to **soft peaks**

clarified butter for frying (see page 60)

**1** Dissolve the sugar and yeast in the lemon juice and warm water. Add the buckwheat flour and leave in a warm place for 25 minutes. It will bubble up and rise slightly, as the yeast gets to work.

**2** In a separate bowl combine the salt, egg yolks and plain flour with the warm cream. Mix to form a smooth batter. Fold into the yeast mixture and allow to stand for a further 15 minutes in a warm place.

**3** Add the whipped cream to the batter, and allow to stand for 10 minutes. Beat the egg whites to soft peaks and gently fold into the batter.

**4** Add a little clarified butter to a hot non-stick pan and cook a large tablespoon of the batter until golden on both sides, turning once, 2 minutes on the first side, 1 minute on the second. Keep warm or allow to cool to room temperature while cooking the remainder.

# Ricotta and Semolina *Gnocchi*

Most *gnocchi* we eat in the UK are made with potato, but you should try these made with semolina, they are very good.

**Preparation and cooking: 1 hour**
**Serves: 4–6**

500ml (18 fl oz) milk

½ onion

1 clove

1 bay leaf

175g (6 oz) semolina

2 egg yolks

85g (3 oz) unsalted butter, melted

140g (5 oz) Parmesan, freshly grated

85g (3 oz) ricotta cheese

¼ teaspoon grated nutmeg

salt and ground black pepper

1 tablespoon finely chopped basil

2 tablespoons finely chopped parsley

¼ teaspoon soft thyme leaves

plain flour for dusting

300ml (½ pint) double cream

55g (2 oz) soft breadcrumbs

**1** Heat the milk to **scalding** with the onion which has been pierced by the clove and bay leaf. Leave the flavours to **infuse** for 15 minutes. Discard the onion and its attachments.

**2** Whisk the semolina into the milk in a steady stream. Allow to cook over a low heat for 5 minutes, then spoon the semolina into a bowl.

**3** Beat the egg yolks one at a time into the semolina. Beat in three-quarters of the melted butter, 85g (3 oz) of the Parmesan, and the ricotta, nutmeg, ½ teaspoon salt and the herbs.

**4** Place a large spoonful of the *gnocchi* mix on a heavily floured board and roll the mix into a 2cm (¾ in) diameter sausage. Cut the sausage into 2.5cm (1 in) pieces. Repeat with the remaining *gnocchi* dough.

**5** Preheat the oven to 200°C/400°F/Gas 6. Bring a large saucepan of salted water to the boil. Cook the *gnocchi* for 1–1½ minutes in small batches – until they pop up to the surface of the water – draining each batch and placing in a lightly buttered baking dish. Lightly pepper the *gnocchi* and pour over the remaining melted butter.

**6** Warm the cream with a little salt and pepper and pour over the *gnocchi*.

**7** Combine the remaining Parmesan cheese with the breadcrumbs and scatter over the *gnocchi*.

**8** Bake in the oven for 15 minutes or until bubbling and golden. (The dish can be pre-prepared to step 7. If baking from cold, cook for 25 minutes.)

# Honey, Orange and Thyme Bran Muffins

A delicious muffin that not only tastes good, but does you good. Good for breakfast with butter and/or maple syrup, served with your morning coffee.

**Preparation and cooking: 40 minutes**
**Makes: 12 muffins**

55g (2 oz) unsalted butter, melted, plus extra for greasing the tin

55g (2 oz) soft light brown sugar

150ml (¼ pint) buttermilk

2 free-range eggs, lightly beaten

½ teaspoon soft thyme leaves

60ml (2 fl oz) clear honey

grated zest of 2 oranges

225g (8 oz) plain flour

225g (8 oz) wheat bran

1 tablespoon baking powder

pinch of salt

**1** Preheat the oven to 180°C/350°F/Gas 4. Lightly butter a 12-cup muffin tin.

**2** Place the brown sugar in a bowl and combine with the melted butter, buttermilk, eggs, thyme, honey and orange zest.

**3** In another bowl combine the flour, bran, baking powder and salt. Make a well in the dry ingredients and then fold in the buttermilk mix. Don't overwork, but combine until just mixed.

**4** Fill each muffin cup two-thirds full of the batter, then bake for 25–30 minutes until the muffins are golden and cooked through. Remove from the oven, allow to stand for 10 minutes then turn the muffins out on to a cake rack to cool completely.

## Bran Batter

- *Make this batter for fish or chicken by processing in a blender 115g (4 oz) wheat bran, 115g (4 oz) plain flour, 3 teaspoons English mustard powder and ½ teaspoon salt.*
- *Add 250ml (9 fl oz) dark beer and 2 teaspoons Dijon mustard.*
- *Process until smooth. Season to taste.*
- *Dip fish or chicken into flour then into batter, and deep-fry.*

# Yogurt and Dill Bulgur (V)

A perfect partner for a grill or roast instead of the usual spuds.

**Preparation and cooking: 55 minutes**
**Serves: 4**

55g (2 oz) unsalted butter
1 onion, finely chopped
1 carrot, finely sliced
1 stick celery, finely sliced
1 leek, sliced
1 teaspoon soft thyme leaves
2 cloves garlic, finely chopped
900ml (1½ pints) chicken or vegetable stock
225g (8 oz) bulgur
3 tablespoons Greek yogurt
4 tablespoons chopped dill
salt and ground black pepper

**1** Melt the butter in a saucepan over a low heat. Add the onion, carrot, celery, leek, thyme and garlic and cook for 10 minutes.
**2** Add the stock and heat until boiling, then fold in the bulgur. Cook until the bulgur and vegetables are tender, about 20–25 minutes. Turn off the heat and allow the mixture to stand for 10 minutes.
**3** Fluff up the bulgur with a fork. Fold in the Greek yogurt and dill, and season to taste.

## Bulgur Pilaff

*Substitute this bulgur dish for rice pilaff.*
● *Cook 2 chopped onions with 4 chopped cloves garlic in 4 tablespoons olive oil until the onion has softened.*
● *Add a good pinch of chilli flakes and 1 teaspoon chopped sage.*
● *Add 175g (6 oz) bulgur and 350ml (12 fl oz) vegetable stock, cook for 15 minutes, then fold in 2 handfuls each of washed chopped spinach and chopped rocket.*
● *Cook for a further 5 minutes until the greens have wilted. Fold in 55g (2 oz) unsalted butter, remove from the heat and allow to rest for 10 minutes.*
● *Fluff up the bulgur with a fork and season to taste.*

# Vermont Corn, Chilli and Bacon Bread

I always think American cornbread is more like a cake, but it is a pleasant mouthful and very useful for the next main recipe overleaf.

**Preparation and cooking: 45 minutes**
**Serves 4–6**

350g (12 oz) smoked streaky bacon, diced
1 tablespoon corn oil
2 spring onions, finely chopped
115g (4 oz) corn kernels
½ teaspoon dried chilli flakes
350g (12 oz) cornmeal or polenta
350g (12 oz) plain flour
1 tablespoon caster sugar
1 teaspoon baking powder
½ teaspoon baking soda
½ teaspoon salt
375ml (13 fl oz) buttermilk
2 eggs, lightly beaten
1 tablespoon maple syrup
½ teaspoon ground black pepper
2 tablespoons unsalted butter, melted

**1** Preheat the oven to 200°C/400°F/Gas 6, and lightly butter a 23cm (9 in) square cake tin.
**2** Fry the bacon in a frying pan in the oil until it is crispy and releases its fats. Add the spring onion and cook for 5 minutes, then add the corn kernels and chilli and stir to combine. Allow to cool slightly.
**3** Combine the cornmeal, flour, sugar, baking powder, baking soda and salt. Add the bacon mixture, the buttermilk, eggs, maple syrup, black pepper and half the melted butter. Mix well.
**4** Pour the batter into the prepared cake tin and brush the top with the remaining melted butter. Bake until golden, 20–25 minutes. Serve warm.

## Leek Polenta

• *Melt 55g (2 oz) butter in a non-stick saucepan and* **sweat** *4 chopped leeks, 4 chopped cloves garlic, 1 finely chopped chilli and 1 teaspoon soft thyme leaves over a medium heat until the vegetables have softened, about 12 minutes. Reserve.*

• *Bring 1.2 litres (2 pints) vegetable stock to the boil, reduce the heat and simmer.*

• *Add 200g (7 oz) quick-cook polenta to the stock, and stir constantly with a wooden spoon until thick.*

• *Add the reserved leek mixture and stir to combine. Fold in 55g (2 oz) grated Parmesan, 85g (3 oz) Gorgonzola, cut into small cubes, and 125ml (4 fl oz) double cream. Season to taste.*

## Polenta Deep-fried Chicken

*Make a polenta coating for chicken.*

• *Marinate 8 chicken thighs or 4 breasts overnight in 125ml (4 fl oz) soured cream with ½ teaspoon cayenne pepper, ½ teaspoon celery salt and ½ teaspoon garlic powder.*

• *Combine 85g (3 oz) polenta with 55g (2 oz) plain flour, a pinch of nutmeg, a pinch of cayenne pepper and ½ teaspoon salt.*

• *Roll the chicken pieces in the polenta coating, then deep-fry.*

• *Keep warm in a 180°C/350°F/ Gas 4 oven until ready to serve.*

## Cornbread, Sausage and Wild Rice Stuffing

A great stuffing to go with a turkey or goose.

**Preparation and cooking: 55 minutes**
**Makes: 1kg (2¼ lb)**

| |
|---|
| 115g (4 oz) wild rice |
| 300ml (½ pint) water |
| ½ recipe *Vermont Corn, Chilli and Bacon Bread* (see page 203), cooled and cubed |
| 85g (3 oz) unsalted butter |
| 225g (8 oz) sausagemeat |
| 1 large onion, finely chopped |
| 1 teaspoon soft thyme leaves |
| ½ teaspoon fennel seeds |
| ½ red pepper, finely diced |
| 1 teaspoon chopped sage |
| 2 handfuls rocket leaves, chopped |
| salt and ground black pepper |

**1** Cook the wild rice in the water for 30 minutes, drain and transfer to a bowl.

**2** Fry the cornbread cubes in batches in the butter until golden all over. Add the cornbread to the rice.

**3** Fry the sausagemeat in the same pan, breaking it up with a wooden spoon. Cook until brown and crusty, and the sausage has released its fat. Drain the sausagemeat and add to the rice bowl. Retain the fats that have been released, and return them to the frying pan.

**4** Add the onion, thyme, fennel seeds, red pepper and sage to the pan. Cook for 10 minutes until the onion has softened and started to colour.

**5** Add the rocket and stir until the rocket has **wilted**, about 3 minutes. Fold this mixture into the stuffing. Mix until all is well combined. Season to taste, and cool.

**6** This is a loose stuffing. Reheat in a frying pan or a baking dish in the oven. I prefer not to stuff the bird, but if you like a stuffed bird spoon into the turkey or goose and sew up the entrance to the cavity. Cook as soon as possible.

# Wild Mushroom Risotto

Risottos are great stand-by supper or lunch dishes. The trick of a good risotto is to add the stock little by little, allowing the liquid to almost disappear before adding the next ladleful.

**Preparation and cooking: 1 hour**
**Serves: 4–6**

1.4 litres (2½ pints) chicken stock

25g (1 oz) dried ceps or *porcini*, soaked in lukewarm water for 20 minutes, chopped

225g (8 oz) wild or fresh mushrooms

140g (5 oz) unsalted butter

1 tablespoon olive oil

85g (3 oz) smoked streaky bacon, chopped (optional)

1 onion, finely chopped

1 clove garlic, finely chopped

1 sprig thyme

1 bay leaf

350g (12 oz) arborio or other risotto rice

300ml (½ pint) full-bodied red wine

175g (6 oz) Parmesan, freshly grated

4 tablespoons chopped flat-leaf parsley

**1** Heat the stock in a medium saucepan and keep simmering. Strain the dried mushrooms and reserve the soaking water. Chop the fresh mushrooms and set aside.

**2** Melt 55g (2 oz) of the butter with the oil in a heavy-based saucepan over a medium heat. Add the bacon, and cook until crispy, then add the onion, garlic, thyme and bay leaf and cook for about 25 minutes until the onion is soft but not brown. Add the *porcini* or cep mushrooms and cook for a further 3–4 minutes.

**3** Add the rice and stir until the grains are well coated with fat, about 3–4 minutes. Add the wine and stir until it has been absorbed. Add the reserved mushroom soaking water and cook until this too has almost all been absorbed. Add the warm stock, a ladleful at a time, allowing the rice to absorb the liquid each time before adding the next ladleful. Continue like this until the rice is tender but still a little firm to the bite.

**4** Cook the fresh mushrooms in the remaining butter then add them to the rice. When the rice is ready, fold in the grated Parmesan and stir. Garnish with chopped parsley and serve.

# Saffron Pea Pilaff

A combination of rice and peas seems to be the rage world-wide, and this one from Kashmir is no exception. It has great colour with a lovely blend of spices, nuts and fruit. Serve on its own or as a partner to a stew or *tagine*.

**Preparation and cooking: 50 minutes**
**Serves: 4–6**

225g (8 oz) basmati rice

55g (2 oz) unsalted butter

25g (1 oz) flaked almonds

8 walnut halves, roughly chopped

2 tablespoons raisins

8 dried apricots, diced

4 cloves

2 cardamom pods

2.5cm (1 in) cinnamon stick

12 black peppercorns

375g (13 oz) fresh or frozen peas

½ teaspoon saffron stamens, soaked in 1 tablespoon hot water

4 spring onions, finely sliced

600ml (1 pint) vegetable or chicken stock

3 tablespoons chopped coriander

salt

**1** Wash the rice well and drain.

**2** Heat the butter in a saucepan and fry separately the almonds, walnuts, raisins and apricots until the nuts are golden brown and the raisins are plumped up. Remove and set aside.

**3** To the same pan add the spices and over a low heat fry until they become aromatic, stirring continuously, about 2 minutes.

**4** Stir in the peas, saffron and soaking liquor, spring onion and rice, and cook for 2 minutes, making sure the rice is coated with butter. Add the stock and bring to the boil. Reduce the heat, cover with a tight-fitting lid and simmer for about 20 minutes or until the rice is cooked and the liquid absorbed.

**5** Fold in the coriander, nuts and fruit, and season to taste.

# Paella

A Spanish rice dish originating in Valencia, and the name actually refers to the cooking vessel, a *paellera*. There are hundreds of versions of the dish, each household or restaurant having its own. This is one-pot dining at its best, and could include anything you fancy: rabbit, snails and green beans seem to have been the original constituents with, of course, Spanish short-grain rice and saffron. Have fun playing with different combinations. With rice dishes it is best to measure the rice and stock by volume, 1 part to just over 2 – e.g. 600ml (1 pint) rice to 1.3 litres (2¼ pints) stock.

**Preparation and cooking: 1 hour, 10 minutes**
**Serves: 6–8**

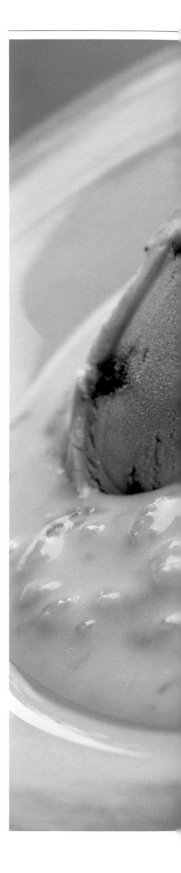

1.3 litres (2¼ pints) chicken stock
½ teaspoon saffron stamens
125ml (4 fl oz) good olive oil
175g (6 oz) *chorizo*, cut in 5mm (¼ in) slices
115g (4 oz) *pancetta* or smoked streaky bacon, cut in small dice
8 chicken thighs, each chopped in half
1 large Spanish onion, finely diced
1 teaspoon soft thyme leaves
2 teaspoons finely chopped garlic
½ teaspoon dried chilli flakes
1 red pepper, diced
600ml (1 pint) *calasparra* (Spanish short-grain) rice
3 bay leaves
1 teaspoon paprika
125ml (4 fl oz) dry white wine
1 tablespoon lemon juice
115g (4 oz) fresh or frozen peas
18 small clams, cleaned
18 mussels, cleaned
55g (2 oz) unsalted butter
4 large tomatoes, seeded and diced
5 tablespoons chopped flat-leaf parsley
grated rind of 1 lemon
salt and ground black pepper
12 jumbo raw prawns, in shell
450g (1 lb) squid, cleaned and chopped into bite-sized pieces

**1** Heat the stock and saffron to boiling point.

**2** Heat half the olive oil in a *paella* dish or heavy-based saucepan. Add the *chorizo* and *pancetta* and fry until crisp, then remove and set aside. Add the chicken pieces to the pan and fry until golden; remove and set aside with the *chorizo*.

**3** Add half the remaining olive oil to the pan with the onion, thyme, three-quarters of the garlic, the chilli flakes and red pepper, and cook over a medium heat for 8 minutes or until the onion has softened without colour.

**4** Add the rice, bay leaves and paprika, and stir to coat the rice in the oil, cooking and stirring continuously for 2 minutes. Stir in the white wine, lemon juice and hot stock, and cook for 5 minutes.

**5** Fold in the *chorizo* mix, the browned chicken, peas, clams and mussels. Put the molluscs in with the edges that will open facing outwards.

**6** Place the dish, uncovered, in a preheated oven (170°C/325°F/Gas 3) and cook for 15–18 minutes. Remove from the oven and leave to rest for 10 minutes. Fold in the butter, tomatoes, parsley and grated lemon rind. Season to taste.

**7** Meanwhile, heat the remaining oil in a frying pan with the remaining garlic and fry the prawns for 2–3 minutes, turning once. For the last minute of cooking, add the squid and fry over fierce heat.

**8** Scatter the prawns and squid over the *paella* and serve immediately.

# Rice Pudding

This classic rice pudding is an old favourite of mine, very simple but very delicious. It is best served hot with your favourite ice-cream.

**Preparation and cooking: 2 hours, 10 minutes**
**Serves: 4–6**

75g (2¾ oz) short-grain rice
butter
a pinch of salt
55g (2 oz) caster sugar
1.2 litres (2 pints) milk
grated nutmeg or cinnamon

**1** Preheat your oven to 150°C/300°F/Gas 2.
**2** Wash and drain the short-grain rice and put in a 1.4–1.7 litre (2½–3 pint) buttered pie dish
**3** Add a pinch of salt, the caster sugar and milk, and stir. Sprinkle grated nutmeg or cinnamon over and top with knobs of butter.
**4** Bake in the centre or towards the bottom of the oven for about 2 hours.
**5** Stir in the skin that forms on the top at least once during the cooking time.

# HERBS

I am going to list only the most popular herbs, due to their sheer numbers. They are invaluable in good cooking, notwithstanding the fact that most of them seem to be a miracle cure for some ailment or other.

## BASIL (*Ocimum basilicum*)

This originated in India, and made its way to southern Europe in the sixteenth century. It is an annual herb, which means you have to re-grow it each year. It likes fairly rich soil and in the UK needs plenty of sun and plenty of water. As it grows, the tips should be pinched out to make it more bushy.

There are several varieties, each with its own distinct flavour, but the overriding one is of aniseed. The varieties we see most are sweet basil, bush basil and purple basil. If you have access to an Asian or Thai store, Asian basil is good, but it does not last when cut, going floppy very quickly; the leaves of all basil blacken when bruised or subjected to very cold temperatures. Unless you are going to use basil immediately, do not use a knife to cut the leaves as this also makes them blacken; rip the leaves with your hands instead.

## BAY (*Laurus nobilis*)

An excellent perennial bush or tree, of Asian origin, that needs a sheltered frost-free position in a UK garden. In the UK it is rare to find bay trees taller than about 3m (10 ft), but I am fortunate to have one in the garden that is getting on for 6m (20 ft). The bay, like the box, makes a very attractive hedge.

The leaves are used sparingly, as they can be overpowering. They flavour soups and stews, and a few can be scattered around a Sunday roast. The bay leaf is more pungent in its dried form, so generally when a recipe indicates 1 bay leaf, use 2 if you have fresh.

## BORAGE (*Borago officinalis*)

Once you start to grow this annual herb, you won't be able to get rid of it as it self-seeds. It originated in the Middle East, and looks equally good in a flower garden as in a herb garden, because of its bluey-green leaves and cobalt blue flowers. The plant has little or no fragrance, but when the leaves are crushed there is a strong taste of cucumber, hence its historical association with that summer drink, Pimms (although mint is now used more regularly). The flowers are often used in edible flower salads and sugared for cake decorations.

## CHERVIL (*Anthriscus cerefolium*)

A hardy biennial herb, chervil is one of the classic *fines herbes*, and its delicate and refreshing aniseedy flavour is good in green salads, with sauces (*Béarnaise* particularly), and as a herb butter for steak or fish.

## CHIVES (*Allium schoenoprasum*)

A member of the onion and garlic family. In cooking it is the stems, which are onion or garlic flavoured depending on the variety, that are used. Chives are easy to grow and are perennial, the stems dying down and returning each spring. The clumps should be split every 2 or 3 years. The stems need cutting several times during the season, but it is also nice to leave a few clumps to flower, as the flowers are delicious scattered over salads. Chives are very adaptable, with uses in all sorts of cooking. They are used cold in salads or added at the last minute to hot dishes. They are a component of *fines herbes*. Onion chives have long (30–45cm/12–18 in) round stems whereas garlic chives have flat blades similar to grass. Don't chop chives, cut them just before using with a sharp knife or scissors.

## CORIANDER (*Coriandrum sativum*)

This fragrant herb is indigenous to the Mediterranean area and Asia, where it is used extensively (one of its colonial names is Chinese parsley). It has become very popular due to the trend for fusion food (East meets West). The Americans call it *cilantro*. The plant produces the herb — leaf, stem and root — as well as a spice, which is the small round seed produced after the flower has been allowed to go to seed. This seed is used extensively in Middle Eastern cooking. It is a very powerful herb, so use with caution, as the taste is acquired and not to everybody's liking. When you buy coriander in a greengrocer or supermarket the herb will usually have been cut, whereas if you purchase it in an Asian shop the herb will still have its roots attached (they crush the roots for aromatic flavouring).

## DILL (*Anethum graveolens*)

This annual or biennial herb grows to a metre or so (3–4 ft). Both the leaves and seeds can be used in cooking. Native to southern Europe and western Asia, it is related to parsley, fennel, cumin and coriander – and the carrot (the Umbellifer family). It has similar feathery leaves to the perennial herb fennel; fennel leaves are lime green, whereas dill leaves are a deeper bluey-green. The dill flavour is akin to that of caraway seeds. The leaves are used for fish and egg dishes, and make a welcome addition to a salad.

## FENNEL (*Foeniculum vulgare*)

This is a perennial herb, related to dill, that can grow to 2m (6½ ft). It is related botanically, and in taste, to Florence fennel, the bulb vegetable (see page 118). Where dill tastes like caraway, fennel tastes like aniseed. The seeds, stalks and leaves can all be used, especially in fish cookery. The dried thin stalks are often used to stuff the cavity of fish, and whole fish, like sea bass, can be grilled over larger fennel stalks. The seeds are very aromatic, and are used in sauces and slow-cooked dishes. You rarely see fennel herb in shops as they prefer to sell dill, but it can be used in similar ways. The feathery leaves attached to Florence fennel can be used as a herb.

## MARJORAM AND OREGANO (*Origanum* spp)

There are three principal varieties of marjoram: sweet marjoram (*O. marjorana*), pot marjoram (*O. onites*), often called Greek marjoram, and wild marjoram (*O. vulgare*) which is oregano. The latter has a much stronger flavour. Pot marjoram is used in many Greek salads. Oregano is used widely in Italian tomato sauces and on pizzas. All are easy to grow, and have wonderful pale or dark green leaves which makes for excellent ground cover. Oregano is a perennial that needs splitting every 2 or 3 years; marjoram is annual.

## MINT (*Mentha* spp)

A wonderful herb that can also be the garden's biggest pest, as it will spread and spread. You need to dedicate a bed just for mint, or many people grow it in its own tub. As it is almost a weed, I can never understand why it is so overpriced when you buy a small pack in the supermarket. Mint originated in the Mediterranean and western Asia, and it is still widely used in the cooking of these areas, particularly Greece and the Middle East. There are about 30 varieties of mint, from the common spearmint and peppermint through to such exotics as pineapple mint. Chop mint just before you wish to use it as it quickly blackens.

## PARSLEY (*Petroselinum crispum*)

The two principal types of parsley – curly and flat-leaf – have made a comeback in the last few years. No longer is parsley just used as a garnish for everything under the sun, we now enjoy its flavour and texture in many dishes and sauces including *Tabbouleh* (see page 211) and *Salsa Verde* (see page 215). The chopped leaves with chives, tarragon and chervil go to make *fines herbes*, its stalks are used in a **bouquet garni**, and chewing on raw parsley is a good antidote to garlic-smelling breath. Flat-leaf Italian parsley has become more widely used recently than the curly variety, probably because it tends to be slightly milder on the palate, and more pleasant to eat. Parsley is one of the few herbs that is biennial, so it lasts for two years, but I would advise you to plant a few seedlings every year to keep a good rotation. Curly parsley can be very gritty, so it needs good washing and drying in a salad spinner before being chopped.

## ROSEMARY (*Rosmarinus officinalis*)

A perennial that originated in the Mediterranean, which is used liberally in the cooking of Italy and southern France. It will grow in the UK but often under protest, as it prefers sandy soil and likes a good dose of sun. It is a woody herb with green and silvery spiky leaves. If you are lucky your bush will develop vibrant blue flowers. In cooking it brilliantly complements roast or grilled meats, especially lamb. It is used in *sofrito*, the base of many Italian and Spanish casseroles, and in France it features in the *herbes de Provence* mixture. The woody stalks make excellent kebab skewers after you have removed the leaves. The leaves of rosemary are very tough, so if a recipe states chopped, it means very finely chopped, almost a powder.

## SAGE (*Salvia officinalis*)

Sage originated in the Mediterranean, and is a powerful herb, often associated with pork or veal. It features in British cooking mainly in stuffings, including the popular sage and onion. The Italians are the leaders in sage cookery, using it with butter and olive oil in their *sofritos*, the beginning of casseroles, and pan-fried with pork or veal. If growing sage, trim it back after it flowers. Its spiky purple flowers attract bees and butterflies. Although it is perennial, try to replace every two or three years, or prune very well, as it tends to become very leggy. It is worth cutting off some branches just prior to winter to hang up to dry; when thoroughly dry, remove the leaves and store in an airtight container. Remember that sage is a very powerful herb, so use sparingly.

## TARRAGON (*Artemisia dracunculus*)

There are two varieties of this invaluable culinary herb: French and Russian (*A. dracunculoides*). The latter is undistinguished in flavour, so always buy or grow the French. Tarragon tastes of vanilla and aniseed, slightly sweet and bitter at the same time, and is used with chicken famously, but is also good in egg dishes, butters, creams, salads; it is one of the *fines herbes*, and flavours classic sauces like *Béarnaise*.

## THYME (*Thymus vulgaris*)

I probably use this perennial herb more than any other herb, as I find it essential in most casseroles, stocks and many soups. As it is powerful, it is generally added at the start of a dish so that the flavour can naturally disperse. One would rarely use thyme raw, although some of the soft thymes such as lemon thyme (*Thymus citriodorus*) can be added in small quantities to salads. (Hothouse-grown thymes seem to be 'softer' than those grown in a garden, which can be woody.) Thyme dries well, so cut a few stalks before winter to hang up to dry. Store the leaves in an airtight container. There are many varieties of thyme: some ornamental ones can be planted on paths or in grass, so that when you walk on it, its amazing fragrances permeate the air.

# Pesto

A dressing created in Liguria, which is usually made fresh the day you want to use it as it loses its colour very quickly. On visiting this area just south of Piedmont I discovered a few cooks who added some blanched leaves of flat-leaf parsley and spinach to preserve the colour. Use in vegetable soups, on *bruschetta* or *crostini* (see page 53), or folded into pasta or *gnocchi*. Originally this sauce would be made with a mortar and pestle which does enhance the flavour, but for most of us time is of the essence so I use a food processor.

**Preparation: 15 minutes**
**Serves: 4–6**

60g (2¼ oz) basil, leaves only

4 large spinach leaves, tough stalks discarded, **blanched** for 30 seconds in boiling water

1 tablespoon flat-leaf parsley leaves, blanched

1 teaspoon rock salt flakes

3 cloves garlic

60g (2¼ oz) Parmesan or Pecorino Sardo cheese, freshly grated

55g (2 oz) pine kernels

150ml (¼ pint) extra virgin olive oil

2 tablespoons ricotta cheese (optional)

1  Blend the basil, spinach, parsley, salt and garlic in the processor until smooth. Add the Parmesan, pine kernels and olive oil, and blend until emulsified.

2  Scrape the mixture into a bowl and fold in the ricotta cheese. Ricotta is not traditional but it helps to keep the sauce emulsified. Only put it in if you are going to use the sauce within a couple of days.

3  To preserve the sauce for longer, place the contents into a clear glass jar and coat the surface with a film of olive oil. Cover and refrigerate.

• • • • • • •
*Substitute parsley (or rocket) for basil in pesto to create a parsley (or rocket) pesto.*
• • • • • • •

• • • • • • •
*Slice some ripe plum tomatoes on to a plate. Sprinkle with flaked Maldon salt, drizzle with extra virgin olive oil, and add a splash of balsamic vinegar. Strew over a few ripped leaves of basil and place the plate in the warm sun for 30 minutes to taste a simplicity that is out of this world.*
• • • • • • •

# *Tabbouleh*

Once you've tried this *tabbouleh*, you'll never order one in a British restaurant again. Middle Eastern versions are green with a few flecks of white; home-grown attempts are white with a few flecks of green. *Tabbouleh* should be really herby.

**Preparation: 50 minutes**
**Serves: 4**

| |
|---|
| 75g (2¾ oz) bulgur |
| salt and ground black pepper |
| juice of 2 lemons |
| 75ml (2½ fl oz) extra virgin olive oil |
| 115g (4 oz) flat-leaf parsley, chopped |
| 25g (1 oz) mint, chopped |
| 1 bunch spring onions, finely sliced |
| 3 plum tomatoes, seeded and diced |

**1** Soak the bulgur in cold water for 20 minutes, then drain and squeeze dry.

**2** Put it in a glass bowl, season with salt and black pepper, and add the lemon juice and olive oil. Allow to rest for 30 minutes.

**3** Stir in the parsley, mint and spring onion.

**4** Check the seasoning and top the salad with the diced plum tomatoes.

*Add coriander leaves, spring onions, chopped ginger, chopped chilli and chopped garlic to soy sauce. With a splash of sesame oil, this makes a good basting sauce for steamed or grilled fish and a dipping sauce for deep-fried prawns.*

*Mix equal quantities of chopped coriander and chopped spring onion with a little crushed garlic into Greek yogurt for an aromatic dip.*

*Deep-fried florets of parsley make a very edible garnish for fried fish. Fry until the bubbling stops, then drain well on kitchen paper. The parsley will crisp when it hits the air.*

## *Kibbeh*

*In the Middle East they are particularly fond of raw lamb with herbs and I have often enjoyed a dish called* kibbeh.

● *Soak 125g (4½ oz) bulgur for 20 minutes in boiling water.*

● *Squeeze dry and place in a food processor with 500g (18 oz) fat-free minced lamb, 2 tablespoons extra virgin olive oil, juice of ½ lemon, 2 tablespoons each of chopped coriander and mint, 1 teaspoon ground cumin, ½ teaspoon ground allspice and ¼ teaspoon cayenne pepper.*

● *Blend everything together until you have a smooth paste.*

● *Serve with hot pitta bread.*

## *Gremolata*

*This is an Italian garnish sprinkled on slow-cooked dishes such as* osso buco.

● *Finely chop 3 cloves garlic and combine with 5 tablespoons chopped parsley and the grated zest of 2 lemons.*

*A herb crust for topping lamb or fish is made by blending in a food processor 2 handfuls of fresh white breadcrumbs, 1 clove garlic, 1 teaspoon soft thyme leaves, 5 tablespoons chopped parsley and 2 tablespoons extra virgin olive oil.*

# Dill Pickles

If you can find the small European cucumbers it is well worth making this sweet pickle. The British call them 'wallies' (well, at least *I* do), and have them with their fish and chips on a Friday night. Good in sandwiches and with burgers too.

**Preparation and cooking: overnight + 15 minutes**
**Makes: 12**

| |
|---|
| 12 small cucumbers |
| 1 litre (1¾ pints) cider vinegar |
| 375ml (13 fl oz) water |
| 3 tablespoons salt |
| 115g (4 oz) caster sugar |
| 2 vine leaves, **blanched** |
| 4 sprigs dill |
| 4 dill flower heads with seeds |
| 2 small dried chillies |
| 1 teaspoon white peppercorns |
| 1 teaspoon mustard seeds |
| 2 bay leaves |

**1**  Combine the vinegar, water, salt and sugar with the cucumbers in a **non-reactive** bowl. Let stand overnight.

**2**  Divide the cucumbers between two large sterilised glass jars. In each jar place 1 vine leaf, 2 sprigs dill, 2 dill flower heads, 1 chilli, ½ teaspoon each of peppercorns and mustard seeds and 1 bay leaf.

**3**  Bring the cucumber soaking liquor to the boil, and simmer for 5 minutes. Place the jars of cucumbers in hot water in a large pan with newspaper or a rack on the base, and bring to the boil to expand the glass.

**4**  Pour the hot vinegar over the cucumbers and seal by the **overflow method**. Keep for at least a month before eating.

## Dill and Mustard Sauce

*This dill and mustard sauce (see photograph) accompanies gravadlax (marinated salmon, see page 119).*

● *Combine 2 tablespoons Dijon mustard, 2 teaspoons red wine vinegar and 2 teaspoons sugar.*
● *Whisk in 6 tablespoons good olive oil slowly to form an emulsion.*
● *Fold in 3 tablespoons chopped dill and season to taste.*

## Dill Butter Sauce

*Good with smoked fish – based on a classic beurre blanc. Other herbs such as parsley or sage can be substituted.*

● *Place 3 chopped shallots in a **non-reactive** saucepan with 100ml (3½ fl oz) white wine vinegar and boil until you have **reduced** the liquor to 2 tablespoons.*
● *Pass the liquid through a fine sieve and return to the saucepan. Over a medium heat, whisk 200g (7 oz) of cold cubed butter into the liquid, beating continuously.*
● *The sauce is served warm, not hot.*
● *Just before serving fold in 3 tablespoons chopped dill and season to taste.*

*Place bay leaves in some sugar syrups for that reaction. 'I don't know what the flavour is, but it tastes very nice.' Bay leaves can also be added to the rice for rice pudding.*

*Insert bay leaves on to skewers in between the meat when making kebabs.*

# Herb Fritters

You might not think a mouthful of herbs would work – but it does, magnificently. They are a revelation. They do you good as well, although there's a touch of naughtiness in that they're fried.

**Preparation and cooking: 30 minutes**
**Makes: about 15**

225g (8 oz) mixed soft herb leaves (chervil, basil, rocket, tarragon etc.), washed, dried and chopped

1 medium onion, very finely chopped

1 teaspoon vegetable *bouillon* powder

85g (3 oz) Parmesan, freshly grated

4 medium eggs, lightly beaten

85g (3 oz) fresh breadcrumbs

salt and ground black pepper

55g (2 oz) unsalted butter

vegetable oil

**1** Place the herb leaves in a medium bowl. Stir in the onion, *bouillon* powder, cheese, eggs, enough breadcrumbs to bind, and salt and pepper to taste. Mix well with a wooden spoon.
**2** Melt the butter in a large frying pan over a medium heat. Add enough oil so that there is 5mm (¼ in) of fat altogether in the pan.
**3** Using 1 generous tablespoon of the mixture for each fritter, fry the fritters a few at a time until deep golden, about 3 minutes per side. Drain on kitchen paper, and keep warm in a low oven until the remaining fritters are cooked.

- - - - - - - - - -
*Throw some branches of
rosemary into a roasting dish
with olive oil when roasting
potatoes or vegetables.*
- - - - - - - - - -

- - - - - - - - - -
*Infuse olive oil with
finely chopped rosemary
for a pleasantly flavoured
oil to go over roast or
grilled meats.*
- - - - - - - - - -

# Asian Pesto

Makes a nice change from your average basil pesto. It is delicious tossed with Oriental noodles and served as a cold salad.

**Preparation: about 15 minutes**
**Makes: about 600 ml (1 pint)**

115g (4 oz) roasted peanuts (or a combination of peanuts, cashews and macadamia nuts)

2 tablespoons chopped garlic

1 tablespoon chopped fresh ginger

2 *serrano* chillies, chopped

6 tablespoons each of chopped mint, coriander and basil leaves

3 tablespoons soft breadcrumbs

300 ml (½ pint) peanut oil

2 tablespoons grated orange zest

1 tablespoon grated lime zest

2 teaspoons sesame oil

salt and ground black pepper

**1** Place the nuts, garlic, ginger and chilli in a food processor, and process to a paste.
**2** Add the mint, coriander, basil and breadcrumbs, and process until roughly chopped.
**3** Pour and mix in the peanut oil in a thin steady stream, the machine still switched on. Scrape out into a bowl.
**4** Fold in the orange and lime zests and sesame oil, then season to taste. Spoon into a jar and store in a refrigerator for no longer than 3–4 days.

- - - - - - - - - -
*When cooking new potatoes
pop a couple of sprigs of mint
and 1 tablespoon caster sugar
into the boiling salted water.
Likewise with peas.*
- - - - - - - - - -

- - - - - - - - - -
*If you grow mint, you must
make your own mint sauce. Chop
a handful of mint leaves and mix
with 2 teaspoons caster sugar.
Add 2 tablespoons boiling water
and 3 tablespoons cider vinegar.
As simple as that!*
- - - - - - - - - -

# Salsa Verde  Ⓥ

A great Italian sauce that is excellent for grilled fish, grilled tongue and other grilled dishes. It should be made freshly, do not make too far in advance.

**Preparation: 15 minutes**
**Serves: 4–6**

| |
|---|
| 2 handfuls flat-leaf parsley leaves |
| 12 basil leaves |
| 1 small handful mint leaves |
| 2 pickled cucumbers, roughly chopped (optional) |
| 3 cloves garlic, roughly chopped |
| 2 tablespoons capers, rinsed |
| 4 anchovy fillets, rinsed |
| 1 tablespoon red wine vinegar |
| 1 tablespoon lemon juice |
| 6 tablespoons extra virgin olive oil |
| 1 tablespoon Dijon mustard |
| ½ teaspoon Maldon sea salt |
| ¼ teaspoon ground black pepper |

**1** You get a better product if you hand-chop this *salsa*. Chop together the herbs, cucumber, garlic, capers and anchovies until medium coarsely chopped, or **pulse** in a food processor.
**2** Transfer the mixture to a **non-reactive** bowl and slowly add the remaining ingredients while whisking.

## Herb Mix

*This herb mix is wonderful as a 'stuffing' for roast monkfish (or cod) with prosciutto (see page 135).*
● *Sweat 2 very finely chopped onions in about 50ml (2 fl oz) olive oil until soft. Roughly chop a large bunch of parsley and a small bunch of tarragon.*
● ***Blanch** the herbs in boiling water for seconds only, then purée in a blender with the onion and 1 teaspoon ground black pepper.*

## Salmoriglio

*A very powerful oregano dressing that I first tasted at London's River Café.*
● *In a food processor or mortar grind 6 tablespoons fresh oregano leaves with 1½ teaspoons Maldon sea salt. Add 3 tablespoons lemon juice, then slowly work in 12 tablespoons extra virgin olive oil with ½ teaspoon ground black pepper.*
● *Brush grilled fish or lamb with the dressing.*

## Herb Oil

*Thyme is essential in herbes de Provence, that magical combination that transports you to the Med. Combine those flavours in an oil.*
● *Place a 15cm (6 in) branch of rosemary, 4 sprigs of thyme, 4 basil leaves, 4 bay leaves, 3 split cloves of garlic, 1 teaspoon dried green peppercorns, 2 slices dried orange peel and 2 dried seed heads of lavender into a sterilised bottle and top up with olive oil.*
● *Store for a month before using.*

*Flour sage leaves and deep-fry them until crisp for an interesting garnish for veal, pork or pasta. (Raw sage is not palatable because of its furry leaf and powerful flavour.)*

*Melt 115g (4 oz) unsalted butter in a saucepan over a low heat, and throw in 8 chopped sage leaves and the juice of 1 lemon. Stir to combine for the most delicious sage and lemon butter sauce.*

*Fold snipped chives into scrambled eggs or scatter over delicious Jersey new potatoes.*

*Use 2.5cm (1 in) pieces of garlic chives instead of spring onions in stir-fries.*

# LAMB

English lamb is available from early spring (from the winter-born lambs of southern England), through to the end of summer from lambs born in the highlands of Scotland and the mountains of Wales. Lamb sold during the autumn has much darker flesh as it progresses towards its post-Christmas name of hogget; thereafter it would be called mutton, although a good leg of mutton is a hard thing to buy nowadays.

Welsh lamb is often said to be the best, a generalisation I would say, as I have enjoyed some fabulous salty lamb that comes from animals which have eaten salt-sprayed grasses on the wild shores of Scotland. I have a love, too, for the French lamb that is fed on herbs, which has a distinctly herby flavour. 'You are what you eat' applies particularly strongly to lamb, and luckily we can still buy lamb that has not been intensively reared, and has stayed clear of hormones and enforced protein. I am not a great fan of lamb sold before it has been weaned (8–10 weeks), as this milk-fed lamb may be very tender but it is also fairly tasteless and ridiculously priced. Buy lamb with a good coating of creamy white fat that is firm to the touch and has a rosy pink flesh; the younger the animal, generally the paler the flesh.

## Roasting

Buy a leg or half leg, or a boned and rolled shoulder. The shoulder will be more fatty but as such tends to have more flavour. You can buy a half rack of best end, but it is an expensive cut producing only 7 or 8 cutlets. Trim your joint of excess fat, but leave enough on to baste it during cooking. I like to spike a leg of lamb with rosemary, anchovy and garlic, then leave it overnight; this imparts an extra dimension to the meat and, once roasted, you will not notice any overwhelming flavour of anchovy. Never season the meat with salt until just prior to cooking as the salt will draw out the blood and toughen the meat.

Smear dripping or oil over the joint then seal the meat all over in a hot pan until golden. Place the lamb in a roasting tray on top of a few garlic cloves, some thyme and bay leaves. **Deglaze** the searing pan with some red wine or stock and pour into the bottom of the roasting tray. During roasting add more stock from time to time to the roasting pan unless you surround the lamb with potatoes. These juices will provide a good base for your gravy. Roast the lamb in a 200°C/400°F/Gas 6 oven for 30 minutes then lower to 180°C/350°F/Gas 4 for the remaining time. Allow 12–15 minutes per 450g (1 lb) for medium rare, up to 25 minutes for well done. Always allow the meat to **rest** after cooking for 10–15 minutes in a warm place to relax the fibres and distribute the delicious juices.

While the lamb is resting, pour off the surface fat from the roasting tray and deglaze the pan with wine or stock with a splash of vinegar; add a dash each of Worcestershire sauce, anchovy essence and mushroom essence. Mash the roast garlic into the **jus** with a fork. Strain into a gravy boat after checking the seasoning. If you are a packet gravy fan, and many are, follow the above recipe but add a teaspoonful of your favourite gravy powder . . . it will still taste better than just using a packet.

## Grilling and Frying

These are fast methods of cooking that demand tender cuts, noisettes, cutlets, chump chops or leg steaks. For an impressive barbecue grilling cut, ask your butcher to 'butterfly' a whole leg of lamb. Rub the meat with oil (use my herb oil, see page 215) to prevent it sticking. If using an overhead grill make sure it is turned on well ahead to heat it up. I always think this form of grilling is messy as the fat spits, creating a very greasy grill, and often with modern grills the heat is not powerful enough to give the meat a delicious crust. I prefer to 'cheat' by using a ridged griddle pan. Always season during cooking or after as you don't want the salt to draw out the meat's natural juices. Single chops will take 7–10 minutes to cook, double chops or large chump chops could take 15 minutes. You should seal the meat over a high heat, then reduce the temperature to finish the cooking.

*If you are not keen on veal or pork, but fancy an escalope, beat flat lamb fillets or slices from a leg of raw lamb. Flour, egg and breadcrumb them and fry for 2–3 minutes each side in butter and oil.*

# Lamb *Tagine*

Moroccan cooking has become very popular in restaurants. Having visited the country, I know they tend there to just sling everything in a pan and cook it on the hob. I like to make my *tagines* a little richer, so brown the meat, fry off the spices, reduce the sauce, and cook it all gently in the oven. The lamb here is left whole, so it is a dinner-party dish; you could cube the meat instead, but reduce the cooking time by 1 hour.

**Preparation and cooking: overnight + 3½ hours**
**Serves: 4–6**

1 shoulder of lamb, knuckle removed
1½ tablespoons ground ginger
2 teaspoons ground black pepper
2 teaspoons powdered cinnamon
3 teaspoons ground turmeric
1½ tablespoons paprika
1 teaspoon cayenne pepper
1 head garlic, all but 3 cloves crushed with a little salt
2 tablespoons olive oil
450g (1 lb) onions, grated
175g (6 oz) dried apricots, soaked in a little water, cut in half
85g (3 oz) flaked almonds
55g (2 oz) sultanas or raisins
2 tablespoons clear honey
1 teaspoon saffron stamens, soaked in cold water
600ml (1 pint) tomato juice
600ml (1 pint) lamb stock
1 x 400g (14 oz) tin tomatoes, roughly chopped
1 pickled lemon, rind chopped (see page 171)
25g (1 oz) coriander leaves, chopped

**1** Coat the lamb in half the ground spices and leave overnight. Pierce the lamb all over with the 3 uncrushed garlic cloves which you have sliced.
**2** Brown the lamb in half the oil in a heavy casserole over a high heat. Add the remaining spices, the crushed garlic and grated onion. Allow the onion to soften without browning.
**3** Add the apricots and their soaking water, the almonds, raisins or sultanas, honey, saffron, tomato juice and lamb stock. Bring to the boil, place in a low oven and cook for 1 hour at 170°C/325°F/Gas 3.
**4** After an hour, add the tomatoes, return the casserole to the oven and cook for a further 2 hours. Remove the meat and **reduce** the sauce over a high heat until thickened.
**5** Fry the lemon rind in the remaining olive oil for a few minutes, then fold in the chopped coriander.
**6** Pour the sauce over the lamb, and garnish with the lemon and coriander mixture.

## Braising, Stewing and Pot-roasting

These are moist, slow methods of cooking so you need to use cuts that have a good level of fat which will slowly disperse during cooking. Use shoulder, shank or neck chops. Flour the meat and brown in oil, butter or dripping before adding vegetables, herbs, wine and stock. By the end of cooking time you should be able to carve the meat with a spoon as the meat slips from the bone. The flavours will have melded together. The liquid in the casserole should just come to the top of the meat. Don't be shy of using herbs such as thyme or bay, spices or whole cloves of garlic. Allow as much time as possible on a very low heat. A braise is best in the oven, but if you're careful, it could be done on the hob at a simmer. A braise or pot-roast usually uses a large cut of meat, whereas a stew uses meat that has been cut into 2.5–5cm (1–2 in) pieces.

## Poaching or Boiling

A rarely used method of cookery for lamb, but if you can find a leg of mutton then cook it slowly in vegetable-**infused** water until the leg is tender. It is a delicious method of cooking, but the meat unfortunately comes out very grey, so smother it with an old-fashioned sauce, such as an onion or caper sauce.

# Moussaka

Moussaka is one of these foreign holiday dishes that has been unfairly derided. Greek restaurants tend to make dishes like moussaka in the morning, and then they sit in hot cabinets all day until unsuspecting tourists eat it in the evening. Greeks quite sensibly eat it freshly made at lunchtime, but in the heat of midday we find it all a bit too much. Eat it fresh and it is as good, if not better, than our own favourite shepherd's pie.

**Preparation and cooking: 2½ hours**
**Serves: 4–6**

1 onion, finely diced

3 cloves garlic, finely diced

½ teaspoon soft thyme leaves

175ml (6 fl oz) good olive oil

2 bay leaves

2 teaspoons freshly chopped oregano or 1 teaspoon dried oregano

675g (1½ lb) lean lamb, minced

¼ teaspoon powdered cinnamon

175ml (6 fl oz) dry white wine

¼ teaspoon ground allspice

1 x 400g (14 oz) tin chopped tomatoes in rich tomato sauce

lamb stock if necessary

1kg (2¼ lb) aubergines, cut lengthways in 8mm (⅓ in) slices

salt and ground black pepper

plain flour for dusting

25g (1 oz) Parmesan, grated

**Béchamel topping**

85g (3 oz) unsalted butter

85g (3 oz) plain flour

600ml (1 pint) milk

1 onion, spiked with 1 bay leaf and 2 cloves

115g (4 oz) Parmesan, grated

2 egg yolks

55g (2 oz) Gruyère cheese, grated

1  Cook the onion, garlic and thyme in 2 tablespoons of the olive oil until the onion has softened without colour, about 10 minutes. Add the bay leaves, oregano and mince, and fry until the lamb has turned brown. Break up the meat with a wooden spoon until it has a loose texture. Add the cinnamon, white wine and allspice, and cook for 5 minutes. Add the tomatoes, reduce the heat, and simmer for 45 minutes. If the meat becomes too dry, add a little lamb stock.

2  Sprinkle the aubergine slices with salt and leave for 30 minutes. This draws out any bitter juices. Rinse the aubergines and pat dry. Dust the aubergines in seasoned flour and fry in batches in the remaining hot olive oil until thoroughly cooked and golden on both sides, about 10 minutes. Drain the aubergine slices on kitchen paper to sop up some of the excess oil. (By flouring the aubergine slices you prevent them soaking up too much oil.) Set aside until ready to construct the moussaka.

3  Fold the Parmesan into the mince mixture. Remove the bay leaves.

4  To start the *béchamel* topping, melt the butter in a non-stick pan and fold in the flour. Cook very slowly over a low heat for 8–10 minutes, stirring from time to time. Do not allow the **roux** to colour too much.

5  Meanwhile, in a separate saucepan heat the milk with the whole onion, bay leaf and cloves. Bring to **scalding point**, remove from the heat, and allow to stand for 10 minutes to infuse the flavours. Add the strained milk slowly to the roux, stirring continuously, until thick and smooth. Remove the pan from the heat, then stir in 55g (2 oz) of the grated Parmesan and the egg yolks. Season to taste.

6  Cover the base of a casserole dish with slices of aubergine, then spoon over some of the meat mixture. Continue layers until the meat and aubergine have been used up. Leave a 2.5cm (1 in) gap at the top of the casserole for the sauce. Pour over the cheese *béchamel*. Combine the remaining Parmesan with the Gruyère and scatter over the *béchamel*. Bake in a preheated oven at 180°C/350°F/Gas 4 for 1 hour until golden and bubbling. (The dish can be pre-prepared until the point before it goes in the oven. Allow an extra 15 minutes in the oven if cooking from cold.)

# Lamb Meatballs

● *Combine 500g (18 oz) minced lamb with 1 egg yolk, 1 finely chopped small onion, 2 chopped cloves garlic, 1 teaspoon ground cumin, ½ teaspoon ground allspice, ¼ teaspoon cayenne pepper, 4 tablespoons chopped coriander, 1 tablespoon chopped mint and ½ teaspoon ground black pepper.*

● *Shape into meatballs and fry in olive oil, then pop into a good tomato sauce to finish cooking.*

# Irish Stew

Having married an Irish girl, I've been subjected to Irish stew in its most basic form, but obviously you can add other ingredients, such as carrots, turnips and pearl barley, but they are not traditional. And you could use wine instead of stock, or cook in the oven (at 170°C/325°F/Gas 3) instead of on the hob.

**Preparation and cooking: 2½ hours**
**Serves: 6**

1.3kg (3 lb) middle neck of mutton, scrag, breast or gigot chops

900g (2 lb) potatoes

450g (1 lb) onions, thinly sliced

1 **faggot of herbs** (thyme, bay leaf etc.)

salt and ground black pepper

600ml (1 pint) water or stock

3 tablespoons chopped parsley

**1** Trim the meat of excess fat, remove bones and cut the meat into 2.5cm (1 in) cubes.

**2** Slice the potatoes. Put the meat, onion and potato in layers in a deep flameproof pan with the faggot of herbs in the middle; season each layer with salt and pepper. Finish with a potato layer.

**3** Add the water or stock and simmer gently until tender, about 2 hours.

**4** Spoon the stew into a serving dish and sprinkle with chopped parsley.

## Butterflied Leg of Lamb

*Ask your butcher to butterfly a leg of lamb.*
- *In a food processor blend together 115g (4 oz) kalamata stoned black olives, 2 tablespoons grated orange zest, 1 teaspoon grated lemon zest, 2 tablespoons chopped sage, 2 tablespoons chopped garlic, 2 tablespoons chopped anchovy, 1 teaspoon crushed black pepper and 2 tablespoons olive oil to a fine paste.*
- *Smear this paste over the interior of the lamb, roll up the leg and tie at 5cm (2 in) intervals.*
- *Allow to **rest** overnight before roasting in the normal way.*

# Crispy Lamb

If you ever experience that yearning for deep-fried food, then try this, it's a little different.

**Preparation and cooking: overnight + 10 minutes**
**Serves: 4 as a starter**

450g (1 lb) raw lamb from the leg, cut into thin shreds

6 cloves garlic, mashed

1 x 5cm (2 in) piece fresh ginger, grated

1 teaspoon chilli powder

1 tablespoon chopped coriander

4 tablespoons Greek yogurt

2 eggs, beaten

140g (5 oz) breadcrumbs, toasted

vegetable oil for frying

**To serve**

Little Gem lettuce leaves

chopped coriander

**1** Combine the lamb in a bowl with the garlic, ginger, chilli powder, coriander and yogurt. Allow to marinate, overnight if possible.

**2** Dip the lamb shreds into the egg, separating them if possible, then fold into the breadcrumbs. As you coat the lamb, separate the pieces.

**3** Deep-fry small batches of lamb pieces in the hot oil until crispy and golden, about 3–4 minutes only.

**4** Serve with lettuce leaves and coriander. Get your guests to wrap the lamb and coriander in the lettuce leaves.

## Barbecued Lamb

*Butterflied leg of lamb is good for grilling on the barbie.*
- *Marinate overnight for added flavour in 600ml (1 pint) water mixed with 150ml (¼ pint) good olive oil, 6 tablespoons chopped oregano, 8 chopped cloves garlic, 1 tablespoon paprika, 1 tablespoon salt, 1 teaspoon dried chilli flakes, 1 teaspoon ground black pepper and 3 finely chopped bay leaves.*
- *Grill for 12–15 minutes on each side and drizzle with the marinade during cooking.*

## Lamb Stew

*I love food that you can just throw in a pot, turn on the heat and forget about. This soup-cum-stew works for me.*

● *To 2.5 litres (4½ pints) of water add 500g (18 oz) trimmed diced neck of lamb fillets, 225g (8 oz) pearl barley, 2 sliced carrots, 2 sliced sticks celery, 2 roughly chopped onions, 2 roughly chopped leeks, 2 sprigs of thyme, 2 bay leaves, 2 cloves garlic, 2 chopped turnips, 2 chopped parsnips, 1 chopped potato, ½ chopped Savoy cabbage and 1 teaspoon ground black pepper.*

● *Bring to the boil, reduce heat and simmer for 1½–2 hours until the meat is tender.*

● *Season to taste and fold in 4 tablespoons chopped parsley and extra lamb stock if too thick for your taste.*

## Lamb Curry

● *Combine 1kg (2¼ lb) trimmed boneless lamb shoulder cut into 1.5cm (⅝ in) dice with 225g (8 oz) Greek yogurt, 1 x 400g (14 oz) tin chopped tomatoes with rich tomato juice, a pinch each of grated nutmeg and powdered cinnamon, 1 teaspoon turmeric, 1 grated onion, 25g (1 oz) grated fresh ginger, 3 cloves garlic mashed to a paste with a little salt, grated zest of 1 orange, 1 teaspoon ground coriander and 2 finely chopped red chillies.*

● *Leave overnight refrigerated, then place on the heat and bring to the boil.*

● *Place in a preheated oven at 150°C/300°F/Gas 2 and cook for 2 hours.*

● *Fold in chopped coriander and serve with pilaff rice.*

# Lamb Shank with Garlic, Rosemary and Flageolet Beans

Based on a classic French peasant dish, this became my trademark when I opened Bistrot 190. If you can't get lamb shanks, ask your butcher to chop up a leg or shoulder.

**Preparation and cooking: 3¼ hours**
**Serves: 4**

4 lamb shanks

6 tinned anchovies, cut in two

12 small rosemary sprigs

12 slivers garlic

salt and ground black pepper

### Braising

55g (2 oz) duck fat, butter or dripping

2 carrots, roughly chopped

2 sticks celery, roughly chopped

1 leek, roughly chopped

2 onions, roughly chopped

1 head garlic, broken up into cloves

1 sprig thyme

1 sprig rosemary

1 bay leaf

½ bottle red wine

600ml (1 pint) chicken or lamb stock (optional)

### Sauce

115g (4 oz) streaky bacon **lardons**, **blanched**

2 tablespoons extra virgin olive oil

1 carrot, finely diced

1 stick celery, finely diced

1 onion, finely diced

6 cloves garlic, peeled

2 sprigs thyme

2 sprigs rosemary, chopped

4 tomatoes, seeded and diced

2 x 375g (13 oz) tins flageolet beans, drained and rinsed

4 tablespoons *gremolata* (see page 211)

2 tablespoons grated Parmesan

**1** Remove the majority of fat from the shanks. Make 3 deep incisions in each joint and insert in each half an anchovy wrapped around a skewer of rosemary and a slice of garlic. Season the meat.

**2** Preheat the oven to 140–150°C/ 275–300°F/Gas 1–2.

**3** Fry the joints to brown all over in a little duck fat in a casserole, then remove and set aside. Add the carrot, celery, leek, onion, garlic cloves and herbs to the casserole, and cook over a high heat until the vegetables are brown. **Deglaze** with red wine, scraping the residue on the bottom of the pan.

**4** Add the stock to the casserole, place the joints on top of the vegetables, cover and cook in the slow oven for 2½ hours.

**5** To start the sauce, brown the bacon in the oil, then reduce the heat and add the carrot, celery, onion and garlic. Cook for 8 minutes until the vegetables have softened. Add the thyme, rosemary, tomatoes and flageolet beans, then set aside.

**6** When the lamb has finished cooking, remove the four joints to a dish and keep warm.

**7** Whizz the lamb vegetables and juices in a blender or food processor, or pass through a **mouli-légumes**. Pass this sauce through a strainer on to the bean mixture and warm through. Season to taste, and pour over the lamb.

**8** Serve the lamb garnished with a mixture of the *gremolata* and Parmesan.

# LEEK

The leek – *Allium porrum* – is another member of the lily family, closely related to the onion, and one of the most indispensable vegetables in cooking today. It is European in origin, but was known to the Ancient Egyptians in about 2000 BC.

When growing leeks choose a strong variety for large leeks such as Alaska or Autumn Grant 2 Argenta. To produce more white stem you need to earth them up, and the easiest way to do this is to let them grow until they have 1cm (½ in) thick stems then place a narrow tube over them; fill the tube with light earth to 1cm (½ in) from the top of the leek. As the leek grows taller, keep topping up the soil, and you'll achieve tall leeks without too much green top wastage. Leeks grown in this way will need thorough washing as the soil tends to get between the leaves. Grow a variety of leeks, some which can be harvested in the autumn, through to a variety (Toledo) that can be enjoyed the following May.

The edible section of the leek is the white part through to the pale green. The dark green leaf is fine for stocks, but tends to be too tough and strongly flavoured to eat. When buying, choose medium to small varieties which have quite good flavour compared to other miniature vegetables. Always buy leeks that are very white with strong green tops and no sign of browning. Late in the season they tend to get a woody core as the leek develops a seed head.

In preparation, discard all but 1cm (½ in) of the green top. If the leeks need slicing, slice and soak the slices in cold salty water to remove earth or any insects. If you are leaving the leeks whole, remove outer leaves then make a 7.5cm (3 in) vertical cut down the centre of the leek. Fan the leaves out under running water to dislodge earthy particles. Leeks can be cooked in various ways – boiled, steamed, pan-fried, **sweated** – but are not happy cooked **al dente** unless you want to use very young leeks shredded raw in a salad. Leeks hold and retain a lot of water so, after cooking, drain well on kitchen paper, then when cool enough to handle, give them a gentle squeeze to release the liquid.

Like their relatives, leeks contain good quantities of vitamins B and C, and a variety of minerals.

## Leek Stew

Leeks work well as part of a vegetarian stew.

**Preparation and cooking: 40 minutes**
**Serves: 4–6**

50ml (2 fl oz) extra virgin olive oil
1kg (2¼ lb) leeks, chopped
1 onion, chopped
2 garlic cloves, chopped
½ teaspoon salt
½ teaspoon cayenne pepper
2 tablespoons black olives, pitted and chopped
1 x 400g (14 oz) tin tomatoes, chopped
12 basil leaves, torn
1 ball of mozzarella, diced

**1** Heat the olive oil, then add the chopped leeks with the onion, garlic, salt and cayenne pepper.
**2** Cook until the vegetables have softened, about 10 minutes, then add the black olives and tomatoes and cook until the mixture has thickened, about 15 minutes.
**3** Fold in the basil leaves and mozzarella, and heat until the mozzarella starts to melt. Serve on *bruschetta* (see page 53).

*Sweated sliced leeks, diced roasted peppers (see page 254) and grated mozzarella make a good topping for a pizza.*

## Barbecued Leeks

● *Blanch small leeks for 3 minutes in boiling salted water, drain and squeeze dry.*
● *Paint with extra virgin olive oil and char-grill on the barbecue until golden.*
● *Toss with chopped parsley, more olive oil and a splash of vinegar. You can scatter them with some chopped hard-boiled egg and a few black olives.*

*Wrap cooked leeks in thinly sliced cooked or raw (Parma) ham, and cover with a cheesy Béchamel Sauce (see pages 60 and 85). Top with grated Gruyère and Parmesan and bake in a hot oven until golden and bubbling.*

# Marinated Leeks

Leeks cooked in an aromatic stock, to be served as a salad or a starter.

**Preparation and cooking: 1¼ hours**
**Serves: 4–6**

1 teaspoon cumin seeds
1 teaspoon coriander seeds
1 teaspoon caraway seeds
1 teaspoon black peppercorns
600ml (1 pint) vegetable stock
2 cloves garlic, crushed
1 bay leaf
2 sprigs thyme
½ teaspoon grated lemon zest
1.6kg (3½ lb) leeks, white and pale green parts only, chopped in 2.5cm (1 in) pieces
175ml (6 fl oz) olive oil
juice of 1 lemon

**1** Toast the cumin, coriander, caraway seeds and peppercorns in a dry frying pan until they become aromatic. Remove from the heat and grind to a powder, either in a coffee grinder or mortar and pestle.

**2** Bring the stock to the boil and sprinkle the ground spices on to the stock. Add the garlic, bay leaf, thyme and lemon zest. Remove the pan from the heat and allow the mixture to infuse for 15 minutes or so.

**3** Add the leeks, olive oil and lemon juice, and cook over a low heat for 30 minutes.

**4** Strain the leeks, reserving the cooking liquor, and keep warm. **Reduce** the cooking liquor until it has reached a syrupy consistency and strain over the leeks. Serve hot or at room temperature.

*Dip cooked drained leeks into beaten egg mixed with chopped parsley. Roll the leeks in seasoned flour and deep-fry in vegetable oil. Sprinkle with tarragon vinegar and salt before serving.*

# Vichyssoise

An all-time favourite soup of mine, and a classic cold soup that is also excellent served hot.

**Preparation and cooking: 45 minutes + cooling**
**Serves: 4**

2 tablespoons olive oil
4 leeks, white and pale green parts only, sliced
3 onions, finely chopped
2 cloves garlic, finely chopped
½ teaspoon soft thyme leaves
3 potatoes, cubed
1 bay leaf
1.5 litres (2¾ pints) chicken or vegetable stock
pinch of freshly grated nutmeg
salt and ground white pepper
300ml (½ pint) double cream
3 tablespoons snipped chives

**1** Heat the olive oil in a saucepan, add the leek, onion, garlic and thyme, and cook over a medium heat for 15 minutes until the vegetables are soft but not coloured.

**2** Add the potato and bay leaf and cook until the potato starts to stick to the bottom of the pan. Add the stock and nutmeg, bring to the boil, reduce the heat and simmer for 20–25 minutes until the potato is cooked.

**3** Blend the soup in a liquidiser until smooth, then pass through a fine sieve into a saucepan. Season to taste.

**4** Allow the soup to cool, refrigerate, then add double cream just before serving. Finally fold in the chives.

**5** If you want to serve the soup hot, you can substitute 55g (2 oz) butter for the oil and add the cream after liquidising. Heat through gently.

*Serve grilled leeks with a grain mustard vinaigrette.*

*Rather than paying a fortune for baby leeks, substitute spring onions instead.*

*When making macaroni cheese, fold in crispy bacon and sweated sliced leeks before baking in the oven.*

# Leek and Roquefort Tart

A quiche-like tart with a wonderful cheesy soft centre. Great warm or cold, served with a green salad.

**Preparation and cooking: 1¾ hours**

**Serves: 6–8**

1 x 23cm (9 in) blind-baked shortcrust pastry base

2 tablespoons olive oil

25g (1 oz) unsalted butter

350g (12 oz) onions, finely sliced

675g (1½ lb) leeks, white and pale green parts only, sliced

1 teaspoon caster sugar

2 cloves garlic, finely chopped

2 teaspoons soft thyme leaves

1 tablespoon plain flour

salt and ground black pepper

3 eggs

300ml (½ pint) double cream

55g (2 oz) Gruyère cheese, grated

2 tablespoons grated Parmesan

55g (2 oz) Roquefort cheese, cut into 1cm (½ in) dice

**1** Heat the oil and butter in a saucepan until melted. Add the onion, leek, sugar, garlic and thyme, and cook over a low heat for 40 minutes until the vegetables are meltingly soft and have started to turn golden. Stir the mixture regularly. Allow to cool slightly. Fold in the flour and season to taste.

**2** Beat the eggs and cream together, and then add to the onion mix. Fold in half the Gruyère, half the Parmesan and all the Roquefort.

**3** Pour the mixture into the prepared pastry case, sprinkle with the remaining Parmesan and Gruyère, and bake in a preheated oven at 190°C/375°F/Gas 5 until golden and semi-set, about 35–40 minutes.

**4** Serve hot, warm or at room temperature.

# LENTILS

Lentils (*Lens culinaris* or *esculenta*) are a pulse and have been staple foods in India and the Middle East for thousands of years. They are very nutritious, containing protein and many vitamins and minerals. When sprouted, they are rich in vitamin C. It is only in the last 10 years that lentils have become really popular in the UK, and they are great vehicles for transporting other flavours, especially spices.

Several types are available. BROWN LENTILS are dark brown or reddish brown and are sometimes called green or continental lentils. They have a good strong flavour, but can break down if overcooked. GREEN LENTILS vary in colour from beige to brown, and are also sometimes known as continental lentils. They retain their shape better than brown lentils when cooked. The PUY LENTIL is 'the' lentil of the last few years and the one that has put lentils back on the culinary map. It is a tiny speckled green lentil grown in the Auvergne in France. These lentils cook relatively quickly and are best for keeping their shape.

There are over 60 types of lentil in India which are made into, and known collectively as, *dhal*. RED LENTILS (*Masoor dhal*) are salmony-orange split lentils, which cook down to a purée very quickly.

Choose lentils, where possible, from a Middle Eastern or Indian shop as you can rely on a good turnover. Lentils don't need to be soaked, but they should be washed before cooking. Check for any stones or foreign matter. Lentils don't need to cook for long, so keep an eye at the latter stages of cooking, otherwise you may be eating soup instead of a lentil stew.

## Lentil Spread

*A lentil spread made with similar ingredients to* Tapenade *(see page 243) is great on* crostini *or* bruschetta.
● *Cook 225g (8 oz) Puy lentils in 300ml (½ pint) of stock with 2 tablespoons chopped garlic, 2 tablespoons sun-dried tomatoes and 1 tablespoon sun-dried peppers.*
● *Simmer until the lentils are tender. Place all the ingredients from the saucepan into a blender with 2 tablespoons extra virgin olive oil, 2 tablespoons capers, 3 anchovy fillets, 3 tablespoons stoned Greek black olives and 2 tablespoons lemon juice.*
● *Blend until smooth then fold in 4 tablespoons chopped flat-leaf parsley.*

## *Dhal* with Added Spice

I couldn't write a section on lentils without acknowledging the classic Indian way of serving red lentils. Not that plain cooked lentils wouldn't taste very pleasant on their own, but there is a reason for spicing them up. The body deals efficiently with the protein found in meat, fish and dairy products, but the vegetable proteins of lentils and certain other pulses require much more effort to digest. So the Indians learnt to add certain digestion-friendly spices such as ginger and turmeric.

**Preparation and cooking: 50 minutes**
**Serves: 4–6**

| |
|---|
| 1.5 litres (2¾ pints) water |
| 250g (9 oz) split red lentils, rinsed |
| 55g (2 oz) *ghee* or clarified butter (see page 60) |
| 5 garlic cloves, finely chopped |
| 1 onion, finely chopped |
| 1 x 2.5cm (1 in) piece fresh ginger, finely chopped |
| 3 green chillies, finely chopped |
| 1 teaspoon ground coriander |
| 1 teaspoon ground cumin |
| ½ teaspoon chilli powder |
| 1 teaspoon black mustard seeds (optional) |
| 1 teaspoon turmeric |
| salt and freshly ground black pepper |
| 3 plum tomatoes, seeded and diced |
| 3 tablespoons chopped coriander |
| 2 teaspoons lime juice |

**1** In a saucepan over a medium heat, heat the water, then add the lentils and cook for 15 minutes, stirring regularly to start with, as this is when the lentils will stick together.
**2** Meanwhile, heat the *ghee* in a frying pan, add the garlic, onion, ginger and chilli and cook for 10 minutes over a medium heat until the onion has softened. Add the spices and cook for a further 2 minutes. Fold this mixture into the lentils.
**3** Cook the *dhal* for a further 10–15 minutes until the lentils are tender. Beat with a whisk until completely mashed.
**4** Season to taste, then fold in the tomato, coriander and lime juice.

# Red Lentil Soup

Pulses can be offputting for some, but we ought to eat them because of their high fibre content. This is a particularly nice way of eating fibre!

**Preparation and cooking: 55 minutes**
**Serves: 6**

55g (2 oz) unsalted butter

1½ tablespoons grated fresh ginger

¼ teaspoon each ground allspice, ground cumin and chilli powder

½ teaspoon each curry powder and ground coriander

2 onions, finely chopped

1 parsnip, chopped

1 stick celery, chopped

1kg (2¼ lb) carrots, sliced

85g (3 oz) split red lentils, rinsed

25g (1 oz) long-grain rice

1.7 litres (3 pints) vegetable stock

1 x 400ml (14 fl oz) tin coconut milk

2 tablespoons fresh lime juice

3 tablespoons chopped coriander

**1** Melt the butter in a heavy-based saucepan and add the ginger, allspice, cumin, chilli powder, curry powder and ground coriander. Cook over a low heat for 3 minutes, stirring continuously.

**2** Add the vegetables, stir to combine, and cook for a further 8 minutes. Stir in the lentils and rice before adding the stock. Bring to the boil and simmer for 30 minutes or until the vegetables are tender and the lentils have started to break down.

**3** Blend the soup in a liquidiser or food processor until smooth. Return to the heat, and add the coconut milk, lime juice and coriander. Heat through but do not let it boil again. Serve immediately.

# Red Lentil Dip

A great dip for vegetarians and meat-eaters alike, to be served with bread (*naan*) or crudités. Thin the recipe down after puréeing and it makes a delicious soup.

**Preparation and cooking: 1 hour**
**Serves: 4**

4 tablespoons extra virgin olive oil

4 cloves garlic, finely chopped

1 onion, finely chopped

1 teaspoon ground cumin

1 teaspoon ground coriander

½ teaspoon cayenne pepper

225g (8 oz) split red lentils, rinsed

600ml (1 pint) vegetable stock

2 tablespoons sun-dried tomato pesto

1 tablespoon lemon juice

salt and freshly ground black pepper

4 spring onions, finely diced

2 tablespoons chopped parsley

**1** Heat the olive oil in a saucepan, add the garlic and onion and cook over a medium heat for 8 minutes until the onion has softened. Add the spices, and cook for a further 2 minutes.

**2** Add the lentils and stock, bring to the boil, reduce the temperature and simmer for 25–35 minutes until the lentils are tender. Add more liquid if required.

**3** Fold in the tomato pesto and lemon juice, and beat with a heavy whisk or wooden spoon until the lentils break up into a thick purée. Alternatively blend the mix in a food processor until smooth, but my preference is for a textured finish.

**4** Season to taste and fold in the spring onion and parsley. Add more olive oil if the purée appears too dry.

## Easy Lentil Soup

● *Cook together 115g (4 oz) Puy lentils with 1 chopped red onion, 1 chopped clove garlic, 1 bay leaf, 1 sprig thyme, ½ teaspoon salt and 1.7 litres (3 pints) vegetable stock.*

● *Cook until the lentils are tender, then liquidise half the soup and fold back into the unblended portion.*

● *Meanwhile, in a separate saucepan heat 55g (2 oz) unsalted butter and throw in 3 handfuls of sorrel. Cook until the sorrel has broken down.*

● *Fold the sorrel into the soup and finish the soup with 150ml (¼ pint) double cream. Season.*

# Cep Lentils

This recipe is packed full of earthy flavours, and it is delicious with roast chicken or as a dish on its own. Vegetarians should omit the bacon and *chorizo*. For a meaty soup, double the quantity of stock and liquidise half the finished item, folding it back into the broth.

**Preparation and cooking: 1½ hours**
**Serves: 4–6**

1 tablespoon good olive oil

225g (8 oz) *pancetta* or smoked streaky bacon, diced

1 onion, finely chopped

1 carrot, finely chopped

1 stick celery, finely diced

1 leek, finely chopped

2 bay leaves

1 teaspoon soft thyme leaves

4 cloves garlic, finely chopped

55g (2 oz) dried ceps, soaked for ½ hour in 300ml (½ pint) boiling water

225g (8 oz) Puy lentils, washed

375ml (13 fl oz) gutsy red wine

850ml (1½ pints) chicken or vegetable stock

225g (8 oz) *chorizo*, skin removed and cut into 5mm (¼ in) slices

55g (2 oz) unsalted butter, cubed

4 tablespoons chopped flat-leaf parsley

salt and ground black pepper

**1** Heat the olive oil in a heavy-based saucepan. Add the bacon and cook over a medium heat until it is golden and has released its natural fats.

**2** Add the onion, carrot, celery, leek, bay leaves, thyme and garlic and cook for 8 minutes.

**3** Drain the ceps and squeeze dry, retaining the soaking liquor. Chop the ceps finely and add to the cooked vegetables.

**4** Add the lentils and stir to combine. Strain the cep soaking liquor through muslin or a fine sieve and add. Take care not to add any grit or murky liquid, so allow the liquor to settle before straining.

**5** Add the wine and stock to the lentils, and bring to the boil. Reduce the heat and cook until the lentils are tender, about 35–45 minutes.

**6** Some 10 minutes before the lentils are cooked, fold in the *chorizo*.

**7** Just before serving, fold in the butter and parsley. Season to taste.

. . . . . . . . . . . .

*A nice vegetable accompaniment is lentils with celeriac. Follow the recipe for* Cep Lentils, *but leave out the ceps,* bacon and chorizo *and add small 1cm (½ in) cubes of peeled celeriac at the same time as the other vegetables. Finish the lentils with a table-spoon of walnut oil and a splash of sherry vinegar.*

. . . . . . . . . . . .

. . . . . . . .

*Serve the* Cep Lentils *with your favourite grilled sausages.*

. . . . . . . .

. . . . . . . . . . . .

*Allow the* Cep Lentils *to cool, then add extra virgin olive oil and balsamic vinegar, and fold in crumbled goat's cheese, chopped parsley and chopped spring onion for a healthy salad.*

. . . . . . . . . . . .

# MUSHROOMS

Mushrooms are fungi, simple plants which grow on living, dead or decaying matter, using this as a food source. Mushrooms are rich in nutrients — protein, B vitamins and potassium among them. When preparing mushrooms, treat them delicately, as they are very fragile. Unless old, they rarely need peeling, and apart from the earthy root are 100 per cent edible. Wild mushrooms tend to be quite dirty. Professional mushroom hunters always carry a brush to remove grass, earth and pine needles. Mushrooms are not fond of water, so only wash them as a last resort.

## CULTIVATED MUSHROOMS

Mushroom cultivation was developed by the French in the seventeenth century (although the Japanese have been cultivating shiitake since the first century AD), and this has since mushroomed ('scuse the pun) into a major industry, which was based originally on the field mushroom (*Agaricus campestris*) — still to be found wild, and fabulous they are too, picked and cooked immediately. The principal mushroom cultivated now is a close relative, *Agaricus bisporus*, the common mushroom. This sells at various stages of its development: buttons are tiny; cups are larger with open heads (excellent for stuffing); and flat are the closest to field, fully mature with flat heads fully opened (often needing peeling).

Other wild mushrooms now commercially grown include CHESTNUT BROWN, similar to a cup with perhaps a little more flavour; SHIITAKE which, although it has made a big impact in the shops recently, is because of novelty, I feel, rather than quality, as it is very chewy with not much perfume (often used in its dry form); and OYSTER mushrooms. These are also popular, but the cultivated variety does not have as much flavour as the wild; it is a very delicate mushroom, pale in colour with the occasional tinge of apricot.

## WILD MUSHROOMS

Historically mushrooms were picked from the wild, and I wonder how many unfortunate testers became horribly ill or even died finding out which were edible and which were poisonous. Wild mushroom picking today has become a lucrative hobby, with very high prices achieved if sold to restaurants and high-class greengrocers. Unless you know what you are about, or are partnered with someone who does, I suggest you don't eat what you pick. In France you are able to take wild mushrooms into a pharmacy to be checked and identified.

There are hundreds of wild mushrooms, but I am only going to mention the most popular. MORELS are available fresh in the spring, and are easy to recognise because of their brown, ridged and pitted cap; it's a great mushroom, with a meaty texture. CEPS or PORCINI, available in the autumn, are my favourite wild mushroom; they are meaty as well, with a lovely flavour, and a fat swollen stem which is very edible. Unfortunately, ceps suffer frequently from maggots: if the stalk feels spongy, cut into it and you will see many maggot tunnels. Dried ceps are invaluable in my store cupboard as a few soaked in boiling water lift stews, risottos, soups and sauces. But a word of warning: even dried ceps contain moth eggs which hatch out if kept in a warm larder, so store them in the refrigerator. GIROLLES and CHANTERELLES are now available in the autumn in supermarkets; these lovely yellow mushrooms tend to deteriorate if wet, and can also be very dirty. The HORN OF PLENTY is a black trumpet-shaped mushroom called endearingly *trompettes de mort* (trumpets of death) by the French.

*Cèpes Bordelaise*

This is one of my favourite simple ways of cooking this luxury mushroom.
● For 2 people, take 4 large ceps. Remove the stalks and chop these finely, then combine with 2 chopped garlic cloves.
● Fry this mix in 3 tablespoons olive oil. Add the sliced caps and cook over a low heat for 10 minutes to release the liquid.
● Season and, just before serving, fold in a little lemon juice and 2 tablespoons chopped flat-leaf parsley.

Brush field or flat mushrooms with garlic-infused olive oil. Grill the mushrooms on both sides until cooked. Cook scrambled eggs until soft (see page 113) then add some ricotta cheese, remove from the heat and fold in chopped basil and parsley. Top the mushrooms with the scrambled egg, and serve with crispy bacon.

# Ceps in a Herb Crust

Ceps have such a wonderful flavour. Serve this dish with a green salad.

**Preparation and cooking: 45 minutes**
**Serves: 4**

3 tablespoons finely diced shallot

2 teaspoons finely diced garlic

55g (2 oz) unsalted butter

450g (1 lb) fresh ceps or button mushrooms, cleaned and sliced

225ml (8 fl oz) red wine

425ml (¾ pint) double cream

6 tablespoons chopped parsley

½ teaspoon ground black pepper

1 teaspoon Maldon salt

115g (4 oz) soft white breadcrumbs

85g (3 oz) Parmesan, grated

2 teaspoons soft thyme leaves

55g (2 oz) butter, melted

**1** In a large frying pan, fry the shallot and garlic in the butter until soft but not brown. Increase the temperature and add the ceps or mushrooms, and cook for a further 6 minutes. Remove the mushrooms from the pan and set aside to keep warm.

**2** Add the red wine to the pan, bring to the boil, and boil to **reduce** by half; add the cream and continue to reduce until approximately 300ml (½ pint) of liquid remains. Return the mushrooms to the pan and mix together with half the parsley. Season with the black pepper and salt.

**3** Meanwhile, make the crust by mixing together the bread-crumbs, Parmesan, remaining parsley, the thyme and melted butter. Place the mushroom mix in a *gratin* dish and top with the herb crust. Brown under the preheated grill or bake in a hot oven at about 220°C/425°F/Gas 7 for 8 minutes.

• • • • • • • • • • • • • • • •

*Slice very clean button mushrooms and toss with extra virgin olive oil, a little chopped shallot, some chopped parsley and coriander, some lemon juice and lots of black pepper. Dress on rocket leaves.*

• • • • • • • • • • • • • • • •

# Oriental Marinated Mushrooms

Shiitake mushrooms can be substituted for the field mushrooms for more authenticity.

**Preparation and cooking: 30 minutes**
**Serves: 4**

450g (1 lb) small field mushrooms, stalks removed

6 tablespoons extra virgin olive oil

1 teaspoon sesame oil

1 teaspoon finely chopped chilli

2 cloves garlic, finely chopped

2 teaspoons soy sauce

2 tablespoons dry white wine

1 teaspoon clear honey

2 tablespoons chopped coriander

2 tablespoons chopped mint

salt and ground black pepper

**1** Wipe the mushroom caps with a damp cloth. Heat the two oils in a large frying pan, add the chilli and garlic and cook until soft, but not brown.

**2** Add the mushrooms, turning them well in the oil, then cover the frying pan and cook slowly for about 7 minutes.

**3** Spoon the mushrooms into a shallow dish. Add the soy sauce and wine to the pan and boil quickly for 2 minutes. Remove from the heat and stir in the honey.

**4** Add the coriander, mint and seasoning, adding more extra virgin olive oil and soy if required. Pour this over the mushrooms, and serve hot or cold, on *bruschetta* or *crostini* (see page 53), or as part of an *antipasti* buffet.

## Button Mushroom and Tomato Stew

Delicious and rich in flavours, this is a dish that can be served on its own as a starter or as part of a cold buffet.

**Preparation and cooking: 30 minutes**
**Serves: 4**

juice of ½ lemon
450g (1 lb) button mushrooms, wiped
2 tablespoons olive oil
3 cloves garlic, crushed to a paste with a little salt
4–5 shallots, finely chopped
1 tablespoon coriander seeds
1 tablespoon fennel seeds
1 bay leaf
4 whole tinned plum tomatoes
175ml (6 fl oz) dry white wine
1 whole red chilli
1 tablespoon tomato paste
1 tablespoon caster sugar
2 tablespoons chopped parsley

**1** Pour the lemon juice over the mushrooms.

**2** In a deep frying pan heat the olive oil, then add the garlic and shallot and allow them to **sweat** for a few minutes. Add the coriander and fennel seeds and the bay leaf. Squash the tinned tomatoes into the pan with your hands, then add the white wine, whole chilli, tomato paste and sugar. Simmer for 5 minutes.

**3** Add the mushrooms and simmer for a further 10 minutes, then remove the mushrooms and **reduce** the sauce.

**4** Finally toss the mushrooms in the sauce. Garnish with chopped parsley and serve.

---

*Cook sliced mushrooms in butter with a little thyme, season and add double cream or crème fraîche. Cook until the cream has thickened, and dish up on hot buttered toast.*

## Mushroom Stuffing

● *To make this stuffing for poultry, finely chop some button mushrooms and shallots and cook slowly in butter to release the natural liquids.*

● *Season with a little cayenne, a pinch of nutmeg and a small amount of chopped thyme.*

● *Cook until the mushrooms are tender and most of the liquid has evaporated.*

● *Mix in some fresh breadcrumbs, grated lemon rind, and seasonings to taste.*

● *Fold in a little melted butter and a raw egg yolk to bind.*

*Grill field or flat mushrooms on both sides with a little olive oil, garlic and thyme. Place a 5mm (¼ in) slice of cooked bone marrow (optional) on each mushroom and top with a thin slice of Taleggio cheese. Place the mushrooms under the grill and cook until the cheese has melted. A starter with a difference.*

## Mushroom Powder

*This is useful to fold into sauces and pasta.*

● *Cook some large peeled and de-stalked field mushrooms with a couple of onions stuck with bay leaves and cloves, a couple of blades of mace, some white pepper and salt.*

● *Add a couple of tablespoons of water and place over a low heat to draw out the mushrooms' natural juices. Cook until the liquid has completely evaporated.*

● *Place the mushrooms on a cake rack in a very low oven overnight (longer if necessary) until completely dry.*

● *Place dry mushrooms in an electric coffee grinder and blend to a powder.*

● *Store in dry jars or bottles and use as required.*

## Mushroom Sauce

*An old-fashioned mushroom sauce to serve with chicken or fish.*
- *Stew clean button mushrooms, chopped onion, chopped thyme and a bay leaf in butter until the mushrooms have released their natural liquids.*
- *Add some* Béchamel Sauce *(see page 60), lemon juice and double cream.*
- *Blend in a liquidiser or serve as is with seasoning and chopped parsley.*

## Preserved Mushrooms

- *Steam button mushrooms or ceps until tender, then toss with lemon juice, salt and pepper.*
- *Heat extra virgin olive oil with lots of sliced garlic, 6 sprigs of rosemary and 3 sprigs of thyme.*
- *Layer the mushrooms in sterilised jars with the garlic and herbs and top up with oil. Seal the jar and refrigerate.*
- *This will keep for a month and is used as part of an antipasti buffet or tossed with salad leaves.*

# OFFAL

'Awful offal' is the catch-phrase most associated with this rich variety of meats (actually called 'varietal meats' in the States). The British have a fondness for kidney and liver, albeit on a diminishing scale, but as for the other bits — anything internal plus the head, feet, ears and tail — we have never really got to grips with them. Other nations won't waste a thing: watch a French *charcutier* at work with a pig, and you'll be amazed, and the Chinese also eat some pretty unsociable parts of animals. It's a shame we don't eat more offal as it is rich in protein, vitamins and minerals, particularly iron.

## BONE MARROW

With a British ban on beef on the bone, one can only purchase this delicacy on the black market, or use animals from abroad. Marrow comes from the shin bones of cows and calves. It is a delicious experience scooping marrow from roast or poached bones. It's wonderful on toast with rock salt, mustard, chopped gherkins and a parsley salad. It can be added to stuffings and sauces.

Buy bones sawn into 5–10cm (2–4 in) lengths, and soak in cold salted water to remove blood and whiten the marrow. If wanting raw, slide the tip of a knife between marrow and bone to loosen the marrow, working from both ends, and push or scoop out the marrow, then poach or use it raw. If poaching *in* the bone, put foil, a flour paste or a slice of carrot over the holes to prevent the marrow slipping out.

## BRAINS

A delicious out-of-favour part of any beast, mainly calf and lamb. Again because of BSE and scrapie you will only buy imported. A very delicate organ needing little cooking, usually poached, sautéed or deep-fried in batter. It has a heavenly creamy texture. My favourite recipe is calf's brains served in black butter and caper sauce.

## CAUL

The honeycomb, soft, fatty membrane that surrounds an animal's stomach is used as a wrapping to enclose fillings, usually meat. After cooking, the caul will have lost most of its stringy fatty content and will be golden and crisp. Pigs' caul is often sold salted in blocks. Soak in several changes of water to soften and remove excess salt. Fresh caul does not require soaking, merely washing.

## CHEEKS

A great favourite of classic French cooks, the cheeks are lovely nuggets of meat, usually from ox, calf or pig. With our history of BSE, ox cheek will now be imported. It is a tough muscle for obvious reasons, and needs cooking slowly and for a long time, but has a lovely flavour, releasing rich fabulous juices.

## EARS

These usually come from calf or pig, and are a great delicacy when cooked very slowly until meltingly tender to break down the cartilaginous flesh. They are usually allowed to go cold then breadcrumbed and deep-fried, grilled or roasted. Lovely with a herby *salsa* or a mustardy dressing and salad.

## FEET AND TROTTERS

These are rich in gelatine and are often added to stocks to give body and setting qualities. You will often see pigs' trotters in France that have been split lengthways, poached for many hours, cooled and painted with mustard, bread-crumbed and baked. In the UK you will find a handful of Michelin-starred chefs laboriously boning out trotters and stuffing them with all sorts of delicacies. Watch out for all the tiny bones and toenails!

## HEADS

I don't intend to labour the point on this part of the anatomy as you will rarely find animal heads for purchase these days. Again, they are very gelatinous and require long hours of cooking.

## HEARTS

Ox, pig and lamb hearts can be sliced thinly and grilled or pan-fried for a short period of time, or stuffed and roasted or braised for ages. Rarely seen in modern cookery, although lambs' hearts are still sold in supermarkets and butchers.

## KIDNEYS

Ox and calf's kidneys are made up of several lobes attached to a suet core; pig's and sheep's kidneys only have one lobe.

All kidneys are surrounded by a thick layer of white suet fat that in retail circumstances is removed before sale. The bigger or older the animal, the longer the kidney needs to be cooked. Young or small kidneys are suitable for grilling or frying.

## LIVERS

Calf's liver is undoubtedly the star of the offal world, wonderfully tender and delicately flavoured. For grilling or pan-frying, stick to calf's or lamb's liver. For braising, buy ox or pig's, and soak in milk for a couple of hours to mellow the flavour. Chicken and duck livers are also delicious and very adaptable to various forms of cooking. *Foie gras* is the very expensive corn-fattened duck or goose liver that is one of the heights of luxury – rich, high in calories and very expensive indeed.

## SWEETBREADS

These come in two varieties, which together form the thymus gland of a calf (or lamb): the elongated one near the throat, and the more favoured round heart or thymus sweetbread. Highly prized by gourmets and those in the know, sweetbreads may be pan-fried, deep-fried or braised. Buy calf's when you can, but lamb's are available. Prior to secondary cooking, sweetbreads need soaking in salted water and then **blanching**: place in a pan of cold water, bring slowly to the boil and cook for 5–6 minutes (calf) or 2–3 minutes (lamb). Transfer to cold water then remove the surface membrane, fat and tubes. Calf's sweetbreads then need pressing under weights to compact the flesh before further cooking.

## TONGUE

These are usually sold salted or pickled. Ox, calf, pig or lamb tongues are available, although ox tongue will now be imported. They have a thick skin which is easily removed after lengthy poaching to tenderise them.

## TRIPE

Not a great favourite with many, so it won't feature in the recipes here, although if you are a fan, cooked well I understand it can be delicious.

## Poached Brains

● Soak brains for 12 hours, poach them in a **court-bouillon** for 10–15 minutes depending on size, then cut into 1cm (½ in) dice.
● Cook some butter until nutty brown, then add lemon juice, parsley and capers, and pour over the poached brains.

## Spiced Brains

● Fry 2 chopped onions, 4 teaspoons chopped garlic and 1 teaspoon caraway seeds in 25g (1 oz) unsalted butter and 1 tablespoon extra virgin olive oil until soft.
● Add 1 tablespoon Harissa (see page 259) and 1 x 400g (14 oz) tin tomatoes.
● Bring to the boil then add 1 teaspoon paprika, 3 roasted, skinned and sliced red peppers (see page 254) and 225g (8 oz) blanched and cubed brains.
● Bring to the boil and simmer until thick, then fold in 2 tablespoons chopped parsley.

## Brains in Tomato Sauce

● Soak 2 lamb's brains in water with 2 teaspoons vinegar for an hour or so.
● Remove membranes and rinse brains well under running cold water, then set aside.
● Fry 3 chopped garlic cloves in a little olive oil, add 1 x 400g (14 oz) tin chopped tomatoes with their juice, a pinch each of chilli flakes, ground cumin and paprika, a handful of fresh coriander leaves, coarsely chopped, 1 handful of fresh flat-leaf parsley leaves, coarsely chopped, and the juice of ½ lemon.
● Simmer the mixture for 3–4 minutes, then add the brains and cook on a low heat for 12–15 minutes.

# Braised Calf's Liver

Everyone associates calf's liver with instant cooking but it can be equally nice cooked in this way.

**Preparation and cooking: 3½ hours**
**Serves: 4–6**

1kg (2¼ lb) centre piece of calf's liver
caul fat
25g (1 oz) butter
175g (6 oz) smoked bacon **lardons**
175g (6 oz) onion, chopped
225g (8 oz) carrot, sliced
1 leek, sliced
4 garlic cloves, chopped
2 sprigs thyme
1 stick celery, sliced
½ bottle of red wine
2 tablespoons brandy

**1** Wrap a centre piece of calf's liver in caul, and brown all over in a casserole dish in a little butter.
**2** Surround the liver with the smoked bacon **lardons**, onion, carrot, leek, garlic, thyme, celery and red wine.
**3** Cover with a tight-fitting lid and braise in a 150°C/300°F/ Gas 2 oven for 3 hours.
**4** After 2 hours, add the brandy.
**5** At the end of cooking you should have plenty of juices. Liquidise the juices with the vegetables, then pass through a fine sieve.
**6** Serve this sauce with slices of the liver.

**N.B.** The liver can also be served cold with a green *salsa* (see page 215).

# Quick Chicken Liver Pâté

It's always useful to have a stand-by in the fridge in case of unexpected visitors, or for when I sneak down in the middle of the night for a hangover snack.

**Preparation and cooking: 20 minutes**
**Serves: 4–6**

175g (6 oz) unsalted butter, softened
450g (1 lb) chicken or duck livers, trimmed and cleaned
2 shallots, finely chopped
1 teaspoon soft thyme leaves
2 cloves garlic, finely chopped
2 tablespoons brandy
2 teaspoons anchovy essence
½ teaspoon ground black pepper
55g (2 oz) clarified butter, melted (see page 60, optional)

**1** Heat 15g (½ oz) of the butter in a frying pan until foaming. Add half the livers and fry quickly on all sides until golden, but still pink in the middle, about 4–5 minutes. Repeat with a second batch of butter and livers. Place the livers and any juices in a food processor.
**2** In the same pan heat another 15g (½ oz) butter, add the shallot, thyme and garlic, and cook over a moderate heat until the shallot is soft but not coloured. Add the brandy, anchovy essence and pepper, and scrape the bottom of the pan to release any coagulated juices. Place everything in the food processor, including the remaining unsalted butter. Blend until smooth.
**3** If you want a very smooth pâté, pass the mixture through a fine sieve and put in a bowl. Cover with clingfilm, cool then refrigerate. If not using within 48 hours, cover the top with clarified butter.

## Devilled Kidneys and Livers

● *Roughly chop 6 lamb's kidneys and 6 chicken livers and pan-fry with 1 chopped onion and 1 chopped clove garlic in 55g (2 oz) unsalted butter for 4–5 minutes. Remove and keep warm.*
● *Add to the pan 2 teaspoons Worcestershire sauce, 2 teaspoons grain mustard, a dash of Tabasco sauce, and 4 tablespoons double cream.*
● *Swirl to combine, then return meats to the pan and warm through. Serve on toast.*

# *Crostini* of Chicken Livers with Vin Santo

A recipe adapted from Ann and Franco Taruschio's wonderful book *Bruschetta, Crostoni and Crostini*. A brilliant dish that I use on a regular basis.

**Preparation and cooking: 30 minutes**
**Serves: 4**

200ml (7 fl oz) extra virgin olive oil

1 red onion, finely chopped

1 teaspoon chopped oregano

1 clove garlic, finely chopped

400g (14 oz) chicken livers, trimmed and cleaned

175ml (6 fl oz) dry white wine

175ml (6 fl oz) Vin Santo

1 tablespoon salted capers, well rinsed and drained

4 anchovy fillets

salt and ground black pepper

8 slices of bread for *crostini* (see page 53)

**1** Heat the olive oil in a non-stick frying pan, add the onion, oregano and garlic, and fry until pale golden. Add the chicken livers and fry for 5 minutes, then add the dry white wine and Vin Santo and cook the livers for a further 8 minutes.

**2** Put the chicken livers, cooking juices, capers and anchovies in a food processor and **pulse** until roughly chopped. Season with salt and pepper, and refrigerate until half an hour before use.

**3** Serve at room temperature, dolloped on hot *crostini*, which have been toasted on a griddle.

• • • • • • • • • • • • • •

*Flour 1cm (½ in) slices of calf's liver and cook in butter for 2–3 minutes each side. Remove and keep warm. Add more butter and a little olive oil to the pan with a few sage leaves and a little chopped garlic. Season with salt, pepper and lemon juice and pour over the liver.*

• • • • • • • • • • • • • •

# Seared *Foie Gras* with Grapes and Oysters

An unusual sweet and sour combination that works for me. The blend of the rich *foie gras* with the sweetness of the grapes, the acid of the vinegar and the salt of the oysters teases most of your taste buds.

**Preparation and cooking: 30 minutes**
**Serves: 4**

4 x 1cm (½ in) slices duck *foie gras*

seasoned plain flour

12 rock oysters, shucked, juices saved

24 green grapes, halved, peeled if you like

2 tablespoons aged red wine vinegar

150ml (¼ pint) **reduced** chicken stock

salt and ground black pepper

**1** Coat the *foie gras* in seasoned flour. Heat a non-stick frying pan until very hot. Add the *foie gras* slices and cook for 1 minute each side. Remove and keep warm.

**2** Add the oysters to the *foie gras* fat that remains in the pan. Cook for 30 seconds each side until the oysters tighten and the edges start to curl. Remove and keep warm.

**3** To the same pan add the grapes, oyster juices and vinegar and cook until very little liquid remains. Add the stock and cook until the juices thicken. Season to taste.

**4** Return the oysters to the sauce, warm through and pour over the *foie gras*. Serve on *bruschetta* (see page 53) or with dressed salad leaves. An individual starter.

## Pan-fried Livers

● Pan-fry chicken or duck livers with butter and olive oil in a very hot pan until the livers are brown and crusty all over.

● Remove the livers from the pan.

● **Deglaze** the pan with balsamic vinegar and a little stock or meat gravy from a roast.

● Fold in some butter and the cooked livers, and swirl to glaze the livers. Serve on salad leaves.

O

*Place duck or chicken liver cubes on skewers with soaked salted pork belly cubes, mushrooms, bay leaves and chunks of onion. Roll in melted butter, allow to cool slightly, then roll in breadcrumbs. Grill or roast in the oven at 200°C/400°F/Gas 6 for 15–20 minutes. Season and serve with lemon and a Salsa Verde (see page 215).*

• • • • • • • • • • • • • • • • • • • • • • • • • • • • • • • • • • • • • • •

# Braised Sweetbreads with Sorrel

The creaminess of the sweetbreads contrasts nicely with the tartness of the sorrel, in a classic and wonderful combination of flavours and textures.

**Preparation and cooking: 12 hours + 1 hour**
**Serves: 4**

4 calf's heart (thymus) sweetbreads, soaked for 12 hours in several changes of water
salt and ground black pepper
3 carrots, sliced
2 sticks celery, sliced
16 baby onions
55g (2 oz) unsalted butter
2 cloves garlic, finely chopped
1 teaspoon soft thyme leaves
1 x 400g (14 oz) tin tomatoes with juice
125ml (4 fl oz) dry white wine
125ml (4 fl oz) chicken stock
175g (6 oz) fresh podded peas
3 handfuls picked sorrel leaves
4 tablespoons double cream

**1 Blanch** the sweetbreads in salted water for 5 minutes, plunge into cold water, then cut away all sinew and transparent skin. Leave whole.

**2** In a casserole brown the carrot, celery and onions in half the butter for 10 minutes. Add the garlic, thyme and sweetbreads, and fry gently to colour the sweetbreads lightly. Add the tomato, white wine and stock, bring to the boil, reduce heat and simmer gently for 45 minutes, turning the sweetbreads once.

**3** About 15 minutes before the end of cooking time, add the peas. When cooked, remove the sweetbreads and vegetables from the sauce and keep warm.

**4** Place the remaining butter in a saucepan, add the sorrel and cook until the sorrel has broken down. Strain the cooking juices on to the sorrel, and boil until reduced by half. Add the cream and season to taste. Pour the sauce over the sweetbreads and vegetables. Serve with mashed potatoes.

## Sweetbreads with Anchovies
- *Blanch sweetbreads, remove sinew and cut in 2.5cm (1 in) pieces.*
- *Cook in foaming butter for 3–4 minutes.*
- *Add chopped anchovies and cook until the anchovies break down.*
- *Add a few capers, a squeeze of lemon juice and some parsley.*
- *Season to taste, and serve with new potatoes and a salad.*

*Brown a whole calf's kidney, still wrapped in a thin coating of its own suet, in butter, then cook with chopped shallots and garlic in a hot oven at 200°C/400°F/Gas 6 for 12–15 minutes. Remove and set aside. Add red wine, Dijon mustard and cream to the braising pan and heat through. Slice the kidney and return to the sauce. Season with lemon juice and chopped parsley.*

*Cook whole lamb's kidneys in their suet under the grill or in a hot oven, until deliciously tender. Serve with herb butter.*

*Split lamb's kidneys in half and cut out any sinew. Use rosemary stalks as skewers and push 2 through each kidney half. Grill the kidneys for 2 minutes each side and serve with very soft grilled tomatoes, grilled back bacon and grilled field mushrooms.*

# OILS

In the most basic culinary sense, oils break down into two categories, those used for cooking, and those used for flavouring. There are only two oils that fit both designations, olive oil and sesame oil.

## GROUNDNUT OIL

This is peanut oil, so all of you with peanut allergies, beware. It's my favourite of all the bland oils for cooking, especially deep-frying, as it survives very well at high temperatures. It has little or no distinct taste.

## SUNFLOWER OIL

This is good for mayonnaise and any form of cooking.

## VEGETABLE OIL

Vegetable oils tend to be made nowadays from rape seeds. They are good for mayonnaise and cooking.

## GRAPESEED OIL

Generally coming from Italy, this is a good oil with a hint of flavour. It is very low in cholesterol. Although an expensive alternative to the ones above, it has a good resistance to high temperatures. Its colour ranges from pale yellow to light green. It can also be used for mild salad dressings.

## SAFFLOWER OIL

The majority of safflower oils are produced in Holland, and they are good for pan-frying and salad dressings or mayonnaise, but not for deep-frying as they deteriorate at high temperatures.

## SESAME OIL

This very powerful oil is used sparingly, mainly in oriental cooking. It can be bought toasted or untoasted. Don't buy it in large quantities as it goes rancid quite quickly. Keep in the fridge.

## HAZELNUT OIL

A very expensive, very powerful, designer oil. You need to use only a few drops mixed with olive oil to flavour a salad dressing. It does not last very well, so buy in small quantities, and keep in the fridge once opened.

## WALNUT OIL

This has great flavour, but again it's an oil to use in small quantities, although not so strong as hazelnut or sesame. It's lovely mixed 1 part to 4 parts olive oil for a salad dressing. Other nut oils include almond (used in cakes) and pistachio (which can be used in dressings). Keep in the fridge.

## OLIVE OIL

This is the oil of the moment, with extra virgin the star. It doesn't seem that long ago that you would buy a small bottle of olive oil at the chemists, with cotton buds to clean your ears out, and that was the only way you could buy it. Now, however, it's all the rage, and we have buyers avidly awaiting the first of the new season's olive oils in much the same way as they do Beaujolais Nouveau. The season starts in November.

Extra virgin olive oils vary hugely in quality and taste, depending on whether they come from single farms or co-operatives. Traditional makers will use stone presses that crush the olives along with some olive leaves for colour. The paste that this crushing produces is layered and then gently pressed to release the oils. Oil and water are then separated. The extra virgin oil comes from the first pressing. Extra virgin olive oil must have a maximum acidity of no more than 1%, and virgin olive oil no more than 1.5%. Olive oil is blended from lesser quality virgin olive oil. Differing strengths or qualities of olive oil are then produced from second and third pressings, often being treated chemically to extract extra oil.

The best olive oil is generally thought to come from Italy, but it is well worth trying out some Greek oils which represent excellent value and aren't bad at all. Other oils come from Spain, Portugal, North Africa and the South of France. Countries that use a lot of olive oil in their diet have a notably lower incidence of heart disease. This could be because the oil is high in antioxidants which are supposed to fight body 'rusters' known as free radicals, and disperse cholesterol, and because the oil is monounsaturated. However, also linked to olive oil are the health-giving qualities of associated products of the same countries — garlic, red wine, pulses and fruit. A good balance of all these products could help you live a little longer.

# Chilli Lemon Oil

The oil will get hotter the longer you leave it, so you could strain it if you like. Delicious over grilled fish.

**Preparation and cooking: 30 minutes**
**Makes: 425ml (¾ pint)**

| |
|---|
| 300ml (½ pint) groundnut oil |
| 1 teaspoon sesame oil |
| ½ tablespoon red chilli flakes, dried |
| 1 teaspoon Szechwan peppercorns |
| 2 large garlic cloves, peeled and smashed |
| 2 tablespoons fresh ginger (in fine strips) |
| 450g (1 lb) spring onions, finely sliced |
| 2 stems lemongrass, pounded and cut into fingers |
| 1 teaspoon coriander seeds, crushed |
| zest of 3 lemons, finely chopped |

**1** Combine all of the ingredients except the lemon zest.
**2** Over a moderate heat bring the mixture to 130°C/266°F, stirring occasionally. Simmer for 15 minutes, making sure the temperature does not rise.
**3** Cool for 5 minutes and then add the lemon zest. Remove the lemongrass and bottle the remaining ingredients.

## Rosemary Oil

*This is useful for roast lamb.*
● *Lightly crush 3 sprigs of rosemary, place in a sterilised bottle, add 1 teaspoon white vinegar and top up with 600ml (1 pint) olive oil.*
● *Leave for 1 month before using.*

## Oil Dressing

● *Make a simple dressing with 4 parts extra virgin olive oil to 1 part red wine vinegar or balsamic vinegar (or lemon juice).*
● *Dissolve salt and pepper in the vinegar first.*
● *Shake together in a screw-top jar.*

# Mayonnaise

Making a good mayonnaise is simplicity itself. Don't use extra virgin olive oil, as this would give too powerful a flavour.

**Preparation and cooking: 15 minutes**
**Makes: 300ml (½ pint)**

| |
|---|
| 2 large egg yolks |
| ½ teaspoon English mustard |
| 1 dessertspoon lemon juice |
| a pinch of salt |
| a pinch of ground white pepper |
| 200ml (7 fl oz) safflower or sunflower oil |

**1** Whisk the egg yolks with the English mustard, lemon juice, salt and white pepper.
**2** Measure out the safflower or sunflower oil and gradually add it to the egg yolks, drop by drop, increasing to a steady stream, until it has all been absorbed.
**3** Beat continuously. Correct seasoning.

* * * * * * * * *
*Olive oil, unlike wine, does not improve with age. If you don't use a great deal, buy in small quantities*
* * * * * * * * *

* * * * * * * * * *
*Instead of spreading butter on bread, try dipping the bread into extra virgin olive oil with a splash of balsamic vinegar and a sprinkling of Maldon sea salt.*
* * * * * * * * * *

# Walnut and Basil Dressing ⓥ

Great with bitter leaves, grilled goat's cheese, or any of the warm salads.

**Preparation and cooking: 5 minutes**
**Serves: 4**

| |
|---|
| 50ml (2 fl oz) white wine vinegar |
| ½ teaspoon caster sugar |
| ¼ teaspoon rock salt |
| ¼ teaspoon ground black pepper |
| 50ml (2 fl oz) walnut oil |
| 75ml (2½ fl oz) olive oil |
| 3 tablespoons torn basil |

**1** Heat the white wine vinegar, remove from the heat and then add the caster sugar, followed by the rock salt, ground black pepper, walnut oil, olive oil and basil.
**2** Whisk together.

• • • • • • • • • • • • • • • • • •

*Olive oil has come into its own with the recent fashion for Mediterranean foods, and it is dribbled over carpaccio (see page 45), used as a finishing touch for a good bread and tomato soup (see page 53), dribbled on country bread and char-grilled on a barbie. It's essential for Pesto and Tapenade, and is the strength behind a good Aïoli (see pages 210, 243 and 196).*

• • • • • • • • • • • • • • • • • •

• • • • • • • • • • • • •

*When cooking, don't waste money by using extra virgin olive oil, as most of the flavour disperses when cooked. Use plain olive oil and reserve the extra virgin for finishing off a dish, for salad dressings and salsas.*

• • • • • • • • • • • • •

# Olive Oil Pickles ⓥ

A simple pickle to accompany cold meats or cheese.
**Preparation and cooking: overnight + 15 minutes**
**Makes: 1 litre (1¾ pints)**

| |
|---|
| 450g (1 lb) small cucumbers, sliced |
| 225g (8 oz) baby onions, sliced |
| salt |
| 2 teaspoons mustard seeds |
| 1 teaspoon celery seeds |
| ¼ teaspoon cayenne pepper |
| 600ml (1 pint) cider vinegar |
| 150ml (¼ pint) extra virgin olive oil |

**1** Salt the sliced cucumbers and baby onions, toss to combine, leave overnight then drain.
**2** Put the mixture, after rinsing and draining, into clean jars.
**3** Sprinkle over the mustard seeds, celery seeds and cayenne pepper. Combine the vinegar and oil, and pour in to cover the pickle.
**4** Screw on tops and store in a dark place for several weeks before using.

• • • • • • • • • • • • • • • • • • • • • • • •

## Olive Oil Vinaigrette
*Whisk together 1 tablespoon Dijon mustard, 1 chopped clove garlic, 1 teaspoon chopped shallot, 2 tablespoons aged red wine vinegar, a pinch each of ground cumin and dried oregano, and 75ml (2½ fl oz) extra virgin olive oil.*

• • • • • • • • • • • • • • • • • • • • • • • •

## Preserved Goat's Cheese
• *Buy small goat's cheeses and place them in glass preserving jars.*
• *Add whole cloves of garlic, some sprigs of thyme and rosemary, a few black peppercorns and a couple of bay leaves.*
• *Top up with extra virgin olive oil.*
• *Allow 48 hours' refrigeration before using. Will keep for 3 weeks.*

• • • • • • • • • • • • • • • • • • • • • • • •

# OLIVES

I yearn for the markets of Italy and the South of France, in which you find bowls and bowls of olives of every description and languishing in every type of marinade. Although a love of olives is growing in this country, we are still light years away from the southern Europeans' passion for this ancient fruit. Supermarkets are getting better with their selections, but they still sell far too many only soaked in brine. I love those lush varieties which are marinated in olive oil and herbs; they are so much meatier and so much less acid. For years we have suffered from only having olives stuffed with red pepper, anchovy or almonds.

The olive tree, *Olea europaea*, has been valued for thousands of years, and is cultivated in Mediterranean countries, North Africa, California and elsewhere. Green olives are unripe, violet are nearly ripe, and black are fully ripe. All of them are inedible in their raw tree-bound state, and need to be treated, usually by brining, to remove bitter components.

Buy olives where possible from a reputable delicatessen where you know the turnover is high. If you buy olives still in their brine, try making your own marinade.

## Hot Marinated Olives

● *Rinse 450g (1 lb) cured cracked olives, then marinate with 1 teaspoon Harissa (see page 259) or chilli sauce, 4 tablespoons lemon juice, 1 tablespoon chopped pickled lemon rind (see page 171), 225ml (8 fl oz) extra virgin olive oil, the grated zest of 1 orange and 4 quartered garlic cloves.*
● *Marinate for 4 days before eating. Be warned, they're very potent!*

## Olive Salad

*An excellent salad to go with roast meats, whether hot or cold.*
● *Combine 20 chopped black olives with ½ sliced red onion, 4 segmented oranges and their juice, 3 tablespoons extra virgin olive oil, ¼ teaspoon cayenne pepper, 2 tablespoons chopped flat-leaf parsley, and 1 tablespoon snipped chives.*

# Spiced Marinated Olives Ⓥ

Something a little different . . .
**Preparation and cooking: 20 minutes**
**Makes: about 900g (2 lb)**

| |
|---|
| 2 tablespoons extra virgin olive oil |
| 2 teaspoons fennel seeds |
| 2 teaspoons cumin seeds |
| 2 teaspoons coriander seeds |
| ¼ teaspoon ground cardamom |
| ½ teaspoon dried chilli flakes |
| 1 vanilla pod, split |
| 50ml (2 fl oz) fresh orange juice |
| grated zest of 1 orange and 1 lemon |
| 1 tablespoon chopped garlic |
| 750g (1 lb 10 oz) black olives |

**1** Heat the extra virgin olive oil with the fennel, cumin and coriander seeds, ground cardamom and dried chilli flakes.
**2** Cook for 5 minutes over a low heat to release some of the flavours.
**3** Add the split vanilla pod, scraping the seeds into the mixture, with the fresh orange juice, grated orange and lemon zest and the chopped garlic.
**4** Fold in the black olives, and refrigerate for 4 days before eating at room temperature.

*Combine 115g (4 oz) chopped black olives with 6 chopped anchovies, 150g (5½ oz) softened unsalted butter and a teaspoon of brandy, and **pulse** in a food processor to combine. Season to taste, roll up in foil, and freeze or refrigerate. Cut slices of the butter to go on grilled fish or chicken.*

# Stuffed Deep-fried Olives

They say patience is a virtue. Just as well, for you will need plenty for
these delicious pre-dinner drink snacks. This stuffing is also excellent
in cherry tomatoes or ravioli.

**Preparation and cooking: 1 hour**

**Serves: a crowd at a party**

| |
|---|
| 1kg (2¼ lb) pitted large olives |
| plain flour for coating |
| 2 eggs, lightly beaten |
| breadcrumbs for coating |
| olive oil for frying |

**Stuffing**

| |
|---|
| 225g (8 oz) ricotta cheese, drained |
| 2 large egg yolks |
| 2 tinned anchovies, finely diced |
| 1 clove garlic, crushed to a paste with a little salt |
| ¼ teaspoon cayenne pepper |
| ½ tablespoon chopped mint |
| grated rind of 1 lemon |
| 55g (2 oz) Parmesan, freshly grated |
| 4 tablespoons chopped flat-leaf parsley |
| salt and ground black pepper |

**1**  Prepare the stuffing. Place the ricotta in a crockery or glass bowl,
add the egg yolks, anchovies, garlic, cayenne pepper, mint, lemon rind,
Parmesan and parsley. Season to taste. Mix all the ingredients, then
cover the bowl with aluminium foil and refrigerate until needed.

**2**  Stuff the mixture into the olives using a small piping bag. Roll the
olives in flour, shaking off any excess, then in the beaten egg and
finally in the breadcrumbs so they are well coated.

**3**  Pour olive oil to a depth of 4cm (1½ in) in a heavy saucepan and
heat it to about 180°C/350°F or until a tiny pinch of breadcrumbs
sizzles immediately. Fry the olives, a few at a time, until they are
golden and crisp. Remove from the oil with a slotted spoon, strain
very well on absorbent kitchen paper, and serve immediately.

# Tapenade

A delicious spread for folding into sauces, spreading on *crostini*, stuffing cherry tomatoes and coating meat or fish before grilling.

**Preparation: 30 minutes**
**Makes: about 675g (1½ lb)**

85g (3 oz) capers, drained and rinsed
55g (2 oz) tinned anchovy fillets, drained and diced
2 teaspoons Dijon mustard
12 basil leaves, ripped
175ml (6 fl oz) extra virgin olive oil
450g (1 lb) pitted black olives, marinated in olive oil
1 teaspoon ground black pepper
1 tablespoon aged red wine vinegar
3 tablespoons chopped parsley (optional)
salt and freshly ground black pepper

**1** Combine the ingredients down to and including the vinegar in a food processor and blend until smoothish but allowing some texture to remain.
**2** Fold in the parsley, if using, and season to taste.

• • • • • •

*Add finely chopped*
*green or black olives*
*to a potato gnocchi*
*mix or your favourite*
*bread mix.*

• • • • • •

# ONIONS AND SHALLOT

If you were to ask someone from Britain which vegetable was the most essential, the answer would probably be the potato, but on a world scale the answer would almost certainly be the onion. It appears to be used in every type of cuisine, and I for one can't imagine cooking without onions. When I get a savoury bag on *Ready Steady Cook* without an onion, life suddenly becomes difficult. They are so adaptable and can be eaten raw, pan-fried, roast, braised, stuffed and deep-fried. They are essential in stocks and most soups, and a British favourite is the pickled onion.

The onion, *Allium cepa*, belongs to the lily family – relatives are garlic and leek – and is thought to have originated in Asia. All onions are bulbs which grow underground, singly or in clusters. Onions are available in one form or other throughout the year. The most common variety in Britain is the BROWN ONION which includes British, Polish and Spanish onions. A point to remember is that onions grown in colder regions are much stronger in flavour than those grown in warmer regions. PICKLING are small onions with brown skins. WHITE ONIONS are available occasionally, but you pay more for the 'design' rather than the flavour. I'm a great fan of the RED ONION which is not only attractive but has a milder, sweeter flavour. The SHALLOT plant produces a cluster of small bulbs, which are milder than larger onions; they come in various shapes and colours and are often used in sauces. SPRING ONIONS are immature green onions and are pulled before the bulb has swollen; the French often let the bulbs mature.

The mild Spanish onion is great for baking and stuffing and is less strain on the eyes when peeling – the sulphur compounds are responsible for flavour and tears. English onions are fine for caramelising, for soups, stews and stocks. Spring onions are used with salads or stir-fries and they char-grill well as a substitute for baby leeks. Red onions work well in salads and are lovely when roasted whole with a little olive oil, thyme and garlic.

When buying any of the round onions make sure they are dry and have little or no smell. Wet onions are likely to have been packed before they have dried, and can show signs of mould. Make sure the skins are crisp and crackly without any bruising or green sprouts. Store the onions out of the fridge in a wire basket so that air can circulate freely. Spring onions should be refrigerated. Once an onion has been topped and tailed or peeled it will deteriorate very quickly and start to smell sour.

There are various methods touted about for peeling or chopping onions without tears; here are a few of them. Peel onions under water (possible), but not a great way to *chop* onions, however. Place a lump of bread or a teatowel in your mouth (a distraction maybe, but I'm not so sure). Wear glasses or a pair of swimming goggles.

For quick peeling some chefs make a slit top and bottom and pour over very hot water; this method is quite good with pickling onions or shallots. With large onions, make a skin-deep cut from top to bottom then cut almost completely through the root end and pull away some skin as you pull away the root. To finely chop, cut a peeled onion in half from top to bottom. Place the flat cut side on a board then make very thin cuts lengthways without cutting through the root. Slice the onion three times horizontally without cutting completely through the onion. Then cut downwards crossways into small dice. For onion rings, cut the whole onion crossways into 1cm (½ in) slices. For crescents, cut the onion in half lengthways into thin slices.

## Spring Onion Half-moon Cakes

*Instead of wasting spring onion tops, chop them up and **wilt** in a little peanut oil.*
● *Mix together 175g (6 oz) plain flour with 100ml (3½ fl oz) boiling water. Beat in 1 egg, mix until smooth, and rest for 30 minutes. Knead this dough on a floured surface for 10 minutes until smooth and elastic. Roll the dough into a tube and cut into 6 pieces. Roll each of the six pieces into a 10cm (4 in) circle. Sprinkle with the spring onion, a little rock salt and some sesame oil.*
● *Fold over and fry these half-moon cakes in hot oil until golden brown, turning once.*

# Shallot *Tarte Tatin* Ⓥ

The Belgian Chicory Board asked me to create a chicory recipe – which I did – but it also works well with shallots. The combination of the sweetness of the sugar and the shallots is delicious.

**Preparation and cooking: 40 minutes**
**Serves: 4**

36 shallots

12 garlic cloves

115g (4 oz) unsalted butter

stock to cover

1 packet shop-bought, ready-rolled puff pastry

55g (2 oz) caster sugar

1½ tablespoons balsamic vinegar

salt and ground black pepper

**1** Pan-fry the shallots and garlic cloves in 55g (2 oz) of the butter until golden all over, then add the stock and simmer until the shallots are tender but still whole. Drain the shallots and garlic and allow to cool.

**2** Cut the pastry into a 25cm (10 in) circle. Preheat the oven to 190°C/375°F/Gas 5.

**3** Spread the remaining butter over the base of a 23cm (9 in) ovenproof frying pan (non-stick by preference). Sprinkle with the sugar. Place the pan over a medium heat and allow the sugar and butter to start to caramelise. Place the shallots and garlic carefully in the bottom of the pan and sprinkle with balsamic vinegar, salt and ground black pepper. Top with the pastry, pushing the edges of the circle down the inside of the pan.

**4** Bake in the preheated oven for about 25–30 minutes, or until the pastry is golden, risen and thoroughly cooked.

**5** Place a tart plate over the *tarte tatin* and invert carefully, remembering hot butter and sugar can cause a nasty burn. Serve with a leaf salad.

# Onion Marmalade

Great with cheese or cold meats. Dab a little on a raw chicken breast or steak before grilling. Spread a little on *crostini* before topping with other ingredients. Add to cooked potatoes when making bubble and squeak, or spread on thin sheets of puff pastry or on a pizza base before adding other toppings.

**Preparation and cooking: 2¼ hours**
**Makes: 1 litre (1¾ pints)**

115g (4 oz) unsalted butter

1 tablespoon olive oil

1.5kg (3 lb 5 oz) brown onions, thinly sliced

1 teaspoon rock salt

1 bay leaf

1 teaspoon soft thyme leaves

½ teaspoon ground black pepper

115g (4 oz) caster sugar

2 tablespoons dry sherry

2 tablespoons aged red wine vinegar

375ml (13 fl oz) red wine

1 tablespoon clear honey

115g (4 oz) pitted prunes, chopped

**1** Melt the butter in a heavy-based saucepan over a medium heat. Stir in the olive oil, onion, salt, bay leaf, thyme and pepper. Reduce the heat and cook, covered, for 35 minutes, stirring from time to time.

**2** Remove the lid and add the remaining ingredients. Cook over a very low heat until very dark in colour, about 1¾ hours. Keep a look out for burning towards the end of cooking. Stir regularly.

**3** Cool and store in sterilised glass jars, refrigerated. This will keep for 2 months.

• • • • • • • • • • • • •

*When making a brown chicken or veal stock, leave on the onion skins for extra colour. Also cut the onions in half and brown the cut sides in a pan. This will add extra flavour and colour to the stock.*

• • • • • • • • • • • • •

# Sweet Brown Pickled Onions

The best onion-pickling recipe I have tried, especially if you like your onions a little sweet.

**Preparation and cooking: 30 minutes + overnight**
**Makes: 4 litres (6½ pints)**

2.25kg (5 lb) pickling onions, peeled

115g (4 oz) salt

450g (1 lb) soft brown sugar

450g (1 lb) golden syrup

1 dessertspoon cloves

2 tablespoons black peppercorns

3 red chillies, quartered

pinch of mustard seeds

½ cinnamon stick

2 bay leaves

2 sprigs thyme

6 slices fresh ginger

3 garlic cloves

1.2 litres (2 pints) malt vinegar

**1** Mix the onions with the salt and leave overnight.

**2** At the same time, in a **non-reactive** saucepan combine the brown sugar, syrup, cloves, peppercorns, chillies, mustard seeds, cinnamon, bay leaves, thyme, ginger, garlic and malt vinegar. Bring to the boil, remove from the heat and leave to cool overnight.

**3** The next day, drain and dry the onions and pack into sterilised storage jars. Boil the pickling liquor and pour it over the onions, evenly distributing the herbs and spices. Seal the jars and store for 2 weeks before eating.

• • • • • • • • • • • • • • • • • • • • • • • • •

*This is an excellent glaze for roasting or pan-frying onions. Combine 25g (1 oz) unsalted butter with 50ml (2 fl oz) clear honey, 2 teaspoons Dijon mustard and 1 tablespoon red wine vinegar. Mix to a smooth paste then fold in ¼ teaspoon cayenne pepper, a pinch of nutmeg, ¼ teaspoon salt and ½ teaspoon ground black pepper. Pour over onions when roasting or frying.*

• • • • • • • • • • • • • • • • • • • • • • • • •

# Baked Onion Soup with Gruyère Cheese and Madeira (V)

One of the nicest old-fashioned soups, perfect for that wet, cold, miserable day.

**Preparation and cooking: 1¾ hours**

**Serves: 6–8**

| |
|---|
| 1.5kg (3 lb 5 oz) brown onions, sliced |
| 85g (3 oz) unsalted butter |
| 1 tablespoon olive oil |
| 1 teaspoon soft thyme leaves |
| 2 bay leaves |
| 1 teaspoon salt |
| 2 teaspoons caster sugar |
| 25g (1 oz) plain flour |
| 1 bottle dry white wine |
| 2 litres (3½ pints) chicken or vegetable stock |
| 175g (6 oz) Gruyère cheese, grated |
| 12 x 2cm (¾ in) slices French bread, toasted on both sides |
| 1 garlic clove |
| 3 egg yolks |
| 150ml (¼ pint) double cream |
| 2 tablespoons brandy |
| 4 tablespoons Madeira |

**1** Place the onion, butter, oil, thyme, bay leaves, salt and sugar in a heavy-based saucepan and cook over a medium heat for 40 minutes, stirring from time to time. The onions should be golden and soft.

**2** Stir in the flour and cook over a low heat for a further 10 minutes. Pour in the wine, stir to combine, and cook for 10 minutes. Add the stock and cook over a medium heat for a further 20 minutes. The soup can be prepared up to this point 48 hours in advance.

**3** Scatter a little cheese – don't use it all – over the bottom of a large ovenproof soup tureen or six to eight individual ovenproof soup bowls on a baking sheet. Pour in the soup. Rub the toasted French bread with the raw garlic and float over the soup. Top with the remaining cheese and place in a preheated (190°C/375°F/Gas 5) oven until bubbling and golden brown, about 20 minutes from hot (40 minutes from cold).

**4** Beat together the egg yolks, cream, brandy and Madeira. When the soup is ready to serve, lift the cheesy crust and pour into the soup, or serve in a jug and offer separately to your guests.

## Roast Red Onions

*Red onions are delicious roasted.*

● *Remove the outer layer of skin, rub the onions with olive oil, rock salt and pepper and roast in a 190°C/375°F/Gas 5 oven for 1¼ hours with some whole unpeeled garlic cloves and sprigs of thyme.*

● *Remove the onions when tender, and keep warm.*

● *Add 50ml (2 fl oz) water to the roasting tray and stir to loosen the baked onion juices. Add 2 tablespoons balsamic vinegar, and stir to combine.*

● *Cut the onions in half, sprinkle with the balsamic/onion juices and allow this to sink into the onion layers.*

● *Serve hot or at room temperature.*

## Deep-fried Onion Rings

*There can't be many people who don't fancy the occasional serving of deep-fried onion rings.*

● *Cut peeled onions in 5mm (¼ in) slices and separate into rings.*

● *Soak the rings in 600ml (1 pint) buttermilk mixed with ½ teaspoon cayenne pepper for 1 hour.*

● *In another bowl mix together 225g (8 oz) plain flour, 1 teaspoon celery salt, ¼ teaspoon garlic powder and 1 teaspoon paprika.*

● *Drain the onion rings and drop them in the seasoned flour.*

● *Remove and deep-fry a few rings at a time in hot oil until golden and crisp.*

● *Season and serve immediately.*

## Quick Onion Sauce

*Serve with boiled duck or mutton.*

● *Boil 1 chopped onion in salted water for 5 minutes.*

● *Drain and place in a saucepan with 55g (2 oz) unsalted butter, 1 bay leaf and 2 cloves.*

● *Cook over a low heat until the onion has softened without colour, then add 300ml (½ pint) Béchamel Sauce (see page 60) and 5 tablespoons double cream.*

● *Season to taste and serve as is or liquidise for a smooth sauce.*

# PARSNIP

The parsnip (*Pastinaca sativa*) originated in eastern Europe and is a root vegetable related to carrot, celery and celeriac, and the umbellifer herbs, fennel, parsley and chervil. Wild parsnips are lethal and not even weed-eating animals can be tempted. Cultivated parsnips are now grown in temperate climates all over the world, but they don't appear to be popular with the so-called kings of cookery, the French, who prefer to feed them to their animals. Likewise the Italians, who still feed their ham pigs on parsnips. However, we in Britain still enjoy a roast parsnip, but it's the Americans who have really taken them to their hearts, using them in everything from bread to cakes and puddings.

When growing parsnips, don't become too frustrated, as they take a long time to germinate, and then even longer to grow, some six months or more to maturity. But they have their compensations, as they are hardy enough to winter under the ground. Parsnips are usually best after Christmas when they have matured and their starches have turned to sugars, making them caramelise deliciously when roasted.

Choose evenly sized parsnips free of nicks and spidery roots. Generally, if you are supermarket shopping, the parsnips will be clean and pretty perfect, but it's often nice to go into a greengrocer and buy some still with the earth clinging; somehow they seem to taste better.

There are two schools of thought on cooking parsnips – the choice is yours. One school advocates peeling before cooking, the other not. I'm a peeling-before man for no particular reason other than that's the way I've always done it. Cut off the tip of the tapering root and a 1cm (½ in) slice off the top, and peel as thinly as possible. Depending on the size, cut lengthways into halves or quarters. If they are large and woody, cut out the central core.

For boiled puréed parsnips, after halving or quartering, cut into 2.5cm (1 in) chunks, and **sweat** in butter with some soft thyme leaves for 5 minutes before adding vegetable or chicken stock. Cook for a further 5–8 minutes or until tender then pass through a **vegetable mouli** or purée in a food processor. Add a little more butter or some cream to produce a silky purée.

My favourite method of cooking parsnips is roasting. Unlike most root vegetables, parsnips cook quickly so they don't need par-boiling. Leave small ones whole, and halve or quarter larger ones. Add to hot dripping having dipped them in a light dusting of cayenne pepper and caster sugar. Bake for 35–45 minutes.

Deep-fried parsnip crisps were in vogue recently and are delicious. With a potato peeler shave thin slices lengthways and either dry them in a slow oven or leave overnight in a warm kitchen. This removes some of their natural moisture. Then deep-fry the shavings in hot clean fat at 180°C/356°F until golden brown. Drain on kitchen paper and season with salt. Serve hot or cold.

# Parsnip and Citrus Croquettes Ⓥ

A dish that can be served as a vegetable or as a starter with a yogurt dip (see pages 304 and 307).

**Preparation and cooking: 45 minutes**
**Serves: 4–6**

450g (1 lb) parsnips, peeled and quartered
350g (12 oz) potatoes, diced
salt
2 tablespoons soft dark brown sugar
½ teaspoon ground cumin
¼ teaspoon cayenne pepper
1 teaspoon grated orange rind
½ teaspoon grated lemon rind
55g (2 oz) pine kernels, roughly chopped
2 eggs, separated
1 tablespoon chickpea or plain flour
55g (2 oz) wholemeal or white breadcrumbs
55g (2 oz) unsalted butter

1  Cook the parsnip and potato in salted water until tender, about 12–15 minutes. Drain, return to the heat to dry out, then mash.
2  Combine the mash with 1 teaspoon salt, the sugar, cumin, cayenne, citrus rinds, pine kernels and egg yolks. Sift in the chickpea flour. Mix thoroughly, then refrigerate until ready to use.
3  Roll tablespoons of the mixture into cylinder croquette shapes or into patties. Repeat until the mixture is used up.
4  Lightly beat the egg whites and roll the patties or croquettes in this before rolling in the breadcrumbs.
5  Heat the butter in a frying pan and cook the croquettes for 2–3 minutes each side. Fry a few at a time and keep warm while cooking the others.

# Jane Grigson's Curried Parsnip Soup Ⓥ

This is undoubtedly one of the finest vegetable soups I have ever experienced. I have not adapted the recipe in any way because it is perfect as it is.

**Preparation and cooking: 40 minutes**
**Serves: 4**

1 tablespoon coriander seeds
1 teaspoon cumin seeds
½ teaspoon chilli flakes
1 teaspoon ground turmeric
¼ teaspoon ground fenugreek
1 medium onion, finely chopped
1 large garlic clove, halved
1 large parsnip, peeled and chopped
55g (2 oz) unsalted butter
1 tablespoon plain flour
1 litre (1¾ pints) vegetable, chicken or beef stock
150ml (¼ pint) double cream
salt and ground black pepper
1 tablespoon snipped chives

**1** Blend the spices in an electric coffee grinder or crush them with a pestle and mortar. Place the powder in an airtight container as you won't need the full amount for this recipe.
**2** Cook the onion, garlic and parsnip in a saucepan in the butter over a gentle heat, covered, for 10 minutes. Add the flour and 1 tablespoon of the spice mixture and cook for a further 10 minutes, stirring from time to time.
**3** Add the stock, bring to the boil, reduce the heat and cook until the parsnip is tender, about 12–15 minutes. Place the soup in two or three batches in a food processor and blend until smooth.
**4** Return the soup to the saucepan, add the cream and season to taste. Garnish with chives.

## Parsnip and Apple Purée

*Makes a great sauce for roast pork or duck.*
● *Peel and quarter 450g (1 lb) parsnips and cook for 5 minutes, then drain and cut out any woody cores.*
● *Peel, core and dice 450g (1 lb) cooking apples.*
● *Combine the apples with the parsnips, add 225ml (8 fl oz) apple juice, 115g (4 oz) soft dark brown sugar, and cook until the apples and parsnips are tender.*
● *Mash the mixture then fold in ½ teaspoon finely chopped sage, 1 tablespoon grated orange rind and 2 tablespoons Calvados.*
● *Season to taste.*
● *Just before serving fold in 25g (1 oz) unsalted butter.*

## Parsnip Soufflé

*When I was in the USA I enjoyed an amazing parsnip soufflé.*
● *Melt 40g (1½ oz) butter and add 1 finely chopped small onion and ¼ teaspoon chopped soft thyme leaves.*
● *Gently cook until the onion is soft but not coloured.*
● *Add 40g (1½ oz) plain flour and cook for 5 minutes, then gradually whisk in 300ml (½ pint) milk until thick and boiling.*
● *Allow the mixture to cool slightly then add 4 egg yolks with ¼ teaspoon ground black pepper and 4 tablespoons dark rum.*
● *Stir in 350g (12 oz) puréed parsnips and 1 teaspoon each of grated orange rind and lemon rind.*
● *Whip 6 egg whites to **soft peaks**.*
● *Carefully mix a quarter of the whites into the parsnip mix, then fold in the remainder.*
● *Spoon the mixture into a buttered 1.7 litre (3 pint) soufflé dish, and bake in a 190°C/375°F/Gas 5 oven for about 30 minutes until risen and golden.*
● *Serve immediately.*

*Fry quartered parsnips in butter and fold in Dijon mustard, honey and a little bourbon for a sweet and sour vegetable to accompany roast meats.*

*Cook quartered parsnips for 5–8 minutes, drain and cut in 5mm (¼ in) slices. Pan-fry the slices in butter until light golden. Add some brown sugar and continue to cook until tender and dark golden. Add a dash of red wine vinegar, season and sprinkle with parsley. Great with roast or grilled meat.*

# PEAS, FRESH AND DRIED

The pea (*Pisum sativum*) has been around for thousands of years, one of the oldest of domesticated plants, but was eaten only in its dried form; it was not until the sixteenth century that some bright Italian decided to grow them to eat fresh, green and immature. Before that time, some peas grew to be as large as marbles and were roasted like chestnuts.

Fresh peas almost disappeared in the late 1950s and 1960s as in Britain we were presented with freeze-dried 'Surprise' peas and then frozen peas. These were a revelation in my household, along with Smash, powdered potato, convenience at its worst. But at the time, both products seem to have been enjoyed by all. After that I became hooked on the frozen baby peas which undoubtedly destroyed our fresh pea industry. It wasn't until recently, when I became a vegetable gardener, that I discovered the beauty of young fresh peas cooked in their immature pods.

In the late 1970s and 1980s the markets were inundated with the mangetout or snow pea, and to be honest I wouldn't be upset if I never saw one again. Much more to my taste is the sugar-snap pea which is a fully formed edible pod with an internal pea that is smaller than the green garden pea. (Mangetout, snow peas and sugar-snap peas lack the inedible inner skin to their pods, thus they can be eaten pods and all.) A delicious by-product recently available, at least to restaurants, is pea shoots, which the Chinese have used for many years; these are the growing tendril tips of the plant. In the last couple of years we have also seen fresh podded peas in supermarkets, which are okay, if a little expensive. On a nutritional basis, though, they are less beneficial than frozen as the sugars in peas turn to starch very quickly after picking. Frozen food manufacturers have the benefit of getting peas from pod to freezer in double-quick time, hence the sweetness of frozen peas.

When buying peas in the pod look for bright green and waxy pods with no tell-tale bulges to show over-maturity. 500g (18 oz) will serve two people once podded.

Dried peas are available in green or yellow and are usually split. They make good purées or soups. Tinned peas are not an acceptable alternative unless you buy one of the French *petits pois* varieties which have a very moreish sweet taste.

## Sweet Pea *Guacamole*

An interesting dish I produced on *Ready Steady Cook* when confronted with a bag of frozen peas. Rather good, even if I say so myself.

**Preparation and cooking: 20 minutes**
**Serves: 4**

3 tablespoons extra virgin olive oil
2 tablespoons fresh lime juice
2 tablespoons coriander leaves
2 hot chillies, diced
500g (18 oz) cooked frozen peas, drained
½ teaspoon ground cumin
½ teaspoon ground coriander
1 teaspoon salt
½ teaspoon ground black pepper
2 plum tomatoes, seeded and diced
½ red onion, finely diced
4 tablespoons soured cream (optional)

1 In a food processor combine the oil, lime juice, coriander leaves and chilli, and blend until reasonably smooth. Add the peas, spices, salt and pepper, and blend until smooth. (There may be a few lumps.)
2 Tip the mixture into a bowl and fold in the tomato and onion. Check the seasoning and adjust if necessary. For a variation fold in soured cream. Serve as a dip or accompaniment to a bowl of *chilli con carne* (see page 193 for *my* version).

## Petits Pois à la Française

The French do nice olive-coloured peas called petits pois à la française.
● **Sweat** 1 chopped round lettuce with 6 chopped spring onions in 55g (2 oz) unsalted butter until the onions have softened.
● Add 450g (1 lb) shelled baby peas, 2 tablespoons chopped parsley, 1 tablespoon snipped chives and 4 tablespoons water, cover with a lid and stew gently for 25 minutes.
● When finished, the dish should be saucy but not too wet.
● Season with salt, pepper and a pinch of sugar if required.

# Chilled Pea Soup

A very easy, very pleasant cooling soup for a warm summer's day.
**Preparation and cooking: 30–40 minutes + cooling**
**Serves: 4**

55g (2 oz) smoked streaky bacon, diced

5 spring onions, finely chopped

2 cloves garlic, crushed with a little salt

1 small round lettuce, sliced

1 stick celery, finely sliced

1 tablespoon chopped mint

½ teaspoon finely chopped rosemary leaves

½ teaspoon caster sugar

600ml (1 pint) chicken stock

500g (18 oz) sugar-snap peas, topped and tailed

150ml (¼ pint) soured or single cream

salt and ground black pepper

1 handful pea shoots (optional)

**1** Cook the bacon in a saucepan over a low heat to release the fats, about 8 minutes. Add the spring onion, garlic, lettuce and celery and cook until the vegetables have softened without colour, about 10 minutes.

**2** Add the mint, rosemary, sugar and stock and bring to the boil. Simmer for 10 minutes, then add the sugar-snaps and cook for 5 minutes.

**3** Liquidise the soup in batches, and pass through a fine sieve. Fold in the cream and whisk to combine. Season to taste.

**4** Allow to cool, then refrigerate. Skim off any fat that rises to the surface. Garnish with pea shoots, if using.

## Sorrel and Pea Soup
*Sorrel and peas are natural partners.*
- *Fry 2 finely chopped onions in 55g (2 oz) unsalted butter until soft but without colour.*
- *Add 1 large diced potato and a handful of shredded sorrel and fry until the potatoes start to stick to the bottom of the pan.*
- *Add 1 litre (1¾ pints) vegetable stock and cook until the potatoes are almost tender.*
- *Add 450g (1 lb) peas and simmer for 10 minutes.*
- *Liquidise, season and add 100ml (3½ fl oz) double cream.*

# Pea and Ham Soup

A classic soup made with dried split peas that warms places other soups cannot reach, almost a meal in itself.
**Preparation and cooking: 2¼ hours**
**Serves: 8**

55g (2 oz) unsalted butter

4 rashers smoked streaky bacon, diced

1 large onion, finely chopped

1 carrot, finely diced

½ teaspoon soft thyme leaves

1 clove garlic, finely chopped

1 bay leaf

450g (1 lb) green split peas, rinsed

2.5 litres (4½ pints) chicken stock

1 ham knuckle or hock

1 tablespoon Worcestershire sauce

ground black pepper

**1** Melt the butter in a large saucepan, add the bacon and cook until the bacon becomes golden. Add the onion, carrot, thyme, garlic and bay leaf, and cook over a medium heat until the onion has softened without colour.

**2** Add the split peas and stir to combine, then add the stock and ham knuckle and bring to the boil. Simmer for 1½–2 hours, skimming from time to time, until the peas are tender.

**3** Remove the ham knuckle and purée the soup. Return the soup to the heat, and season with Worcestershire sauce and pepper. Remove the meat from the ham hock, chop it, and return it to the soup. Serve piping hot with warm crusty bread.

*Combine barely cooked cold peas with chopped spring onions, chopped fresh mint, a little Dijon mustard, some mayonnaise, soured cream, some pea shoots and chopped roasted red pepper (see page 254). Serve as a salad with slices of Parma ham.*

# Fettuccine with Peas, Spring Onions and Mint

Fresh bright colours, fresh clear taste, spring meets pasta.

**Preparation and cooking: 20 minutes**

**Serves: 4 as a starter**

| |
|---|
| 85g (3 oz) unsalted butter |
| 6 spring onions, cut into rings |
| salt and ground black pepper |
| 225g (8 oz) shelled fresh peas |
| 3 tablespoons chopped mint |
| 2 tablespoons Dry Martini |
| pinch of saffron stamens, soaked in 1 tablespoon warm water |
| 350g (12 oz) fresh fettuccine |
| 1 handful sorrel leaves, shredded |
| 55g (2 oz) Parmesan, freshly grated |

**1** Heat 55g (2 oz) of the butter in a saucepan, add the spring onion and a pinch of salt, and cook over a medium heat for 3 minutes. Add the peas and 125ml (4 fl oz) water and cook for 8 minutes or until the peas are tender. Fold in the mint and Martini, and cook for 2 minutes.

**2** Heat a serving bowl for the pasta and add to it the saffron and its water with the remaining butter.

**3** Meanwhile, cook the fettuccine in boiling salted water for 2–3 minutes or until **al dente**. Drain and add to the saffron butter, tossing to combine.

**4** Fold the sorrel into the pasta and allow the heat of the pasta to **wilt** it. Pour over the peas and toss to combine. Season to taste, then sprinkle with Parmesan. Serve immediately.

* * * * * * * * * *

*Combine raw peas and raw baby broad beans with olive oil, lemon juice, chopped anchovy and freshly grated Parmesan for a fresh salad.*

* * * * * * * * * *

* * * * * * * * * *

*__Sweat__ some onions in butter, add peas, honey, a little chicken or vegetable stock and cook until the peas are tender and the liquid has almost evaporated. Add a few dashes of Nando's peri-peri sauce and some chopped pickled walnuts. Serve with roast or grilled meats.*

* * * * * * * * * *

• • • • • • • • • • • • • • • • • • • • • • • • • • • • • • • • • • • • • • • •

# One-eyed Bouillabaisse with Peas

Jane Grigson's Vegetable Book *has this wonderfully named recipe.*

● *Heat 6 tablespoons olive oil in a large saucepan with 4 chopped spring onions and 1 chopped onion.*

● *Cook until lightly golden then add 2 chopped skinned tomatoes, 4 chopped cloves garlic, 1 sprig herb fennel, 1 strip dried orange rind, a pinch of saffron stamens and 6 sliced new potatoes.*

● *Add 2 litres (3½ pints) boiling vegetable stock.*

● *Cook over a high heat until the potatoes are tender, about 8 minutes, then add 450g (1 lb) shelled peas and cook for 6 minutes.*

● *Break an egg for every person into the soup, poach for 3 minutes, then season.*

● *Serve soup, vegetables and egg in individual bowls, along with wedges of grilled garlic-rubbed bread.*

• • • • • • • • • • • • • • • • • • • • • • • • • • • • • • • • • • • • • • • •

# PEPPERS AND CHILLIES

The sweet pepper and the chilli pepper are both of the genus *Capsicum* (the family Solanaceae, therefore related to the potato, tomato and aubergine). All sweet peppers and most chilli peppers are cultivars of *Capsicum annuum*; the potent bird chilli – the basis of Tabasco sauce and cayenne pepper – is *Capsicum frutescens*. Peppers were introduced to Europe by Columbus who discovered them in the New World. Spain hogged this discovery for a few generations before the pepper spread to Italy, Hungary, Africa and Asia (where, of course, chilli is now a principal seasoning spice). The British weren't particularly interested until Elizabeth David revealed all in her wonderful Mediterranean book, published in 1950. Now peppers are so common as to have become a bit clichéd. The Dutch produce the majority of the peppers we eat, perfect in shape and size, and in a myriad of colours – green, yellow, orange, red, purple and black. But perfection is only skin deep, as Dutch hothouse peppers lack the flavour of sun-drenched Spanish and Italian varieties. I love craggy, unevenly shaped peppers with the occasional bodily flaw as I know they will have a miraculous flavour. You can occasionally find large 'paprika' sweet peppers, another *C. annuum* cultivar; these are dried and ground for the Hungarian paprika and Spanish *pimentón*.

In the UK, our names for peppers are confusing. We call them all peppers but we also call the seed spice, pepper. We used to call them *pimento* or *pimiento* from the Spanish. The Americans and Australians call them bell peppers and sweet peppers respectively. The French call them *piments doux* or *poivrons*; their chillies are *piments*. We'll have to be content with the colouring adjective of red, green and yellow.

Chillies are becoming more common in the UK, but we don't respect or honour them like the Americans, who can identify over 100 varieties; they also grade them in heat form, from 1 (mild) to 10 (blow-your-head-off-hot). They even have different names for chillies when dried. And there are over 150 different varieties in Mexico alone!

Both sweet and chilli peppers start life as green, when they are unripe, then turn red as they ripen. The red pepper is the sweetest, but no hotter in any way than the green. Chillies come fresh or dried, usually red or green. As a general rule, the smaller they are, the hotter they are. The hottest varieties we get in the UK are the small bird's eye chilli or the ones that look like small sweet peppers, the Scotch bonnet.

When choosing peppers look for the country of origin and, where possible, choose a *hot* country! The peppers should be shiny with tight skins. Look around the stalk for any soft patches that show deterioration. Generally peppers can be kept in the salad drawer of your refrigerator for up to a week. Use chillies fresh, or hang them in an airy place to dry out, when they will become much hotter.

Chillies contain capsaicin, an oily substance, not water soluble, which is the source of the fiery flavour; this is lodged in the seeds and the pale membranes on the inside of the flesh. When preparing chillies, either use surgical gloves or rub your hands first in a thin veil of oil. This will prevent the capsaicin entering the pores of your skin. You must *never* rub your eyes or other sensitive parts of your body after handling chillies. Removing the seeds and membranes renders the chilli a little less hot.

Sweet peppers can be eaten raw or cooked. Personally I'm not a fan of them raw, but I love them roasted or char-grilled. You can do this in many ways. Cut the peppers in quarters, remove stem and seeds, and brush skin side with olive oil. Grill skin side towards the heat until blackened. Do the same by roasting. You can alternatively place a wire grill over an open flame and turn a whole pepper over the flame until blackened. Whichever method you use, pop the charred peppers in a plastic bag or container and seal for 10 minutes so that the peppers 'steam' themselves. This will make them easier to peel. Store the peppers in olive oil until ready to use.

# Thai Green Curry Paste

You can buy very good Thai curry paste in many
supermarkets, but it is never quite the same as making it
yourself.

**Preparation and cooking: 30 minutes**
**Makes: about 375g (13 oz)**

8 shallots, roughly chopped

6 cloves garlic, roughly chopped

3 tablespoons chopped lemongrass, inside tender part only

6 large mild green chillies, roughly chopped

15 small hot green chillies, roughly chopped

6 tablespoons chopped coriander stalks and roots

1 tablespoon chopped fresh galangal

1 tablespoon ground coriander

1½ teaspoons ground cumin

½ teaspoon grated nutmeg

½ teaspoon mace

1½ teaspoons ground white pepper

1 teaspoon grated lime zest

2 teaspoons chopped lime leaves

3 teaspoons shrimp paste (*blachan*)

3 teaspoons Maldon salt flakes

3 tablespoons chopped coriander leaves

**1** If you have the time, grind everything together in a mortar
and pestle. Failing that, blend everything together in a food
processor, scraping the mixture down regularly to make a
smooth paste.

**2** This paste keeps well in a sealed jar in the refrigerator.

# Roast Red Pepper Soup   Ⓥ

A lovely intense soup which always seems popular when I put
it on the menu at Woz, my London restaurant.

**Preparation and cooking: 40 minutes**
**Serves: 6–8**

50ml (2 fl oz) extra virgin olive oil

2 onions, finely chopped

1 tablespoon fennel seeds

½ teaspoon soft thyme leaves

1 bay leaf

3 cloves garlic, finely chopped

3 green chillies, finely diced

6 roasted red peppers, skinned, seeded and sliced

225g (8 oz) plum tomatoes, skinned, seeded and diced

1 tablespoon tomato purée

1.5 litres (2¾ pints) vegetable or chicken stock

300ml (½ pint) double cream

2 tablespoons ripped basil leaves

salt and ground black pepper

**1** Heat the olive oil in a saucepan, add the onion, fennel
seeds, thyme, bay leaf, garlic and chilli, and cook over a
medium heat until the onion softens without colour, about 10
minutes.

**2** Add the roast peppers and any of their roasting juices,
along with the tomato, tomato purée and stock. Simmer for 15
minutes.

**3** Liquidise the soup in batches and pass through a fine sieve.
Return to the heat and fold in the double cream and basil.
Warm through and season to taste.

## Red Pepper Sauce

*A simple light, thin and pure sauce.*
● *Juice 1kg (2¼ lb) seeded sweet red peppers in a
centrifugal juicer.*
● *Heat the pepper juice in a* **non-reactive** *saucepan
with salt, pepper and 100ml (3½ fl oz) extra virgin
olive oil.*
● *Boil to emulsify, then serve with grilled fish or
chicken.*

*Pan-fry feta or haloumi cheese
in olive oil with some dried
oregano and serve, seasoned to
taste, with slices of grilled or
roasted peppers and fresh basil
leaves. A pleasant starter.*

# Penne with Red Pepper (V) Sauce

An easy sauce for pasta, but you can also serve it with cauliflower, chicken or fish. It can be made ahead, then folded into the cooked pasta.

**Preparation and cooking: 25 minutes**
**Serves: 4 as a starter**

2 cloves garlic, finely chopped
1 onion, finely chopped
1 tablespoon olive oil
2 roasted red peppers, skinned, seeded and chopped
300ml (½ pint) double cream
115g (4 oz) unsalted butter
2 tablespoons tomato purée
½ teaspoon chopped sage
1 teaspoon paprika
225g (8 oz) penne
55g (2 oz) Parmesan, freshly grated
salt and ground black pepper

**1** Cook the garlic and onion in the olive oil over a medium heat until soft but not coloured, about 10 minutes.
**2** Place this mix with the peppers in a blender with the cream and purée until smooth.
**3** Melt the butter in a saucepan over a medium heat. Whisk in the tomato purée, sage, paprika and the pepper purée, and cook for 8 minutes.
**4** Meanwhile, cook the penne in boiling salted water until **al dente**, between 4 and 12 minutes, depending on whether fresh or dried.
**5** Fold the pasta into the sauce and add the Parmesan. Season to taste, and serve.

*Add 115g (4 oz) hot red chillies to 1.2 litres (2 pints) dry sherry and infuse for a couple of weeks before using – add a dash to soups, stews or a Bloody Mary (see page 298).*

# Roasted *Peperonata*

A great salad from Apulia in southern Italy, which can be served as part of an *antipasti* selection. I'm not keen on pepper skins, so I've slightly adapted this classic dish.

**Preparation and cooking: about 1 hour**
**Serves: 4–6**

3 onions, sliced
2 tablespoons extra virgin olive oil
4 cloves garlic, finely chopped
3 roasted red peppers, skinned, seeded and sliced
3 roasted yellow peppers, skinned, seeded and sliced
3 plum tomatoes, skinned, seeded and diced
4 anchovy fillets, diced
1 hot fresh chilli, finely diced
25g (1 oz) baby capers, rinsed
6 basil leaves, ripped
3 tablespoons chopped flat-leaf parsley
1 tablespoon balsamic vinegar
salt and ground black pepper

**1** In a large frying pan cook the onion in the olive oil with the garlic until the onion has softened without colour, about 8–10 minutes.
**2** Add the pepper slices, tomato, anchovy, chilli and capers and cook for a further 10 minutes. Fold in the basil, parsley and balsamic vinegar, then season to taste. Serve hot or at room temperature.

## Chilli Mayonnaise
● *Pound together 2 chopped, seeded green or red chillies with 2 cloves garlic until smooth. Stir in an egg yolk, then add 175ml (6 fl oz) groundnut oil gradually until the mayonnaise emulsifies and is thick.*
● *Stir in 1 tablespoon lime juice and season to taste.*

# Sweet Chilli *Compote*

The trendy definitions would be either 'jam' or 'marmalade', but I personally would hesitate to put this on toast! It's a great complement to grilled foods – squid, say – and can be folded into sauces or mashed potato.

**Preparation and cooking: 1½ hours**
**Makes: 600ml (1 pint)**

6 small red chillies

4 red peppers, roughly chopped

4 cloves garlic, crushed

1 tablespoon grated fresh ginger

2 shallots, roughly chopped

2 tablespoons *nam pla* (fish sauce)

1 x 400g (14 oz) tin chopped tomatoes with juice

225g (8 oz) soft dark brown sugar

100ml (3½ fl oz) sherry vinegar

**1** Place the chilli, pepper, garlic, ginger, shallot, fish sauce and tomato in a food processor and blend until smooth.

**2** Put the purée with the sugar and vinegar in a **non-reactive** saucepan and bring to the boil, stirring from time to time. Reduce heat and simmer for 40–60 minutes until thick. Stir regularly, especially in the latter stages of cooking.

**3** If you prefer, strain through a fine sieve. Bottle in warm sterilised jars. Allow to cool, then refrigerate. Will keep for 2 weeks.

· · · · · · · · · · · ·

*Make a roasted pepper pasta salad. Cook penne or pasta shells until **al dente** and combine with red onion, extra virgin olive oil, lots of roasted pepper dice or strips, paprika, puréed garlic, chopped tomatoes, soured cream and Tabasco.*

· · · · · · · · · · · ·

# Hot, Hot, Hot Chilli Oil

A fiery, pungent oil that can be added to a myriad of dishes. The 'gloop' that settles at the bottom can be added to sauces, soups and marinades.

**Preparation and cooking: 1 hour**
**Makes: 1 litre (1¾ pints)**

85g (3 oz) dried hot red chilli flakes

85g (3 oz) unrinsed fermented black beans, finely chopped

½ teaspoon onion powder

6 cloves garlic, crushed to a paste

2 tablespoons finely chopped ginger

2 teaspoons sesame seeds

850ml (1½ pints) groundnut oil

**1** Combine all the ingredients in a heavy-based saucepan. Over a lowish heat, bring to the boil and simmer for 15 minutes, stirring occasionally. Remove from the heat and allow to cool.

**2** Pour the oil and 'gloop' into sterilised jars. Store in a dark place. This oil will keep for a couple of months.

· · · · · · · · · · · · · · · · · · · · · · · · · ·

# Green Chilli *Salsa*

*If you like something with a kick, then try this.*
● *Roast 450g (1 lb) green chillies, pass through a **mouli** or fine sieve and fold together with 225g (8 oz) chopped plum tomatoes, 1 diced red onion, 3 chopped garlic cloves and ¼ teaspoon ground cumin.*

· · · · · · · · · · · · · · · · · · · · · · · · · ·

# *Harissa* Ⓥ

You can buy *harissa*, a Tunisian chilli paste, in speciality shops, but it is not yet widely available. If you make it yourself, it will keep for several months. Add a dollop to soups, serve with a vegetable or meat couscous, or fold into salads for a great flavour kick.

**Preparation and cooking: 30 minutes**
**Makes: 300ml (½ pint)**

225g (8 oz) fresh hot red chillies, chopped

8 garlic cloves, chopped

½ tablespoon ground coriander

1 tablespoon ground caraway

2 tablespoons chopped mint

1 tablespoon chopped chives

2 tablespoons chopped coriander

½ tablespoon rock salt

1 tablespoon tomato purée

1 teaspoon caster sugar

2 tablespoons extra virgin olive oil

**1** Blend all the ingredients in a food processor until smooth. Pass through a fine sieve to remove any lurking chilli seeds.
**2** Pot in sterilised glass jars and dribble some extra olive oil over the surface to create an airtight seal. Refrigerate.

## *Zhug*

This is a Yemeni condiment used for soups, stews, pasta or splashing on a grilled piece of meat. Great mixed into yogurt for a hot dip.
● Place 14 fresh green chillies in a food processor with 1 teaspoon sea salt, 12 garlic cloves, 1 teaspoon ground caraway, 1 teaspoon ground cumin, 1 teaspoon ground cardamom, 5 tablespoons chopped coriander, 1 teaspoon ground black pepper and 1 tablespoon fresh lime juice. Blend until smooth.
● Pack in jars, and it will keep 2 weeks in a refrigerator (you can also freeze it).

## *Ajuar*

A great relish from eastern Europe.
● Roast and peel 2 red peppers and 1 aubergine.
● Chop the flesh and place in a frying pan with 3 hot chopped chillies, 3 cloves garlic mashed with a little salt, 4 tablespoons each of olive oil and balsamic vinegar, ¼ teaspoon sea salt and ¼ teaspoon cayenne pepper.
● Cook gently for 30 minutes, or until very thick like a chutney.
● Cool and store, refrigerated in sterilised glass jars.

*Take large fresh green chillies, remove the stems and seeds, and place 1 anchovy fillet with 2 slices garlic in each chilli. Place the chillies in sterilised jars, add 1 teaspoon dried oregano and 2 bay leaves to each jar, and top up with extra virgin olive oil. Seal and place the jars in a refrigerator for 4–6 weeks before serving with buffalo mozzarella or as part of a Mediterranean buffet.*

*A great red pepper and sun-dried tomato paste is made by puréeing 2 roasted peppers, 10 oil-packed sun-dried tomatoes, 150ml (¼ pint) extra virgin olive oil and 2 teaspoons Harissa (see above). Delicious on crostini or folded into a vinaigrette.*

# PORK

I am a keeper of pigs but, being a bit of a softie, the day has not yet arrived when any of them has reached the table. (That day must come, of course, or I will be overrun with piglets!) In the war years it was common practice for a family to have a pig; born in the spring and killed in the winter, it helped supplement our meagre rations. Pigs were more popular than other animals – and were more useful – as they produce more edible meat in relation to feed costs than other animals: most pigs could be fed on household scraps (or beech mast or acorns).

The French have always worked wonders with their pigs, and nothing is wasted: blood, intestines, ears, snout, tail and trotter all have a part to play in the French kitchen. They even have speciality pork butchers, *charcutiers*. On farms in many parts of France they hold a *fête du cochon*, a Sunday extravaganza following the slaughtering of a pig. Every dish in the meal, apart from pud, contains some bit of the pig, from a *terrine* to a sausage, a soup or salad, a casserole or *ragoût* and a roast or grill. And of course the French, Italians and Spanish produce wonderful hams, from the legs of plump, naturally fed, specially reared pigs.

If you can, avoid intensively reared pigs, as their living and feeding conditions are horrendous. Go for free-range, runabout pigs that will have a magic flavour (and will have had a happy life).

From head to tail therefore, here are the edible bits of a pig. The head gives us brains, tongue, throat, jowl, ear, lips and snout, all great for salting and using in head cheese or brawn. Hocks, trotters, shanks, tails and ears all lend themselves to being poached, spread with mustard and breadcrumbs, and grilled until crisp. Inside the pig lie the heart, liver and kidneys, the bladder, the stomach or tripe and intestines. Moving quickly on, we have the shoulder which provides roasting and braising joints, meat for stewing, mincing and sausages. The loin is the most expensive cut, providing us with chops, loin roast, fillet and, in its salted form, back bacon. The belly provides belly chops, streaky bacon, spare ribs and meat for terrines. Then lastly the leg which provides the best roasting joints, whole hams after curing, and cubes of pork for kebabs.

The colour of pork varies from pale pink to pale red according to the pig's age and the cut of meat. Look for meat that has very white fat and flesh that appears dry. You probably won't be able to find out, but where possible buy pork meat from sow rather than boar. Trim away some of the fat from the pork before cooking. Use the fat to make dripping by rendering, or mince it and freeze it, adding it to stews, stuffings or terrines. Pork needs to be cooked until its juices run clear.

## ROASTING

Marinate, stuff or leave the joint as it is. Brown the meat all over before roasting it at 200°C/400°F/Gas 6 for 20 minutes, then reducing the heat to 180°C/350°F/Gas 4 for the remainder of the cooking time (20–25 minutes per 500g/18 oz). If you like crackling, score the rind in thin strips, pour boiling water over the rind three times, then baste with cider vinegar. Leave uncovered in the fridge overnight. The next day rub the rind with coarse salt and olive oil, then roast in the normal way.

## GRILLING

Brush each side with oil or melted butter. Season just before cooking. A normal chop should take 5–7 minutes per side.

If you are cooking pork chops with the rind, score it to prevent the chop from curling.

## STIR-FRYING

Follow the rules on **velveting**, then fry in hot oil for 1 minute. Remove the meat, add the remaining stir-fry ingredients and cook, then fold the meat back in to warm through.

## BRAISING or STEWING

Braising uses larger cuts of meat, and stews use diced meat. Both require the meat to be browned in oil or butter first, then cooked very slowly with vegetables, liquid and aromatics until very tender.

# Poached Pork Shoulder

This is one of my really useful meat recipes because, although it eats well as it is with mashed potato or a bowl of lentils, it also provides a stand-by for soups, salads and stews.

**Preparation and cooking: 3½ hours**

**Serves: 4**

1 large onion, thinly sliced

1 carrot, sliced

1 pork shoulder joint, boneless (1.5kg/3 lb 5 oz)

1 bottle dry white wine

1 litre (1¾ pints) chicken stock

1 teaspoon sea salt

2 teaspoons chopped fresh ginger

1 teaspoon black peppercorns

4 dried chillies

1 clove

1 tablespoon clear honey

1 star anise

1 head garlic, cut into two horizontally

2 teaspoons coriander seeds

1 teaspoon cumin seeds

2 bay leaves

2 sticks celery, sliced

2 tablespoons chopped coriander

**1** Place the onion and carrot in a large saucepan. Put the pork on top of this vegetable bed, and add all the remaining ingredients.

**2** Bring to the boil over a medium heat, then reduce the heat, cover and simmer for 3 hours, skimming from time to time. Halfway through cooking, turn the pork over.

**3** As the pork cooks, the liquid will **reduce**, exposing the pork, so in the last hour of cooking baste the pork every 10 minutes with the stock.

**4** Serve the pork hot with a pulse or potatoes, and some good strong mustard. If serving the pork cold, allow the meat to cool in the liquor. After removing the meat strain the stock and remove any fat. The stock is a good base for sauces or soups and can be frozen.

# Oriental Pork Salad

This recipe uses the *Poached Pork Shoulder*, and here has a remarkable flavour, similar to duck at a fraction of the cost. The salad contains lots of fresh clean flavours.

**Preparation and cooking: 30 minutes**

**Serves: 6 as a starter**

450g (1 lb) *Poached Pork Shoulder*, cut in thin strips

18 jumbo cooked prawns, peeled

450g (1 lb) asparagus, **blanched** and cut in 2.5cm (1 in) slices

6 spring onions, cut in 1cm (½ in) pieces on the diagonal

1 celery heart, finely sliced

2 tablespoons roughly chopped coriander

1 tablespoon finely chopped mint

1 tablespoon chopped basil

½ cucumber, halved, seeded and cut into 5mm (¼ in) half moons

1 mild red chilli, thinly sliced

55g (2 oz) broken walnuts

**Dressing**

1 tablespoon Dijon mustard

¼ teaspoon ground white pepper

¼ teaspoon sea salt

50ml (2 fl oz) fresh lime juice

1 tablespoon *nam pla* (fish sauce)

1 tablespoon rice or sherry vinegar

1 teaspoon dried red chilli flakes

1 teaspoon sweet chilli sauce

1 teaspoon crushed garlic

1 teaspoon grated fresh ginger

1 tablespoon walnut oil

2 tablespoons extra virgin olive oil

**To serve**

3 Little Gem lettuces

**1** Make the dressing by combining all the ingredients.

**2** Combine all the other ingredients, then add enough dressing to coat, and leave to marinate for a few minutes. Add more dressing if necessary just before serving. Serve on Little Gem lettuce leaves.

# Toad in the Sky

A twist on toad in the hole, a recipe I discovered in a 1960s newspaper. Nice use of your favourite pork sausage.

**Preparation and cooking: 1 hour 10 minutes**
**Serves: 4**

500g (18 oz) pork sausages

250ml (9 fl oz) milk

55g (2 oz) unsalted butter

150g (5 oz) plain flour

salt and ground black pepper

1 onion, roughly chopped

1 tablespoon good-quality olive oil

1 teaspoon finely chopped fresh sage

1 tablespoon grain mustard

4 eggs, separated

**1** Preheat the oven to 200°C/400°F/Gas 6. Grill the sausages for 1 minute on each side, until lightly browned. Cut them in half lengthways.

**2** Heat the milk in a non-stick saucepan with the butter, until it has reached boiling point and the butter has melted. Tip the flour into the milk in one go, remove from the heat and beat vigorously until smooth and thick. Season with salt and pepper.

**3** Meanwhile, cook the onion in the oil over a medium heat in a separate pan, until softened but not brown. Stir in the sage and mustard, and add to the milk–flour mixture.

**4** Beat the egg yolks, one by one, into the milk–flour mixture. In a clean bowl, beat the egg whites to **soft peaks**. Fold them into the batter as well.

**5** Butter a 23cm (9 in) or 25cm (10 in) soufflé dish. Cover the base with 1cm (½ in) of the batter. Arrange the half sausages on top, then cover with the remaining batter, and smooth over with a knife or palette knife.

**6** Bake near the top of the oven for about 40 minutes, until golden, crisp and well risen.

# Pork *'Rillettes'* with Prunes

A recipe based on the classic *rillettes*, but a slightly less unhealthy version with the pork cooked slowly in stock rather than pork fat. The recipe produces a moist, slightly sweet, topping for *crostini* or hot toast.

**Preparation cooking and cooling: overnight + 6 hours**

**Serves: 8–10**

| |
|---|
| 300ml (½ pint) dry white wine |
| 3 onions, roughly chopped |
| 2 carrots, sliced |
| 4 cloves garlic, sliced |
| 1 stick celery, sliced |
| 2 sprigs thyme |
| 175ml (6 fl oz) good olive oil |
| 2 bay leaves |
| 1 teaspoon black peppercorns |
| 6 juniper berries, crushed |
| 1 sprig rosemary |
| 175g (6 oz) salt pork or streaky bacon, cut in cubes |
| 2kg (4½ lb) pork shoulder, cut in 6 chunks |
| 12 stoneless prunes, chopped |
| 125ml (4 fl oz) brandy |
| 125ml (4 fl oz) cold tea |
| 2 tablespoons vegetable oil |
| 1.4 litres (2½ pints) chicken stock |
| 1 tablespoon grain Dijon mustard |
| 225ml (8 fl oz) double cream |
| 20 sorrel leaves, ripped |
| 1 tablespoon lemon juice |
| salt and ground black pepper |

**1** Combine the white wine, onion, carrot, garlic, celery, thyme, olive oil, bay leaves, peppercorns, juniper and rosemary in a **non-reactive** saucepan.

**2 Blanch** the salt pork in boiling unsalted water for 5 minutes, drain and cool, and add to the marinade with the pork shoulder. Marinate overnight, turning the meat from time to time.

**3** Soak the prunes overnight in the brandy and tea.

**4** The next day remove the meat, drain and dry. Set aside the marinade vegetables and liquor. Preheat the oven to 150°C/300°F/Gas 2.

**5** Brown the meat over a high heat in hot vegetable oil. Place the meat in a heavy-based casserole. Drain the vegetables from the marinade and brown them in the same pan as the pork. Add the vegetables to the pork.

**6** Pour the marinade and chicken stock over the meat mixture, and bring to the boil. Cover the casserole, place in the preheated oven, and cook for 4 hours, undisturbed.

**7** Remove the meat from the casserole and set aside. Strain the cooking juices into a saucepan and place over a medium heat. Remove any fats from the surface and skim regularly. Cook until the liquid has **reduced** by half, about 20 minutes.

**8** Add the mustard and cream and boil for 10 minutes or until you are left with 425ml (¾ pint). Add the sorrel, lemon juice, prunes and their soaking liquor. Cook until the liquid has reduced to about 300ml (½ pint). Season.

**9** Meanwhile, shred the meat by ripping it apart with two forks. Place in a bowl or terrine dish.

**10** Pour the hot liquor over the pork, stir well to combine, and allow to cool. Refrigerate until 1 hour before use. Serve at room temperature with hot toast or as a topping for *crostini*.

• • • • • • • •

*Instead of using Chinese crispy duck, try crispy suckling pig with pancakes, cucumber, spring onions and* hoi-sin *sauce.*

• • • • • • • •

## Oriental Pork Kebabs

● *Make these by cutting pork fillet into 1cm (2 in) cubes, then marinating them in 1 tablespoon oyster sauce, 1 tablespoon dark soy sauce, 1 tablespoon rice wine vinegar, 1 tablespoon caster sugar, ¼ teaspoon white pepper, 2 teaspoons finely chopped spring onion, 1 teaspoon finely chopped chilli, and ½ teaspoon grated ginger.*

● *Thread pork on to skewers and char-grill.*

# Pork with Stout, Pepper and Brown Sugar

One of the nicest, slow-cooked pork dishes – the meat falls off the bone, and melts in the mouth with wonderful sweet peppery taste sensations.

**Preparation and cooking: overnight + 4 hours**
**Serves: 4**

2 x 1.5kg (3 lb 5 oz) pork knuckles from the shoulder

12 pitted black olives and 12 sage leaves, or 6 pitted prunes, halved, and 12 tinned anchovy fillets

75g (3 oz) unsalted butter

3 onions, finely sliced

1–2 tablespoons oil

300ml (½ pint) stout

450ml (16 fl oz) chicken stock

**Marinade**

4 teaspoons black peppercorns, crushed

2 teaspoons salt

2 teaspoons dried oregano

1 teaspoon soft thyme leaves

7 cloves garlic

5 tablespoons soft brown sugar

2 tablespoons olive oil

2 tablespoons white wine vinegar

1  For the marinade, combine the peppercorns, salt, herbs, garlic and sugar in a food processor, then gradually add the oil and vinegar.

2  Remove the rind from each pork knuckle and keep to one side. Trim off the excess fat from the meat. Make 6 incisions in each piece of pork and press a black olive and sage leaf, or half a prune and an anchovy fillet, into each slit. Rub with the marinade and leave to marinate in a cool place for at least 3 hours, ideally overnight.

3  Preheat the oven to 150°C/300°F/Gas 2.

4  Melt the butter in a casserole and cook the onion over gentle heat until it caramelises. This will take about 20 minutes.

5  Meanwhile, in a separate pan, heat the oil and brown the meat well, on all sides. Set the pork on top of the onion slices in the casserole. Add the stout to the pan in which the pork was browned and bring to the boil to soften any sediment in the pan. Pour the stout and residues from the pan, plus the chicken stock, into the casserole with the meat.

6  Cover each piece of meat with its reserved rind, then cover the casserole. Cook in the oven for about 3 hours until the meat is very tender and falling off the bone.

7  Remove the meat from the bones and cut into chunks; discard the bones. Keep warm. Pour all the pan juices and onions into a food processor and blend until smooth. If the liquid is too thin, boil vigorously to **reduce**. Pour over the meat.

8  If you like, garnish with *crostini* spread with *Tapenade* (see page 243), and top with deep-fried sage leaves. Serve with roast carrots, roast parsnips and polenta mash.

*You won't find veal in this book. Don't get me wrong, I think it is a great meat, but not so great that I can condone the way the majority of veal calves are reared. Most veal in recipes can be replaced by pork, especially pork fillet.*

## Asian Pork Meatballs

*These make a delicious snack or starter.*

● *Caramelise 55g (2 oz) sugar in a frying pan.*

● *When golden add 3 tablespoons nam pla (fish sauce). Combine this with 450g (1 lb) minced pork, 4 finely chopped spring onions, 1 teaspoon chopped garlic, 2 teaspoons finely chopped lemongrass, 1 teaspoon cornflour, 1 tablespoon finely chopped mint, 2 tablespoons chopped coriander, ½ teaspoon salt and ½ teaspoon ground black pepper.*

● *Form into 2.5cm (1 in) meatballs, brush with oil and pan-fry or grill for 3–4 minutes each side.*

● *Serve with an Oriental dipping sauce.*

# Coarse Country Terrine with Pheasant

Terrines and pâtés are very easy, although people tend to think of them in the same breath as soufflés – 'Oh, no, I couldn't do that!' Piece of cake, so just follow the instructions.

**Preparation and cooking: 48 hours + 3 hours**

**Serves: 8–12**

450g (1 lb) thinly sliced streaky bacon or pork back fat, rinds removed

85g (3 oz) plain flour, mixed to a paste with 50ml (2 fl oz) water

**Marinade**

75ml (2½ fl oz) dry white wine

50ml (2 fl oz) brandy

2 bay leaves

1 clove garlic, finely chopped

2 teaspoons soft thyme leaves

½ teaspoon sea salt

½ teaspoon white peppercorns, crushed

**Meat mixture**

breasts and thighs of 1 pheasant, skin removed, flesh cut into 1cm (½ in) dice

225g (8 oz) chicken or duck livers, trimmed

55g (2 oz) unsalted butter

1 onion, finely chopped

3 garlic cloves, finely chopped

350g (12 oz) lean pork, minced

175g (6 oz) ham, chopped

500g (18 oz) pork back fat, minced

225g (8 oz) lean salt pork, minced

25g (1 oz) soft white breadcrumbs

1 teaspoon grated nutmeg

¼ teaspoon cayenne pepper

¼ teaspoon ground allspice

1 teaspoon ground black pepper

1 teaspoon sea salt

3 eggs, lightly beaten

1 tablespoon green peppercorns, drained

55g (2 oz) pistachio nuts, blanched and peeled

**1** Combine the marinade ingredients in a **non-reactive** bowl, then add to it the pheasant and the chicken or duck livers. Leave to marinate overnight. Drain, reserving the marinade.

**2** Heat the butter in the frying pan, add the livers and fry for 4 minutes, turning once. Remove the livers, and add the onion and garlic to the same pan. Cook over a low heat until the onion has softened. Add the marinade, and boil to **reduce** by half. Allow to cool.

**3** Roughly chop the livers. Combine the onion mix with the livers and pheasant. Combine with all the remaining meat mixture ingredients.

**4** Stretch the bacon slices with the back of a knife. Line a 1.5 litre (2¾ pint) earthenware or cast-iron terrine mould with the bacon across the bottom and up the sides, leaving excess to cover the pâté after the mould has been filled.

**5** Spoon the meat mixture into the bacon-lined terrine. Tap the terrine on the work surface to release any air bubbles. Fold the slices of bacon over the mixture.

**6** Preheat the oven to 180°C/350°F/Gas 4.

**7** Line the top edge of the terrine mould all the way round with a strip of the flour and water paste and push the lid down into the paste.

**8** Place the terrine in a slightly larger deep baking dish, and pour in boiling water to come halfway up the sides. Bake for 1¾ hours, undisturbed.

**9** Remove the roasting dish from the oven and allow it to stand in the water bath for 1 hour.

**10** Break the paste seal, remove the terrine lid, and place a weight of about 1kg (2¼ lb) on a piece of board to fit the terrine. Leave the weight in place overnight in the refrigerator.

**11** Remove the weight and, if possible, allow the terrine to mature another day before eating on hot toast with pickles.

# Home-made *Chorizo*

Obviously you can buy this peppery Spanish sausage, but most tend to be disappointing. The sense of satisfaction in making your own sausage makes the effort worthwhile.

**Preparation and cooking: 1 hour + overnight**
**Makes: 2kg (4½ lb)**

| |
|---|
| 1–3 tablespoons dried chilli flakes soaked in 125ml (4 fl oz) warmed cider vinegar |
| 1kg (2¼ lb) lean pork, neck or shoulder, diced |
| 500g (18 oz) hard back fat, diced |
| 1 teaspoon caster sugar |
| 2 red peppers, diced |
| 2 hot chillies, diced |
| 1 tablespoon minced garlic |
| 1½ teaspoons paprika |
| 1 tablespoon sea salt |

**To finish**

wide sausage skins (from your butcher)

**1** Crush the chilli flakes in a mortar and pestle to a paste with the cider vinegar. Depending on how hot you like your sausage, use 1, 2 or 3 tablespoons of this chilli paste.
**2** Combine the paste with the remaining ingredients, then pass twice through the coarse blade of a mincer.
**3** Fill the sausage skins with the mixture then twist the sausage length every 15cm (6 in), to make a string of sausages. Smoke the sausages (see page 189), or hang to dry overnight in a temperature of 16–21°C/60–70°F.
**4** Poach the sausages for 15–30 minutes, depending on thickness. They can then be grilled or fried to crisp the skins.

• • • • • • • • • • • • • • • •

*A baste to rub over a pork joint before roasting is made by combining 1 tablespoon English mustard powder, 1 tablespoon clear honey and ½ teaspoon olive oil. Spread over the meat and scatter with caraway seeds. Roast in the usual way.*

• • • • • • • • • • • • • • • •

## Spiced Brine for Pork

*The way some pork is produced today, the meat can lack flavour, so compensate by brining it before cooking.*

• *Combine 2 litres (3½ pints) water with 85g (3 oz) sea salt, 115g (4 oz) caster sugar, 4 bay leaves, 2 cloves, 1 tablespoon coriander seeds, 1 tablespoon roasted juniper berries, lightly crushed, 2 tablespoons black peppercorns, 3 smashed cloves garlic, 2 sprigs thyme and 1 broken cinnamon stick.*
• *Bring the mixture to the boil and simmer for 5 minutes. Remove from the heat and allow to cool.*
• *Submerge the meat in the brine and leave for 4 hours (chops) or overnight (for a joint). Dry the meat before cooking.*

## Pork *Saltimbocca*

• *Beat pork fillet out flat to form escalopes, place 2 sage leaves on each escalope, and top each with a thin slice of Parma ham.*
• *Dip both sides in seasoned flour, dust off excess. Heat a knob of butter and a good slurp of olive oil in a large frying pan. Seal the pork for 1–2 minutes each side, remove and keep warm.*
• *Add a further 25g (1 oz) butter and some slices of lemon and shredded sage. Cook until the lemons are brown. Spoon butter, sage and lemon over the escalopes.*

• • • • • • • • • • • •

*The same escalopes can be dipped in flour, egg and breadcrumbs and then pan-fried in the usual way. Top with a fried egg or some slices of anchovies.*

• • • • • • • • • • • •

# POTATO

The potato (*Solanum tuberosum*) was discovered in South America in the sixteenth century by a Spanish explorer who brought some back to Spain. It took a long time for them to be accepted in Europe, which is remarkable when one considers what a necessity they are today, the fourth most important food crop in the world. It wasn't until about 1750 that the British adopted them into their diet.

The potato is a member of the Solanaceae family, thus is related to the tomato, aubergine, sweet and chilli peppers — and henbane and deadly nightshade! (Potatoes can be poisonous as well, perhaps one of the reasons they took so long to become popular. A poisonous alkaloid, solanine, is present in all green parts of the plant — leaves, stems, fruit and the green that develops on the skin.) The potato is neither a fruit nor a root, but a tuber, swollen underground stems of the plant that serve as storage organs. Potatoes are strongly associated with the Irish, firstly because it is believed Sir Francis Drake brought them to Britain (he certainly planted a few tubers at his house in Youghal near Cork). Potatoes became central in the Irish diet, then tragedy struck in the form of the potato blight in 1845 (caused by a fungus). This completely ruined the Irish potato crop and plunged the Irish population into famine. Up to a million are thought to have died, and this was followed by huge waves of emigration to the UK, Australia and, particularly, America.

Once upon a time there were over 1,000 varieties of potato but, with modern farming methods, we've managed to reduce them to about 100. Yield appears to be the only criterion for farmers. Recently supermarkets started to look for more varieties, but, as with most things, this enthusiasm seems to have waned. We are lucky nowadays if we are offered more than half a dozen varieties.

Potatoes are floury or waxy, and this is fundamental to the cook: floury are for mash, waxy for boiling and salads. I give a few variety suggestions below. Potatoes also come as 'old' and 'new'. 'New' or 'early' potatoes arrive in May, and are waxy. 'Maincrop' potatoes, available from autumn, are waxy at first, becoming floury. Potatoes stored over the winter are 'old' and usually floury.

Potatoes are rumoured to be fattening, but in fact, being 80 per cent water, an average-sized potato contains only 100 calories. However, add to your potato some butter, cream, oil or dripping, and the calories race up. Keep potatoes in your diet, but without the saturated fats, for they contain valuable minerals and a healthy amount of vitamins B and C. Baked are best for those trying to slim, and they also contain good amounts of fibre in the skins.

Choose potatoes that are firm and smooth with no signs of sprouting, an indication that the potato has been hanging around too long. Avoid subjecting potatoes to daylight, which is when they go green; store them away from light in a ventilated area. If buying pre-packaged potatoes, always remove them from the plastic bag, as the plastic makes the potato sweat. Maincrop or old potatoes can be kept for a few weeks, but new potatoes should be used as soon as possible.

The choice of potato varieties in an ideal world would be as follows:

*All-purpose:* Desirée, Golden Wonder, King Edward.

*Boiling:* Pentland Javelin, Sharpe's Express, Epicure, Maris Piper; and salad varieties, Jersey Royals, Belle de Fontenay, Ratte, Pink Fir Apple, or any Cyprus or Egyptian varieties.

*Mashing:* Desirée, Golden Wonder, King Edward, Pentland Ivory, Pentland Hawk.

*Roasting:* Cara, Desirée, King Edward, Golden Wonder, Maris Piper and Pentland Dell.

*Pan-frying:* Egyptian, Cyprus, Pink Fir Apple, Charlotte, Belle de Fontenay, Ratte.

*Chips:* Maris Piper, Majestic, Croft, Ulster Sceptre, Desirée, Maris Piper, Pentland Dell.

*Baking:* Golden Wonder, King Edward, Maris Piper, Wilja, Pentland Crown, Pentland Squire, Desirée, Cara.

*Salad:* Jersey Royals, Belle de Fontenay, Ratte, Pink Fir Apple for vinaigrettes; Arran Pilot, Desirée, Golden Wonder, Kippler, Aura for mayonnaise.

## STEAMING

Do not peel before cooking. If you use new potatoes, they should take about 15–20 minutes to cook.

## BOILING

Ideally do not peel before cooking, just give the potatoes a good scrub and skin them afterwards. This is not always convenient, especially if you want to cut the potatoes into smaller pieces. Peeled you lose nutrients during cooking, and stand the chance (depending on the potato variety) of waterlogged and crumbling potatoes (if a floury variety). New potatoes are scrubbed and cooked in their skins with mint, salt and a pinch of sugar. I quite like being old-fashioned and peeling new potatoes after they are cooked; there is something special about cutting into the waxy flesh of a new spud. Old potatoes go into cold water, new into boiling. Old will take, depending on their size, 15–25 minutes to cook, new potatoes between 12–15 minutes.

## MASHING

We're talking British mash first, which is the fluffy stiff mash. Boil potatoes until tender, drain, then return to a low heat to dry out. Peel and mash, using a fork, masher, **mouli-légumes** or, best of all, a potato ricer. For 1kg (2¼ lb) potatoes, add 115g (4 oz) unsalted butter when mashing. Beat in 150–300ml (¼–½ pint) milk with a whisk or wooden spoon until fluffy. Season with a pinch of nutmeg, salt and white pepper. The French prefer more of a purée, so as well as butter and milk they will add hot cream. They sometimes use a food processor, but the technique needs practice and precision, or you will overwork the starches, and produce a very elastic, sticky mess. If you have the patience, the best mash comes from scooping out the souffléd flesh from baked potatoes, then adding butter and milk.

## ROASTING

I am looking for really crunchy outsides and fluffy middles. Sounds obvious, doesn't it, but so often you go to houses or restaurants, and the potatoes have been started off in the deep-fat-fryer and finished off in the oven: this is rank. The best method I have found for guaranteed results is to preheat a roasting tray with 1cm (½ in) deep dripping in a 200°C/400°F/Gas 6 oven. Peel and cut the potatoes lengthways down the narrow side so you have a large flat surface, place the potatoes in cold salted water, bring to the boil and cook for 10 minutes. Drain and return to the heat to

dry. Combine 115g (4 oz) plain flour with 1 teaspoon salt, 1 teaspoon ground black pepper and optionally ½ teaspoon soft thyme leaves. Place the potatoes in a colander and toss them in a handful of seasoned flour. Toss the potatoes quite vigorously so the edges start to break up slightly. Place the potatoes carefully, flat side down, in the hot dripping and baste the tops with the dripping. Position in the oven and cook for 20 minutes before turning the potatoes over. Cook for a further 20 minutes, then pour off the majority of the fat. Cook for a further 20 minutes. If you like, a few whole unpeeled cloves of garlic added to the dripping lend a different dimension. Even better, place your roast meat on an oven tray above the potatoes so the meat juices can drip down on to the potatoes as they cook. Delicious.

## BAKING

Wash and dry the potatoes then place in a preheated 190°C/375°F/Gas 5 oven on a rack so the air can circulate. Leave them for 1½ hours although they will be cooked after 1 hour. Leaving them the extra 30 minutes produces a great crispy skin and a wonderfully souffléd centre. Some cooks wrap the potatoes in foil; big mistake, as this has the effect of steaming the potato, and you lose the crispy skin. (Same as in the microwave.)

## PAN-FRYING or SAUTÉING

Par-boil old potatoes or new, depending on your fancy. Cut the potatoes after they have cooled in 8mm (⅜ in) slices. Use butter, butter and olive oil, olive oil, duck fat, dripping or pork fat with a few sprigs of rosemary and whole garlic cloves if you like. Heat up enough fat to a depth of 5mm (¼ in) and pan-fry the potato slices until golden, about 10 minutes; turn them over and repeat. Don't be tempted to turn the potatoes over early. Season with salt.

## CHIPS and DEEP-FRYING

I hate to advise home cooks on this method of cooking, as more fires are started through oil being heated in a saucepan than by anything else. Please invest in a domestic fryer which has a thermostat. I find a Tefal model one of the best on the market and very reasonably priced. You won't produce a good chip without the right potato, though – check my list – but even that is no guarantee, as the later in the season you are, the more the sugar in the potato turns to starch, and unfortunately you need a balance of the two.

## Twice-baked Mashed Potatoes

The richest mash I have ever eaten, deliciously different, and well worth the effort.

**Preparation and cooking: 2½ hours**
**Serves: 4–6**

1kg (2¼ lb) baking potatoes, washed

1 teaspoon salt

¼ teaspoon ground white pepper

¼ teaspoon freshly grated nutmeg

175g (6 oz) unsalted butter, softened, plus 2 tablespoons melted

4 egg yolks

3 tablespoons chopped flat-leaf parsley

1 tablespoon snipped chives

150ml (¼ pint) double cream

**1** Preheat the oven to 190°C/375°F/Gas 5. Bake the potatoes on a rack until the skins are crisp and the flesh is tender, about 1¼ hours.

**2** Cut the potatoes in half lengthways and scoop out the innards. Mash the potatoes (or use a ricer). Use the skins for deep-fried potato skins.

**3** Place the potatoes in a large bowl, and add the salt, pepper, nutmeg and the softened butter. Beat until smooth. Beat in the egg yolks one by one, then stir in the herbs and cream.

**4** Spoon the mixture into a buttered baking dish. Bake in the moderate oven for 15 minutes, then drizzle with the melted butter. Raise the oven temperature to 230°C/450°F/Gas 8, and bake for a further 9–10 minutes until golden.

* * * * * * * *

*Instead of butter in mashed potato, fold in warm, garlic-infused extra virgin olive oil, warm double cream and chopped green olives.*

* * * * * * * *

## Chilli and Coriander Mashed Potato Cakes

Akin to an Oriental bubble and squeak, this is a great dish for brunch topped with poached eggs, hollandaise sauce (see page 113) and crispy bacon.

**Preparation and cooking: 35 minutes**
**Serves: 4**

350g (12 oz) mashed potatoes

2 carrots, cooked and mashed

2 hot chillies, diced

1 x 2.5cm (1 in) piece of fresh ginger, finely grated

1 tablespoon desiccated coconut

4 spring onions, finely sliced

1 tablespoon chopped roasted peanuts

1 tablespoon chopped coriander

2 tablespoons soured cream

2 tablespoons plain flour

2 teaspoons lime juice

salt and ground black pepper

butter or olive oil for frying

**1** Combine all the ingredients except for the seasoning and frying medium. Season to taste.

**2** Heat some oil or butter in a large frying pan. Shape the mixture into four cakes and pan-fry for 4–5 minutes each side until golden and crusty.

. . . . . . . . . . . . . . .

## Mashed Combos

*Other mashed potato combinations.*
*● Add English mustard powder and turmeric powder for mustard mash.*
*● Cook shallots, garlic and a bottle of Cabernet Sauvignon red wine to **reduce** by two-thirds, and fold in for red wine mash.*
*● Cook 6 cloves garlic with 450g (1 lb) chopped wild mushrooms and 50ml (2 fl oz) extra virgin olive oil; fold in with loads of parsley for mushroom mash.*
*● Fold in mashed sardines, chopped roasted peppers and roasted garlic, for delicious 'nursery' mash.*

. . . . . . . . . . . . . . .

# Textured Potato Salad

There must be hundreds of varieties of potato salad – warm ones with vinaigrette, spicy ones and herby ones – but I like the mayonnaise version, albeit with one or two useful additions. On this occasion I'm a bit of a Hellmann's mayonnaise fan, so don't bother making your own (unless of course you feel you have to!).

**Preparation and cooking: 30 minutes**
**Serves: 6–8**

| |
|---|
| 675g (1½ lb) floury potatoes, peeled and cut into 2.5cm (1 in) cubes |
| 6 rashers smoked streaky bacon, cooked until crisp |
| 2 large dill cucumbers, diced |
| 2 hard-boiled eggs, chopped |
| 4 spring onions, chopped |
| salt and ground black pepper |

**Dressing**

| |
|---|
| 1 tablespoon lemon juice |
| 1 tablespoon chopped dill |
| 1 tablespoon snipped chives |
| 1 tablespoon chopped flat-leaf parsley |
| 4 tablespoons Hellmann's mayonnaise |
| 3 tablespoons soured cream |

**1** Cook the potatoes in salted water until soft, then drain and return to the heat to dry out. It is important that the potatoes are thoroughly cooked, there is nothing worse than **al dente** potatoes.

**2** Combine the potatoes with the crumbled crispy bacon, the diced cucumber, eggs and onion. Season to taste.

**3** Combine the remaining ingredients to make the dressing.

**4** Fold enough of the dressing into the salad to make it creamy. When folding everything together, try and do it while the potatoes are still warm, and allow the potatoes to break down a little in the mixing.

# Chunky Potato Soup

A cross between a soup and a stew, perfect winter-warming stuff. If you prefer a smooth soup, feel free to liquidise, but you will need to add more stock or cream to thin it down a little.

**Preparation and cooking: 45 minutes**
**Serves: 3–4**

| |
|---|
| 55g (2 oz) unsalted butter |
| 1 onion, roughly chopped |
| 2 cloves garlic, finely chopped |
| 4 rashers rindless smoked streaky bacon, diced |
| 2 sticks celery, finely sliced |
| 1 teaspoon soft thyme leaves |
| 1 bay leaf |
| 2 medium carrots, sliced |
| 2 medium baking potatoes, peeled and cut into 2.5cm (1 in) cubes |
| 1 litre (1¾ pints) chicken or vegetable stock |
| 3 tablespoons chopped flat-leaf parsley |
| 3 tablespoons soured cream |
| salt and ground black pepper |

**1** In a medium-sized saucepan, heat the butter. Add the onion, garlic and bacon, and cook over a medium heat for 8 minutes.

**2** Add the celery, thyme, bay leaf, carrot and potato, and cook until the potato starts to stick on the bottom of the pan, about 5 minutes.

**3** Add the stock and cook for 15 minutes until the potato is tender and starting to fall apart.

**4** Add the parsley and soured cream. Warm through but do not re-boil. Stir to combine all the ingredients, then season to taste and serve.

## Roasted Royals

● *Roast 450g (1 lb) baby Jersey Royal potatoes with 2 tablespoons extra virgin olive oil, 175g (6 oz) dried pancetta or streaky bacon, cut in 2cm (¾ in) dice, 6 smashed cloves of garlic, 1 teaspoon soft thyme leaves, rock salt and pepper.*

● *During the 35 minutes' cooking time, shake the pan from time to time to coat the potatoes in oil.*

# Potatoes and Ceps Baked in Parchment

A recipe full of earthy flavours, inspired by a dish from Périgord in France. Perfect on its own or with roast chicken.

**Preparation and cooking: 45 minutes**
**Serves: 4 (8 as a starter)**

2 rashers rindless smoked streaky bacon, diced

2 shallots, finely diced

3 cloves garlic, finely chopped

2 tablespoons duck fat (see page 111), dripping or butter

675g (1½ lb) Pink Fir Apple potatoes or other waxy variety, peeled and sliced

450g (1 lb) ceps, sliced (or soaked dried)

1 teaspoon chopped soft thyme leaves

3 tablespoons chopped flat-leaf parsley

salt and ground black pepper

50ml (2 fl oz) Dry Martini

**1** Cook the bacon with the shallot and garlic in the duck fat until the bacon is golden and the shallot has softened.

**2** Add the potatoes and ceps and stir to combine. Cook for 3 minutes, then fold in the herbs and seasoning.

**3** Place the contents of the pan on one large sheet of parchment or greaseproof paper, or 4 (or 8) smaller ones. Fold the parchment over the vegetables so the edges of the paper meet. Fold the paper tightly along the edges, forming a semi-circle as you go. Just before completing the sealed packet(s), pour a little Dry Martini in. Tuck the last corner of the packet(s) under to seal well.

**4** Place the packet(s) on a baking sheet and cook in the oven preheated to 180°C/350°F/Gas 4 for 30 minutes.

## Gratin Dauphinoise

*This is a favourite of mine.*
- *Rub a gratin dish with a clove of garlic, and butter liberally. Make layers with 450g (1 lb) sliced waxy potatoes (Pink Fir Apples are nice), seasoning each layer.*
- *Pour over 300ml (½ pint) double cream and cook in a 170°C/325°F/Gas 3 oven for 1¼ hours.*
- *Turn up the heat to 200°C/400°F/Gas 6 and cook for a further 15 minutes until the top is golden.*

## Perfect Chips

*Follow this sequence of events for good, if not always perfect, chips.*
- *Peel the potatoes and place in a bowl of cold water.*
- *Cut the potato into the size of chip you require: roughly 2.5cm (1 in) thick for fat chips, 8mm (⅜ in) for medium and 5mm (¼ in) for shoestring. Place the chips in water again to rinse off starches.*
- *Heat the oil to 160°C/320°F.*
- *Dry the chips.*
- *Place a few chips at a time in the hot oil and cook for 4–6 minutes until they become limp but have not browned.*
- *Drain the chips and place in a container until you are ready to serve. The chips can be prepared to this point up to 12 hours in advance.*
- *Increase the heat of the oil to 190°C/375°F.*
- *Return the blanched chips to the hot oil and cook for 2–3 minutes until golden and crispy.*
- *Drain the chips on kitchen paper, season with salt and serve immediately.*
- *The bigger the chip, the fewer calories it contains as the absorption percentage rate of the oil to potato is less. So skinny chips pound for pound contain more calories.*

## Extra Hot Potato Salad

- *Fry 450g (1 lb) sliced New Jersey potatoes in duck or bacon fat with 175g (6 oz) bacon pieces until bacon and potatoes are golden.*
- *Add 1 tablespoon chilli oil (see page 258) with 2 sliced heads of chicory and cook until the chicory starts to **wilt**.*
- *Fold in 1 tablespoon chopped coriander leaves and 2 tablespoons sliced spring onions. Serve with grilled foods.*

*When making gratin dauphinoise, for a change add grated Gruyère cheese between each layer and scatter some on top.*

# Potato *Gnocchi*

While you can buy perfectly acceptable *gnocchi* in supermarkets or Italian delis, there is nothing quite like making your own, as you can achieve something that is so much lighter. Serve the *gnocchi* with sage butter, a cheesy sauce or a spicy tomato sauce. *Gnocchi* also suits a sauce made from pesto and cream.

**Preparation and cooking: 1¼–2¼ hours**
**Serves: 6–8**

1kg (2¼ lb) baking potatoes
salt, ground white pepper and grated nutmeg
2 egg yolks
250g (9 oz) plain flour
1 teaspoon baking powder
2 heaped tablespoons herbs, chopped (flat-leaf parsley, chives, basil)

**1** Ideally bake the potatoes in a 190°C/375°F/Gas 5 oven for 1–1¼ hours. Allow to cool slightly, cut in half lengthways, scoop out the potato flesh and mash to a smooth consistency. Alternatively boil the potatoes until tender, peel and mash in the normal way.

**2** Season the mash with salt, pepper and nutmeg, and place on a work surface floured with extra flour. Make a well in the potatoes and add the egg yolks. Combine the flour and baking powder, then add a little to the potato. Work in the eggs, herbs and flour, adding a little more flour from time to time as you knead the potato dough. Work the dough with the heel of your hand for 5 minutes. Allow the dough to rest for 20 minutes.

**3** Place a large pot of salted water on to boil.

**4** Divide the potato mixture into four and roll each portion into a long rope, about 1cm (½ in) in diameter. Cut the ropes into 1–2cm (½–¾ in) pieces. Drop the *gnocchi* into the boiling water in small batches and cook until they start to float, about 4–5 minutes.

**5** Scoop them out with a slotted spoon and keep them warm while you cook the remainder.

**6** Pour over a sauce, or pan-fry in butter with sage and sprinkle with Parmesan, the combinations are up to you.

# *Gratin* of Potato, Anchovy, Rosemary and Cream

A similar dish to that Swedish favourite, Jansson's Temptation. It's a rich, moreish dish of potatoes that could be eaten on its own, or served with roast or grilled meats.

**Preparation and cooking: 1½ hours**
**Serves: 4**

55g (2 oz) unsalted butter
350ml (12 fl oz) double cream
1 tablespoon chopped rosemary
8 anchovy fillets, finely chopped, plus the oil from anchovy tin
6 medium waxy potatoes
2 large onions, finely sliced
2–3 tablespoons fresh white breadcrumbs
½ teaspoon ground white pepper

**1** Butter a *gratin* dish, using some of the butter. Preheat the oven to 200°C/400°F/Gas 6.

**2** Heat the cream with the rosemary and anchovy oil from the tin, and bring to **scalding** point. Turn off the heat, and allow the flavours to infuse for 15 minutes.

**3** Peel and grate the potatoes and arrange layers of potato, chopped anchovy and sliced onion in the *gratin* dish. Pour over a little hot cream and then repeat layers, finishing with a layer of potatoes. Pour over half the remaining cream, and sprinkle with breadcrumbs.

**4** Place in the oven and bake for 35 minutes. Pour over the remaining cream and dot with the remaining butter. Sprinkle with the pepper. Bake for a further 20 minutes until bubbling and golden.

*Roast 2 heads of garlic for 30 minutes, squeeze the garlic cloves and fold the garlic purée into mashed potato for roast garlic mash.*

# Boxty

In deference to my Irish wife, Jacinta, the potato chapter needs to include this famous Irish dish.

**Preparation and cooking: 20 minutes**

**Serves: 4**

225g (8 oz) potatoes, peeled

225g (8 oz) cooked mashed potato

225g (8 oz) plain flour

½ teaspoon bicarbonate of soda

350ml (12 fl oz) buttermilk

salt and ground black pepper

butter

**1** Grate the peeled potato into a clean tea-towel and squeeze dry.

**2** Combine with the mashed potato, plain flour and bicarbonate of soda.

**3** Mix well, then add the buttermilk and a pinch each of salt and pepper to make a stiff batter.

**4** Heat some butter in a non-stick frying pan, drop tablespoons of the batter into the pan and cook for about 5 minutes each side until golden.

**5** Eat straight from the pan with golden syrup and crispy bacon.

## Colcannon

*This is another Irish potato dish.*

● *Combine 675g (1½ lb) hot mashed potato with 450g (1 lb) chopped cooked kale or Savoy cabbage.*

● *Cook 6 sliced spring onions in 125ml (4 fl oz) double cream and 125ml (4 fl oz) milk. Fold into the mashed potato.*

● *Place in a warmed dish. Indent the surface of the colcannon and pour in a puddle of 55g (2 oz) melted butter.*

## Sage Crisps

*When cooking game, instead of serving crisps or game chips, make your own sage crisps.*

● *Preheat the oven to 170°C/325°F/Gas 3. Line a baking sheet with greaseproof paper and brush the paper with some clarified butter.*

● *Using a **mandoline** or electric slicer, cut a large baking potato into very thin slices. Keep the slices in order as if you were going to reconstruct the potato.*

● *Place 2 adjacent slices together, sandwiching 1 blanched sage leaf between them. Place on a baking sheet and brush with clarified butter. Do the same with the remaining slices.*

● *Bake in the oven for 15–20 minutes, turning once as the edges brown. Allow to cool on racks to crisp up.*

## Curry Sauce

*Chips with curry sauce are quite popular in parts of the UK. Why not make your own sauce?*

● *Blend in a food processor 3 chopped onions, 12 peeled cloves of garlic and 6 tablespoons water.*

● *Heat 6 tablespoons olive oil in a large saucepan and add ½ teaspoon fenugreek seeds, ½ teaspoon fennel seeds, 1 tablespoon mustard seeds, 3 bay leaves and 5 hot chillies.*

● *Cook for 30 seconds then add the onion purée and cook for 10 minutes.*

● *Add 1 teaspoon sugar and 2 x 400g (14 oz) tins chopped tomatoes. Add 300ml (½ pint) vegetable stock and simmer until thick. Season to taste.*

*For a simple supper dish, melt 175g (6 oz) diced Taleggio cheese with 125ml (4 fl oz) double cream and 40g (1½ oz) unsalted butter. Combine cooked hot sliced new potatoes with 3 tablespoons extra virgin olive oil, ½ tablespoon white wine vinegar, 1 finely chopped shallot and 1 teaspoon Dijon mustard. Season and scatter with 1 tablespoon snipped chives and 1 tablespoon chopped parsley. Pour the cheese sauce over the potato and serve warm.*

# SALAD LEAVES

'Eat your salad' was the constant nag of my mum when I was a boy. But at that time what we were faced with was: boring outside leaves from a round lettuce dressed with corn oil and malt vinegar, topped with slices of pickled beetroot and a dollop each of Heinz vegetable salad and potato salad, both out of tins; this was rounded off with a couple of wedges of tomato and cucumber and a slice of tinned ham. Such was life a couple of years after rationing was stopped, but as far as lettuce went, the round lettuce was the only one on offer. A few years on and we all got very excited at the arrival of Webb's Wonder and cos lettuces. The next one to arrive on the scene was the iceberg, a real treat then, lettuce that made teeth less redundant. A few years passed, and cooks started trying out spinach and chicory as salad leaves; prior to that time, both had been used solely in cooked dishes. After that the bitter brigade arrived – radicchio, oak leaf, escarole, curly endive, lamb's lettuce and dandelion, a true array of flavour. Chefs became designers, arranging skilfully an artist's palette of leaf colour. The 1990s progressed the revolution with the arrival of rocket, mizuna and mustard greens. Only one salad leaf didn't ever sit right with me, the *lollo rosso*, a designer lettuce with no relevant flavour, a garish leaf of which appeared as a ridiculous garnish on every dish on every buffet in the land. *Lollo rosso* must now take the hint: it's time for it to disappear.

All green leaves contain vitamins A and C, and they have a number of other nutrients as well. Primarily salad leaves contain no fat and therefore no cholesterol.

Here's a brief description of much of what is available to you.

### ARUGULA OR ROCKET (*Eruca sativa*)

A favourite of mine. A delicious leaf related to the mustard family, it has a peppery flavour with a fair bit of tartness. Unfortunately, supermarkets sell it as a herb, and for a lot of money. For organisations that are generally fairly switched on to trends they've been a bit slow at recognising this leaf as the salad of the moment, and that it's here to stay – and in quantity – because of its delicious flavour. (It's easy to grow in the garden.)

### BELGIAN ENDIVE OR CHICORY

(*Cichorium intybus*)

Grown originally in darkness and its root used as a coffee substitute, the plant is harvested at 13–15cm (5–6 in) long, a compact head of crisp, pale yellow-tipped, white leaves. Chicory is crunchy with a pleasant bitter flavour that complements milder leaves or stands well alone. Buy *chicons* that have pale yellow rather than green tips (if they are green it means they have been subjected to daylight and their bitterness will be increased).

### CURLY ENDIVE OR *CHICORÉE FRISÉE*

(*Cichorium endivia*)

This relative of chicory forms a low growing head of large curly-edged leaves. It is one of the bitter leaves, with the outside darker leaves more bitter than the pale yellow 'blanched' centres.

### DANDELION (*Taraxacum officinale*)

Recognised by most of us as a stubborn lawn weed, but it is cultivated in many parts of the world, especially France. It is grown under darkened cloches or has its leaves tied together to 'blanch' the centre leaves to make them less bitter. (The root of this plant has also been used to make a coffee substitute.)

### ESCAROLE OR BATAVIAN ENDIVE

This is a cultivar of curly endive, and is similar in flavour to chicory. It has broad flat leaves and is dark green with a more yellowy centre. It is one of the bitter leaves.

### BEET GREENS (*Beta vulgaris* spp)

Use the young tender leaves from the garden beetroot plant, or the leaves of spinach-beet, or seakale-beet or chard, grown especially for their leaves. They are slightly bitter with a mild, earthy and nutty taste.

### MUSTARD GREENS (*Brassica nigra, B. hirta*)

A leaf that you won't find except in specialist shops. Those from *B. nigra*, black mustard, are used as a vegetable in the East. The leaf is increasingly popular in restaurant salad bowls. It has a tart pungent flavour ranging from quite mild to hot and peppery. Eat the small tender leaves, stalks and buds. (The leaf shoots of *B. hirta*, also known as *Sinapis alba*, or white mustard, often turn up in a mustard and cress mixture.)

## SWISS CHARD (*Beta vulgaris* spp)
This leafy plant is a beetroot cultivar and comes in red and white stalked varieties. Mild in flavour, it should only be eaten raw when the leaves are very small.

## TURNIP GREENS (*Brassica* spp)
A small tart leaf grows from the top of the turnip. If this is left to enlarge, the leaves can become the vegetable sold as spring greens.

## ICEBERG OR CRISPHEAD LETTUCE
(*Lactuca sativa* spp)
A 'cabbage' lettuce, with large very tight heads of pale green leaves. They contain a very high percentage of water and very little flavour. Grown as a pest- and bolt-resistant salad leaf whose primary or only advantage is the crispness and crunch.

## ROUND OR BUTTER LETTUCE
(*Lactuca sativa* spp)
Our most common, everyday lettuce is loose-headed with wasteful outside leaves. The leaves taste nicer than they look, tender and delicate with hints of sweetness. Summer varieties have a good crop heart, and in recent years growers have developed the heart only in the form of Little Gem lettuces which have proved a godsend to those who constantly fight over the heart!

## COS OR ROMAINE LETTUCE (*Lactuca sativa* spp)
Originally called 'cos' by the Romans who claimed to have discovered it on the Greek island of Cos. When the Romans brought it north, it was called romaine, a name the Americans adopted, while we reverted to cos. It is an elongated head of dark green oval leaves with a crisp pale-green heart. It has a pungent flavour and stays crisp. Unfortunately, growers allow it to grow too long, and so it loses its unique flavour. It is the salad leaf used in Caesar salad.

## CORN SALAD, LAMB'S LETTUCE OR *MÂCHE*
(*Valerianella locusta*)
This used to be gathered in the wild, long before it was cultivated. It has small round leaves with a deep green colour. It has a mild flavour and makes a good partner to some of the more bitter leaves. It over-winters very well and is one of the few salad leaves that can be around when others have disappeared. As the whole plant is often picked, the leaves will usually require a good wash.

## MINER'S LETTUCE OR PURSLANE
(*Portuluca oleracea*)
This has pale to deep green, saucer-shaped leaves with quite a thick texture. A rarity in the greengrocer's, but quite highly rated by chefs. They have great crunch and an unusual, mildly sour flavour.

## NASTURTIUM (*Tropaeolum majus*)
A peppery, shield-shaped, pale green to dark green leaf that is usually grown for its flowers. Both leaves and flowers are edible and add colour and flavour to any salad. The seeds that form after the flowers have faded are often pickled and used in a similar way to capers.

## RADICCHIO OR RED VERONA CHICORY
(*Cichorium intybus*)
All chicories in Italy are known as *radicchio*, but we know it as the tight-headed, round ruby leaf lettuce. It has a tangy bitter flavour and its wonderful colour adds an extra dimension to a salad. We can occasionally get a cos-like version, which comes from Treviso, and is often known as *trevise*.

## SORREL (*Rumex acetosa*)
I could, and probably should, have placed sorrel in the Herb section, but its characteristic lemony tang is welcome in leaf salads. There are several varieties, but most common in culinary use is French sorrel. It is high in oxalic acid hence its sharp citrus flavour.

## SPINACH (*Spinacea oleracea*)
I'll be dealing with spinach later, but it is definitely worth mentioning in salad leaves. For salads buy baby spinach leaves which are widely available in washed form in supermarkets. A leaf rich in iron.

## WATERCRESS (*Nasturtium officinale*)
Another peppery leaf, which is very nutritious. It grows along streams in limestone-rich areas. It has smooth round leaves, dark green in colour, and is available all year round. Choose bunches with no yellow leaves, and keep refrigerated, with the stems sitting in water.

# Bitter Leaves with Pear, Roquefort and Hazelnuts

The creaminess of blue cheese such as Roquefort contrasts well with the bitterness of chicory, radicchio and dandelion, and the crunch of the hazelnuts.

**Preparation: 10 minutes**
**Serves: 4**

2 ripe Conference pears
1 teaspoon lemon juice
1 head radicchio, coarsely chopped
1 head chicory, leaves separated and ripped
1 handful dandelion or watercress leaves
115g (4 oz) Roquefort or other blue cheese, cut in small pieces
2 tablespoons hazelnut oil
2 tablespoons extra virgin olive oil
1 tablespoon balsamic vinegar
salt and ground black pepper
55g (2 oz) hazelnuts, toasted and roughly chopped

**1** Peel and core the pears, dice the flesh into 5mm (¼ in) pieces and toss with the lemon juice. Set aside.
**2** Combine the radicchio, chicory and dandelion in a mixing bowl. Add the pears and fold in the cheese.
**3** Mix the oils and vinegar and season to taste. Pour the dressing over the salad, sprinkle over the nuts and toss to combine.

* * * * * * * *

*Combine shredded rocket and radicchio with jumbo cooked prawns, shredded Parma ham, diced avocado and shards of fresh Parmesan.*

* * * * * * * *

# Rocket and Radicchio Salad with Parmesan Shavings

A simple satisfying salad, perfect for a light first course with its contrasting flavours of the bitter radicchio, peppery rocket and powerful Parmesan.

**Preparation: 10 minutes**
**Serves: 4**

2 handfuls rocket leaves, washed
1 head radicchio
1 tablespoon balsamic vinegar
½ tablespoon lemon juice
6 tablespoons extra virgin olive oil
salt and ground black pepper
1 × 55g (2 oz) piece of Parmigiano Reggiano or Grana Padano

**1** Make sure the rocket is dry, using a salad spinner.
**2** Cut the radicchio in quarters and remove the white central core. Cut each piece crossways into strips approximately the same size as the rocket. Combine with the rocket.
**3** Mix the balsamic vinegar and lemon juice. Whisk in the olive oil and season with salt and pepper.
**4** With a potato peeler or cheese slice, form Parmesan shavings by slicing or 'peeling' as thinly as possible.
**5** Pour the dressing over the leaves, using as much as is necessary to coat the leaves. Toss well, then scatter the Parmesan over the top of the leaves and serve.

* * * * * * * * * *

*Watercress combines well with boiled baby beets, hard-boiled eggs and chopped anchovies.*

* * * * * * * * * *

# Warm Dandelion and Crispy Bacon Salad with a Sweet and Sour Dressing

Most salad dressings are heavily based on oil; this one reverses the situation by using mainly vinegar. A salad that needs to be eaten the moment it is made.

**Preparation and cooking: 25 minutes**

**Serves: 4**

| |
|---|
| 4 handfuls dandelion leaves |
| 1 handful baby spinach leaves |
| 1 handful rocket leaves |
| 15g (½ oz) unsalted butter |
| 175g (6 oz) smoked streaky bacon, diced |
| 2 cloves garlic, finely chopped |
| 4 egg yolks |
| 6 tablespoons cider vinegar |
| 1 tablespoon caster sugar |
| ½ teaspoon English mustard powder |
| 2 tablespoons snipped chives |
| 1 tablespoon chopped chervil |
| 2 teaspoons chopped tarragon |
| salt and ground black pepper |

**1** Combine the dandelion, spinach and rocket leaves.

**2** Melt the butter in a heavy frying pan, add the bacon and garlic, and over a medium heat cook until the bacon is crispy. Remove the bacon and garlic and place on kitchen paper. Allow the pan fats to cool slightly.

**3** Add the egg yolks to the bacon fat in the pan and whisk vigorously. Add the vinegar, sugar and mustard and cook over a low heat until smooth and thickened. Do not allow to boil or the mixture will curdle.

**4** Transfer the dressing to a bowl, fold in the herbs and season to taste. Pour the dressing over the salad leaves and toss to combine. Sprinkle with the crispy bacon and serve immediately.

## *Gratin* of Greens

● *Blanch 675g (1½ lb) green leaves, drain and finely chop. Preheat the oven to 180°C/350°F/Gas 4.*

● *Heat 2 tablespoons olive oil with 2 diced shallots, 3 chopped cloves garlic and cook until soft.*

● *Fold in the greens and cook for 2 minutes. Set aside.*

● *Beat together 4 large eggs, 350ml (12 fl oz) double cream and 175g (6 oz) grated Gruyère cheese.*

● *Add the greens mixture, season, and pour mixture into a baking dish. Sprinkle with 3 tablespoons grated Parmesan.*

● *Place dish in a warm **bain-marie** and bake for 25 minutes. Serve with roast or grilled meats.*

*Combine baby spinach leaves with clean raw, sliced button mushrooms, crumbled crispy bacon and Parmesan-dusted croûtons.*

*Serve grilled goat's cheese on shredded chicory with an anchovy dressing.*

# Risotto of Greens, Garlic, Anchovies and Capers

A delicious risotto making full use of different salad leaves. One advantage of wilting leaves is that you don't have to be too fussy about the quality of the leaf – outsize, outside and secondary leaves are all fair game.

**Preparation and cooking: 30 minutes**
**Serves: 4**

2 tablespoons extra virgin olive oil

1 onion, finely chopped

3 cloves garlic, finely chopped

5 anchovy fillets, drained and chopped

350g (12 oz) arborio rice

2 litres (3½ pints) chicken or vegetable stock, boiling

8 handfuls salad leaves (rocket, spinach, escarole, mustard greens), ripped

55g (2 oz) unsalted butter

115g (4 oz) Parmesan, freshly grated

ground black pepper

2 tablespoons tiny capers, drained and rinsed

**1** In a large saucepan heat the olive oil, add the onion and garlic, and cook over a medium heat until the onion has softened without colour, about 8–10 minutes.

**2** Add the anchovies and rice and stir to coat the grains in the oil. Cook for 2 minutes until the rice becomes translucent.

**3** Add a ladle or two of stock. Stir the rice until it has absorbed most of the stock. Add a little more stock and repeat. Continue to add stock little by little until the rice is almost cooked. The mixture should be creamy without being too wet.

**4** Add the greens and cook for a further 3 minutes until the leaves have **wilted**. Fold in the butter and Parmesan and stir to combine. Season to taste with pepper.

**5** Just before serving fold in the capers. Remember that risotto continues to cook after you remove it from the heat, so serve immediately.

## Chicken Liver Salad

● *Fry together 2 tablespoons olive oil, 1 chopped shallot with 1 chopped garlic clove and cook until soft. Remove and set aside.*

● *Add 4 tablespoons of small bread croûtons and fry until golden, remove and keep warm.*

● *Add to the pan 225g (8 oz) cleaned and halved chicken livers and fry for 3–5 minutes, turning once.*

● *Add 1 tablespoon balsamic vinegar to the pan with the livers.*

● *Fold the croûtons and shallot back into the pan, mix, add 1 tablespoon walnut oil and warm through.*

● *Toss hot liver dressing with 4 handfuls ripped curly endive leaves and serve immediately.*

## Chicory with Mustard

*Chicory works for me with a creamy mustard dressing.*

● *Crush 1 clove garlic with a little salt, add 2 teaspoons Dijon mustard, 1 tablespoon aged red wine vinegar, 3 tablespoons extra virgin olive oil, ¼ teaspoon ground black pepper and 3 tablespoons snipped chives.*

● *Whisk in 3 tablespoons double cream until emulsified.*

*Rocket leaves on their own dressed with extra virgin olive oil and a wedge of lemon is a simple little starter for those watching their waistline. So what's a little olive oil between friends!*

# SPINACH

Spinach (*Spinacea oleracea*) is a highly prized vegetable, not only because it supplies us with copious amounts of vitamins, calcium and iron, but because it is also exceptionally adaptable and can be eaten raw or cooked. It was first grown by the Persians and eventually found its way to Spain and subsequently the remainder of Europe. It is eaten regularly in India, China, Italy, France and the Middle East, a worldly vegetable. There are several varieties available, but chefs often favour New Zealand spinach, a close relation, which appears to have a much crisper leaf. Some of that must be the British attitude to transport and packaging, because I grow many varieties in my garden, and have always found home-grown spinach to be every bit as good as that which has suffered 14,000 miles' travelling.

Spinach is available all year; it is also possible to buy bags of baby spinach leaves which are perfect for salads but a waste of space for cooking. Allow 350g (12 oz) spinach raw per person because, when cooked, it shrinks enormously. Buy spinach that looks fresh and lively, rather than limp. Frozen spinach is available in leaf, chopped and creamed, which, although one of the better frozen vegetables, bears no comparison to fresh. Fresh takes a little effort, and usually needs several good washes in deep water to allow the mud or sandy soil to drop to the bottom. For large leaves, remove the central stem by folding the leaf in half and sliding your hand down the stem towards the leaf, pulling the leaf away from the stem in one easy action.

The modern trend for cooking spinach is to place the leaves in a pan with only the water clinging to them. The spinach will **wilt**, and should be turned over regularly with tongs to make sure each leaf has hit the heat. This process will take about 3–5 minutes. For larger quantities, cook in plenty of boiling salted water for 2 minutes. Drain in a colander and use a saucer or small plate to push down on the spinach to extract as much liquid as possible. After that return it to the heat and pump in plenty of butter with black pepper, nutmeg and a little salt. If you need to use the spinach cold for pasta, a soufflé or a roulade, plunge the cooked spinach into a large bowl of iced water, then squeeze out excess moisture, using your hands. For purée, cook ripped leaves of spinach then drain and transfer to a food processor with butter, salt, black pepper and nutmeg. Double cream is an alternative extra.

# Spinach and Coconut Soup

Hints of Thailand influence this light creamy soup, which is very smooth and very moreish. For a variation you can add some cooked mussels or flaked white crabmeat.

**Preparation and cooking: 40 minutes**
**Serves: 4–6**

40g (1½ oz) unsalted butter
1 red onion, finely chopped
3 cloves garlic, finely chopped
1 tablespoon finely chopped fresh ginger
2 teaspoons *Thai Green Curry Paste* (see page 255)
½ teaspoon ground turmeric
600ml (1 pint) coconut milk
600ml (1 pint) chicken or vegetable stock
2 lime leaves, finely chopped
1 stem lemongrass, tender leaves only, finely chopped
450g (1 lb) spinach, washed, stems removed, roughly chopped
2 teaspoons *nam pla* (fish sauce)
1 tablespoon fresh lime juice
2 tablespoons chopped basil
2 tablespoons crispy shallots (buy in Oriental supermarkets)

**1** Heat the butter in a large saucepan, add the onion, garlic and ginger, and cook until the onion has softened, about 8–10 minutes.
**2** Add the curry paste and turmeric, and cook for a further 3 minutes over a medium heat, stirring continuously.
**3** Add half the coconut milk and cook until the mixture starts to split, about 5–8 minutes. Add the stock, lime leaves and lemongrass, and cook for 10 minutes.
**4** Add the spinach and cook for 5 minutes. Add the remaining coconut milk, and spoon the mixture in batches into a liquidiser. A word of caution, don't fill the liquidiser more than half full when you're working with hot liquid. Pass the liquid through a sieve, for a very smooth soup, into a saucepan.
**5** Return to the heat and add the fish sauce, lime juice and basil. Warm through gently.
**6** Pour the soup into warm bowls, and offer your guests some crispy shallots to scatter on top.

# Spinach Soufflé

This is an adaptation of the signature dish of Langan's restaurant in London and is particularly good. They serve it perfectly partnered with anchovy sauce, so you could accompany mine with the recipe on page 10.

**Preparation and cooking: 1 hour**
**Serves: 4–6**

500g (18 oz) cooked spinach, puréed

55g (2 oz) unsalted butter

6 anchovy fillets, finely chopped (optional)

25g (1 oz) plain flour

150ml (¼ pint) milk

pinch of grated nutmeg

salt and ground black pepper

½ teaspoon grated orange rind

4 egg yolks

55g (2 oz) Parmesan, freshly grated

5 egg whites

2 tablespoons fresh breadcrumbs

**1** Place the spinach in a saucepan with 15g (½ oz) of the butter and the anchovies, and warm through over a medium heat.

**2** Make a *béchamel* sauce by melting 25g (1 oz) butter, adding the flour and cooking the resulting **roux** for 5 minutes until it starts to turn a pale nutty colour. Add the milk by degrees, whisking continuously for a smooth thick sauce. Simmer over a low heat for 10 minutes to cook out the flour, stirring constantly.

**3** Fold the spinach mixture into the *béchamel* sauce, and season with nutmeg and ground black pepper. Because of the anchovies, it shouldn't need any extra salt.

**4** Fold in the orange rind then the egg yolks one by one, beating between each addition. Add half the cheese. Preheat the oven to 200°C/400°F/Gas 6, and heat a flat baking tray in it.

**5** Beat the egg whites with a pinch of salt to **stiff peaks**. Fold 1 large spoonful into the spinach mix to slacken the mixture, then gently fold in the remainder, taking care not to beat out the airiness.

**6** Use the remaining butter to grease a 1.4 litre (2½ pint) soufflé dish. Combine the remaining Parmesan with the breadcrumbs and sprinkle over the buttered areas of the dish. Shake out any surplus.

**7** Pour in the soufflé mixture. Run a palette knife around the top inch of the soufflé to release the mixture from the sides. This helps the soufflé to rise evenly.

**8** Place the soufflé on the hot tray in the oven and bake for 25 minutes without disturbing. If you have a windowed oven door and the soufflé is browning too quickly, reduce the heat to 180°C/350°F/Gas 4. Serve immediately, with anchovy sauce.

· · · · · · · · · ·

*Dress raw baby spinach leaves with vinaigrette and top with pan-fried chicken livers, crispy bacon and poached egg.*

· · · · · · · · · ·

· · · · · · · · · · · · · · · · · · · · · · · · · · ·

## Spinach Dip

● *Blend 2 handfuls of raw picked spinach leaves with 5 chopped spring onions, 3 tablespoons chopped parsley, 1 teaspoon chopped garlic and 2 anchovy fillets.*

● *Fold mixture into 150ml (¼ pint) soured cream and 150ml (¼ pint) mayonnaise.*

● *Season to taste with lemon juice, salt and pepper.*

● *Serve as a dip with shellfish or raw vegetables.*

· · · · · · · · · · · · · · · · · · · · · · · · · · ·

# Spinach and Garlic *Gnocchi*

An excellent way of getting your children to eat spinach. In my experience they enjoy all forms of *gnocchi*, especially with a cheese sauce.

**Preparation and cooking: overnight + 4 hours**
**Serves: 2–4**

100g (3½ oz) garlic and herb Boursin cheese

175g (6 oz) ricotta cheese, drained in a sieve for 3 hours

350g (12 oz) cooked, dried and finely chopped spinach

55g (2 oz) Parmesan, grated

4 tablespoons plain flour

2 eggs, lightly beaten

pinch of freshly grated nutmeg

salt and ground black pepper

**1** Combine the Boursin, drained ricotta and chopped spinach until an even consistency and colour. Fold in the Parmesan and flour. Beat in the eggs, then season with nutmeg, salt and pepper. Refrigerate the mixture overnight.

**2** Flour a board and roll the mixture into long ropes, 1cm (½ in) in diameter. Cut the ropes into 2.5cm (1 in) pieces and drop into lightly boiling salted water. Simmer until the *gnocchi* rise to the surface, about 3–5 minutes; the *gnocchi* can be made ahead to this point. Remove with a slotted spoon to an oiled dish.

**3** Either fry the *gnocchi* in butter with some sage leaves (see photograph), or bake them covered with cheese sauce (see page 85) and sprinkled with a mixture of breadcrumbs and Parmesan, and a little melted butter, in a hot oven at 200°C/400°F/Gas 6 for 10–15 minutes until golden.

*Place cooked buttered spinach in the bottom of a* gratin *dish and place poached eggs or lightly poached sole fillets on top. Coat with a light cheese sauce and bake until golden.*

## Spinach Pancake Stack
*Make a pancake stack by layering pancakes with thinly sliced ham and cooked spinach combined with Béchamel Sauce (see page 60).*
*● Layer the pancakes 6 high and coat the whole with hot reduced cream and grated Gruyère cheese.*
*● Bake in a hot oven until bubbling and golden.*

## Spinach and Basil Sauce

*Make a cold spinach and basil sauce for cold poached salmon.*

● *Melt 25g (1 oz) unsalted butter with 1 teaspoon olive oil, and add 2 finely chopped shallots, ½ teaspoon thyme leaves and 1 teaspoon chopped garlic. Cook until the shallot has softened without colour.*

● *Add 150ml (¼ pint) Dry Martini and boil to reduce to 2 tablespoons; add 300ml (½ pint) vegetable stock and reduce by one-third.*

● *Add 2 handfuls de-stemmed spinach and cook for 2 minutes with 4 tablespoons chopped watercress and 2 handfuls basil leaves.*

● *Liquidise the whole and pass through a sieve, allow to cool then fold in 4 tablespoons double cream and serve.*

*Spinach and children don't generally see eye to eye. A solution is to blanch spinach leaves one by one for 10 seconds in boiling water to **wilt**. Lay them out on kitchen paper to dry. Stick 4 leaves together then dip each mini pile in flour and then in beaten egg. Fry in oil until crispy on both sides. Pour over warmed honey or golden syrup and dredge with icing sugar.*

*Pan-fry onions, garlic and anchovies in a large quantity of extra virgin olive oil. Work this mixture into copious amounts of cooked drained spinach. Season and allow to cool to room temperature, sprinkle with lemon juice and serve as a cooked spinach salad.*

# SWEDE AND TURNIP

Just thinking of swede used to make me nauseous when I had to suffer the watery, woody orange slop of school dinners. It was so bad that I used to research what was on the menu for that day, and if it was swede, I would smuggle in a plastic bag into which I would pour the slop when the master at the end of the table wasn't watching. Now that I know how to cook it, swede has become one of my favourite winter vegetables.

Swede (*Brassica napus*) and turnip (*Brassica campestris* or *rapa*) are closely related to each other (and to rape), and are grown for their roots. They were once generally considered to be a poor man's vegetable. The turnip, of European origin, has been around for thousands of years, and is highly prized in France, especially in its modern mini version. The swede is thought to be a lot younger than the turnip, possibly produced in the seventeenth century, a hybridisation of a cabbage with a turnip. The swede is eaten mainly in northern European and Scandinavian countries; elsewhere it is often fed to livestock. In America it is known as turnip or rutabaga, and in Scotland as turnip or, colloquially, neeps.

Turnips have a white flesh and a white skin, often with a purple top. Young turnip leaves can also be eaten and have a peppery flavour, excellent in salads or stirred into pasta or risotto. The swede has an orange flesh which becomes darker when cooked; it usually has a yellowy brown skin, although one can also find varieties with white skins. Both vegetables contain vitamin C, especially the leaves, and natural sugars.

When buying either vegetable, look for those with smooth skins, and that feel heavy for their size. Avoid buying wrinkled roots as this indicates age and water loss. Large turnips can be quite woody and spongy, and are not good for much apart from dicing into stews or making into purée; buy young turnips in the spring; swede is usually fine all year round. Turnips last for about a week, whereas swede will last a couple of months if kept in a dark place. (For another turnip-style vegetable in winter you could buy kohlrabi, a related green root vegetable, with a great crunch and white flesh.)

Both vegetables need to be peeled before cooking, although occasionally the baby turnips can be cooked unpeeled. Cut off 1cm (½ in) top and bottom and you will notice a distinct line just below the skin, which shows you how deep to peel the vegetables. The younger the vegetables, the shallower the line. Both vegetables are hard, so a sharp knife and great care must be taken when dicing or slicing. Always cut off a rounded edge, or cut in half to create a flat surface.

Both vegetables can be boiled, steamed or braised, or small dice can be added to soups or stews. Small turnips will cook in about 15 minutes, and 2.5cm (1 in) dice of swede will take about 20–25 minutes.

## Swede Chutney

*Swede makes an unusual and cheap chutney.*

- *Grate 500g (18 oz) swede and 500g (18 oz) onions. Core and chop 1 large cooking apple and combine with the swede and onion, 115g (4 oz) sultanas, 350g (12 oz) caster sugar, 1 teaspoon ground ginger, ½ teaspoon dried chilli flakes, ¼ teaspoon ground cloves, ¼ teaspoon powdered cinnamon, 2 teaspoons English mustard powder, 1 teaspoon turmeric, 1 teaspoon chopped garlic, 1 tablespoon honey, 1 tablespoon salt and 1.2 litres (2 pints) cider vinegar.*
- *Mix everything together in a **non-reactive** saucepan and simmer over a medium heat for 1 hour.*
- *Bottle in clean sterilised hot jars, and seal when cold.*

*When making a gratin dauphinoise (see page 273) halve the amount of potatoes and substitute thinly sliced turnip.*

# Red Pepper Turnips  Ⓥ

A lovely, brightly coloured purée with peppery flavours, which is a great partner to grilled fish.

**Preparation and cooking: 35 minutes**
**Serves: 4–6**

| |
|---|
| 25g (1 oz) unsalted butter |
| 1 onion, finely diced |
| 450g (1 lb) turnips, peeled and diced |
| 115g (4 oz) potato, diced |
| 1 red pepper, diced |
| 6 tablespoons dry vermouth |
| ½ teaspoon soft thyme leaves |
| ½ tablespoon caster sugar |
| 1½ tablespoons paprika |
| 150ml (¼ pint) double cream |
| 2 tablespoons chopped flat-leaf parsley |
| 1 tablespoon snipped chives |
| salt and ground black pepper |

**1** Melt the butter in a heavy-based saucepan and add the onion, turnip, potato and red pepper. Toss to combine.
**2** Combine the vermouth, thyme, sugar and paprika and pour over the vegetables. Cover and cook over a medium heat for 15–20 minutes until the turnip is tender.
**3** Place everything in a food processor and blend until smooth. For a very smooth purée, pass through a fine sieve.
**4** Return the purée to the heat and fold in the cream and herbs. Season to taste, and serve hot.

. . . . . . . . . . . . . . . . . . . . . . . . . . . . . . .

## Sweet Honeyed Turnips

● *Melt 1 tablespoon unsalted butter with 2 tablespoons honey in a saucepan. Add 450g (1 lb) baby peeled turnips with ¼ teaspoon ground black pepper, and cook covered for 15–20 minutes until tender.*
● *Season to taste and sprinkle with parsley and chives.*

. . . . . . . . . . . . . . . . . . . . . . . . . . . . . . .

# Spring Vegetable Stew

A perfect starter, or a partner to roast spring lamb. For vegetarians omit the bacon.

**Preparation and cooking: 45 minutes**
**Serves: 4–6**

| |
|---|
| 85g (3 oz) unsalted butter |
| 175g (6 oz) smoked streaky bacon, diced |
| 12 baby onions |
| 1 clove garlic, finely chopped |
| ½ teaspoon soft thyme leaves |
| 20 baby carrots, scrubbed |
| 20 baby turnips, lightly peeled |
| 350g (12 oz) podded peas |
| 8 very small Jersey new potatoes, scrubbed |
| 1 bay leaf |
| ¼ teaspoon ground black pepper |
| 4 Little Gem lettuces, halved |
| 1 tablespoon truffle oil (optional) |
| salt |

**1** Place 15g (½ oz) of the butter in a saucepan with the bacon and cook over a medium heat for 6 minutes without the bacon taking on much colour.
**2** Add the onions, garlic, thyme, carrots, turnips, peas, potatoes, bay leaf and black pepper. Stir to combine. Pour in 125 ml (4 fl oz) water and cover the vegetables with the lettuce. Cover with the lid and cook over a low heat for about 30 minutes until the potatoes are tender. Check from time to time that the liquid hasn't evaporated. Top up as necessary.
**3** Fold in the remaining butter and truffle oil (if using) and swirl the vegetables around to emulsify the liquids and fats. Season to taste. If you don't use the truffle oil, fold in 1 tablespoon chopped flat-leaf parsley and ½ tablespoon chopped dill.

# Bashed Neeps

A favourite in Scotland, served with haggis, whisky and tatties (potatoes). This is the recipe that returned swedes to my favour.

**Preparation and cooking: 40 minutes**
**Serves: 4–6**

1kg (2¼ lb) swede, cut in 2.5cm (1 in) pieces

salt

115g (4 oz) unsalted butter, diced

½ teaspoon ground black pepper

pinch of ground ginger

pinch of grated nutmeg

**1** Cook the swede in plenty of salted water for 25 minutes until very tender, drain and return to a dry pan to evaporate any remaining moisture over a low heat.

**2** Mash or pass through a **mouli-légumes**. Return to the saucepan over a low heat and beat in the butter, pepper, ginger and nutmeg. A little double cream may be added if desired. Adjust seasoning with a little more salt if necessary.

## Root Soup

*A cheap winter soup.*
- *Melt 25g (1 oz) unsalted butter in a large saucepan with 1 chopped onion, 1 chopped stick celery, 1 chopped clove garlic, 1 bay leaf, 1 teaspoon soft thyme leaves, 450g (1 lb) chopped turnips, 450g (1 lb) chopped swede and 2 diced floury potatoes.*
- *Cover the whole lot with 1.2 litres (2 pints) chicken or vegetable stock, and cook uncovered over a medium heat for 30 minutes.*
- *Pour into a food processor in two batches and liquidise until smooth.*
- *Return to the heat and fold in 150ml (¼ pint) double cream. Season to taste.*

Haggis and Bashed Neeps,
a Scottish institution.

## Warm Salad of Turnip Leaves

- *Pan-fry 4 chopped cloves garlic with 150ml (¼ pint) extra virgin olive oil, 1 chopped fresh chilli and 4 chopped anchovies.*
- *When the garlic is tender, fold in 55g (2 oz) fresh breadcrumbs and cook until golden. Set aside.*
- *Blanch 3 handfuls of washed turnip leaves, squeeze dry and toss with the savoury breadcrumbs. Season to taste.*

## Apple and Swede Purée

*A vegetable purée to serve with roast pork.*
- *Cook and mash 1kg (2¼ lb) swede; set aside.*
- *Cook 2 peeled, cored and chopped cooking apples with 1 teaspoon grated lemon rind, ½ teaspoon chopped thyme leaves, 85g (3 oz) soft dark brown sugar and a pinch of powdered cinnamon.*
- *Cook covered over a low heat until pulped, about 30 minutes.*
- *Combine the apple with the swede and fold in 85g (3 oz) soft butter, 150ml (¼ pint) double cream and 1 tablespoon dark rum. Season to taste.*

# SWEETCORN

Maize or sweetcorn (*Zea mays*) originated in Mexico, and was the staple diet of the Mayan, Aztec and Inca peoples. Half of the world's production of maize is in the twelve American states which constitute the famous Corn Belt. Maize is also grown in Europe, China, South America and South Africa. It can be grown in the UK, but is primarily a warm climate crop (most British maize is fed to chickens). There are many varieties of maize and the one grown to be eaten as a young vegetable contains a high proportion of sugar. It is high in beta-carotene.

If you grow sweetcorn to eat, it will be a pale imitation of the deep yellow ripened cobs you find in the States, and if you allow it to mature to yellow, you may find it is very mealy and tough. I hate to say it, but you will probably be better off eating frozen corn on the cob, as fresh corn kernels convert sugars to starch very quickly (40 per cent within 6 hours of picking), so lose their sweetness. (Baby corn, mainly coming from the Far East, is picked from the plant before pollination or fertilisation.)

From maize and corn comes one of today's most popular ingredients, *polenta*, and other products and foods deriving from corn include popcorn, cornmeal, cornflour, hominy grits, cornbread, *tortillas* and *tamales*, corn syrup, corn oil, and that classic American whiskey, bourbon.

If you are buying fresh corn, choose cobs that have green husks with exposed silk (the threads at the top) no darker than amber in colour. If possible, peel back the husk to check that the kernels are plump; they should ooze a milky fluid if pricked with your fingernail.

To cook corn, remove the silk and husk and cook in boiling water for up to 15 minutes. For those who grow their own, 5–8 minutes' cooking will be sufficient. Never salt the water as this will toughen the kernels and lengthen the cooking time. Alternatively, cook the corn in half water and half milk with a good knob of butter. This makes the corn taste sweeter (use the cooking liquor for a soup). To barbecue the corn, fold back the husk and remove the silk, then fold the husk back over the cob to protect the kernels. Dip the whole corn in boiling water for 2 minutes then place on the barbecue for 15 minutes, turning every 5 minutes. Pull back the husk before eating with barbecue sauce or butter. Serve boiled corn with best-quality butter, sea salt and a decent amount of ground black pepper.

To remove the kernels from the cob, stand the cob on its flatter end and, with a downward movement, cut just under the rows of kernels down the length of the cob.

## Spicy Sweetcorn *Compote*

*Great for barbecues.*

● *Combine 225g (8 oz) sweetcorn kernels, 225g (8 oz) cherry tomatoes, 1 bunch finely chopped spring onions, 1 seeded and finely chopped chilli, 1 tablespoon caster sugar, 50 ml (2 fl oz) red wine vinegar, 1 tablespoon chopped fresh coriander leaves and 1 tablespoon chopped fresh flat-leaf parsley leaves in a bowl.*

● *Once the sugar has dissolved, put into sterilised jars.*

## Sweetcorn Salad

*Combine 450g (1 lb) cooked corn kernels with 450g (1 lb) diced cooked chicken, 2 diced tomatoes, 4 chopped spring onions, 1 clove garlic crushed with a little salt, 2 tablespoons chopped flat-leaf parsley, 1 tablespoon snipped chives, ½ teaspoon salt, 4 tablespoons mayonnaise, 3 tablespoons soured cream and ½ teaspoon toasted cumin seeds.*

# Corn Pudding

Serve at Christmas with your roast turkey or other roast meats. This also makes a good filling for a quiche.

**Preparation and cooking: 1½ hours**

**Serves: 6–8**

15g (½ oz) unsalted butter

½ onion, finely chopped

1 clove garlic, finely chopped

1 teaspoon thyme leaves

½ green pepper, finely chopped

2 green chillies, finely diced

corn kernels from 3 corn cobs

2 tablespoons plain flour

150ml (¼ pint) milk

3 eggs

300ml (½ pint) double cream

1 teaspoon salt

¼ teaspoon ground black pepper

¼ teaspoon freshly grated nutmeg

pinch of cayenne pepper

2 tablespoons chopped flat-leaf parsley

1 tablespoon snipped chives

55g (2 oz) Parmesan, freshly grated

55g (2 oz) Gruyère cheese, grated

**1** Preheat the oven to 180°C/350°F/Gas 4.

**2** Heat the butter in a frying pan, add the onion, garlic, thyme, green pepper and chilli, and cook over a medium heat for 8 minutes. Add half the corn and cook for 10 minutes. Set aside.

**3** Place the remaining corn in a food processor with the flour, milk and eggs, and blend until smooth. Set aside.

**4** To the corn in the frying pan add the cream, salt, pepper, nutmeg and cayenne. Fold in the corn purée, the herbs and both cheeses.

**5** Pour the mixture into a greased 1.7 litre (3 pint) soufflé dish, place in a hot **bain-marie** and bake until the mixture is firm, about 1 hour. Let the pudding stand for 10 minutes before serving. This can also be served cold with meats and salad.

## Corn Chowder

● Cook 3 hot chopped chillies in 1 tablespoon olive oil for 2 minutes.

● Add 2 chopped cloves garlic, 1 tablespoon each of ground cumin and coriander, 2 puréed tomatoes, 225g (8 oz) puréed sweetcorn and 225g (8 oz) puréed onions.

● Cook for 10 minutes then add 600ml (1 pint) milk, 600ml (1 pint) chicken or vegetable stock, 225g (8 oz) fresh corn kernels, 3 diced large potatoes, 2 diced roasted red peppers (see page 254), 2 teaspoons salt, 1 teaspoon ground black pepper and ½ teaspoon cayenne pepper.

● Cook until the potatoes are tender, about 20 minutes.

● Add 4 tablespoons double cream, 1 tablespoon snipped chives and 2 tablespoons chopped flat-leaf parsley. Check the seasoning.

*Cook corn kernels in boiling water, drain and set aside. Fry chopped spring onion with diced red chilli and chopped garlic. Add a little chilli sauce, some chopped coriander leaves and soured cream. Fold in the cooked corn and warm through, do not boil. Season to taste. Great with grilled foods.*

# Sweetcorn Fritters

A useful brunch dish served with crispy bacon, poached eggs and hollandaise (see page 113), or great served with *Southern Fried Chicken* (see page 88) as in the photograph.

**Preparation and cooking: 25 minutes**
**Serves: 4**

| |
|---|
| 4 corn cobs |
| 300ml (½ pint) milk |
| 60g (2¼ oz) plain flour |
| pinch of paprika |
| 1 teaspoon baking powder |
| ¼ teaspoon salt |
| ¼ teaspoon celery salt |
| pinch of cayenne pepper |
| 2 eggs, separated |
| 1 teaspoon clear honey |
| unsalted butter for frying |

**1** Remove the corn kernels from the cobs. Blend half the kernels with the milk and pass through a fine sieve to make a smooth purée. Combine the remaining kernels with this purée.

**2** Combine the flour with the paprika, baking powder, salt, celery salt and cayenne pepper.

**3** Beat the egg yolks together then whisk into the dry mixture. Fold in the corn mixture, followed by the honey. Allow to rest for 10 minutes.

**4** Beat the egg whites to **stiff peaks**. Mix 1 spoonful into the corn batter to slacken the mixture, then carefully fold in the remainder.

**5** Heat a little butter in a non-stick frying pan. Drop tablespoons of the corn mixture into the pan and cook until you see small bubbles appearing on the surface of the fritters, about 1½ minutes, then turn over and cook for a further 30–45 seconds. Keep warm while cooking the remainder.

• • • • • • • • • • • • • • • • • •

*Boil corn kernels until tender, then blend in a food processor with butter, double cream, a dash of Worcestershire sauce and a few drops of Tabasco for a sweetcorn purée. Good with chicken.*

• • • • • • • • • • • • • • • • • •

# Corn Relish

The perfect relish for barbecued meats, sandwiches or strongly flavoured hard cheese.

**Preparation and cooking: 1½ hours**
**Makes: 2 litres (3½ pints)**

| |
|---|
| corn kernels from 10 cobs, about 1kg (2¼ lb) |
| 2 onions, finely diced |
| 4 sticks celery, finely sliced |
| 2 red peppers, finely diced |
| 1 green pepper, finely diced |
| 280g (10 oz) caster sugar |
| 1.2 litres (2 pints) cider vinegar |
| 1 tablespoon English mustard powder |
| 1 teaspoon celery seeds |
| 1 tablespoon salt |
| ½ teaspoon turmeric |

**1** Combine all the ingredients in a **non-reactive** saucepan, and over a medium heat bring to the boil. Simmer uncovered for 1 hour.

**2** With a slotted spoon pack the vegetables into hot sterilised jars, leaving 2.5cm (1 in) space at the top. Spoon in the hot syrup to the top and seal.

**3** Place the jars on a rack or 2.5cm (1 in) depth of newspaper in a deep saucepan, and pour water in up to the necks of the jars. Bring slowly to the boil and simmer for 15 minutes. Cool and store for 1 month before using.

• • • • • • • • • • • • • • • • • • • • • • • • • • • • • •

# Popcorn

● *Heat 1 tablespoon vegetable oil in a frying pan and add popping corn kernels in one layer, cover with a lid and wait until you hear the corn popping, shaking the pan from time to time.*

● *When the popping stops, remove from the heat and tip the popcorn into a bowl.*

● *Mix with salt, melted butter and cayenne pepper.*

• • • • • • • • • • • • • • • • • • • • • • • • • • • • • •

# TOMATO

The tomato (*Lycopersicon esculentum*) is native to Central and South America, and its English name comes from the Aztec word, *tomatl*. Brought back to Europe by Spanish explorers in the sixteenth century, it was called love apple and then the golden apple (*pomodoro*). It didn't really reach northern Europe – or America – until the eighteenth century, and the British took a long time to lose their suspicion of this cousin of deadly nightshade and henbane (and aubergine, potato and sweet pepper). Tomatoes contain some vitamins and minerals, particularly potassium.

Most tomatoes sold today are a shadow of their historical selves. Grown hydroponically, they may look perfect but, as we all know, perfection is often only skin deep, and so it is with the modern tomato. Below this perfectly shaped, perfectly sized, perfectly coloured tomato lies watery, pale and tasteless flesh. I yearn for the markets of the South of France, Spain, Greece and Italy where you can buy craggy, slightly misshapen, warty tomatoes that you know are packed full of flavour. There was a time when chefs, bored with Dutch or Canary Island tomatoes, paid fortunes for Italian plum tomatoes; now even these have become tasteless and perfectly shaped. I grow tomatoes myself, and know that tomatoes do not all ripen at the same time and are never all the same size. Apparently the tomatoes are gassed to make them turn red. I advise all cooks to use tinned varieties in cooking because if you buy a good-quality canned tomato, you know it has been sun-ripened and so contains flavour.

So recipes in this section that use raw tomatoes are designed for the gardener unless by chance you can buy sun-ripened tomatoes in late summer or early autumn. Beefsteak tomatoes are large, often misshapen, tomatoes and are deep scarlet, wonderful for salads or sandwiches. Plum tomatoes are elongated and are excellent for sauces and tomato salads. The tiny cherry tomatoes are available in round and plum shapes, and in red, orange or yellow. Even commercial varieties of cherry tomatoes seem to have more flavour than the larger fellows. Only buy small amounts of tomatoes unless you are bottling sauces or making chutneys. If you grow tomatoes, at the end of the season before the first frosts you will often find that they stay green; these are excellent for frying in slices, coated in cornmeal, or making into chutney.

Often a recipe will ask for tomatoes to be skinned. Do this in one of two ways. Cut a cross on the bottom of the tomato and drop it in boiling water for 30–45 seconds, depending on ripeness. Remove the tomato to a bowl of iced water to arrest the cooking, then strip off the skin. Tomatoes skinned in this fashion are useful for soups or stews. The other method involves spearing the tomatoes and holding them over a gas flame until the skin blisters, and can be peeled off. If you want to use peeled tomatoes completely raw, cut the tomato in half, then each half in three. Cut between the flesh and skin with a very thin, sharp knife.

Sun-dried tomatoes, either in their dried form or preserved in olive oil, have been a useful recent addition to supermarket shelves, especially as fresh tomatoes have so little flavour. They can be added to salads or to casseroles to intensify the tomato flavour. You can make your own oven-dried tomatoes by cutting the tomato lengthways then removing the seeds. Sprinkle the cut surfaces with a little rock salt then place the tomatoes cut side down on a cake rack to allow the moisture to drain out. Heat the oven to 60°C/140°F/the very lowest gas possible, place the tomatoes on their racks in the oven, and leave overnight or for 10 hours. In the last couple of hours check that the tomatoes are not too leathery. Layer the dried tomatoes in a jar with fresh basil, thyme, rosemary, chilli and garlic and cover with a good olive oil, making sure that there are no trapped air bubbles.

# Chilled Tomato Bisque

Based on a *gazpacho*, but smooth instead of chunky, this soup is wonderfully refreshing on a hot summer's day.

**Preparation and cooking: 1 hour**
**Serves: 4–6**

1 slice white country bread, crusts discarded, broken into large crumbs
1 dessertspoon sherry vinegar
½ clove garlic, finely chopped
1 teaspoon caster sugar
½ fresh red chilli, finely diced
2 tablespoons extra virgin olive oil
225g (8 oz) plum tomatoes, skinned, seeded and chopped
1 dessertspoon Heinz tomato ketchup
200ml (7 fl oz) tomato juice
2 spring onions, finely sliced
½ red pepper, roasted or grilled (see page 254), skinned, seeded and diced
¼ large cucumber, peeled, seeded and roughly diced
1 dessertspoon pesto
salt and freshly ground black pepper
olive oil ice cubes (place olive oil in ice cube moulds and freeze)

**1** Place the bread in a food processor or blender. With the machine running add the vinegar, garlic, sugar and chilli, and blend until smooth.

**2** Add the extra virgin olive oil until the bread will absorb no more then, a little at a time, add the tomato pieces, tomato ketchup, tomato juice, spring onion, red pepper, cucumber and pesto. Continue to blend to form a smooth emulsion.

**3** Season to taste with salt and black pepper, and serve with frozen olive oil cubes floating on the top, if desired.

# Tomato Oil Pickle

A pickle with a good kick that is excellent with cold meats, cheese or curries.

**Preparation and cooking: overnight + 1½ hours**
**Makes: 2 litres (3½ pints)**

2 tablespoons mustard seeds
1 tablespoon celery seeds
350ml (12 fl oz) cider vinegar
115g (4 oz) grated fresh ginger
20 garlic cloves, roughly chopped
300ml (½ pint) vegetable oil
1 tablespoon ground turmeric
3 tablespoons ground cumin
½ tablespoon cayenne pepper
1 teaspoon onion salt
20 mild green chillies, halved
2 bay leaves
2 sprigs thyme
2kg (4½ lb) ripe tomatoes, skinned, seeded and chopped
225g (8 oz) caster sugar
½ tablespoon salt

**1** Soak the mustard and celery seeds overnight in the vinegar. The next day blend the vinegar mix in a food processor until reasonably smooth. Add the ginger and garlic and blend again until smooth.

**2** Heat the oil in a heavy-based **non-reactive** saucepan until smoking. Allow to cool a little then add the turmeric, cumin, cayenne and onion salt and cook for 3 minutes, stirring continuously.

**3** Add the chillies, bay leaves, thyme, tomato and the vinegar purée, bring to the boil, and cook over a low heat for 15 minutes. Add the sugar and salt, and cook until the tomato has reduced to a pulp and the oil has started to float to the top, about 45 minutes. Check seasoning.

**4** Allow to cool then pour into sterilised jars. Seal, and it will be ready to use after 2 weeks.

# Baked Herby Tomatoes

I love these for breakfast with good-quality grilled bacon.
They also make good partners to grilled or roast meats.

**Preparation and cooking: 45 minutes**
**Serves: 4**

450g (1 lb) large, ripe but firm tomatoes

salt and ground black pepper

1 shallot, finely diced

2 cloves garlic, chopped

1 teaspoon soft thyme leaves

2 tablespoons extra virgin olive oil

4 anchovies, chopped

2 tablespoons roughly chopped parsley

¼ teaspoon dried chilli flakes

55g (2 oz) fresh breadcrumbs

balsamic vinegar

**1**  Cut the tomatoes in half horizontally and gently remove the
seeds. Sprinkle the cut sides with salt and place cut side down
on kitchen paper to remove some liquid. Allow to stand for 20
minutes. Then place cut side up on a baking sheet.

**2**  Meanwhile, preheat the oven to 200°C/400°F/Gas 6.

**3**  Place the shallot, garlic, thyme, oil and anchovy in a food
processor and blend to a smooth paste. Fold in the parsley,
chilli and breadcrumbs. Season with black pepper.

**4**  Spoon the bread mixture into the tomato cavities and bake
for 15 minutes in the oven. Serve hot or at room temperature
sprinkled with extra virgin olive oil and balsamic vinegar.

. . . . . . . . . . .

*Toss cherry tomatoes with
mini bocconcini (baby
mozzarella), fresh basil
leaves, extra virgin olive oil,
chopped red onion, sea salt
and ground black pepper.*

. . . . . . . . . . .

# Basic Tomato Sauce for Pasta

This sauce can be adapted by adding fresh basil or pesto, or a
few chillies. The bacon is optional but adds a nice flavour. Fresh
tomatoes can be roasted whole until charred and blackened, for
a more smoky flavour.

**Preparation and cooking: 1½ hours**
**Makes: 600ml (1 pint)**

4 tablespoons good olive oil

3 cloves garlic, finely chopped

1 onion, finely chopped

1 stick celery, finely diced

115g (4 oz) smoked streaky bacon or *pancetta*, diced
(optional)

1 carrot, diced

1kg (2¼ lb) ripe tomatoes, peeled, seeded and chopped,
or 2 × 400g (14 oz) tins chopped tomatoes in sauce

1 teaspoon dried oregano

½ teaspoon soft thyme leaves

150ml (¼ pint) dry white wine

1 tablespoon caster sugar

1 tablespoon tomato purée

¼ teaspoon grated orange rind

salt and ground black pepper

**1**  Heat the oil in a heavy based **non-reactive** saucepan. Add
the garlic, onion, celery, bacon and carrot and cook over a
medium heat for 10 minutes until the vegetables have started
to soften.

**2**  Add all the remaining ingredients and cook uncovered over
a gentle heat for about 45 minutes until the sauce is thick.
Season to taste.

**3**  The sauce can be left chunky or passed through a food mill
or coarse blade of a **mouli-légumes**.

# Green Tomato Pickle

A powerful sweet and sour pickle, suitable for cheese, cold meats and sandwiches.

**Preparation and cooking: 2 hours**
**Makes: 6 litres (10 pints)**

| |
|---|
| 3kg (6½ lb) green tomatoes, sliced |
| 5 Spanish onions, thinly sliced |
| 500g (18 oz) black treacle |
| 10 garlic cloves, sliced |
| 6 hot chillies, finely sliced |
| 2 tablespoons hot curry paste |
| 2 tablespoons English mustard powder |
| 1 tablespoon salt |
| 2 litres (3½ pints) malt vinegar |
| 5 tablespoons plain flour |

**1** Combine the tomato and onion with the treacle, garlic, chilli, curry paste, mustard, salt and vinegar in a heavy-based, **non-reactive** large saucepan. Bring to the boil and simmer gently for 1 hour, stirring from time to time.

**2** Mix the flour to a paste with a little extra vinegar, stir into the pickle and continue to simmer for a further 15 minutes, stirring regularly.

**3** Pour into hot sterilised jars and seal. It will be ready to use after 1 month.

*Cut green tomatoes into 1cm (½ in) thick slices. Beat an egg with 1 tablespoon double cream, 3 tablespoons tomato juice and a dash of Tabasco sauce. Dip the tomato slices in this egg mixture then in polenta, and cook in hot butter for 5 minutes each side. Serve on hot buttered toast.*

## Tomato *Gratin*

● *Chop 4 rashers of streaky bacon and combine with 1 chopped onion.*

● *Mix these with 2 tablespoons chopped parsley, 1 teaspoon chopped thyme, ½ tablespoon chopped basil and 55g (2 oz) fresh breadcrumbs. Moisten this mixture with 85g (3 oz) melted butter and season with salt and pepper.*

● *Cut tomatoes into thick slices and place on the bottom of a buttered gratin dish. Sprinkle with half the bread mixture, then repeat the layers, finishing with the crumbs.*

● *Bake in a 200°C/400°F/Gas 6 oven for 25 minutes until golden and bubbling.*

## Sauce Vierge

● *Heat 125ml (4 fl oz) extra virgin olive oil in a small pan. Add the juice of ½ lemon and remove from the heat.*

● *Add a teaspoon of crushed coriander seeds and 10 ripped basil leaves and leave to infuse in the warm oil for a few minutes.*

● *Add the dice of 2 skinned and seeded ripe plum tomatoes. Serve immediately with steamed vegetables or seafood.*

## Tomato *Bruschetta*

● *Char-grill 6 slices of Italian country bread on both sides, having first dribbled them with garlic-infused extra virgin olive oil.*

● *Rub the toasted bread with more garlic, then rub with halved tomatoes until you are left with only the skins.*

● *Dribble with extra virgin olive oil, sprinkle with sea salt and ground black pepper, and top with shredded basil.*

# Bloody Mary

The perfect start to your Sunday. A little different from the
average Bloody Mary, perhaps, but well worth the effort.

**Preparation and cooking: 24 hours + 10 minutes**
**Fills: 6–8 highball glasses**

| |
|---|
| 50ml (2 fl oz) Worcestershire sauce |
| 1 tablespoon Heinz tomato ketchup |
| 1 teaspoon Tabasco sauce |
| 1 teaspoon celery salt |
| 75 ml (2½ fl oz) lemon juice |
| ½ tablespoon orange juice |
| 1 teaspoon freshly grated horseradish (not creamed) |
| 1 teaspoon finely chopped shallot |
| 1 teaspoon grated orange rind |
| ½ teaspoon finely ground black pepper |
| 1.7 litres (3 pints) thick tomato juice, chilled |
| 2 tablespoons fino sherry, chilled |

**To serve**

| |
|---|
| ice cubes |
| vodka to suit |
| celery |
| lemon wedges |

**1** Place all ingredients in a liquidiser and blend thoroughly.

**2** Transfer to a jug, cover and leave in a cool place for 24
hours for the flavours to develop.

**3** Pass the mixture through a fine sieve and add extra
seasoning to taste.

**4** Place ice cubes in highball glasses, pour on a shot of vodka
and top up with the tomato mix. Stir to combine. Garnish with
a stick of celery and a lemon wedge.

### Green Tomato Jam

- *Slice 3kg (6½ lb) peeled green or unripe tomatoes.*
- *Layer the tomatoes with 2.5kg (5½ lb) preserving sugar and leave overnight, stirring from time to time.*
- *Pour the tomatoes and juices into your preserving pan and bring slowly to the boil. Cook for 1 hour, removing any scum as it rises to the surface.*
- *Add 3 lemons cut in half lengthways, and then each half cut into 3mm (⅛ in) slices. Cook over a low heat for an additional hour, stirring from time to time.*
- *Pour into hot sterilised glass jars, then seal.*
- *Place jars on a rack or newspaper in a deep saucepan and fill with water up to the necks, bring to the boil and simmer for 15 minutes.*
- *Cool, seal and store in a dark place.*

*Cut 13cm (5 in) circles from shop-bought pre-rolled puff pastry, brush with beaten egg yolk and bake until thoroughly cooked. Cream together 225g (8 oz) ricotta cheese with 175g (6 oz) Roquefort cheese. Spread the cheese on the cool puff pastry, top with thin tomato slices and dribble with pesto. Place under a hot grill and cook for 3–4 minutes until hot and bubbling.*

# TURKEY FOR CHRISTMAS

Christmas Day always seems to create a modicum of panic. Quite often, what should be a peaceful holiday becomes a very stressful part of one's year. All it takes is careful planning, which involves cooking as much as possible before the big day.

## THE TURKEY ITSELF

• Where possible don't buy a frozen turkey, especially if you are only rushing out on Christmas Eve. Always defrost a turkey in the refrigerator, never at room temperature or under hot or cold water! Even the smallest turkey can take about 2 days to defrost, and an 11kg (25 lb) turkey can take up to 5 days . . .

• Don't buy a self-basting turkey. Either wrap it in foil or, if small enough, pop it in a roasting bag. Fold back the foil half an hour before the finish of the cooking time. One of the best ways is to buy some muslin, dip it in melted butter and lay it over the whole turkey. Some chefs cook the turkey breast side down, so that most of the juices run into the breast instead of the back which is not used. Follow my recipe below and you will have a moist bird at the end of cooking.

• Allow 350g (12 oz) per person dressed weight. Unstuffed cooking times can be as follows for a hot oven (230°C/450°F/Gas 8).

| | | |
|---|---|---|
| 3.6kg (8 lb) | 8–10 portions | 2½–2¾ hours |
| 4.5kg (10 lb) | 14 portions | 2¾–3 hours |
| 6.3kg (14 lb) | 18 portions | 3–3½ hours |
| 8.1kg (18 lb) | 24 portions | 3½–4 hours |
| 9.9kg (22 lb) | 28 portions | 4–4½ hours |

• You will see from the above table that cooking times are quicker than you might imagine. Allow 20 per cent extra time for a 180°C/350°F/Gas 4 oven, or for a stuffed turkey. With the fast cooking, you may have to wrap the drumsticks in extra foil to stop them burning. To be sure the turkey is cooked, either insert a meat thermometer into the thickest part of the thigh and check the temperature, or insert a skewer into the thickest part of the thigh – the juices should run clear, but if they are still pink, return the bird to the oven. Check again every 15 minutes.

• Unless you strongly object, don't stuff the turkey as the heat finds the stuffing hard to penetrate and therefore has to cook the turkey 'outside-in', so lengthening the cooking time and making for a dry-breasted bird. Cook any stuffings separately.

• Don't do as my mother used to do, and put the turkey in a slow oven overnight (unless of course you enjoy eating shoe leather).

• Buy a female turkey rather than a male as the ratio of meat to bone is much better.

• There is often not room to roast your potatoes and other vegetables in the same roasting tray as the turkey. Roast ahead and reheat, or ideally cook them in a second oven. The vegetables can be three-quarters cooked and then finished off while the turkey is **resting** after cooking.

• Instead of stuffing the bird traditionally, just pop ½ a lemon, ½ an onion, a few garlic cloves and a sprig of rosemary and thyme in the cavity.

• For turkey accompaniments, think of balance of colour, textures and ease on the day.

• With my traditional Christmas I try with difficulty not to over-indulge. Start with a dish that is cold and can be plated ahead, something like good smoked salmon or a seafood platter. The accompaniments are always more exciting than the turkey in my mind. You need one green vegetable. Brussels sprouts are traditional, but zap them up with bacon, thyme, chestnuts and grated orange rind, or you could have *petits pois à la française* (see page 250) which can be prepared ahead. I always enjoy one purée, perhaps *Bashed Neeps* (see page 289), the *Broccoli and Leek Purée* opposite or the *Celeriac and Apple Purée* (see page 75). My *Corn Pudding* (see page 291) is rather 'American Thanksgiving', but a lovely change to the norm. You should have *Bread Sauce* (see page 52) and try my *Cranberry Cumberland Sauce* (see page 302). Check out page 269 for how to make great roast potatoes.

Good luck and Happy Christmas.

## Christmas timetable

| Make ahead | On the day |
|---|---|
| 2 contrasting stuffings | Reheat stuffing |
| Bread sauce | Reheat bread sauce |
| Corn pudding | Reheat corn pudding |
| Stock for gravy | Make gravy |
| Peel potatoes (keep in water) | Roast potatoes |
| Trim Brussels sprouts | Cook green vegetables |
| 1 green vegetable purée | Reheat purée |
| Bake ham (see page 32) | Roast turkey! |
| Cranberry sauce | |

# Broccoli and Leek Purée Ⓥ

A delicious winter purée that accompanies turkey well.
**Preparation and cooking: 1¼ hours**
**Serves: 6**

85g (3 oz) unsalted butter
675g (1½ lb) leeks, washed and shredded
1 teaspoon soft thyme leaves
225g (8 oz) potatoes, quartered
salt and ground black pepper
450g (1 lb) broccoli, stems sliced and florets separated
150ml (¼ pint) double cream

**1** Melt the butter in a large saucepan over a medium heat, add the leek and thyme, cover, reduce the heat and cook until the leeks are very soft, about 15–20 minutes.
**2** Meanwhile, in a separate saucepan of boiling salted water, cook the potatoes until nearly tender, about 12–15 minutes. Add the broccoli stems and cook for a further 5 minutes, then add the florets and cook for a further 3 minutes.
**3** Drain well and place in a food processor. Add the leeks and process until smooth.
**4** Return the purée to a saucepan, add the cream, mix and check seasoning. Reheat just before serving.

# Rice Stuffing with Greens, *Pancetta* and Pecans

This stuffing is American in influence, using wild rice and pecan nuts. If you would prefer a sausage stuffing, see page 188.
**Preparation and cooking: 2 hours**
**Serves: 4–6**

1.4 litres (2½ pints) chicken stock
1 bay leaf
1 sprig thyme
115g (4 oz) wild rice
115g (4 oz) easy-cook long-grain rice
55g (2 oz) unsalted butter
225g (8 oz) *pancetta* or smoked streaky bacon, roughly chopped
2 onions, finely chopped
3 sticks celery, finely chopped
½ Savoy cabbage, chopped
3 tablespoons finely chopped marjoram
1 × 85g (3 oz) packet sage and onion stuffing, made according to packet instructions
115g (4 oz) pecans, chopped
salt and ground black pepper
3 eggs, beaten

**1** Bring 850ml (1½ pints) of the stock, the bay leaf and thyme to the boil. Fold in the wild rice, reduce the heat, cover and cook for 30 minutes. Add the long-grain rice and cook for a further 12 minutes. Drain and transfer the rice to a large bowl, discarding the bay leaf and thyme.
**2** Melt the butter in a large saucepan, add the *pancetta*, onion and celery, and cook over a medium heat for 8 minutes until the onions have softened but not browned. Add the cabbage and marjoram and cook for 5 minutes, stirring regularly.
**3** Add this mixture to the rice, along with the sage and onion stuffing, pecans, salt and plenty of ground black pepper. Finally fold in the beaten eggs. Beat well with a wooden spoon to combine all the ingredients.
**4** Butter a large baking dish, fold the remaining chicken stock into the stuffing and place in the baking dish. Cover with buttered foil and bake in a hot oven at 200°C/400°F/Gas 6 for 30 minutes, either beforehand or while the turkey is **resting**.

# Cranberry Cumberland Sauce

This is a combination of the classic Cumberland sauce and cranberry sauce, and would make an excellent accompaniment to your turkey or baked ham.

**Preparation and cooking: 30 minutes**
**Serves: 6**

450g (1 lb) fresh cranberries
300ml (½ pint) ruby port
115g (4 oz) caster sugar
125ml (4 fl oz) fresh orange juice
1 teaspoon cornflour
1 teaspoon English mustard powder
1 teaspoon lemon juice
pinch of ground cloves
75g (3 oz) sultanas
55g (2 oz) flaked almonds
1 tablespoon grated orange rind
1 teaspoon grated lemon rind
salt

**1** Combine the cranberries, port, sugar and orange juice in a **non-reactive** saucepan over a medium heat. Cook until the berries burst, stirring from time to time, about 8–10 minutes.

**2** Combine the cornflour, mustard, lemon juice and cloves with a little water to make a paste. Stir into the berry mix. Add the sultanas, almonds, orange and lemon rind.

**3** Simmer over a medium heat until thickened, about 5 minutes. Season to taste, and chill. Can be made up to 1 week in advance.

# Roast Turkey

This recipe proved really popular when I made it on BBC's *Food and Drink*. The butter and herby cheese mix that you push under the skin acts as a self-baster.

**Preparation and cooking: 3½ hours**
**Serves: 10–14**

115g (4 oz) ricotta or cream cheese
115g (4 oz) unsalted butter, softened
1 tablespoon snipped chives
1 tablespoon chopped flat-leaf parsley
2 teaspoons chopped tarragon
1 teaspoon chopped chervil
½ teaspoon ground black pepper
¼ teaspoon sea salt
1 × 4.5kg (10 lb) fresh turkey, at room temperature
½ lemon
½ onion
3 garlic cloves
1 sprig thyme
1 sprig rosemary
extra butter for greasing foil

**1** Combine the ricotta and butter with the chopped herbs, pepper and salt.

**2** Gently ease the skin away from the flesh at both ends of the turkey by carefully inserting your fingers between skin and flesh. Push the butter mixture under the skin, easing it over the whole bird; be careful not to puncture the skin. Place the lemon, onion, garlic and herb sprigs in the cavity of the turkey.

**3** Lay a large sheet of foil over a baking tray lengthways, leaving enough at each end to wrap over the turkey, and lightly butter this. Repeat this exercise with another sheet, this time *across* the roasting tray. Lightly butter once again.

**4** Place the turkey, breast side up, in the centre of the foil. Wrap the turkey completely in foil.

**5** Place in a preheated 230°C/450°F/Gas 8 oven, and roast for 2¾ hours. For the last 20–30 minutes fold back the foil to allow the turkey to brown. Make sure the ends of the drumsticks are still covered. Check with a metal skewer to see if the turkey is cooked. The juices should run clear.

**6** Remove from the oven and allow to **rest** in a warm place for the juices to settle and to ease carving, about 20 minutes. Tip away the fat from the roasting tray and use the meat juices that remain as the base for your gravy.

## Leftover Turkey Sandwich

- *Spread 2 slices of country-style bread with butter.*
- *Lay one slice of bread on a work surface, butter side up, and top with a layer of turkey stuffing, then a layer of cranberry sauce, followed by the turkey meat.*
- *Spread the turkey with cold turkey gravy, top with an unbuttered slice of bread, then layers of sliced baked ham, sliced tomato and mayonnaise.*
- *Season, and top with the final slice of bread, butter side down. Serve with McCoys plain crisps.*
- *Don't use a knife and fork, just seize in both hands and wrap your laughing gear around a yummy, moreish mouthful.*

My Roast Turkey
with Cranberry
Cumberland Sauce
and a seasonal
stuffing.

# YOGURT

Yogurt is a cultured, fermented milk product, and is made from milk that has had friendly bacteria, among them *Lactobacillus bulgaricus* and *Streptococcus thermophilus* added. These bacteria digest the lactose thereby setting the milk into yogurt curd. Yogurt was and still is a staple throughout the Middle East and India, and is used in soups, salads, marinades and drinks. It is relatively new in Britain, with little evidence of it before the mid 1950s. It has now become a massive, highly successful industry. Regular plain yogurt has lost its popularity to be replaced by creamy Greek yogurt, low-fat yogurts and a variety of fruit yogurts. Yogurt, because it is 'pre-digested', is very easy to digest, and is good for children. It contains all the nutrients of milk, particularly calcium, as well as the bacteria, which are widely considered to contribute to health.

There are quite a few varieties of yogurt. SET YOGURT is yogurt which has been poured directly into the carton to set; it is generally natural. STIRRED YOGURT is mixed and fermented in a tank then poured into individual pots; it often has additional milk or whey powder to extend it and give it a creamier texture. STRAINED YOGURT is literally that, where the water content is strained off to intensify the fats and give creaminess; yogurts in this category include Greek yogurts. BIO or LIVE YOGURTS contain other bacteria (including the gut-friendly *acidophilus*) and are sold because of their health benefits and their milder, less acid flavour. WHOLE MILK YOGURT is generally out of favour as more people want to eat less fat; LOW-FAT YOGURT is made with skimmed milk and fat levels range from 1 to 5 per cent. (Although low in fat, you should read their labels carefully as many have extra sugar.) FLAVOURED YOGURT, enough said, may be great for kids but not for me (and is *laden* with sugar). SHEEP'S MILK and GOAT'S MILK YOGURTS are hard to find; fat levels are generally lower, and they have quite a tart taste.

Shop-bought yogurt will usually keep up to 2 weeks unopened, but always check the sell-by date. Do not shake or whip yogurt as this breaks up the curd and allows the whey to separate out. Unstrained yogurt will also separate when heated, so use Greek yogurt which, although quite fatty, is still a healthier alternative to double cream. Adding a teaspoon of cornflour per 140g (5 oz) yogurt helps prevent separating or curdling, but often this is part of the recipe.

## *Tzatziki*

*Tzatziki* is probably one of the most popular Middle Eastern dishes available in our supermarkets today, but they all pale into insignificance when compared to this recipe. You can substitute natural or low-fat yogurt for Greek if you prefer less fat, but I love the creaminess.

**Preparation: 15 minutes**
**Serves: 4–6**

1 cucumber, peeled, seeded and diced
sea salt
1 tablespoon extra virgin olive oil
2 cloves garlic, crushed with a little salt
1 teaspoon white wine vinegar
¼ teaspoon ground black pepper
225g (8 oz) Greek yogurt
8 mint leaves, chopped

**1** Sprinkle 2 teaspoons of salt over the cucumber and leave for 30 minutes to drain some of the cucumber's natural liquid away. Rinse and dry the cucumber.
**2** Meanwhile, combine the oil with the garlic, vinegar and black pepper.
**3** Whisk the yogurt into the oil dressing and fold in the cucumber and chopped mint. Check seasoning.

*For a hot dip, mix 1–2 tablespoons, or to taste, of zhug (see page 259) into 250g (9 oz) Greek or other natural yogurt.*

# *Labna* (Yogurt Cheese)

A simple and very satisfying recipe for your own simple cheese, which is delicious as part of an *antipasti* buffet or just spread on *crostini* or eaten with sharp fruits.

**Preparation: 36 hours + 30 minutes**
**Makes: 36 balls**

1kg (2¼ lb) sheep's milk yogurt (or live cow's milk yogurt)
4 teaspoons ground black pepper
3 teaspoons sea salt
1 teaspoon green peppercorns
1 teaspoon finely chopped rosemary
1 teaspoon finely chopped thyme
600ml (1 pint) extra virgin olive oil
2 bay leaves
3 garlic cloves, lightly crushed
2 dried red chillies

**1** Mix together the yogurt, pepper and salt. Line a colander with cheesecloth or muslin and place over a bowl. Pour the yogurt into the muslin and allow to drain, refrigerated, for 18 hours.

**2** Scoop out tablespoonfuls of the drained yogurt and roll into balls. Place the balls on a lightly oiled tray and refrigerate, uncovered, for 12 hours to become more solid.

**3** Pack the small cheeses into a 2 litre (3½ pint) glass jar, sprinkling each layer with peppercorns, rosemary and thyme. Top up with olive oil. Slip in the bay leaves, garlic and chillies.

**4** Seal and store in the refrigerator for 1 week before eating. The cheese will keep refrigerated for 6 weeks. Allow to come to room temperature before eating.

## Yogurt Marinade for Meat or Fish

● *Fry 4 chopped fresh red chillies with 4 chopped garlic cloves, 6 crushed green cardamom pods, a 7.5cm (3 in) cinnamon stick, 3 cloves, and 225g (8 oz) chopped shallots.*

● *Cook over a low heat until the shallots have softened, about 8 minutes.*

● *Add 2 teaspoons ground coriander, 1 teaspoon ground fennel seeds, 1 teaspoon ground cumin, 1 teaspoon finely chopped fresh ginger and ½ teaspoon turmeric, and stir to combine.*

● *Fold in 600g (1 lb 5 oz) Greek yogurt and cook for 2 minutes. Allow to cool before marinating your chicken or fish.*

## Strawberry Yogurt Sponge

● *Take 1 small pot of natural yogurt and fold in 115g (4 oz) puréed, fresh strawberries.*

● *Using the pot as a measure mix together 3 pots of plain flour sifted with a pinch of salt, 1 pot caster sugar, 1 pot sunflower oil, 1 teaspoon baking powder and 3 lightly beaten eggs. Whisk together and pour into a greased 20 cm (8 in) spring-form tin.*

● *Bake in a preheated oven at 180°C/350°F/Gas 4 for 35–40 minutes. Check with a skewer to see if it is cooked all the way through; if the skewer comes out clean, then the cake is done.*

● *Allow to cool, carefully slice in half and spread the bottom with home-made strawberry jam. Replace the top sponge and sprinkle with icing sugar.*

# Mango and Yogurt Fool

A delicious tropical creamy pudding that is simple to make. A must for children and adults alike.

**Preparation: 15 minutes**
**Serves: 4**

| |
|---|
| 600g (1 lb 5 oz) Greek yogurt |
| 1 tablespoon grated fresh ginger (and juices) |
| 1 teaspoon ground cardamom |
| 2 mangoes, peeled (see page 182) |
| 150ml (¼ pint) double cream |
| 2 tablespoons caster sugar |
| ½ teaspoon vanilla extract |

**1** Combine the yogurt with the ginger, its juices (always grate ginger over a bowl to catch the juices), and ground cardamom.
**2** Finely dice 1 mango and set aside. Cut the flesh off the other and purée it in a food processor. For an extra smooth purée, pass through a fine plastic sieve. Mix the diced mango and purée into the yogurt.
**3** Whip the cream with the sugar and vanilla essence to **soft peaks**. Fold the cream into the mango yogurt. Spoon the mixture into glasses and refrigerate until required. Decorate as you please: we used blanched orange rind strips and mint leaves in the photograph.

## Spinach Raita

*Chop 115g (4 oz) cooked and drained spinach and combine with 300g (10½ oz) yogurt, ½ teaspoon roasted cumin seeds, 1 clove garlic crushed with a little salt, 3 chopped dates, 3 chopped dried apricots, ½ teaspoon cayenne pepper and 1 tablespoon pine kernels.*

## Apricot and Herb Raita

*An excellent dip for crudités, or to serve with curries and other hot and spicy food.*
● *Combine 200g (7 oz) Greek yogurt, 6 dried apricots, finely chopped, 1 clove garlic, finely chopped, 1 tablespoon chopped coriander, 2 teaspoons chopped mint and ¼ teaspoon ground black pepper.*
● *Allow flavours to develop for 1 hour before serving.*
● *Season with salt just before eating.*

## Vegetable Raita

*Combine 1 peeled, seeded and diced cucumber with 1 diced seeded plum tomato, 1 diced small onion, 1 diced cooked potato, ½ teaspoon roasted cumin seeds, 425g (15 oz) Greek yogurt or other natural yogurt and 1 tablespoon chopped mint. Season to taste.*

## Potato and Mint Raita

*Combine 1 large diced cooked potato with 4 tablespoons chopped mint, ½ teaspoon black cumin seeds, and 600g (1 lb 5 oz) Greek or other natural yogurt. Season to taste.*

## Aubergine Raita

● *Roast 1 large aubergine (350g/12 oz) in a hot oven until the skin has blackened (see page 24).*
● *Rinse off the skin, mash the aubergine flesh, and combine it with 600g (1 lb 5 oz) Greek or other natural yogurt, 1 teaspoon chopped mint leaves, ½ teaspoon roasted cumin seeds, ½ teaspoon ground black pepper and ½ teaspoon cayenne pepper. Season to taste.*

# CHEF TALK

**Acidulated water** Water with a little vinegar or lemon juice added into which vegetables and fruits that discolour quickly are submerged, e.g. apples, pears, artichokes and celeriac. Allow 1 tablespoon acid medium to 1 litre (1¾ pints) water.

**Al dente** An Italian term meaning 'to the tooth', and describes correctly cooked pasta with just a hint of resistance when eaten.

**Bain-marie** An age-old cooking technique, apparently invented by the Italians, where a deep dish or baking tray is half-filled with hot water in which terrines, custards or other fragile concoctions stand. This method avoids direct heat, stabilises the oven's temperature fluctuations, and allows the food to cook in a more gentle, steamy atmosphere. This method is also used in professional kitchens: sauces stand in water on the hob to keep them at a constant temperature. It is similar to a double-boiler, see below.

**Batons** Describe the shape you can cut vegetables or meat to, approximately 2.5cm x 5mm x 5mm (1 x ¼ x ¼ in).

**Blanch, to** Means parboiling, a method used by chefs to part- or half-cook a vegetable, prior to reheating or freezing: the vegetables cook for a short burst in fast boiling water. It sets the colour of green vegetables and herbs. This method can also be used to whiten meats and fish, to remove any trace of blood or impurities. Blanching can remove skins from nuts, tomatoes, peaches and peppers.

**Bouquet garni** A 'nosegay' of herbs tied together and wrapped in muslin – usually a sprig of thyme, parsley stalks, a celery stick, and a bay leaf (sometimes wrapped in leek leaf). A **faggot of herbs** is much the same thing.

**Court-bouillon** A flavoured liquid in which you poach fish or offal, usually containing vegetables, a few spices, a *bouquet garni*, and a piece of lemon rind.

**Cream, to** To beat ingredients together to lighten them in texture and whiten them in colour, e.g. butter and sugar or egg yolks and sugar.

**Deglaze** The addition of a liquid such as stock or wine to loosen fats, sediment or browned juices from a roasting tray when making gravy, or a pan after frying meat. The resulting juices provide great flavour for a sauce or gravy.

**Dice, to** To cut into small cubes. A similar consistency to the French terms, *duxelle*, *brunoise* or *macedoine*, which are all different sized dice.

**Double-boiler** A similar method of cooking to **bain-marie** (see above) where a sauce is whisked in the top of a purpose-built double saucepan, the top section sitting over simmering liquid in the pan below. A home-made double-boiler can be made by placing a metal or heatproof bowl on the top of a saucepan, with water boiling underneath. Never allow the water to touch the bottom of the bowl.

**Egg wash** Beaten egg, sometimes just yolks, with or without the addition of milk or water, painted on to pastry for glazing or sealing the bottom of a blind-baked pastry case.

**Faggot of herbs** See **Bouquet garni**

**Flambé, to** Alcohol is added to a pan, then ignited to burn off the alcohol, leaving behind the residual flavour.

**Fold, to** A delicate mixing motion rather than vigorous whisking, e.g. folding beaten egg whites into mousse without destroying all the air. A large metal spoon, which has thinner edges than a wooden spoon, is normally used.

**Infuse, to** To steep something in, or heat in a liquid, to release the flavours, e.g. a vanilla pod in milk before making a custard, or onion, bay and cloves in milk before making a *béchamel* sauce.

**Julienne, to** To cut vegetables or citrus rinds into very thin strips or matchsticks.

**Jus** A *jus* in the past was made by long, slow reductions; nowadays, a liquid is added to the cooking juices in a pan and quickly boiled to a sauce.

**Lardons** Small strips or **batons** (see above) of bacon, salt pork or pork fat, usually blanched before frying. Often used as a garnish for dishes such as *coq au vin*.

**Lard, to** The threading of fats or bacon into very lean cuts of meat, or anchovy into fish, to allow the meat to be self-basting and to give flavour during long, slow cooking. A larding needle is generally required for this operation.

**Macerate, to** To soak food, usually fruit, in sugar or a syrup to extract natural flavour.

**Mandoline** A gadget, made of metal (better and more expensive), wood or plastic, which cuts vegetables thinly in slices or shreds.

**Marinade, Marinate, to** The former is a liquid, usually containing an acid such as vinegar or wine, and vegetables and oil, into which meat or fish are put to be tenderised and given extra flavour. The latter is the act of putting the meat or fish into the liquid.

**Mouli-légumes, Vegetable mouli** A hand-operated mechanical strainer usually with three discs of differing fineness through which is strained vegetable, fish or meat matter after cooking to extract as much liquid and subsequently flavour as possible. Used where you want juices mainly, rather than using a blender to purée all the ingredients.

**Non-reactive** Usually referring to a saucepan, tray or bowl made out of a metal that doesn't react to an acid content. Often stainless steel. Old saucepans were often made from aluminium which can become pitted with the use of an acid (vinegar or lemon juice, for instance). Cast-iron frying pans also react.

**Overflow method** A means of excluding air from pickles. The jar with its contents is filled right to the top with the vinegar or liquid until it literally overflows, then is quickly sealed.

**Pulse, to** Modern food processors have a pulse button which has a quick on-off action. Use this when full puréeing is likely to mean that the contents will stick to the walls of the blender or processor.

**Reduce, to** To reduce liquid by rapid boiling. Evaporation occurs, intensifying the flavours of the liquid and often thickening it. (Remember to salt *after* reducing, or you will have a very salty reduction.)

**Refresh, to** The process of dunking vegetables after boiling or blanching in a bowl of iced water or under a cold tap to arrest the cooking and set the colour.

**Rest** or **Relax, to** A process used in pastry to allow the gluten in the flour to contract, thereby avoiding shrinkage when cooking. Also used for batters to allow the starches to swell, giving a lighter result when cooked. Roast meats benefit from relaxing after being removed from the oven to allow the juices to be balanced and reabsorbed. This also enhances the colour of red meats.

**Ribbon, to the** A stage in whisking or stirring cream, custard, a soup or a sauce where the consistency still shows movement but has not reached a **soft peak** or **stiff peak** stage (see below). If you were to drop a sauce from the end of a spoon it would fall reluctantly. Thick hot custard and thick, not-set cream are probably the best examples.

**Roux** This is made by cooking together a fat (usually butter) and flour to a liaison for thickening a liquid. You can either have a blond *roux* where it does not colour at all, or a brown *roux* where it is cooked more thoroughly and takes on colour.

**Scald, to** To heat a liquid (usually milk) to the point of boiling, just as the liquid starts to tremble at the edges but before there is uniform bubbling.

**Seal, to** To brown meat or fish rapidly, usually in fat or oil, to colour and add flavour, before further cooking.

**Seize, to** Chocolate 'seizes' after melting when you add a cold liquid. Seizing makes the chocolate very stiff and impossible to stir. Chocolate can also become stiff or grainy if placed over a direct heat. Always melt in a **double-boiler**.

**Soft** and **stiff peaks** Referring to the beating or whipping of cream or egg whites. Soft peak is where a peak forms but will flop over and appear quite light and delicate. Stiff peak is where there is no movement and you could turn the bowl upside down without the contents falling to the kitchen floor.

**Sweat, to** To cook gently over a low heat, usually in oil or butter but occasionally in the food's natural juices, to a point where the food has softened but has not taken on colour.

**Vegetable mouli** See **Mouli-légumes**

**Velvet, to** A term used in Chinese cookery. Meat strips to be stir-fried are coated first in cornflour, or egg white and cornflour, to protect them while frying.

**Wilt, to** A term adopted from America. A green leaf or herb is placed in a pan with moisture from washing still clinging from the leaves and turned constantly with tongs over heat until the leaf releases its own natural juices and becomes lifeless and floppy but retains its colour.

# BIBLIOGRAPHY

Alexander, Stephanie, *The Cook's Companion*, Viking, 1996

Allen, Darina, *Irish Traditional Cooking*, Gill & Macmillan, 1995

Bay Esbensen, Mogens, *Thai Cuisine*, Nelson, 1986

Beer, Maggie, *Maggie's Farm*, Allen & Unwin, 1993

Bertolli, Paul and Waters, Alice, *Chez Panisse Cooking*, Random House, 1988

Bissell, Frances, *The Real Meat Cookbook*, Chatto & Windus, 1992

Bocuse, Paul, *The New Cuisine*, Granada, 1978

Campbell, Joan, *Bloody Delicious*, Allen & Unwin, 1997

Casas, Penelope, *The Food and Wines of Spain*, Knopf, 1979

Costa, Margaret, *Four Seasons Cookery Book*, Thomas Nelson & Sons, 1970

Durack, Terry, *Yum*, William Heinemann, 1996

Glick Conway, Lindsay, *Café Cuisine*, Houghton Mifflin, 1988

Gray, Rose and Rogers, Ruth, *The River Café Cookbook*, Ebury Press, 1995

Greene, Bert, *Greene on Greens*, Workman Publishing, 1984

Greene, Bert, *The Grains Cookbook*, Workman Publishing, 1988

Grigson, Jane, *Charcuterie and French Pork Cookery*, Michael Joseph, 1967

Grigson, Jane, *English Food*, Macmillan, 1974

Grigson, Jane, *Jane Grigson's Vegetable Book*, Michael Joseph, 1978

Hazan, Marcella, *Essential Classic Italian Cooking*, Macmillan, 1992

Hazan, Marcella, *Marcella Cucina*, Macmillan, 1997

Holuigue, Diane, *The French Kitchen*, Methuen, 1983

Jump, Meg, *Cooking with Chillies*, The Bodley Head, 1989

Liew, Cheong, *My Food*, Allen & Unwin, 1995

Luard, Elisabeth, *European Peasant Cookery*, Bantam Press, 1986

Manfredi, Stefano, *Fresh from Italy*, Hodder Headline, 1993

Meyers, Perla, *Fresh from the Garden*, Potter, 1996

Nathan, Amy, *Salad*, Chronicle Books

Ogden, Bradley, *Breakfast, Lunch and Dinner*, Random House, 1991

Panjabi, Camellia, *50 Great Curries of India*, Kyle Cathie, 1994

Perry, Neil, *Rockpool*, Heinemann, 1996

Roden, Claudia, *A New Book of Middle Eastern Food*, Viking, 1985

Rosso, Julee and Lukins, Sheila, *The Silver Palate Cookbook*, Workman Publishing, 1979

Salaman, Rena, *Greek Food*, Harper Collins, 1993

Schwartz, Leonard, *Salads*, Harper Collins, 1992

Slater, Nigel, *The 30-Minute Cook*, Michael Joseph, 1994

Slater, Nigel, *Real Cooking*, Michael Joseph, 1997

Slattery, Geoff, *Australian Home Cooking*, The Text Publishing, 1991

Taruschio, Ann and Franco, *Bruschetta, Crostoni and Crostini*, Pavilion, 1995

Tropp, Barbara, *China Moon Cookbook*, Workman Publishing, 1992

Wolfert, Paula, *Mediterranean Cooking*, Ecco Press, 1977

Wolfert, Paula, *The Cooking of South-West France*, The Dial Press, 1983

Wolfert, Paula, *Good Food from Morocco*, John Murray, 1989

# INDEX

Note: page numbers in **bold** refer to illustrations; main recipes are indicated by capitals;
'a + a' denotes additions and accompaniments to main entry.